THE
HACIENDA

THE
HACIENDA

Isabel Cañas

BERKLEY
NEW YORK

BERKLEY
An imprint of Penguin Random House LLC
penguinrandomhouse.com

Library of Congress Cataloging-in-Publication Data

Names: Cañas, Isabel, author.
Title: The hacienda / Isabel Cañas.
Description: First edition. | New York : Berkley, 2022.
Identifiers: LCCN 2021034439 (print) | LCCN 2021034440 (ebook) |
ISBN 9780593436691 (hardcover) | ISBN 9780593436714 (ebook)
Subjects: LCSH: Haciendas—Mexico—Fiction. | GSAFD: Suspense fiction. |
Occult fiction. | LCGFT: Thrillers (Fiction) | Paranormal fiction.
Classification: LCC PS3603.A533 H33 2022 (print) |
LCC PS3603.A533 (ebook) | DDC 813/.6—dc23
LC record available at https://lccn.loc.gov/2021034439
LC ebook record available at https://lccn.loc.gov/2021034440

Printed in the United States of America
4th Printing

Title page art: Gothic background © Arm001 / Shutterstock
Book design by Alison Cnockaert

For my mother, who first gave me the freedom to write.

And for my husband, who gives me the courage to never stop.

1

ANDRÉS

THE LOW SWEEP OF the southern horizon was a perfect line, unmarred by even the smudge of horses tossing their heads in the distance. The road yawned empty.

The carriage was gone.

I stood with my back to the gates of Hacienda San Isidro. Behind me, high white stucco walls rose like the bones of a long-dead beast jutting from dark, cracked earth. Beyond the walls, beyond the main house and the freshly dug graves behind the capilla, the tlachiqueros took their machetes to the sharp fields of maguey. Wandering the fields as a boy taught me agave flesh does not give like man's; the tlachiqueros lift their machetes and bring them down again, and again, each dull thud seeking the heart's sweet sap, each man becoming more intimately acquainted with the give of meat beneath metal, with the harvesting of hearts.

A breeze snaked into the valley from the dark hills, its dry chill stinging my cheeks and the wet in my eyes. It was time to turn back. To return to my life as it was. Yet the idea of turning, of gazing up at San Isidro's heavy wooden doors alone, slicked my palms with sweat.

There was a reason I had once set my jaw and crossed San Isidro's threshold, a reason why I passed through its gates like a reckless youth from legends of journeys to the underworlds.

That reason was gone.

And still I stood in the center of the dirt road that led away from San Isidro, away from Apan, my eyes fixed on the horizon with the fervor of a sinner before their saint. As if the force of my grief alone could transcend the will of God and return that carriage. Return the woman who had been taken from me. The echo of retreating hoofbeats and the clouds of dust they left curled in the air like copal incense, mocking me.

It is said that mortal life is empty without the love of God. That the ache of loneliness's wounds is assuaged by obedience to Him, for in serving God we encounter perfect love and are made whole.

But if God is the Father, Son, and Holy Spirit, if He is three in one in the Trinity, then God knows nothing of loneliness.

God knows nothing of standing with his back to a gray morning, of dropping to his knees in the dust. Of his shoulders slumping beneath the new weight of knowing what it meant *not* to be alone, and an acute awareness of his chest's own emptiness.

God knows nothing of loneliness, because God has never tasted companionship as mortals do: clinging to one another in darkness so complete and sharp it scrapes flesh from bone, trusting one another even as the Devil's breath blooms hot on their napes.

Sharp pebbles dug into my kneecaps through my worn trousers as I knelt, my breathing labored, too exhausted to sob. I knew what the maguey felt. I knew the whine of the machete. I knew how my chest gave beneath the weight of its fall. I knew how it felt to have my heart harvested, sweet aguamiel carving winding wet tracks down my hollowed chest. My wounds sinful stigmata, flinching and festering in the sun.

God knows nothing of being alone.

Alone is kneeling in dust, gazing at an empty horizon.

In the end, it was not the ink-slick shadows and echoing, dissonant laughter of San Isidro that broke me. It was not fear that carved my chest open.

It was losing her.

2

BEATRIZ

SEPTIEMBRE 1823
TWO MONTHS EARLIER

THE CARRIAGE DOOR CREAKED as Rodolfo opened it. I blinked, adjusting to the light that spilled across my skirts and face, and took the hand Rodolfo offered me as gracefully as I could. Hours of imprisonment in the carriage over rough country roads left me wanting to claw my way out of that stuffy box and suck in a lungful of fresh air, but I restrained myself. I knew my role as delicate, docile wife. Playing that role had already swept me away from the capital, far from the torment of my uncle's house, into the valley of Apan.

It brought me here and left me standing before a high dark wooden door set deep in white stucco walls, squinting under the blinding sweep of azure September skies, the broad shoulders and steady hands of Don Rodolfo Eligio Solórzano at my side.

In the sunlight his loose curls gleamed bronze, and his eyes were almost as light as the sky beyond. "This is San Isidro," he said.

Hacienda San Isidro. I let my eyes drag over the heavy door, its wrought-iron accents, the high dark spikes on the front of the walls, the wilting bougainvillea that wound through them, blossoms and thorns alike drained of color and dying.

It was not quite what I expected, having been raised in the verdant, lush gardens of an hacienda in Cuernavaca, but it was my new conquest. My salvation.

Mine.

WHEN I FIRST MET Rodolfo, dancing at a ball to celebrate the founding of the Republic, he told me his family had owned an hacienda that produced pulque for nearly two hundred years.

Ah, I thought, watching the sharp panes of his clean-shaven face flirt with the shadows of the candlelit ballroom. *So that was how your family kept its money throughout the war.* Industry will rise and fall, men will scorch the earth and slaughter one another for emperors or republics, but they will always want drink.

We danced the next round, and the next. He watched me with an intensity I knew then was a priceless tool.

"Tell me about the hacienda," I had said.

It was a big house, he replied, sprawling over the low hills north of Apan, overlooking sharp-pointed fields of maguey. Generations of his family had lived there before the war of independence from Spain, cultivating the agave and producing pulque, its sour beer, to be shipped to the capital's thirsty markets. There were gardens filled with birds of paradise, the air thick with swallows, he said, and broad, bustling kitchens to feed all the tlachiqueros and the servants and family. They celebrated feast days in a capilla on the property, a chapel adorned with paintings of saints and an altar carved by the scion of the family in the seventeenth century and gilded by later, wealthier generations.

"Do you miss it?" I asked.

He did not answer, not directly. Instead, he described the way the sun set in the valley of Apan: first rich golden, deepening to amber, and then, with a swift, sure strike, night overtook the sun like the extinguishing of a candle. The darkness in the valley was so deep it was almost blue, and when thunderstorms slinked over steep hills into the valley, lightning spilled like mercury across the fields of maguey, silvering the plants' sharp tips like the peaked helmets of conquistadors.

It will be mine, I thought then. A flash of intuition that swept me with the strong, trusting arm of a lover into the next steps of the dance.

And mine it became.

For the first time since March, a house was mine.

So why didn't I feel safe when the enormous door of Hacienda San Isidro groaned open and Rodolfo and I walked into the first courtyard of the estate?

A delicate tremor, the tremble of a monarch's wings, fluttered at the back of my throat as I took in the hacienda.

Its buildings were muscular and ungainly, the awkwardly splayed limbs of a beast frozen halfway into adolescence. The rainy season was ending; the garden should have been shades of emerald at this point in September, but what scarce vegetation grew in the outer courtyard was as brown as the earth. Wild magueys scattered weed-like and drooping on either side of a grayed capilla—it must have once been white—and dotted the lawn that led up to the house. Rotting birds of paradise crowded in scattered beds, their heads submissively bowed before us as our boots crunched up the gravel path. The air felt heavier inside San Isidro's walls, thicker, as if I had stepped into a strange, soundless dream where the stucco swallowed even the songs of the birds.

Outside of the chapel, we passed into an inner courtyard. Here, Rodolfo gestured to two rows of servants who stood at attention in front of their quarters and kitchen, waiting to greet us. Before they dipped their heads, a dozen pairs of black shining eyes swept over me, cool and assessing.

After explaining that the tlachiqueros were in the fields until dusk,

Rodolfo made introductions: José Mendoza, once the right-hand man to the dismissed foreman Esteban Villalobos, had acted as record keeper for over a decade. He was the chief authority when Rodolfo was in the capital. Mendoza removed his weather-stained hat and placed it on his chest; his hands were gnarled with age and work. He looked old enough to be my grandfather.

Ana Luisa, the head of household, was a woman of about fifty, her steel-gray hair parted severely in the center, her plaits wound tightly around her head in a solemn crown. Her daughter, Paloma—Ana Luisa's double with raven black hair and rounder cheeks—stood at her side. Other names rolled over me like water; I heard them but remembered none, for a figure caught my eye at an arched doorway at the far entrance to the servants' courtyard.

A woman strode toward us, tall as a soldier and possessing all the same swagger. She wore a faded blue skirt that was short enough to reveal leather riding boots, stained with sweat; a wide-brimmed hat hung down her back by a cord around her neck, but if her complexion was any indication, she rarely wore it. Her skin was bronze and her hair streaked gold from long hours in the sun.

Stay out of the sun or you'll never get a husband, Tía Fernanda once whispered snidely, pinching the skin on the back of my hand. Though she had never met my father, and my mother refused to reveal any information about how mixed his heritage was, it didn't matter to Tía Fernanda: my hair and face gave her enough ammunition to find me undesirable. To refuse to let me stand next to her cream-pale daughters at the ball where I had met Rodolfo.

In the end, Fernanda's behavior meant that I had a golden husband, and her daughters did not. Fate had been unkind to me, but sometimes, its pettiness worked in my favor.

The woman stopped directly in front of me. Her pale eyes were the mirror of Rodolfo's, and her hair was the same color, sun-gilded and windswept. She gave me a swift, frank look from polished black shoes—quickly gathering dust—to my gloves and hat.

"You're early," she announced. "Is this my new sister?"

My lips parted in surprise. Who? Rodolfo had only ever mentioned a sister once in passing. She was called Juana; he said she was a few years younger than his own twenty-eight years, an age that led me to assume she was married. Never once had he mentioned her in the same breath as San Isidro.

"You look displeased," Juana said after Rodolfo introduced me, a hint of amusement in her voice. It was not warm. "Did Rodolfo not warn you about me?" Her lips were dry, and thinner than was considered attractive. They disappeared entirely when she smiled; her teeth were almost too bright, even and ivory as a set of piano keys. "Don't worry, I keep to myself. I won't even be underfoot—I live over there." She jutted her sharp chin over the line of servants, to a set of low buildings between the house and the capilla.

Not in the family's house? "Why?" I blurted out.

Juana's face shifted, resettled. "The house is terribly drafty this time of year," she said lightly. "Isn't it, Rodolfo?"

Rodolfo's face looked a bit strained as he agreed and returned her smile. He was embarrassed by her, I realized with a start. Why? She was unusual, to be sure, but there was a frankness to her that reminded me of Papá's no-nonsense manner. A simple, easy kind of authority, one that drew the attention of all the servants to her.

I could almost feel the air shift around me, toward her and her undeniable gravity. Rodolfo was not the master of this house.

Juana was.

A breathless fear uncurled in my chest; in response, I adjusted my posture, drawing my shoulders back as my father used to. There was nothing to be afraid of. This hacienda was mine. I married its patrón, and Juana chose to live among the servants. I ought to be glad Juana was so embarrassing to Rodolfo that he barely spoke of her. She was no threat to me. Let her stay in this middle courtyard, in the servants' quarters. The main house would be mine to rule. My domain.

Those thoughts quieted the unsettled lurch of my gut as we chatted with Juana for another moment longer, and then left the servants to their work and walked through the arched doorway into the innermost courtyard.

Rodolfo had asked me twice if I wanted to stay in the capital, in his family's old Baroque apartment, but I refused. I wanted the house. I wanted to steal Mamá away from Tía Fernanda, bring her here and show it to her. I wanted to prove to Mamá that marrying Rodolfo was *right*. That my choice would open a door into a new life for us.

And now, as I at last faced the house, the slant of its gap-toothed roof, its dark windows and age-weathered white stucco walls, a feral feeling seized me.

Get back.

My spine stiffened. I wanted to fling myself back from the courtyard as if I had been burned.

But I refused to let myself falter. I tightened my grip on Rodolfo's hand and banished the feeling. It was foolish. I was taken aback by Juana, but that was no reason to flee. Not when I had won so much.

Not when I had nothing to run to.

The air was thick and silent, our footsteps the only sound as we reached a set of low, broad steps leading up to the front door. I stepped onto the first, then froze, a gasp stealing the breath from my lips.

A dead rat splayed across the third step, its head tilted back at a broken angle, its stiff tongue jutting through yellowed teeth. Perhaps it had fallen from the roof, but its skull had split open as if it had been flung from a height with incredible force. Shining brains spilled onto the stone step, a splatter of rotten pink covered with crawling black flies.

Rodolfo let out a weak cry of surprise and yanked me back from the steps.

Juana's light laugh lilted over our heads. She was directly behind us, then at once at my elbow.

"Oh, the cats here get a little carried away," she said gaily, as if explaining away a troublesome nephew. "Do you mind cats?"

3

⁓

THE TOUR RODOLFO GAVE me of the main house was brief.
The housekeeper, Ana Luisa, would give me a more thorough introduction
to its inner workings later in the day, he said. Though he had spent his childhood in this house and had many fond memories of it, he came and went too
infrequently during the war to understand running it as well as she.

The house's walls were thick, stucco and whitewashed; though the sun
shone bright outside, cool shadows draped the halls. The building was arranged in a U shape around a central courtyard and was two-storied only
over its central, largest section. The southern branch housed the kitchen
and storerooms and was Ana Luisa's domain. At the north end of the central wing, a staircase led to an upper floor composed of bedrooms, the suite
of the patrón, and several empty drawing rooms.

As Rodolfo and I returned downstairs, I noticed a narrow passage to
the right of the foot of the stairs. Its doorway was boarded up, a hasty job
of mismatched wood and rusting nails.

"Juana told me there was damage in the northern wing," Rodolfo said when he noticed how I paused, my attention drawn to the doorway. He took me gently by the hand and led me away. "An earthquake, or water, I can't remember which. I will have Mendoza look into repairs."

I tilted my chin up as we entered a formal dining room, tracing Moorish tiles imported from the peninsula by his forebears to a high ceiling. A narrow ledge ran around the circumference of the room, nearly twelve feet off the ground.

Rodolfo followed the line of my gaze. "When my parents used to have parties here, the servants would take candelabras up there," he said. "It was as bright as an opera house." Then his smile at the memory faded, and a shadow passed over his face. "Never go up there. A maid fell from there once."

His words struck the air off-key, distant and slightly dissonant.

I shivered. Contrary to what Juana said, *drafty* was not the term I would have chosen to describe the chill inside the house. It sank into my bones like claws. The still air tasted of the staleness of an underground storeroom. I wanted to throw open all the shuttered windows, to let in fresh air and light.

But Rodolfo escorted me swiftly onward, closing the door with a snap behind him.

"We will dine somewhere more comfortable tonight," he said.

Tomorrow, I promised the room. Tomorrow I would throw light into all its shadowed corners, order paint to be mixed to tidy its soot-soiled stucco.

From behind the door, the room laughed at me.

I froze. Rodolfo kept walking; my hand slipped out of his.

Had I misheard? Was I imagining it? I was certain I had heard light, bubbling laughter, like that of a wicked child, reaching through the heavy wooden door.

But it was empty. Behind that door, I *knew* the room was empty. I had just seen it.

"Come along, querida." Rodolfo's smile was overbright, strained. "There is much to see before dinner."

And there was. Gardens, stables, household servants' quarters, the village, where the tlachiqueros and farm workers lived, the general store, the capilla . . . San Isidro was a world unto its own.

Rodolfo left me in the care of Ana Luisa for a tour of the rest of the house, and I immediately wished he hadn't. She was brusque and humorless.

"This is the green parlor," she said, gesturing into one room but not entering. It had a single fireplace that was soot-stained; the walls were white, the floorboards scratched and tired.

"It's not green." My voice landed hollow on the empty space.

"The rug used to be," was Ana Luisa's only answer.

Like her voice, the house was devoid of color. White, brown, shadows, soot—these were the smudgy palate of San Isidro. By the time the sun was setting, and Ana Luisa had finished guiding me around the servants' courtyard and the tidy capilla, I was exhausted. The house and the grounds were in various states of disrepair; the amount of effort it would take to prepare them for Mamá daunted me. But as Ana Luisa and I returned to the house and I took it in from the courtyard, from its foreboding dark door to the cracked tiles on the roof, I could not stop a flutter of emotion from rising in my throat.

This house was *mine*. Here I was safe.

SEVEN MONTHS AGO, I sprang from bed in the middle of the night, woken by pounding from somewhere in the house and shouting from the street. Heart in my throat, I stumbled into the dark hall and seized the handle of the parlor door with clammy hands, tripping over the rug. Light and shadows danced mockingly across dainty chairs and delicate wallpaper, across Papá's worn map of his battles pinned to the wall opposite the second-floor windows.

I rushed to the windows. Flames filled the street below: there were men in military uniform, dozens of them, brandishing torches and dark muskets crowned with long bayonets, their steel grinning greedily in the light of the flames.

One of them pounded on the door, shouting my father's name.

Where was Papá? Surely he would know the meaning of—

And then Papá opened the door. Papá was among them, his hair disheveled, a robe wrapped tidily around his wiry frame. He looked more tired than I had ever seen him, heavy shadows accenting the gauntness of his face.

But his eyes burned with hatred as he took in the men surrounding him. He began to speak, but even if I had pressed my ear to the window, I would not have been able to hear him, not from so far above, not over the din of the shouting. I was paralyzed as the men seized Papá by the upper arms and dragged him away from the house, into the street. He seemed so frail, so breakable . . .

Traitor. A single word rose from the din. *Traitor.*

Then they were gone.

Only a handful remained behind, their faces cast in shadow as they took the butts of their muskets and thrust them at the windows below. Glass shattered; men flung shining liquid and torches through the jagged teeth of broken panes. The men melted away into the night, and I could not move, not even as the smell of burning wood rose into the room and the floorboards beneath my knees grew warm.

Papá was not a traitor. Even though the man who became emperor and Papá began the war on different sides—Papá with the insurgents and Agustín de Iturbide with the Spanish—they worked side by side in the end. Papá fought for independence. For México. Every battle he and I marked in red ink on his map was for *México*, every—

Mamá's shriek split my skull. I flung myself back from the window; my heel caught on the leg of a chair and sent me sprawling on the carpet. Heat scorched my lungs; the air rippled thick with it. Smoke rose in delicate columns through the floorboards as I pushed myself to all fours.

The map. I lurched upward, then to the wall, and reached for the pins on which it hung, hissing as they seared my fingertips.

"Beatriz!"

I ripped it down, folding it with shaking hands as I ran toward her voice. Smoke stung my eyes; my ribs seized with coughing.

"Mamá!" I couldn't see, I couldn't breathe as I tripped downstairs to the back door. Mamá grabbed me and yanked me into the street. Our backs sweated and blistered from the heat behind us; we were coughing, bare-footed, shocked by the cold of the night.

Mamá had gone to the servants' quarters to wake the household staff but found their beds cold and empty. Had they known? Had they known, and fled to save their hides, and never warned us?

They must have known. Someone must have told them what we learned in the pale, fragile light of the next morning: that Agustín de Iturbide, emperor of México, was deposed. Exiled. On a ship to Italy. And his allies? Even those who had been insurgents, like Papá? Rounded up and executed.

"Shot in the back like the cowards they were, that's what I heard," said my watery-eyed cousin Josefa across the breakfast table, sneering archly down her Roman nose.

With nowhere to go, Mamá took us to the home of the only family she had left in México, the only ones who still spoke to her after she married Papá, a man of a lower casta than she: that of Sebastián Valenzuela, the son of her father's cousin.

"But Tío Sebastián hates us," I whimpered as we walked, shivering, the veil of sweat the heat of the house doused us in turning frigid in the night.

Papá's map crinkled against my nightdress, clenched protectively between my bicep and rib cage as we ran through the dark winding alleys of the capital. We rounded the back corner of the walls of my uncle's house and collapsed on the muddy steps of the entrance to the servants' quarters.

Mamá said she couldn't trust any of her or Papá's friends. Not after what had happened. We had to come here.

"We don't have a choice," she said.

But Sebastián did.

His wife, Fernanda, made that perfectly clear as she took Mamá and me in. She could have left us on the doorstep. She could have turned us away, and Sebastián would not question her judgment.

It was true, and I knew it. My uncle had no love for us, never had, and only took us in out of whatever remaining scrap of childhood loyalty he felt for a cousin long disowned by the family.

He took us in, but he preached self-righteously at dinner our first day in his house how my father had made the wrong choices all through the war, first by throwing his weight behind the insurgents, then by compromising and forming a coalition with the monarchist conservatives.

Though I was exhausted and starving, my appetite vanished. I stared at the cooling food on my plate, unmoving.

"It is a tragedy, but it was bound to happen," Tío Sebastián mused sagely. His too-long gray muttonchops quivered with each gluttonous bite he took.

I could not decide if the feeling that seized my throat meant to make me vomit or cry. Humiliation seared my cheeks. Papá risked his life for independence, and I had a map to prove it. His rivals must have betrayed him, lied about him. And he was killed. I lifted my head, eyes fixed on my uncle. I opened my mouth—

A soft touch at my elbow.

Mamá's touch. Nothing she ever did was above a murmur, none of her movements were anything but graceful and soft, but her message was piercingly clear: *do not speak.*

I bit my tongue, the pork on my plate going blurry as hot tears pricked my eyes.

She was right.

If Tío Sebastián chose to turn us out, Mamá and I would have nowhere to go. The realization was like a slap to the face: no one would take us. Our lives depended on pleasing my mother's cousin and the beady-eyed, petty wife who poured poison into his ear.

I forced food into my mouth. It stuck to my dry throat like glue.

That night, as Mamá and I curled together, forehead to forehead, in the one narrow bed Tía Fernanda would spare us, I sobbed until I thought my ribs would crack. Mamá brushed away the sweaty hair that stuck to my forehead and kissed my hot cheeks.

"You must be strong," she said. "We must bear this with dignity."

With dignity.

With *silence* was what she meant.

I could not inherit my father's property. I could not work. I could not care for Mamá, whose face grew wan and peaked. Reliant on my uncle's charity, on my sour aunt's thin goodwill, I had nothing. I wore castoffs from my cousins, I was not allowed to study or go out, for fear my presence would lower the esteem of the Valenzuela name in the eyes of the other criollos and peninsulares. I was a body without a voice, a shadow melting into the walls of a too-crowded house.

And then I met Rodolfo.

When he entered that ball to celebrate the founding of the Republic, when his broad shoulders filled the doorway, a sense of peace swept through the room. The tide changed, the hum quieted. He was solid. Reliable. He had a commanding voice, rich and golden, his bronze hair bright in the candlelight. He was smooth and collected, with all the confident, quiet authority of an idol in his temple.

My breath caught. Not because of his easy, lopsided smile, or the coy, almost timid way he approached me to ask for a dance. Not because his youth and his status as a widower gave him a romantic, tragic reputation among Josefa and her tittering friends. But because of the silence with which the room watched him. I craved that. I wanted to cup a room in my palm, to tell it to be still, to tell it to *hush*.

If Rodolfo was aware of his powers of enchantment, he did not reveal it. Of course he wouldn't. He was a military man, a protégé of Guadalupe Victoria, one of the generals who formed the Provisional Government that ousted and replaced the emperor.

By the end of our first dance, I realized that a politician like Rodolfo would not overlook my father's legacy for long. If it did not frighten him off when we were first introduced, when he was told my surname—Hernández Valenzuela, indicating my father's family and then my mother's—then it might later.

And at twenty, I faced a ticking clock: marry soon, when I was seen as fresh and virginal and desirable, or marry not at all.

So when it became clear he was attracted to my laugh like bees to piloncillo syrup and to my eyes, my mother's eyes, bright as Chiapas jade, I seized it.

When I announced to my mother that I would be marrying Don Rodolfo Eligio Solórzano Ibarra, she set down her embroidery into her lap without grace, mouth dropped open in surprise. The months since my father's death had taken a toll on her: her pale skin no longer called to mind fine china, but faded, crumbling paper. Violet shadows weighed beneath her eyes, which had lost their vigor. Her cheeks, once haughty in their height, were hollow, thinned by exhaustion.

"You . . . *Solórzano*," she breathed. "He's one of Victoria's men."

I folded my arms across my chest. Yes, he served one of the leaders of the political party that had turned on my father.

"If you want to leave this house and stop mending Tía Fernanda's sheets, he's the only choice. Don't you understand?" I snapped. *Look around you*, I wanted to scream. Mamá married for love and burnt bridges behind her. I didn't have that privilege. I couldn't afford her idealism. Not when I had Rodolfo's proposal, not when I had the chance to get us out of Tía Fernanda's house. I could secure us a dignified life. Rodolfo's name, his money, his land—these could give us wings to *fly*.

Mamá closed her mouth, dropped her eyes to her mending, and did not speak another word to me. Not then, not in the weeks leading up to the wedding.

I ignored her absence at the wedding. I held my head high beneath my lace mantilla and ignored the whispers about Rodolfo's family. About past romantic entanglements and mysterious illnesses that Tía Fernanda jealously relayed to anyone who would listen, her lips smacking like boots in thick mud, her stage whisper scraping like dry, too-long fingernails across the back of my neck.

I heard his first wife was murdered by highwaymen on the Apan road. Really? I heard she died of typhus. I heard she was kidnapped by insurgents. I heard she was poisoned by the cook.

Rodolfo was my salvation. I seized him like a drowning man seizes driftwood in a flash flood. His solidness. His name. His title. His shoulders that cut into Apan's blinding sky like the mountains surrounding the valley and the calloused, honest hands that led me to the gate of San Isidro.

He was safe. He was right. I had made the one decision that was guaranteed to lift me from the grim fate to which my father's murder had doomed us.

I only prayed that one day, Mamá could see my decision to marry him for what it was: the key to a new life.

4

RODOLFO, JUANA, AND I reconvened for dinner in a small
drawing room near the kitchen that had been repurposed for dining. Its
windows opened to the back of the house: a terrace, lined with pillars and
arches, overlooked a dead garden with wilted birds of paradise and black
skeletons of flower beds. Heavy-bellied clouds had rolled into the valley;
Ana Luisa's daughter, Paloma, fastened the window shutters against the
rain as we sat. The drawing room was cozier for three than the formal dining room, but I soon wished it were less cozy.

"I apologize for the state of the flowers," Rodolfo said, his gaze trailing
over the shutters as Paloma flitted shyly away to the kitchen. "Juana cares
for maguey more than she cares for gardens."

Juana snorted. I looked up from my food in surprise. As much as I
disliked my cousins in Tío Sebastián's house, I was well accustomed to
their fine manners. It was how I had also been raised.

"Maguey is resilient," she said flatly. "It is an admirable trait."

Rodolfo's eyes slid across the table to her, their blue no longer brilliant, but icy. "Beauty is also an admirable trait," he said. A playful retort and delivered utterly without warmth. "This the maguey lack, I believe."

"Then you're not looking hard enough." The edge to her voice laid clear how little she cared for his thoughts on any matter, be it maguey or anything else.

No wonder Rodolfo had never spoken to me of his sister. The air between them crackled with friction.

"The garden is beautiful, querido," I lied, forcing a brightness into my voice that rang hollow in the closeness of the room. Rodolfo cast me a sideways glance, disbelieving. I rested my hand on his knee under the table, rubbing my thumb against the fabric of his trousers in a calculated attempt to break the tension. "My mother taught me something about gardening, when we lived in Cuernavaca," I added. "Give me some time with it. You won't recognize it when you return."

In two weeks, Rodolfo would head back to the capital. He had accompanied me on the road to Apan to protect me from highwaymen, but his political work meant he could not stay in the country. The Provisional Government meant to hold elections for a president, and if sneakily peering at Rodolfo's correspondence had taught me anything, it was that his mentor, Guadalupe Victoria, meant to win these elections.

Rodolfo opened his mouth to reply but was interrupted by his sister.

"We don't need gardens," she said harshly, not bothering to direct the comment at me. It dismissed me as efficiently as a slap across the face. "What we need is to keep San Cristóbal from poaching our land."

"I decide what we need or don't," Rodolfo snapped. His sudden shift of temper sent a tremor of surprise down my spine. "If Doña Beatriz wants a garden, she will have a garden. My wife's word is mine in this house, do you understand?"

If Juana did, she did not say. "I'm retiring," she announced to the room at large, falsely bright, and set her napkin on the table with a rude slap.

I stiffened as she pushed back from the table; then, with a brusque *good night*, she was gone.

IF THE RANCOR BETWEEN Rodolfo and Juana cooled over the two weeks he spent with us at San Isidro, I did not see it. I did not see her at all. It was as if she had vanished into the harsh rows of maguey that carved the fields below the main house, ephemeral as a ghost.

She did not join us when Rodolfo and I went into the town of Apan for Mass on Sunday.

It was my first visit to Apan, and the first time I would be seen by the hacendados of the other estates and their wives. Something in the air shifted as we passed through the gates of the hacienda, and I relaxed back into my seat. I rested my head on Rodolfo's shoulder and rocked with the carriage's movement, listening as he told me about the hacendados to whom he would introduce me after Mass.

"Their politics are slow to change, but they were my father's allies and will continue to be ours, if their tolerance of Juana is any measure of their patience." He took my gloved hands into his lap and held them, running a thumb over the lace absentmindedly. Though my eyes were closed, I could picture his wry half smile as he said, with a touch of knowing amusement, "Besides, country society is rather toothless compared to the capital."

It took an hour to ride to the center of Apan. When Rodolfo helped me out of the carriage, I was struck by how small the town was. Some three thousand people lived here, Rodolfo said, and perhaps a thousand more scattered on surrounding haciendas, but what was such a number to me, who had grown accustomed to the density of the capital? Now I saw it concretely. The town itself—the central plaza de armas before the parish, post, barracks, other assorted buildings—was so small we could have passed through it in the carriage in ten minutes.

Sickly cypress trees lined the path up to the church. Though its front facade was simple, decorated only with carved stone, its stucco walls were impeccably whitewashed, as bright against the azure sky as the clouds. A bell rang from a single tower announcing the beginning of Mass.

I had assembled my attire from demure colors, soft gray and green, and was glad I did so as we entered the church. Even though my dress was by no means the most elaborate, it was by far of the highest quality, and I drew stares from the townspeople as I fell into step beside Rodolfo up the aisle of the church. My mantilla fluttered gently against my cheek as I genuflected and took a seat in a pew reserved for us and other hacendados near the altar.

In the capital, I had been merely one general's daughter among many; here I was Doña Beatriz Solórzano, the wife of one of the wealthiest estate owners, urbane and mysterious. Whispers rippled through the pews behind me in the quiet moments before the beginning of Mass.

I relished it. I cupped that power and held it close to my chest as Mass began. San Isidro was not what I had pictured when I married Rodolfo, but that power *was*. This was my new life. This was what I had won.

Mass was a long hour of incense and murmurs, rising and sitting. We all moved as one, speaking and responding, the steps of the dance carved into us from years of repetition like the rhythm of a lullaby. I had always found the Latin rites monotonous at best but paid even less attention than usual now there were hacendados around me to size up. Rather than watch the gray-haired, plump priest and his raven-like mestizo attendant behind the altar, my attention flitted like a hummingbird from head to head in the pews. Which of these strangers would be a friend? Who might be a foe?

After Mass, Rodolfo began his introductions: Severo Piña y Cuevas and his wife, Encarnación, of Hacienda Ocotepec, a pair of Muñoz brothers from Hacienda Alcantarilla, and elderly Atenógenes Moreno and his wife, María José, of San Antonio Ometusco. All were pulque-producing haciendas, and—judging from the fine silk and stately peninsular fashions of the wives—they had survived eleven years of civil war as well as Rodolfo's family had.

"It is good your husband's sister is no longer alone," Doña María José Moreno said, taking my hand and putting it on her arm affectionately as we followed her husband, Atenógenes, and Rodolfo toward the door of the church. Her hair was spun silver beneath her mantilla, her back slightly humped from age. "There are widows who run their own haciendas, it is true. I must introduce you to the widow of old Herrera. She used to live in the capital as well and has been running Hacienda Buenavista for nearly ten years now. But Doña Juana . . . she is a figure of some curiosity. I am glad she now has someone as refined as you to be her example."

She patted my hand with the absentminded affection of a grandmother, but a hint of warning underscored the softness of her voice. I kept my expression carefully still as I tucked that information away. Perhaps the hacendados were not as tolerant of Juana as Rodolfo thought.

Doña María José lifted her rheumy eyes, squinting through her mantilla. "You're nearly as lovely as Doña María Catalina, though quite darker. Perhaps you will weather the country better than her. Poor thing. Such a delicate constitution."

The words struck me like freezing water to the face. Rodolfo's first wife. Of course they would bring her up. I pasted a concerned look on my face, nodding in agreement. This was the first time I had met someone who knew Rodolfo's previous wife, who wasn't merely sharing ill-spirited gossip. I should have asked her for the truth about the first Doña Solórzano's untimely death.

But the idea repulsed me. Less lovely or not, *quite darker* or not, I was Doña Solórzano now. Rodolfo and all that was his were *mine*, won in a fair fight.

Loathing itched under my skin as I looked down at Doña María José. Women like her thought themselves sage when doling out advice to young brides, so I steered the conversation away from dead women and my complexion by asking her empty questions regarding marriage, nodding and smiling where I knew I ought to as she replied. But my mind was elsewhere.

She is a figure of some . . . curiosity.

Curiosity meant gossip, and gossip—be it ill-intentioned or not— always had a seed to spring from. Perhaps it was Juana's irreverence about her appearance that inspired talk. Perhaps it was her brusqueness. She certainly did not beget the same kind of sympathy her deceased sister-in-law stirred in acquaintances.

These thoughts trailed after me into the evening, coiling through my fingers like my hair as I plaited it by candlelight, sitting in a chair before my vanity. I did not tell Rodolfo about my conversation with Doña María José, though questions uncurled in my chest like weeds, their roots finding firm purchase in my ribs.

I couldn't ask him much of anything still. Our newlywed intimacy was an uneven thing: I knew the warm smell of his throat, the rhythm of his breathing as he slept, but not the thoughts that played behind his face. Uncharted silences stretched between us, long and pitted with secrets. What did he fear? Why had he hidden Juana from me? If he loved San Isidro so much, why avoid it for so many years?

So many questions, yet I bit my tongue. I glanced over my shoulder at the bed behind me. Rodolfo was already breathing deeply, tangled in white blankets, a lock of bronze hair flopped over his forehead and straight, sharp nose. A sleeping prince beneath a delicate shroud.

As beautiful as he was, I had no romantic notions about Rodolfo when I accepted his offer. Though he wooed me with sweet litanies of my fine qualities—my strength, my kind smile, my laughter, and my eyes—I did not believe he married me for who I was at all. My appearance may have convinced him to look past my father's politics; after all, I was a newcomer to capital society, and I knew I was beautiful. These two truths made me an enticing mystery to conquest-minded men.

But I was also someone who turned a blind eye to the susurration of rumors circling his widowerhood, and Rodolfo wanted a bride who did not ask too many questions. I chose to gamble on his secrets. Our relationship was founded on one thing and one thing only: my world was a dark, windowless room, and he was a door.

I turned back to the mirror and continued braiding my hair. An ache built slowly in my chest, a heavy, sweet ache edged with sharpness like broken glass. I missed Mamá. I missed Papá. I missed who I was before we lost everything: someone who saw her parents tease each other and laugh, who watched them hold hands while reading beside the fire at night or while whispering conspiratorially behind a door they thought was fully shut.

I used to be someone who wanted that. Who *yearned* for it. I wanted what it was Mamá had when Papá kissed her forehead and ran his thumb over her cheek before he left for battle. Whatever it was that made Mamá watch the window, restless and unable to be comforted, whenever he was due to return. Whatever it was that made them see each other for who they were, not their class or their casta.

My parents fought to be married despite their differences, despite the prejudice of Mamá's family, because they had *that* to fight for. *That* was what I wanted. Someone who saw me not as darker than someone else, nor not quite as lovely as someone else. Not the daughter of someone. Not a piece to be played in a larger game. Someone who saw me for who I was and treasured me for it.

And what did I have?

A stranger whose lips left me cold, whose heavy touch in the darkness inspired no desire in me. Questions swirling unanswered through my mind. Letters to my mother sent and unanswered. A house bare of family. An emptiness in my own rib cage, yawning and clawing and growing as much as I tried to repress it.

I bit my lip as it began to tremble. Yes, I had seized the name Solórzano despite barely knowing the man who bore it. Yes, I had married a man who came between me and Mamá, a man whom I did not love.

I sacrificed that dream because survival was more important than being lonely.

And now I had a roof over my head. An hacienda in my name. An income rooted in the land, firm and sheltered from the twin tempests of war and plague.

A *future*.

I was grateful to Rodolfo for lifting me from obscurity. For saving me from poverty. Perhaps, on my warmer days, I even felt fond of him for transforming my life. Perhaps one day I could even learn to love him for it.

A wink of color caught my attention in the mirror. Two red lights stared at me from a darkened corner beneath the window.

I blinked, and they were gone.

The hair on the back of my neck stood on end. An oily feeling slipped over my shoulders.

I was being watched.

I whirled to face the corner, eyes wide and desperate, searching the dark.

The light cast by the dying candle barely reached the foot of the bed. Black shadows shrouded the room, deepening near the walls.

The room was empty but for sleeping Rodolfo. There was nothing there.

I took a deep breath and exhaled, brusque and hard, to clear my head. I was exhausted from the trip into town and meeting so many new people. I was overwhelmed by the mountainous task fixing the house presented me. I had imagined the winks of red. I had imagined the feeling of being watched. That, or it was one of the cats Juana mentioned when I first arrived at San Isidro.

Yes, it had to be one of the cats.

Mind settled on this explanation, I turned back to my vanity and blew out the candle. I felt my way through the clammy dark to the bed, and slid under the blankets, letting myself be drawn to Rodolfo's warmth like a moth to flame. He flinched once at the cold brush of my feet, then shifted sleepily into me. The peace of his own sleep, of his solidness, settled over me. I closed my eyes.

His weight on the mattress was so different from when I had shared a bed with Mamá in Tía Fernanda's house. As grateful as I was for it, I fantasized idly about when he left for the capital and, for the first time in many, many months, I would have a bed to myself. And more. My own house. My own world. I slowed my mind with choosing paint colors for the different rooms downstairs, tempting dreaming to take me.

It was not until much later, as I swayed on the dark cusp of sleep, that I realized that since arriving at Hacienda San Isidro, I had not seen a single cat.

5

ANDRÉS

As I RODE ACROSS the countryside of the district of Tulancingo, the valley of Apan claimed me like a summer twilight: the bittersweet realization that I was nearly home was soft at first, teasing at the fringes of my senses, then took me all at once, swift and complete. Some kilometers outside the town, I told my traveling companions my mule had a stone in her shoe, and that they should ride on. I would rejoin them momentarily.

I dismounted.

For seven years at the seminary in Guadalajara, the Inquisition hovered over my shoulder like the shroud of death, ever watchful, its clammy breath foul on the back of my neck. From the age of sixteen until my ordination, I smothered my senses, drowning them in Latin and philosophy and penance. I prayed until my voice was hoarse. I wore a hair shirt when instructed it would purify me. I folded up the darkest parts of myself and shoved my contorted spirit into a box that remained locked.

But when my feet touched the earth of the valley, the axis of the world shifted beneath them. The windswept winter countryside and low gray skies turned their sleepy gaze toward me. They saw me, recognized me, and nodded in the slow, satisfied way of the ancient giants. I scanned the low, dark hills that curled around the valley like knuckles: for the first time in seven years, I sensed the spirits who hummed through this small corner of creation even when their names were forgotten.

The valley's awareness of me overtook me in a roar, in a wave, and I trembled beneath my too-big sarape. For years I had buried myself behind thick walls, alone—my secret severed me from the other students at the seminary. Fear of discovery governed my every thought and step; I hid myself so completely that I lived a hair's breadth from suffocation.

Now I was *seen*.

Now, the thing I feared most spread like a shadow in my breast: here, far from the eyes of the Inquisition, the parts of myself that I had shoved into a box began to unfurl, soft and curious as plumes of smoke, testing lock and hinge.

I forced them down.

Tell him I pray for his return to San Isidro. The birds pray for his return to San Isidro.

My grandmother's prayer was answered. I was nearly home. But what would become of me, now that I was?

MY ARRIVAL WAS IMMEDIATELY consumed by preparations for the feast day of la Virgen de Guadalupe. Padre Guillermo and Padre Vicente had a specific vision for the procession of the statue of la Virgen and San Juan Diego through the streets of Apan, and made it clear what my place in it was: shouldering the litter carrying la Virgen and the saint at her feet alongside men from the town. Padre Guillermo was too old for such things, Padre Vicente said, and he—well, he would be leading the procession, wouldn't he?

This was my place as a young cura, a sin destino priest with no parish and no hope of a career in a city. This was the proper place of a mestizo priest in the eyes of Padre Vicente. He was correct. More than he knew. Even if I had been a man of ambition, even if I had entered the priesthood with the intention of lining my life with silver and comfort like so many men I met in the seminary, I could not change what I was.

I knew Padre Guillermo from before I left for Guadalajara. How often he had found me asleep beneath the pews in the church as a boy and carried me back to my mother through the dawn, curled in his arms like a drowsy kitten. If Guillermo guessed at the reason I fled from the house in the middle of the night, seeking the silence of the house of God, he never mentioned it. It was he who wrote to Guadalajara and welcomed my transfer to the small parish of Apan, and when I arrived, dusty and exhausted from weeks on the road, he who embraced me. Guillermo, for all his fluster and pomp and his desire to please the wealthy hacendados who funded renovations in the church, was someone I trusted. But still, he had never lived on the haciendas as I had as a child. There were so many things he could never understand.

Vicente was new, a replacement for old Padre Alejandro, who had walked alongside the specter of Death for years. From the moment I met Vicente's hawkish light gaze, a curl of fear turned in my bones. He could not be trusted—not with me, nor my secrets, nor with the struggles of my people.

The priests exited the church through the back to begin the procession, and I took my place among the three other townspeople elected to carry the litter of la Virgen—the aging master of the post, an equally graying baker, and his whip-thin son who looked no more than twelve. Nine years of insurgency had left no family unscathed. No townsperson, no hacendado, no villager had not lost a son or brother or nephew in their prime. If not in the battles that tore up the countryside and painted it black with blood, then to tuberculosis, or gangrene, or typhus.

I took my place and lifted the litter of la Virgen on my left shoulder. We were imbalanced; my height was not matched by the baker, so I would need to slouch to keep la Virgen at an even keel.

"¿Todo bien, Padre Andrés?"

I looked over my shoulder at the baker's son and grunted in the affirmative. Past him were the low stone walls of the graveyard. I turned my face away quickly.

More of my family now lay beneath the earth than walked it, but I had not paid my respects to those who lay behind the parish of Apan. My brothers were not there. Antonio and Hildo had died in battles in Veracruz and Guadalajara; only the Lord knew where they rested. The third, Diego, had vanished somewhere near Tulancingo last year. He was alive, I *knew* it, and was held somewhere, but none of my frantic letters to every insurgent I knew resulted in any reply. My grandmother was not there. She was buried near her home in the village of Hacienda San Isidro. I wished my mother could be buried near her, on the land where she had been born, the land that was *home*, the land where her family had lived for seven generations, but she was in the cemetery behind me.

I would visit soon. But not now. Not yet.

On Padre Vicente's command, we began to walk around the church to the plaza de armas. Apan was four proper streets and a tangle of alleys; gray and quiet on most days, it burst at the seams on the feast day of la Virgen. People from the haciendas traveled into town for the Mass and the procession. They were dressed in their feast day best, men in starched shirts and women in bright embroidery, but as we proceeded slowly behind Padres Vicente and Guillermo, it became clear how faded and patched these clothes were. There were too many gaunt faces, too many feet without shoes, even in the middle of winter. The war left no part of the countryside untouched, but it left its deepest mark on those who had the least.

But whenever I glanced up, I saw eyes bright as an autumn sky. Burning with curiosity. Fixed not on la Virgen and rapturous Juan Diego, but lower.

On me.

I knew what they saw.

They did not see the son of Esteban Villalobos, onetime Sevillan fore-

man to old Solórzano on Hacienda San Isidro, then assistant to the caudillo, the local military officer who maintained order in Apan and the
surrounding haciendas. Resident thug and drunk who had returned to
Spain seven years ago.

They did not see the newly ordained Padre Juan Andrés Villalobos, a
cura trained in Guadalajara, who regularly prayed before a cathedral retablo resplendent with more gold than they had ever seen in their lives.

They saw my grandmother. Alejandra Pérez, my sijtli, called Titi by her
many grandchildren and by a good measure of the countryside besides.

It was unlikely they saw her in my features—these were more my Spanish father's than my mother's. No. I knew they felt Titi's presence. Perhaps
they even felt the shift of the earth beneath their feet, the attention of the
skies tilting toward me. *There*, they said. *That one. Look.*

And look they did. They made a show of gazing at la Virgen and crossing themselves when blessed by Padre Vicente's swinging golden censer,
but I knew they watched me beneath Juan Diego's wooden knees.

I kept my eyes on the dusty road before me.

The people of Hacienda San Isidro were clustered in a group near the end
of the procession, at the front of the church. I raised my head and found my
cousin, Paloma, standing with a few other girls her age. She shifted her
weight from one foot to the other in anticipation, craning her neck, scanning
the procession. When her eyes caught mine, a smile illuminated her face like
lightning. I nearly stumbled, like Christ on the road to Calvary, from the
shock of seeing someone so familiar after so many years apart. I had returned
to Apan, yes, but now, in Paloma's presence, I felt I was *home*.

They were all there, the people of the hacienda I had known my whole
life: my aunt and Paloma's mother, Ana Luisa, the old foreman Mendoza
who had replaced my father in the wake of his indiscretions. They watched
me with intense black eyes, taking me in for the first time in seven years,
knowing me as their own.

I knew they expected me to step into Titi's shoes.

But how could I? I was ordained. I had followed the path Titi and my mother urged me to take: I was not lost to the last decade of war, be it by gangrene or a gachupín's bayonet. I had skirted the attention of the Inquisition and become a man of the Church.

They will teach you things I cannot, Titi said as she put me on the road to the seminary so many years ago. *Besides,* she added, a sly twinkle in her eye as she patted my chest, aware her palm rested directly over the darkness that lived curled around my heart, *won't you be well hidden there?*

The people of San Isidro needed more than another priest. They needed my grandmother. *I* needed her. I missed how she always smelled of piney soap, how the veiny backs of her hands were so soft to hold, her knobby fingers and wrists so strong and sure as they braided her white hair or ground herbs in the molcajete to cure a family member's stomach pain. I missed the mischievous glint in her dark eyes that my mother, Lucero, had inherited, and that I wished I had. I even missed her exasperatingly cryptic advice. I needed her to show me how to be both a priest and her heir, how to care for her flock and calmly deflect the withering suspicion of Padre Vicente.

But she was dead.

I closed my eyes as the procession shuffled to a halt before the front door of the church.

Please. The prayer reached out, up to the heavens to God, out to the spirits that slept in the bellies of the hills ringing the valley. I knew no other way to pray. *Give me guidance.*

When I opened them, I saw Padre Vicente shaking hands and blessing members of a group of hacendados. Their silks and fine hats stood out against the crowds, garish as peacocks in a famine. The old patróns of Hacienda Ocotepec and Alcantarilla tipped their hats to Padre Vicente, their pale-haired ladies and daughters clasping his hand in their gloved ones. Even the hacendados had not escaped the ravages of war. Their sons had left to fight for the gachupínes, the Spanish, and left only old men and boys to defend the estates against insurgents in the countryside.

The only young man among them was one with light brown hair and piercing blue eyes, whose saintly face looked like it was carved and painted for a statue in a gilded retablo. He stood apart from the others and met Padre Guillermo's effusive greeting with a calculated half smile.

It took me a moment to place why he seemed so familiar.

"Don Rodolfo!" Padre Guillermo cried.

He was the son of old Solórzano. Now, presumably, he was the patrón of Hacienda San Isidro. I had seen him from a distance as a boy on the property; I knew children in the village did not mind him, and even played with him chasing frogs in the creek below the house from time to time. Now, he could not be more different from the villagers: his clothing was finely tailored and cut a sharp silhouette. A criolla woman hung on his arm, whom he introduced to Padre Guillermo as his new bride, Doña María Catalina.

He had brought her from the capital to be safe from typhus, he said. She would join his sister on Hacienda San Isidro and stay for the foreseeable future.

"Does this mean you are returning to the capital soon, Don Rodolfo?" Padre Guillermo asked.

"I am." He glanced over his shoulder at the other hacendados, then leaned into Padre Guillermo and lowered his voice. "Things are changing very quickly, and the capital is not safe." His voice lowered further; another man would not have been able to hear him over the general commotion of the crowd, but my grandmother left me with many gifts. My ear, long accustomed to hearing the shifting moods of the fields and the skies, was sharp as a coyote's.

"You must watch over Doña Catalina, Padre," Rodolfo said. "You understand . . . my politics are not popular with my father's friends."

"May he rest in peace," Padre Guillermo murmured, his tone and the slow dip of his head subtle assent.

Curiosity sharpened my ears, though I fought to keep my face as passive as a saint's. To be unpopular with the conservative criollo hacendados, those who clung to their wealth and the monarchy, meant that Rodolfo was sympathetic to the insurgents and independence. It was not unusual for sons of hacendados to turn the tables and support the insurgents, but I did not expect it of the son of old, cruel Solórzano. Perhaps Rodolfo was different from the other criollos. Perhaps, now that old Solórzano was dead, the people of San Isidro would suffer less under the younger man's watch.

I peered at the woman on his arm. She looked as if she had stepped out of a painting: her small, pointed face was crowned by hair pale as corn silk. Her eyes were doe-like, dark and wide-set; when they flicked in my direction, they slid right over me. They passed over the townspeople, unseeing, and then refocused on Padre Guillermo.

Ah. Those were eyes that did not see faces that were not peninsular or criollo. There were many such pairs of eyes among the hacendados and their families. How could such a woman survive without her ilk, alone in the country, in that enormous house at the center of Hacienda San Isidro? She looked as if she were made from expensive white sugar, the likes of which I had only ever seen in Guadalajara. Unreal as a phantom lilting pale on a riverbank. I had seen women like her in Guadalajara, pious, wealthy women with hands as soft as a lamb's spring coat, utterly incapable of working. Such people could not survive long in the country.

I wondered then if the changes Don Rodolfo hinted at would end the war at last. Whenever it did, I was sure that his spun-sugar wife would flee back to the comforts of the capital, typhus or no.

How very wrong I was.

6

BEATRIZ

PRESENT DAY

AFTER BREAKFAST ONE MORNING, Rodolfo saddled his horse and bade farewell to me at the gates of San Isidro.

He cupped my chin in one hand, searching my face. "Are you sure?"

This was now the third time he had asked if I was going to be all right at San Isidro. I had slept fitfully and woken before him, staring at the cobwebs between the Nicaraguan cedar beams in our bedroom. There was so much in the air of the house that felt *other*.

Perhaps it was that many generations had lived here before me, slept under the same beams. Each had made it their own. So, too, would I.

"Of course, querido," I said. "I need to settle in. Make it presentable for my mother. You know how she is about tidy houses." He didn't. His smile was knowing all the same. A politician, an actor, even with his wife. I paused, weighing the wisdom of what I was about to say next, then went ahead anyway: "Promise me you'll deliver my letters to her. In person, if you can spare the time."

Mamá hated everything that Rodolfo stood for. She would not welcome his presence, especially if he was delivering messages from me, her turncoat daughter. But I had to try, even if none of my other letters had been answered.

"Of course," he said, and kissed me. A brief, chaste brush of lips. His skin had a bite of citrus from his aftershave. "Don't hesitate to write if there is anything you need. Anything at all."

With that, Rodolfo mounted his bay mare and rode south. I waited until his dark hat was nothing more than a smudge on the horizon, then retraced my steps through the courtyards, midmorning sun already hot on my hat. Now that he was gone, there was something I needed to do before anything else.

Once inside the house, I headed upstairs. The suite of the patrón was divided into four rooms: the first was a parlor of sorts, bare of much furniture and cluttered with chests filled with my clothes from the capital. The only windows were set high in the wall and were far too narrow for my liking; they had no glass panes and were covered with old cedar shutters. Such was the way with country houses, Rodolfo had explained. It would be hard to adjust to this after years of sewing by the large glass-paned windows in Mamá's parlor in the capital.

The next room was a drawing room, a study of sorts. Rodolfo had left a number of books here from his studies: military texts, a Bible, Plato's *Republic*. A door on the left-hand side of the room led to the bedchamber, and off the bedchamber was the room for washing.

I knelt before the first of my chests. The lock clicked open, and I lifted the heavy lid. Atop my bedclothes, undergarments, and stockings was a small square of folded paper. I took it, held it to my nose, and inhaled deeply. Something about the smell of paper *was* Papá. It was his map, the one piece of home I snatched as I fled.

I took it, and a handful of embroidery pins, to the study and pinned it to the wall above Rodolfo's desk. Yes, the room was still dusty, still in desperate need of airing out. Too dark. But Papá was on the wall now. His neat *x*'s in red, the sweep of his charcoal pencil directing armies.

This tiny bit of the house was *home* now, and I would not rest until the remainder of it was as well.

UNTIL THE FIRST SHIPMENT of furniture arrived from the capital, I was going to see what could be done about the gardens. I tightened the ribbons of my hat, took a pair of gloves from my chests, and made for the back terrace. While Rodolfo was present, I sat on my hands, fighting every urge to clean the house myself. Rodolfo was still unaware of how I had toughened my hands to work Tía Fernanda's house, and I intended to keep it that way.

I strode through the cool halls and made my way to the parlor that had heavy cedar double doors to the terrace. I threw them open and inhaled deeply of fresh morning.

I had resented every callus I built following Tía Fernanda's orders, every cut I accidentally gave myself in the kitchen. But here? The garden before me was *mine* to fix, and though it was wilted and brown, a fierce affection for it welled up in me. This was *mine* to make ready for Mamá. I could already picture her standing next to me on this terrace, her green eyes lifting up to the bright azure sky.

My earliest years were spent on an hacienda in Cuernavaca on a vast sugar plantation with my father's extended family—the Hernández side, the one that had less *Andalusian blood*, as he euphemistically described his darker complexion and thick black hair. The vine-covered stone main house sprawled lazily among palm trees and two-hundred-year-old fountains and was crowded with generations of cousins, but we lived in a smaller house apart from most of the family. For while Papá was loved by his aunt, the matriarch of the hacienda, she alone tolerated his choice to join the insurgency against Spain. Our small cottage once belonged to a long-dead foreman, or a gardener, and was connected to the main house by arches covered with thick vines, their lush green accented by trailing bougainvillea.

Mamá did not mind this slight. She loved how the boisterous growth of the gardens always threatened to overtake the buildings of the hacienda and draw them into a verdant embrace. She had a miraculous way with everything living and green, and when Papá was away fighting, she spent hours with her broad-rimmed hat walking the property with the head gardener, discussing irrigation and pruning.

The arid climate and dead grasses of the lawn before me were not quite the same palate she had worked with in Cuernavaca, but I had no doubt she would work her miracles on the gardens of San Isidro. Long grasses whispered against one another, gossiping like aunts as I crossed to the back wall of the garden. A tall wooden ladder was propped against it; though its bottom rungs were splintered and cracked, the next few bore my weight. I climbed until I could peer over the row of bricks that lined the top, gap-toothed with age.

San Isidro was built on high ground to the northwest of the town. The rainy season had just ended; the green that swept from their foothills to the town's edges looked as soft as one of Mamá's rugs. Its hue was browner and earthier than Cuernavaca's bold strokes, its color broken only by white dots of sheep and the severe rows of the hacienda's maguey fields.

There, in the farthest corner of the fields, the dark forms of tlachiqueros swung machetes in steady arcs or strode through the rows of maguey. Every once in a while, a male voice rose from among them; a shout of surprise, or a swoop of laughter as they drained aguamiel, the honey water that collected in the heart of the maguey plant and that was fermented to make pulque.

I squinted against the rising sun. A woman's form strode among them—I knew it was Juana from the determined sway of her skirts and her broad-rimmed hat.

Perhaps I could understand Juana's fierce dedication to the hacienda.

For Rodolfo, San Isidro was a source of guaranteed income during the transition of power between Spain and México, emperor and republic. It was a godsend. But for Juana? The money it generated for her family allowed her freedom. She lived well without marrying, an enviable privilege in wartime and peace alike. As far as I knew, she had lived on the hacienda all her life. Why, then, was she so dismissive at dinner with Rodolfo of my desire to improve the gardens? Were my attempts to revive the wilting grounds so repugnant?

Juana, Juana.

A voice lilted from behind me. So faint it could have been the twisting of the breeze in the grass.

I looked over my shoulder at the house. Its red-tile roof looked too heavy for its walls; the way the building was situated on a gentle slope made it look stocky and squat; the way the wings were crowded atop one another, their shoulders overlapping at various angles and heights, made them look like too many teeth in a mouth.

The ladder rung my feet rested on broke with a brittle snap.

My breath left my lungs in a yelp rather than a scream as I fell. I flung both my arms out and caught the top of the wall, hissing as my face struck stucco.

Madre de *Dios.*

I hung there, heart pounding, for a long moment. I was going to be fine. A fall from this height could not hurt me. The wall was only about as tall as Rodolfo—not very high at all.

I prepared myself, then let go of the wall. I caught myself in a low crouch and straightened. A breeze stung my cheek; I must have broken skin when I grazed it on the wall.

"Buenos días, Doña Beatriz."

I whirled to face the kitchen doorway.

Ana Luisa, gray haired and dressed in a white top and a villager's pale blue skirts, filled it. "What are you doing out here?"

"Inspecting the grounds," I said, holding my chin high as I smoothed my skirts. I prayed she hadn't witnessed my fall, nor had noticed the scrape on my cheek. "Why is this garden in such a state?" I added, hoping my question would distract her from my flustered state.

"I hadn't noticed, Doña Beatriz," she said archly. Her tone was drier than the brown grass crunching beneath my shoes as I crossed to her. As I grew close, I noticed that a strong smell of incense rose from her clothing. "I have not been in this garden in months. Not since . . ." Something in her eyes grew distant, and I was sure she was changing the direction of her sentence mid-step. "Not since the patrón was here last. We stay in our houses and make use of the kitchen there, and Doña Juana sees no use in living in the house alone."

As head of the household, Ana Luisa held a high position among the people who worked on the hacienda, second only to the foreman José Mendoza. I knew from working with Tía Fernanda's servants that such a place in a household's hierarchy and the trust of the señora meant autonomy. *Freedom.* I knew the taste of that craving as keenly as a toothache, and I had learned to recognize it in other women: it was a flash of hot yearning in their eye when they thought no one was looking. The determined curl of a hand into a fist beneath a table. With so many brothers and husbands, fathers and patrones slain in the war, more and more women in the capital could unsheathe their knives and take what was now theirs. I was no different. And I doubted the women of the countryside were any different, be they the daughters or widows of hacendados or heads of household like Ana Luisa.

My arrival had supplanted Juana as natural authority, rattling the hierarchy of the hacienda. Perhaps Ana Luisa looked at me and saw a threat to the comfortable order of her world.

Perhaps she was right.

"I have plans to make this place habitable again, and the garden is no exception," I said, lifting my chin as I had seen Tía Fernanda do a thousand times. "My mother will be joining us from the capital in a few weeks' time, and I want everything perfect for her arrival."

Ana Luisa's dark brows had raised slightly at my tone; she nodded once, solemnly and without embellishment, then took a rag from a hook near the kitchen door and resumed cleaning. "As you say, Doña Beatriz."

The smell of copal incense grew stronger as she stepped into the doorway. My throat tightened. Not from the strength of the smell—which I found unusual, but not unpleasant—but from a sudden wash of shame.

I heard Tía Fernanda's own voice within my command. All at once I was back in her house, taken by the arm and escorted to the kitchen in the midst of preparations for a dinner party.

A dinner party to which I was decidedly not invited.

Of course you understand you cannot be seen, my aunt had said, her nails carving half-moons into my upper arm. My cheeks—already too dark, in her esteem—flushed with heat. She had made her opinion on my father's heritage well known. It did not bear repeating. *In the meantime, you need to be useful*, she said, the oily sweetness in her voice slipping down the nape of my neck. *Maybe then you'll be worth something.*

No matter how I tried to ignore her, Tía Fernanda's voice lingered, a faint smell of rot I could not banish. It echoed every time I put on my wide-brimmed hat and gloves, every time I checked my complexion in the mirror. Thanks to her, every time I took Rodolfo's arm, a small, wounded part of me wanted to shrink away from him, from what I clearly did not deserve.

And I heard *her* in my voice as I gave an order to Ana Luisa.

Embarrassment stung the back of my throat.

With Rodolfo gone, I was the lady of the house. For weeks I had looked forward to this moment, but now that authority in the house was mine and mine alone, I had no idea how to enact it.

I turned my back on Ana Luisa and the kitchen and walked into the dark, clammy air of the hall toward the front garden. Once there, I set my hands on my hips and glowered at the wilting birds of paradise, the stray wild maguey, the weeds consuming the flower beds near the front door, a general surveying the battlefield.

I was afraid of how openly Ana Luisa disliked me. I was unsteady on my feet and lashed out. I should not speak that sharply again—cementing authority the way Tía Fernanda had, with haughtiness, with coldness, had sowed hate and hurt in me and most of her servants.

But then how would I establish my place as the head of the household? I did not have Rodolfo's easy inborn authority as a man. Nor Juana's as a criolla and an hacendado's daughter.

I would have to find my own way. Somehow. I had to, before Mamá arrived.

If she ever answered my letters begging her to come. I could only hope that she would stomach the sight of Rodolfo.

I shoved the thought aside and pulled on my leather gloves, laying siege to the flower beds. I weeded violently, leaving piles of deadened flowers in my wake. With the exception of a break for lunch and a short siesta in the cool of the house, I continued until the shadows grew long in the courtyard.

"What on earth are you doing?"

I jumped.

Juana stood over me, eyes narrowed as she scanned the sweat-stained rim of my hat and the dirt on my dress. Her cheeks were pink from the sun; sweat darkened her blouse beneath her armpits and below her throat.

"My brother would say this is what we have servants for, Doña Solórzano," she drawled.

I jerked my hands out of the dirt, brushing off the gloves.

Was she mocking me? I could not parse her expression as I rose and shook out my skirts. It was evident from our one dinner together that Juana did not hold what Rodolfo thought in high esteem. Nor vice versa. Nor that she believed caring for the gardens was as important as tending the maguey. But why?

"My husband would say he admired women who understand the amount of work that goes into running a property." I had heard him talk about women's education and the importance of widows running haciendas in the country in the wake of the war with his colleagues and twisted his words to make them sound as if they were approving of my behavior.

Juana snorted softly. She surveyed the pockmarks my labor had left in the soil. "He may admire them, yes. But he doesn't often marry them."

I busied myself with taking off my gloves to hide the curiosity in my expression. So Juana had never caught María Catalina weeding the garden, that was for certain. What else did she know about my husband's first wife? They had lived together on the hacienda for a time, hadn't they?

"I'm joining you for dinner tonight," Juana said abruptly.

She announced this as if she were the host and not I, as if the house were hers and not mine. I bit back the retort that sprang to my lips.

The animosity between my husband and his sister, the fact that Juana was such a curiosity to Doña María José and the other hacendados' wives, the rumors about the departed María Catalina . . . there was so much I didn't know about Hacienda San Isidro.

So much that Juana did.

If she warmed to me, if she saw me as unthreatening to her way of life here, perhaps she would confide in me.

I would find my place as lady of the house. I would make it my own. But I could not risk alienating Juana, not yet.

I followed as she strode into the house.

"How do you like it?" she wondered, her chin tilted up, gaze skipping over the high ceiling of the entryway. It was an idle question, perfectly innocent on the surface, but something uncertain lurked beneath it.

"It's . . ." I let the word trail off. Juana turned and faced me, the evening light from the open doorway illuminating her face, dancing off the flyaway bronze hairs that had come loose from their knot at her nape. Her wide, pale eyes met mine so frankly I couldn't help but respond in kind. To say exactly what I was thinking as I untied my hat and took it off my sweaty hair. "I want to blast the roof off. It seems like the only way to let in the amount of fresh air I want."

A peal of surprised laughter burst forth from Juana. It swept up to the high ceiling, tangling in the cobwebs. "I thought Rodolfo said you were a general's daughter, not of an artillery man." A warm curl of pleasure had unfurled in my chest at making Juana laugh, but it cooled quickly. Rodolfo had told her about me—why hadn't he told me a single thing about her? What other secrets was he keeping from me about San Isidro? About his first wife?

"What other violent plans do you have to clear the air?"

What I wanted to do was take a tlachiquero's machete to the walls to carve more windows.

"Color," I replied curtly.

"What if the house doesn't like color?" Juana teased. Was she toying with me or trying to be friendly? In the capital, women played chess with their words, moving coyly around china and silk to check one another, to protect their territory, to take one another off the board. I had never been close with anyone but Mamá—even my cousins and friends from before Papá's death were sharp clawed and evasive, keeping me at bay with barbs and sideways looks.

"The house will like what I tell it to like," I said, folding my arms across my chest. Because it is *my* house, I added silently. "We will start with blue."

Juana's thin lips vanished as she grinned. "I like you," she said bluntly. "What shades of blue do you have in mind, General Beatriz?"

My folded arms loosened. My experiences since my father's death had laid stone after stone in my chest, building walls so impenetrable that Mamá commented on how hard it had become to reach my heart. But still, I liked being told I was liked.

I waved to Juana to follow me to the stairs. "I brought silks from the capital," I said. "Blues the likes of which you've never seen."

A moment of hesitation, then Juana's boots followed me down the hall.

She did not speak, so I filled the silence by lecturing her about what I would do with each room as we passed. I would model the dining room after ours in the capital, where Papá and Mamá once hosted generals; the parlors I would decorate in colors that would please Mamá, like soft yellows and pinks.

"I lied about the house being drafty," Juana said in a small voice as we took the stairs. I cast her a look over my shoulder. Her face was drawn; she followed right at my heels, but her attention slinked down the wrought-iron banister to the northern wing. "The truth is . . . I am overwhelmed by it all. There is so much to do," she said. She continued, her voice brightening and picking up speed. "There used to be so many people here, in the old days," she said. "I remember it before the war more than Rodolfo does. It was always full of people when our parents threw parties. The kitchens were teeming with servants, and the house was always spotless."

"Where are all the servants now?" I opened the door and led her into my bedroom parlor, listening carefully as she continued.

"I dismissed them," Juana said curtly. "We couldn't afford any of that during the war. When our father died and Rodolfo joined the insurgents, I was the only one left. None of the hacendados would help me after what Rodolfo did—imagine, a Solórzano joining the *insurgents*. He may as well have joined the Indios ransacking the haciendas. Our father was well respected in the district, but after that?" She shook her head and made a dismissive sound.

Her voice raked over the words *Indio* and *insurgents* derisively. I clicked my tongue softly in disapproval. For a moment, I weighed pointing out that those same people were the forces that all the conservative hacendados and monarchy-supporters had joined in the end of the war, that those insurgents were now the men who ruled the Republic. Those same people were the ones who made peace possible, thus allowing Hacienda San Isidro to continue to profit from the sale of pulque. They made Juana's life *possi-*

ble. I glanced over my shoulder to see her features had settled into a stony, determined expression; I thought it better to bite my tongue.

"It was up to me to keep the hacienda running. Ana Luisa was my only help," she continued, oblivious to my silence. "I had to manage the money carefully. It was that or sell the land."

I understood the decrepit state of the house more now. It wasn't that Juana cared more for maguey than for the garden. She neglected the house that had been in her family for generations because she would do anything to keep the land. An hacienda like this was freedom. I, too, had sacrificed to have autonomy like hers in my grasp.

Perhaps she and I had more in common than I initially thought. Perhaps we would not have to battle over the property—perhaps we could be allies. Even friends, despite our differences.

I knelt before the chest that held my silks. I had a deep blue skirt, one of the few things Mamá purchased for me before I announced my engagement to Rodolfo. I had been angry at her for spending our precious savings on something so frivolous as a birthday gift, but now I wanted to use its color all over the house in her honor: chair covers, china, glass. A click of the lock; I opened the chest.

"Jesus Christ!" Juana cried, her boots scraping against the floor as she leaped backward.

Dark liquid soaked the silks in the chest. I could not move; a metallic tang filled my nose. Sent my head spinning. My silks. Gifts from my mother, artifacts from a life I no longer had, that I clung to, that I treasured.

They were . . . *wet.* How was that possible? It had rained on the carriage as we drove through the mountains two weeks ago, but the chests had been covered.

I reached—

"Don't touch it!" Juana shrieked.

My fingertips met sticky warmth. I drew them back sharply.

They were red. Bright bloodred.

Humming like a thousand bees filled my ears. A single, thick glob of scarlet dripped from my hand back into the chest, where it landed with a smack.

My silks. They were soaked in blood.

7

JUANA SEIZED MY SHOULDER and yanked me back from the
chest.

"We're going to the kitchen," she ordered, her voice slicing through my
shock. She shifted her grip to my arm and drew me sharply to my feet.
"Come. *Now.*"

The kitchen? Why on earth would we do that, when there was enough
blood in my chest to flood the carpet if it were tilted over? Juana's face was
stark white, her eyes wide as they darted about the room.

"I need to speak to Ana Luisa," she said. Her voice was hollow, as if she
were forcing it to sound a certain way. "To get to the bottom of who is
behind this prank."

I was still incapable of speech. Someone had ruined thousands of reales
worth of my silks, and she called it a *prank?*

She half dragged me to the staircase. We took them fast, two at a time,
thundering down into the shadows of the main hall. The temperature

dropped as we did; I gasped as Juana yanked me past the corner that led to the north wing and its unnaturally sharp chill.

The heavy taste of copal on the air reached me before we saw Ana Luisa. We turned a final corner to the glow of the kitchen doorway, plumes of smoke reaching into the hall like curious fingers. Sprigs of herbs—the plants I had been weeding—were scattered on the ground at the kitchen's threshold, and Juana stepped carefully over them. My skirts brushed the herbs aside as she dragged me to the back of the kitchen, which was open to the side garden.

Ana Luisa herself clicked her tongue loudly and set to rearranging the herbs I had knocked out of place; Juana reached violently for a jug of water and turned to me.

"Hold out your hand," she barked.

I obeyed, eager to wash the blood off.

But it had vanished.

There was no blood.

I yelped as Juana poured half the ice-cold contents of the jug over my hand anyway, half drenching my skirts. She seized a bar of natural soap and rubbed my hand hard, as hard as if she were scrubbing away ink.

"It's clean now, it's clean," I cried when she drenched my hand again. It was stiff and achy from the cold.

She set the jug down. Her eyes were hard as steel. The uncanniness of her resemblance to Rodolfo struck me, but I had never seen a look like that cross Rodolfo's face.

I was overcome by the urge to step back from her, but she still held my hand. Hard. My wedding ring dug into my finger, almost to the bone.

"I will get to the bottom of this. I will speak to the servants. They know me and obey me." Her tone clearly indicated that they certainly would not do the same with me. "Do *not* speak to them of this. Understood?"

I nodded. I breathed in sharply when she released my hand, half expecting to see blood again from where my ring had dug into flesh.

Juana released me and strode to a pantry; when she reemerged, it was with a clay jug gripped in one hand.

Blue smoke blurred my vision; copal burned in a shallow clay bowl by the open-air ranch stove where Ana Luisa was cooking.

I glanced over my shoulder. Deep shadows lengthened from the house to the whitewashed walls that encircled the gardens. Beyond, the southern and western skies deepened, as if the weight of the shadows drew them into darkness. The faint baying of dogs rose into the twilight; indistinct voices, perhaps from the hacienda village. They sounded as if they came from unreachably far away, from the unseeable side of a dream, as if reality broke off where the house's stucco walls did. Or perhaps that was where reality began, and I was the one trapped in an uneven, unending dream.

"Come inside," Juana barked. She was motioning for me to sit at the small table. She had conjured cups made from jícara and poured clear liquid from the jug into them.

Ana Luisa fanned the stove. The rich smells of warming tortillas and frijoles drew my feet back into the kitchen. I sat as Juana set the jug on the table heavily.

"A su salud," she said dryly and, lifting one of the cups to her lips, took a long draft.

A judgmental click of the tongue from Ana Luisa. "Before dinner, Doña Juana?"

Juana did not reply. The color had not returned to her face, but the tight line of her sharp shoulders was loosening. She was no longer a snake coiled to strike. Slowly, the warmth and smells of the kitchen were dispelling the shock of the sight of the chest.

The kitchen was having the same effect on me. It was the kind of room that had no touch of men, either Rodolfo or previous generations. The kitchen in Tía Fernanda's house had felt like a prison to me, the place I was shunted because nothing better could be made of me. This kitchen felt like a refuge. Smoke curled up in the doorways from their bowls of incense like sentries; my eye followed soot markings around the doorway that led to the rest of the house. Geometrical shapes darkened the white paint where it met Moorish tile. They looked fresh, as if they had been newly drawn.

Juana pressed a cup into my hands.

"What is this?" I asked.

"Mezcal." She was already refilling hers. "Instead of harvesting agua-miel for pulque, the tlachiqueros carve out some maguey hearts and cook them in an open pit to crush and distill."

I studied the clear liquid. Women were not supposed to drink.

You'll never get a husband. Tía Fernanda's voice wound through my mind.

Well. I already had. And he had given me a house with servants who played dark-spirited pranks.

The alcohol bit my tongue and filled my mouth with the smokiness of an open fire.

"Finish it," Juana ordered.

I paused. Her own cup was full again. I thought of the clink of glasses at balls in the capital, of the glint of champagne in the candlelight and raised, energetic voices of dancers between turns. Drink loosened tongues. I had to be careful, watch mine . . . but what if Juana didn't? What could I learn from her if I kept her drinking? Questions bubbled to the surface: who would pour blood on my silks?

Doña María José's crepe-paper voice slipped under my skin. *Poor thing. Such a delicate constitution.* How *had* my husband become a widower? What did Juana think of her departed sister-in-law?

So I obeyed Juana. I lifted my cup to her, then waited for her to echo the motion. When she did, we tipped our cups back in unison. I coughed as the alcohol stung my throat.

"Welcome to San Isidro," Juana said flatly.

"What is wrong with the people here?" I said when I had caught my breath. "Who would do that?"

Juana solemnly poured herself a third cup as Ana Luisa set plates and food on the table and sat to my left, opposite Juana.

Juana poured Ana Luisa a jícara cup and handed it to her, then reached for a basket of tortillas wrapped in cloth to keep them warm. "I think it is best we forget it," she said, not meeting my gaze.

"Forget it?" I repeated, incredulous. Easy for her to say, when she hadn't sunk her hand into warm, sticky . . . I shook my head to clear it. My hand had been *clean* before Juana drenched it in icy water. How was that possible? "But—"

"Just eat," Juana said briskly. "Our senses are not about us."

They weren't when we finished eating Ana Luisa's hearty country food either, thanks to the mezcal. Juana kept my cup refilled, even when I protested that I had had more than enough.

But I was right. Drink loosened her, made her cold face animated. I had never seen Rodolfo drunk—was this what he was like? Jovial and open, casually touching my hand with calloused fingers and cooing over how beautiful my green eyes were? Juana had Rodolfo's same powerful magnetism, and I found myself laughing alongside her as she told stories from the fields or mocked petty community dramas with Ana Luisa, though I knew none of the names of the characters in the stories or their meanings.

I was lulled into a sense of comfort, blanketed by liquor-bright voices and the smell of the fire and the copal, the smoky sentries keeping watch. I was certain they had both drunk enough that I could ask them the questions that itched beneath my skin. I slipped into a dip in their conversation, keeping my voice as girlishly innocent as I dared.

"I'm so curious about her," I said.

"Who?" Ana Luisa said.

"What was her name?" I paused, as if I couldn't remember it. Of course I remembered it. How could I not? "María Catalina."

Deep inside the house, far from the warmth of the kitchen, a door slammed.

All three of us jumped. Juana and Ana Luisa perched like hunted hares on the edges of their seats, their attention fixed on the kitchen doorway.

"What was that?" I breathed.

"Draft," Juana said, voice hollow.

But none touched the copal smoke. It curled, languid as a dancer, into the still, shadowy house beyond.

Juana took the jug and emptied it into her cup.

Ana Luisa reached out as if to stay her but relented when Juana shot her a look I could not parse. I had lost count of her cups, and by the look of it—by the slip of her eyes, the roll of her posture as she leaned her elbows on the table—she had as well.

I mimicked her posture, lowering my chin to my hands to appear small. Innocent. "What was she like?"

Tell me things, I willed her, as if the force of my alcohol-slurred thoughts alone could sway her. *Tell me why Rodolfo won't speak of her. Tell me why the other hacendados dislike you.*

A distant look stilled Juana's expression. I knew the look well from Rodolfo's face—she was no longer with me, but somewhere in her memory. Somewhere far from here. "Exactly as an hacendado's wife should be," she said, an exaggerated twist to her voice. "Refined. Elegant. Rich, of course, for Rodolfo cared something for numbers then. Canny. She saw *everything*."

My face was numb from drink, and I prayed it did not betray how my pride smarted. Was I not as an hacendado's wife should be? I knew I was not rich, that I brought little of value to my marriage, but that did not mean Rodolfo had lost his financial sense entirely when he married me.

Then the meaning of Juana's words sank into me. The lilt of her mockery peeled back a veil, and for a fleeting moment, I glimpsed truth.

"You didn't like her."

Juana's eyes bore into me, searching my face. Now she was present, sharp and frighteningly so.

I had misspoken.

Then she smiled, a thin, saccharine thing. She stood, took my hand, and brought me to my feet. How could she stand so solidly when I swayed, when the kitchen spun around me? She slipped her arm around my waist and guided me to the door of the kitchen, to the entryway that led to the rest of the house.

"I lied about the house," she said into my ear. Her breath was warm and sweet with drink against my skin. "I lied twice, actually. The truth is I'm . . . afraid of it. I cannot go in, not in the dark. Neither will Ana Luisa. But you? Ah, you—" She released me, the suddenness of the movement pushing me into the dark. I swayed as I caught my balance. "It's time for you to go to sleep, Doña Beatriz."

She then thrust a handful of herbs into my hand; the pressure of her sweaty-palmed grip had released their sap and earthy aroma. Ana Luisa put a lit candle in my other hand. The smoke twined around them, their softly mocking *good nights* echoing against one another as the warmth and glow of the kitchen pulled farther and farther away.

I turned a corner, my feet certain they knew the way to my room, my body less sure. Juana's words took their time sinking past the mezcal thickening my senses, and it was only when I had left the kitchen behind, when a cold draft struck my face, that I realized what she had said.

She was afraid of the *house.*

Cold sank through my dress, into the bones of my arms, winding into my chest in icy rivulets.

Juana and Ana Luisa shut the door to the kitchen.

I was alone.

My single candle barely cut the darkness. My head spun as I lifted the handful of crushed herbs to my nose, crinkling my nose at its earthy scent.

A peal of childish laughter sounded behind me. The candle's flame flickered wildly as I shrank away from it, heart slamming against my ribs.

There was no one there.

I grabbed skirts in my herb-filled hand. Forward. I had to get to my room. The candle cast a thin halo of light, barely enough to see a foot in front of me.

More lilting laughter echoed behind me, coy and light, so unlike Juana's amused bray. Was I imagining it? I had never been drunk before, and—based on the sway in my step and the spin of my vision—there was no doubt that I was. Did one hear things? Did one feel the clammy brush of cold against their cheek as if it were someone's flesh?

I didn't want to know. I focused on climbing the stairs as quickly as I could. Cool fingers brushed over my neck—no, I was imagining it, I had to be imagining the sensation of death-cold fingertips brushing over my earlobes, tugging at my hair.

Then two hands placed themselves on my shoulders and shoved me forward. I gasped as I fell to my knees, my temple striking the banister.

The voice grew clearer, shifting from mangled laughter into garbled speech, as if it were conversing with someone, lilting up the scale of pitch and anger as if it were asking questions, demanding answers . . .

Fright numbed the pain in my kneecaps and skull, narrowed my world to the candle before me, to the shuddering sensation of fingers tugging at my hair again.

I had to get away from it. What if those hands yanked me down the stairs? Would I end up like the rat on the front steps of San Isidro, head shattered on the cold flagstones?

Careful to hold the candle aloft, I forced myself to my feet, crouching protectively forward as I stumbled up the remaining stairs and ran to the patrón's rooms. I thrust my weight against the door until it heaved open, then staggered into the parlor and let it slam shut behind me.

The voice stopped.

At the far end of the parlor, the dark shape of the chest came into view, its lid still arched open like an animal's gaping maw. I cut it a wide berth and tripped over the doorway into my bedroom; I threw out my arm to catch myself and realized my mistake too late.

"No, no," I cried as the flame of the candle vanished, extinguished by the rush of movement.

Darkness fell over the room like a wool cloak, stifling. Airless.

No. I could not be in this bedchamber in the dark. I could not. Not without Rodolfo.

My chest tightened at the memory of the flash of red eyes in the dark.

There were no cats on this godforsaken hacienda.

Juana had lied.

And she had sent me here alone.

My heartbeat raced as I fumbled through the dark for the matches I kept on my vanity, my hands clumsy because I would not release the fistful of herbs. There. There they were. Strike, strike, and a flare of flame burst to life.

"Thank God," I whispered hoarsely, and lit the candles on my vanity. All of them. When I had an altar of trembling flame, their reflection in the mirror casting light into the rest of the room, I turned around.

Like an animal, the dark drew back.

A feral instinct unfurled at the back of my neck, under skin and muscle, flush to my spine.

I was not alone.

8

I WOKE THE NEXT morning with a stale taste in my mouth, my lips sticky and dry. Handfuls of blue sky winked at me through the windows set high in the walls. I stretched, wincing when the throb behind my eye sockets reminded me why I had fallen asleep in my dress, why I had let the candles melt down to shapeless mounds on their tray.

I rolled over onto my back and stared at the beams in the ceiling.

Something was wrong with this house.

Something lurked in it during the day and grew stronger at night.

I had slept curled in a tight ball, the herbs clutched to my chest like a talisman. I unfurled my hand stiffly. The herbs' stems and leaves left red indentations on my palm and fingers.

I frowned. Was my mind playing tricks on me? I had not had my senses around me last night.

But . . . the blood in the chest. The cold hands shoving me forward on the stairs.

I shuddered. Were the servants testing me? Did they worry I was going to disrupt their way of life, their easy neglect of the house, and so thought to drive me away?

I was slow to bathe and dress myself but accomplished these as quickly as I could. I then walked into the study. I went straight to where I had hung Papá's map and stood there for a long moment.

A weak part of me was quite ready to be driven away. In the capital, I could truly play the role of Rodolfo's high-society wife, entertaining in the gilded rooms of his family's house . . .

My mouth soured further when I remembered who I would be entertaining. Members of the government. The men who had ousted the emperor.

The men who had fought alongside my father, only to then turn on him.

Could I smile blandly at them and pour them chocolate? Could I chat mindlessly with their wives, coo over their children? As achy and stiff and nauseous as I was, I was overcome by the hot desire to seize one of the perfume glasses on my vanity and throw it as hard as I could against the stucco wall.

No. I could not. *I would not.*

This was my house. I would not shrink away from it the way Juana and Ana Luisa did, jumping every time boards creaked underfoot. I would scald its soot stains clean. I would strip its protective layer of dust and straighten its crooked edges, rebreaking and setting broken bones. I would make it mine, I would make it my home. My safe haven.

I had no other choice, after all.

Even if it meant facing a chest full of blood-soaked clothing. I had to face it at some point or another, to see what could be salvaged. Better to face it now, when the sunlight was hale and bright.

I turned. The chest was open, as Juana and I had left it. I braced myself, anticipating the buzz of flies, acidity preemptively rising at the back of my mouth as I drew close enough to peer inside.

Blue.

The silk was the dark, rich blue of traditional blown glass. And it was *clean*.

I fell to my knees, clenching my teeth as the sudden movement rattled my sore skull. I touched the silk tentatively, then moved it around, searching for any trace of blood. The room was filled with the sound of shifting fabric.

"What on earth?" I murmured.

Distantly, as if from three rooms away, a girlish giggle echoed.

I stood as fast as my aching head would allow and slammed the chest shut.

The room was silent.

I had *not* imagined it. I could not forget the expression that contorted Juana's face as she drenched my hands, desperate to clean skin that was already bare of blood.

Juana saw what I had seen.

I needed to talk to her. If it was late morning, she must be in the fields, or tending to some other running of the hacienda beyond the house that I was not privy to. I would find her in the evening, then. First, I needed food.

The house watched me coyly as I descended the stairs. I shook the feeling off like a horse twitching flies from its hide. Houses did not *watch*. It simply was not true or possible.

But still my steps quickened. A faint smell of copal shrouded me, thanks to my hair; it had reeked of the incense when I brushed it out and pinned it into a knot high off my neck. I thought of the kitchen with its smoky sentries, how *safe* I had felt within that room.

When I reached the kitchen, the hope building in my heart dissipated. The incense had burned down; no smoke wreathed the doorway, no herbs scattered on the floor. No relief from the eerie feeling of being watched.

A bowl clattered to the ground.

I jumped, a cry in my throat, and whirled to face the sound.

It was Paloma, Ana Luisa's reserved daughter. She dipped to the ground to collect the bowl and rose to put it on its shelf. "Doña! I wasn't expecting you."

I gave her as kind a smile as I could muster with my heart racing so wildly. I willed it to slow. How silly of me, to be frightened by her presence.

"I was expecting Ana Luisa," I said. "Isn't she the cook?"

"When the patrón is here, yes," Paloma said quietly. "She still could be, if you wish. She sent me to tidy and with this." Here she pointed at eggs, tortillas, and a small jug of chocolate atole. Steam curled above the jug, visible in the crisp morning air. "For you."

I thanked Paloma effusively and sat to eat as she swept the kitchen. The slight spice in the atole soothed my nausea, and I savored it.

I had been dreading spending the morning scrubbing dried blood from silk, and now I would not have to. That was good. I could return to the task of compiling a list of things I wanted Rodolfo to send from the capital.

I glanced over my shoulder at the doorway. It yawned before me, crowned by black glyphs. Whispers twined through the shadows beyond it.

Not whispers, I corrected myself firmly. The creak of hundred-year-old wood. The wind in the drying leaves of the oaks in the side garden beyond the kitchen. Nothing more.

"Paloma," I began.

"Yes, Doña Beatriz?" She turned and stood at attention, chin dipped submissively, gaze fixed on the floor somewhere near my shoes. Paloma was a mirror image of her mother, but very little like Ana Luisa in how she behaved around me.

"Are you busy this morning?" When she replied no, I asked her to accompany me as I walked the rooms of the house. "I come from a busy house with a very large family," I said. Never mind that the very large family I referenced barely treated me as a part of it, relegating me to the scalding steam of the laundry whenever it suited Tía Fernanda's needs or temper. "I dislike how quiet the house is and wish for company while I work."

"Very well, Doña Beatriz," Paloma said. There was something in her tone that hinted this was not at all an unusual request to her.

I gestured to the doorway.

"Do you know what the meaning of those marks is?"

"I couldn't tell you, doña." But as she spoke, Paloma's eyes were still on the floor. I could not tell whether she was telling the truth or not.

I took a quick trip upstairs for paper and a charcoal pencil and a shawl. The echoes of my footsteps followed me as I returned. Aside from the kitchen, the patrón's suite, and the parlor turned dining room where Rodolfo and I generally ate, the house was utterly empty; even the smaller rooms felt at once cavernous and stifling as I stood in them, imagining how they could be filled, thinking out loud to Paloma about how they would be scrubbed. I took notes all the while.

Green parlor. Will be green again. Fresh coat of paint. Re-brick the fireplace.

Dining room. Scrub the soot from above; add a railing to the balcony for safety. Wrought iron to match the doors. Colors: gold upholstery to match the dark wood table.

Halls: rugs. For the damn echoing.

Paloma giggled softly as I wrote this. I glanced at her. She was scanning the list over my shoulder as I placed the paper on the wall to write.

"You read and write?" I asked.

Paloma met my eyes. Now that she did not turn her face away from me, I noted how expressive it was, how the slim brows that framed her face could speak volumes before she even parted her lips.

She murmured something neither affirmative nor negative.

I raised my brows. Tía Fernanda's servants were not literate; I did not expect this of any member of the staff besides the foreman.

"Wonderful," I said. I meant it. I handed the paper and pencil to Paloma. "Will you write down what I say, then?"

She did not meet my gaze but took the writing instruments silently and did as instructed. We worked together until an hour to midday, when Paloma said she needed to help Ana Luisa prepare lunch for the tlachiqueros and the farm workers.

I stepped out of the last room we surveyed, then slowed near the foot of the staircase. A steep dip in temperature washed over me. Though I did not know why, my eye was drawn to the boarded-up entrance to the north wing.

It was damaged, Rodolfo said. Earthquake, or perhaps water damage. If he had asked the foreman José Mendoza to look into it, clearly it had not been done.

How odd. I put the pencil and paper down on the steps, resolved to investigate the damage myself. The first board came off easily. I tossed it to the side. It struck the flagstones; the sound echoed in the foyer as I took off another, and another, until the passage was open. I collected my pencil and paper and walked forward.

Though sunlight still shone outside the house, the clamminess in this narrow hall was thick as mist. It weighed heavily on my chest, akin to physical pressure. Perhaps there was a well nearby, or an underground spring.

I reached out to brush my fingertips against the wall, expecting them to come away damp. They didn't. The wall was cool to the touch, but dry. Dry and cold as clay that had been left out in the chill of a winter night. Temperatures had an odd way of shifting in this house when I least expected them to. Our house in the capital was built of wood, and the house in Cuernavaca was stone; I was unlearned in the ways of stucco, of thick walls and slim windows.

Perhaps I could convert this part of the house into storage. It would be perfect for storing things that needed to remain cold. Wax in the summer.

Maybe even ice, if that luxury were ever to be had in Apan. I smiled, half laughing at myself in a vain attempt to alleviate the clammy pressure in my chest. I had not seen ice in a home in years. I would have to write to Rodolfo to ask if there was even ice in the capital.

I placed the paper on the hall wall next to me and began to write. *North wing: naturally cold storerooms. Check temperatures again in the late aftern—*

The wall shifted beneath my weight.

I lurched backward so I wouldn't fall.

Flakes of stucco went flying as I did. I hit the solidness of the opposite wall with a thud, cracking my skull against it.

Stars speckled my vision; I hissed in pain. My headache, which had faded over the last hour or so, roared back with a vengeance.

Last night had made me overly jumpy. *Well done, Beatriz,* I mocked myself. As easily spooked as a colt.

There was a dent in the wall before me. Bits of stucco had indeed crumbled away, like dry icing from a stale cake.

I frowned. If the wall before me was as solid as the wall behind me, that sort of dent should only be possible with the force of a battering ram, not a girl of twenty leaning against it to write.

But if it wasn't as solid as the wall behind me? Gritting my teeth against the pain in my head, I stepped forward to the wall to investigate. While every wall in the house appeared to be made of the solid indigenous building materials, bricks of mixed mud and agave fiber and clay that had withstood centuries of earthquakes and floods, this wall was different.

I brushed my fingers over ruined stucco. It came apart at my touch, flaking like dandruff. It couldn't be stucco. Or even good-quality paint. I took a piece and sniffed it. It was lime whitewash, covering stacked bricks.

How odd. Had part of the house been walled up hastily? I frowned at the wall. The hall was narrower than most, and dim, but I could make out the outline of bricks. San Isidro was many things, but shoddily built was not one of them. It was solid to its heart.

I set down my paper and pencil and tested one of the bricks.

It came away from the wall in my hands. I shrank a step back, surprised and somewhat afraid that the whole thing might come crashing down.

It didn't. I set the brick down quickly and peered into the hole in the wall. Something caught the light and glinted. There was something back there.

Driven by curiosity, I took out two more bricks, then jumped aside with a yelp as half the wall came cracking down. White flakes of limestone went flying; clouds of dust rose from the wreckage. That was indeed shoddy workmanship, I thought. I must tell Rodolfo that the—

My thoughts stopped dead. The fallen bricks had been covering something up.

A skull, white as the limestone, grinned coquettishly out at me.

Its neck was bent at an angle not unlike the dead rat's on the doorstep, and its spine curled down in positions I knew were wrong. Though I knew little of the human body, my gut told me it was *wrong*.

Around the skeleton's broken neck, a golden necklace glinted dully. That was what had caught my eye.

I cast down the clay I had been holding.

A body had been bricked into the wall of San Isidro.

I needed to talk to Juana.

I turned on my heel and fled.

I found Ana Luisa in the outdoor kitchen of the servants' courtyard, serving pozole to the tlachiqueros for lunch.

"Where is Juana?" I cried.

The tlachiqueros, the other servants, Paloma—they all turned to stare at me. I must have looked like a madwoman, racing from the house as if pursued, covered in dust and limestone, my eyes wild, my hair falling from its knot. I didn't care.

"I need Juana," I said to Ana Luisa. "Now."

She took me in from head to toe, then jerked her chin at her daughter.

"Do as Doña Beatriz says," she said. "Take her to Doña Juana."

The weight of all the people's eyes pressed down on me like a thousand hands. I wanted to be away from them; I needed to get away from them.

Paloma shot her mother a reluctant look and stood, slowly, too slowly.

"It is urgent," I said to her.

She turned to me, her face still as a statue's. My voice had come out hard, even if I felt like I was going to shatter like glass.

Paloma gestured for me to follow her around the back of the servants' quarters. The sun was bright here; with each passing moment I felt lighter, as if every step leading away from the house were stripping off a heavy layer of clothing.

Maybe I was going mad.

No. I wasn't. I *knew* what I had seen.

The smell of horses greeted me as we reached the stables. Paloma led me inside the barn, into a small room off the main aisle. Juana was seated on a stool with her legs crossed, her shoulders curled inward, and her head down. Strands of light hair fell into her face as she stitched a bridle, mending it.

"Doña Juana." The way Paloma addressed Juana was stony and flat, and her hands hung at her sides instead of respectfully in front of her. Her weight had shifted, as if she were ready to run.

If she was afraid of me, or was shy around me, then she loathed Juana. It was written all over her face: the girl practically itched to be out of Juana's presence.

How odd, given how close her mother Ana Luisa and Juana seemed.

Juana's brows rose when she saw me. "You look wretched," she said bluntly.

"Someone died," I blurted out. "I found a body. A skeleton."

Juana went still.

On the road to Apan from Mexico City, Rodolfo and I spent the night in a roadside inn. Alone, he could have made the journey in one long day on horseback, as the riders who carried the post did, but the carriage was slower. We rose early to set out, before dawn had perfectly broken, when the touch of the morning was velvet, when mauve and pink lined the eastern horizon bright against the purple gray of the dome of the sky. Rodolfo stopped dead in his tracks as we walked toward the stables. He grabbed my arm.

"Don't move," he breathed, then pointed east.

A puma crouched not ten meters from the barn. If it had been stalking chickens or goats, its attention now turned to us. We stared at it; it stared at us. I had never seen a puma before, and I hadn't known its shoulders would be so large, its eyes so wide-set and intelligent as it assessed me.

Nor that it could be as still as a painting.

A horse whinnied from the barn, shattering the silence.

Rodolfo whistled to the grooms in the stables and nudged me to walk slowly backward, never turning our backs on the puma. He raised the alarm and called for a gun, but by the time the grooms rushed from the barn with a musket, the cat was gone. Melted into the dawn like smoke on a breeze.

Juana was as still as the puma as she looked at me.

"What?" she said. There was something of the puma's fluid movements in her as she cast aside the bridle and stood.

"A wall collapsed," I said. Why was my breath coming short? My heart was racing—perhaps it had been racing since I first saw the skull grinning gruesomely at me through the dark. "Come. You must come." I took a step back and turned, to return to the house, even though my muscles protested, even though going back into the house, back to the weight of it, was the last thing I ever wanted to do.

Juana followed reluctantly, Paloma trailing her. Every time I looked over my shoulder, Paloma's eyes were locked on the back of Juana's head, watchful as a hound. Juana looked wan as we entered the house and turned to the north wing, and slowed, so much that I snapped at her at least twice to hurry.

Then instead of turning right toward my bedroom, as she and I had yesterday before finding my clothing drenched in blood, I turned left to the north wing and the ruined wall.

My notes lay on the floor of the hall, my pencil abandoned a few feet past them.

The wall was unblemished. Whole.

"No," I breathed. "But—"

Juana and Paloma stopped as I barreled down the hall, as I ran my hands over the wall, the wall where I had taken down three bricks and nearly been crushed by the resulting tumult. The wall was cool and dry, but I could not see the outline of bricks as I had before. "No."

I struck the wall with the heel of my left hand, biting my lip as the rough surface of stucco bit into my palm. Stucco. Not lime whitewash. This couldn't be. I ran down the hall, trailing my hand along the wall, searching for the bricks, searching for the lime whitewash that had covered me in dust. For the love of God, the backs of my hands were still pale with it.

I stopped again right before the place where the wall had nearly crushed me. I hammered the heels of my hands against the wall in frustration.

"Doña . . ." Paloma interrupted.

"It was here!" I whirled on them. "The wall was open, and there was a body in there. There was a dead person. Someone covered it with bricks. It was here, I swear it was *here*."

Their eyes were wide, but not with fear.

With something else.

They thought I was mad.

My heart hammered in my throat.

"It's true," I cried. "I leaned on the wall and it started caving. It's true." Tears sprang to my eyes; my throat was tight with frustration. I picked up my notes and abandoned pencil from the ground, miming how I had been writing against the wall before.

The solidity of the wall mocked me.

Juana raised a single brow.

"What is that?" she wondered, her gaze falling on my notes. She stepped forward and looked over my shoulder.

"It's a list of things for Rodolfo," I said. "To outfit the house and make it presentable again. Why aren't you listening to me?"

Juana scanned the list: notes about china dealers in the capital, fresh talavera tiles from Puebla, a note to ask my mother about imported rugs.

Her face hardened. Then she turned to Paloma, her face transformed into a mask of sympathy.

"Doña Beatriz had a bit of a shock yesterday," she said in a soft, maternal voice, as if she were explaining away the woes of a weeping child. "I think perhaps this must have been a misunderstanding."

I stared at Juana, mortified.

"No." The word came out strangled. "There is no misunderstanding. There is something—some*one*—in this wall."

"You are dismissed, Paloma," Juana said softly. "I will take care of this."

Paloma's eyes skipped to me. I couldn't read her expression; if I had had longer to parse it, if I had known her better, perhaps I could have, but she turned and left. Her footsteps echoed down the hall.

Juana took me by the upper arm. "Let's go."

I dug in my heels. "You oughtn't humiliate me in front of the servants," I snapped, perhaps more harshly than I should have. Not only was I shaken, embarrassment burned in my cheeks as I faced Juana. "You heard Rodolfo. My word is *his* when he's gone. They won't respect me if you treat me like this."

Perhaps that was what she intended all along. But she gave no indication if this was the case; her face did not shift from its mask of sympathy. She clucked.

"Did you not sleep well last night?" she wondered sweetly. "Perhaps you dreamed it. I used to have terrible nightmares as a child."

A wave of hatred filled my chest. How dare she? I shrugged violently, trying to release my arm from her hold. Her grip tightened.

"Let me go, Juana."

"Why don't you come—"

"No."

And, to my surprise, she released me. I nearly fell backward, the absence of pressure was so sudden.

"As you wish, Doña Beatriz," she said silkily, her voice woven through with threads of venom, so spiderweb thin I barely caught them. "Your word is the patrón's."

She smiled, pale lipped and joyless, and turned. Her long stride took her around the corner and out of sight before I could say another word.

Distantly, I heard the enormous door of the main entryway thunder shut. For a long moment I stood, my pulse hammering in my ears.

Then, from the direction of my bedroom, there came the faint sound of a girl calling a name in a singsong voice.

Juana, Juana . . .

The hairs on my forearms stood on end.

A handful of cold truths unfurled before me as I stood in that hall, paralyzed by fear:

Someone had died in this house.

I needed help.

And no one at Hacienda San Isidro was going to give it to me.

9

Two days later, Paloma delivered Rodolfo's response to my latest letter. I was weeding the garden around the front door, my broad-brimmed hat protecting my skin from the sun as usual. I could have kissed Paloma when she handed me the letter, but my spirits sank when I noticed how wary she was of me. I did not know which was worse—the disdain with which Ana Luisa regarded me, or Paloma's clear unease?

She left as I ripped open the seal, dirt from my fingertips smearing the fine paper.

I had asked for more than furniture this time.

Querida Beatriz, Rodolfo began. He wrote that he understood my desire for a priest to bless the house, to bury a statue of such and such saint in the garden, to sprinkle holy water on the threshold and throughout the rooms. *Give the enclosed letter to Padre Guillermo in town—he and his assistant will be more than obliging.*

My lips curled into a grim smile. I was not a devout woman. My views on the clergy were informed by Papá, who often repeated the words of revolutionary leader Miguel Hidalgo y Costilla. Of his enemies in the Church, the insurgent priest said they were Catholic "only to benefit themselves: their God is money. Under the veil of religion and of friendship they want to make you the victims of their insatiable greed."

I did not trust the clergy, not so long as men like my husband could buy them and their services. Still, I had to help myself somehow. Despite my distrust of priests, part of me suspected—an irrational hope, perhaps, born of sleeplessness and desperation—that they had the power to do something I couldn't.

I didn't care about a sprinkle of holy water here and there, a murmured prayer over my threshold.

I wanted an exorcism.

And Rodolfo's letter was going to get the priests into my house so I could show them how desperately it needed it.

THE NEXT MORNING WAS Sunday. I dressed in my finest as Mamá and I always did, pinching my cheeks in the mirror to bring color to my wan complexion. My nights were restless, my dreams populated by dark shadows that caused me to wake with a cry in the night, my heart racing as I fumbled for matches to relight the double-thick tallow candles I had asked Ana Luisa to bring me. I had ransacked the beds where Ana Luisa grew her weeds and, given no other weapon to assuage my paranoia, cut fragrant, sappy bunches of herbs to scatter around my bedroom's threshold.

I wondered about the soot markings in the kitchen and nearly laughed at myself as I imagined asking a priest about them. That was almost as ludicrous as asking cold Ana Luisa herself.

Paloma accompanied me on the way to town. It was dark in the carriage; Paloma pulled back the corner of one window covering and stared intently out the window, studiously avoiding my gaze. She clearly had no intention of making small talk during the ride into Apan, and neither did I.

Like the first time Rodolfo and I had come to Mass, whispers followed me up the aisle; curious eyes weighed on my shoulders as I genuflected and took my seat near the front of the church. I cupped that power and held it close to my chest, letting its warmth burn away the memory of the look Juana had given me in the hall. I was not mad. I was not shocked, not seeing things.

Something was wrong with the house.

And because I had married Rodolfo, because I had a man's voice to speak for me, I could wrangle a priest into helping me fix it.

I watched the priest as he held the Eucharist before us. The flesh beneath his chin trembled in the way of the well-fed as he spoke; the war had been easy on him. Not so of his congregation: I lost count of the widows as I watched people crowd to the front of the church to receive Communion. Many of the men of fighting age had a pinned-up, hollow trouser leg and crutches, or were missing an arm. Padre Guillermo blessed them all, bidding them farewell one by one at the arched doorway. I hung back, watching him clasp the dark hands of his parishioners in his own plump, age-speckled white ones, wisps of hair from his balding crown silhouetted against Apan's blinding azure sky.

I approached him last, Paloma trailing in my shadow.

"Doña Beatriz," he effused. "I trust you are settling in well."

His hands were as sweaty as I anticipated. I forced my lips into what I hoped was a beaming smile, counting the moments until it was proper for him to release my hands. I counted at least two moments longer than I would have hoped, but kept the smile pasted on my face.

I fished into my well-stocked reserve of society small talk to gush about the beauty of the countryside, the kindness and goodness of my new husband, the quiet of our home. Then I reached into my small purse and withdrew Rodolfo's letter. I had read and resealed it and was pleased to discover that Rodolfo promised the priest silver in return for following my wishes.

Their God is money.

If only he knew what that silver was in return for.

I had written Rodolfo a long letter around my request for a priest to come to San Isidro, but I had not touched on anything that was truly unsettling me: the body in the wall that no one else seemed to see.

The only thing less desirable than the daughter of a traitor was a madwoman.

I was not mad. All I wanted, as any devout Catholic would, was for a priest to come and tread his holy, plump feet over my threshold and throw water at things in return for my husband's money. That was all I wanted.

Or rather, that was all I told Padre Guillermo in the bright light of Sunday morning.

Once he stepped into my home, we would have a different conversation.

"Padre Andrés will join me." He gestured over my shoulder at a second priest lingering at the door bidding farewell to the townspeople, a slender young man with the serious expression of a student. I had noticed him during Mass, flitting like a raven behind Padre Guillermo's ample, ambling form on the altar. "He is well acquainted with the property."

Padre Andrés met my gaze over Paloma's head. They had been engaged in a hushed conversation, and I was immediately struck by how the severe line of his nose and shape of his eyes echoed Paloma's in the way of relatives. But unlike Paloma, his eyes were light, hazel in the direct sunlight. He could not have been much older than me, for his clean-shaven face was still lean in the rangy way of youth. I thought of the men with crutches and the widows; there were so few young men among the townspeople. Perhaps if he hadn't become a priest, he would also be missing a limb. Perhaps he might not be here at all.

He dropped my gaze. It was only then that I realized how inappropriately long I had held it, and felt embarrassed warmth rise up my neck.

"Doña Beatriz," he murmured in greeting, keeping his eyes shyly downcast. "Welcome to Apan."

I AWAITED THE PRIESTS at the gates of San Isidro the next morning, swaying slightly from exhaustion. I had slept especially poorly the night before. It was as if the house knew what I had done. That I had gone and tattled on it to its parents, that men with heavy books and heavier senses of self-importance were coming to shake its ill humors loose.

And it retaliated.

A cold wind kicked up inside the house as I left the kitchen last night. At first I thought a door had swung open, but the wind poured down the hall, ripping my hair loose from its bun, its ice sinking into my bones and tightening around my chest like a clawed hand. I tried to run forward, run through it, but it was too powerful. I took slow strides, teeth chattering, throwing my weight into the wind and fighting to make my way to the staircase as it ripped at my hands.

I clutched a piece of copal to burn in my room the way Ana Luisa did in the kitchen. I hadn't been able to find any in town as I intended, so I ripped apart the pantry when she was gone to help myself to her supply. The pickings were meager—she must have kept her store in her own home in the village.

I don't know how long it took me to get to my room. The cold stiffened my limbs, weighed on my chest; it only increased when I entered the parlor. It was as if I had stepped into an icy stream. I wondered if I could see my breath on the air, but the dark was too complete, too thick, soot black and heavy. My numb fingers fumbled the matches in my bedroom, and time after time, I lit a candle and it was extinguished by the wind. Tears rose in my eyes.

Nothing else in the rooms seemed disturbed by the wind. Not the curtains, not my papers, not Papá's map in the study. Only me. Me and the candles.

I had to focus on lighting the copal. It *must* be the reason the kitchen seemed so quiet when Ana Luisa was in it, empty of something the way the rest of the house never was. It had to be the solution. It had to be.

I nursed the end of the block of resin as its tip reddened and began to smoke, cupping my hands around it and coaxing until the plume grew hale and curled toward the ceiling. Slowly, the temperature of the room began to warm. The chill seeped away; the darkness grew warmer, less dense.

A wink of red light caught my eye from the study, hovering about a meter and a half off the ground. It moved closer and closer to the bedroom, approaching with the quiet determination of a hunter.

I leaped to my feet and slammed the bedroom door shut. I stuffed the key in its hole and locked it as swiftly as I could.

Click.

I withdrew the key.

The room was silent. My racing heartbeat began to slow. The numbness had faded from my fingers, and soon would from my freezing feet and arms. Now that I had copal, I would be able to sleep.

I stepped away from the door.

Thundering erupted over the door from the study, as if a thousand fists were hammering against it, pounding and pounding with immortal force.

I flung myself back, narrowly missing the end of the four-posted bed as I fell to the floor in a heap. The thundering paused, then began again with renewed force, so hard the door handle rattled and bounced against the wood. I imagined the hands that had shoved me on the stairs, icy and disembodied, pounding and pounding. The door was going to break off its hinges. It was going to cave in, and whatever was making that noise, whatever had red eyes and moved with the silence of a ghost, was going to sweep into the room and come for me.

But it never did. The pounding would stop, then begin again, but the door never gave out. I nursed the resin incense and lit candles, then sat with my back against the stucco wall, my knees curled to my chest, my hands over my ears.

That was how the night passed. Pounding on the door, then silence. Pounding, then silence. The silences were never the same length; long after midnight I began to drift off in one of the longer pauses, and then would wake with a strangled scream as the thundering of thousands of hands attacked the back of the door.

The sun rose. My incense burned low. My sanity was in tatters, shredded by a thousand claws.

It wasn't until morning light crept into the room and silence stretched long, longer than it ever had in the night, that I summoned the courage to peer through the keyhole into the study.

It was empty.

Of course.

What had I expected to see? A thousand people, snoring in heaps on the floor after a taxing night of terrorizing the lady of the house?

It took me a full hour after that to brave opening the door, and by then, it was time to greet the priests.

I expected to see Padre Guillermo, looking maddeningly well rested, his pale face cherry bright from the walk up the hill from the stables. But the first of the priests who entered San Isidro's courtyard was younger, his thinning pale hair streaked with gray only at the temples. A light sheen of sweat shone on his brow as he strode toward me. Padre Andrés followed at his shoulder, his chest rising and falling as slowly as if he had ambled lazily across the plaza de armas on his long legs. Though he was also dressed in black, no sweat shone on his brow. Streaks of red winked in his dark hair in the midmorning sunlight as he followed the other priest's example and nodded his hello.

"Buenos días, doña," the first priest said. "I am Padre Vicente."

"Welcome, Padres," I said. "Where is Padre Guillermo?"

"He is busy," Padre Vicente said, taking a handkerchief to dab the sweat at his brow. He did not deem it necessary to elaborate.

He was taller than Guillermo, and not as plump; his middle-aged face had fewer lines and a cool, settled expression that stoked a curl of fear in my belly. Was it that his straight-backed confidence was that of the fiercely pious, or that his assessment scraped over me in a way that was far too close to Tía Fernanda for comfort?

I cleared my throat. "Thank you for coming all this way in his stead," I said. "Please, come into the house."

I made sure I spent the requisite amount of time charming them, seating them on the terrace overlooking the half-weeded back garden. I asked Ana Luisa to bring them cool drinks; she sent Paloma instead. I spoke of weather and the other hacendados with Padre Vicente, leaning on all the high-society airs I had learned while living in the capital in an attempt to impress him. Men like him only pitied women they deemed worthy of the effort: the wealthy, those of high class. I was not born one of these. I had to rely on my new surname and acting the part. Though I was exhausted and felt close to shattering from the night before, I poured all my energy into trying to endear myself to him. Despite my efforts, Padre Vicente only half listened to me; my initial curl of fear spread, winding tight and trembling around my spine.

Padre Andrés remained silent. Out of the corner of my eye, I thought I caught a strange expression cross his face—it took on a distant look, as if he were eavesdropping on another conversation.

But there was no one else in the house to eavesdrop on.

A moment later, his expression cleared. It was calm and attentive as he nodded along with whatever Padre Vicente was saying.

Had he heard something? Did he understand why I had invited them here?

Would he believe me?

A small bud of hope fluttered behind the hollow of my throat. I cradled it tenderly, praying to I knew not whom that at least one of the priests would not think me mad as I brought them to the north wing.

The day before, when the sun was at its zenith—for I could not force myself when there was anything less than the brightest light possible—I went back to the north wing. It was as it had been when I brought Juana and Paloma to see: smooth, unblemished stucco mocking me. Sometimes when I headed upstairs, I would cast a glance over my shoulder, thinking I had spied a tumble of bricks out of the corner of my eye . . . but whenever I turned to face it, it was gone.

Had I imagined it? Was it there or not?

It was time to end this, once and for all.

"'This is where you wish to begin the blessing?" Padre Vicente looked around the dark hall, frowning at the cobwebs, a crease deepening between his brows.

I turned to face the priests. I accidentally met Padre Andrés's gaze; he must have been watching me with a scholarly focus. There was something in his eyes, an understanding frankness that stole the words from my lips.

He knew.

Intuition was a cool hand on my fevered brow.

He would listen.

"I know this sounds shocking, but someone died in this house, Padre Vicente," I said, the authority in my voice echoing through the narrow hall. "Someone died and was buried in a wall. Covered with bricks. I know because I found a body. This house is diseased because of it. There are . . . there is a spirit. A malevolent one . . ."

"That is quite enough, Doña Beatriz," Padre Vicente snapped, his brows now drawn close together.

My cheeks flushed hot. I don't quite know what I expected, but I certainly should not have expected it to go well. Perhaps it was because I described the house as *diseased*. Perhaps it was because I had no proof of this body I claimed to have found buried in the walls of the house.

"I will do what I came to do. That is all." He turned on his heel and stalked toward the front hall, muttering prayers of blessing and sprinkling holy water on this wall and that. That wasn't what I wanted.

"This house needs an exorcism, Padre," I said, following him toward the front door. "I beg you."

"I said, that is enough, Doña Beatriz." Padre Vicente gave me a sharp look that indicated how obvious it was to him that something on San Isidro's property needed an exorcism, and it wasn't the house. "Do not give me further reason to believe you mock me with Satan's tongue."

My breath caught. I trod on dangerous ground. *We must bear this with dignity*, Mamá often said—the well-worn habit of fear bade me be silent. I should have held my tongue. But the cold of the north wing sank its claws deep into marrow. I could not shake it. I would never be free of it. I needed help. I needed someone—anyone—to *listen*.

"Please," I repeated softly, and caught Padre Andrés's forearm as he trailed behind Padre Vicente.

The young man paused, his eyes falling to my hand on his arm. I dropped it as if I had been burned—laying hands on a priest was not something a woman like Rodolfo Solórzano's wife should do. Something no sane woman would do.

Yet I had.

For there was a curl of fear in the way Padre Andrés held his shoulders, a bent to his posture that told me he felt there was a predator nearby. That he was ready to spring away, because he, too, felt there was something breathing down his neck.

He raised his gaze to mine.

He believed me.

"Padre Andrés, my work here is done," Padre Vicente called. He was already in the garden.

"No, please," I breathed. The holy water and begrudging blessings were not enough. I couldn't face another night like the previous. I would lose my mind, or—

"Andrés, boy!" That was the cross bark of a superior who would not tolerate being disobeyed.

"Come to Mass often, Doña Beatriz," Padre Andrés said. His voice was low, sonorous—low enough that Padre Vicente could not overhear him in the garden. "The sacraments remind us we are not alone."

Then he dipped his head and stepped into the light. I watched his dark silhouette, slender as a young oak, as he crossed the courtyard in Padre Vicente's wake.

There was a lilt of invitation in that final phrase, in the urgent shade of his eyes.

Come to the church, it said. *I will help you.*

10

THE NEXT LETTER I received from Rodolfo opened with the same piloncillo-sweet well-wishes as the first, but quickly dovetailed into harsh scolding.

Evidently, Padre Vicente had found it prudent to report my troubling behavior to my husband. And he had either embellished my state or truly believed I had taken leave of my senses.

I stood in my study as I read, my back to the wall. Two sleepless nights had passed since the visit from the priests. No matter where I was, no matter where I hid, it was as if the house *knew* where I was. Cold swept through the halls like flash floods through arroyos, gluttonous from rain, sweeping me away.

That morning, as I uncurled the stiffness in my back and watched the lilting smudges of bats returning outside my bedroom window, I wondered if I should try sleeping outside. Far from the house rather than in its belly.

But the idea of being so exposed, of having no wall to put my back to, no door to shut if those eyes . . .

Gooseflesh crawled over my skin.

No more of this foolishness, Rodolfo wrote. *I know you must be lonely—as I am without you by my side. But if you feel unwell in the country, come back to the capital. Do not draw the attention of the Church like this again.*

Perhaps it was not embarrassment that caused Rodolfo to write. The Inquisition had released its bloody fervor and was abolished several years ago, but its suspicions were still firmly in place. We had never discussed it, for what newlywed politician would divulge anticlerical views to his pretty little wife? But I suspected he did not hold the institution of the Church in high regard, much less trust them.

Rodolfo's message was plain: if San Isidro does not agree with you, come to the capital.

And do what? Wait on the generals who ordered my house be burned and killed my father? Simper and smile with their obedient wives?

No. San Isidro was freedom. San Isidro was *mine.*

But San Isidro was also trying to break me, and I did not doubt the force of its will.

I needed help.

Stop, or go to the capital.

There had to be a third way.

The sacraments remind us we are not alone, Padre Andrés said.

And though I had just met him, though I had no reason to trust any stranger, much less a member of the clergy, I felt in my bones that the young priest was where I would find it.

PALOMA ACCOMPANIED ME TO church, a quiet shadow at my elbow. Disappointment seeped sourly through my mouth when I saw that it was Padre Vicente, not Padre Andrés, who walked up the aisle past our pew to the altar.

Come often, Padre Andrés said. He never said *when.* I would try again tomorrow, then. And if he were not here, then the next day.

But the thought of facing another night alone tightened my throat like a slipknot yanked taut. Bowing my head in prayer, I clasped my trembling lace-gloved hands together, my breath shallow and hitching. I would drown in San Isidro without help. The weight of the darkness would crush my lungs, crush my bones, grind me to dust and sweep me away . . .

Someone was looking at me.

I had grown familiar with the weight of attention after living under San Isidro's roof. I lifted my eyes slowly.

A figure hovered behind the altar, blending into the shadows of the doorway that led to the sacristy. Padre Andrés. He lingered for a moment longer, his attention on my mantilla, and then vanished.

He had seen me. He would find me. Relief loosened the tightness in my throat, though not completely. I still did not know if he meant to help me. Nor how. Nor if he thought me mad.

Mass stretched interminably. Sleeplessness weighed heavy in my face, tender as a bruise. When Padre Vicente finally bid us go in peace, I stopped before one of the chapel eaves in the side of the church—that of la Virgen de Guadalupe. The paint of Juan Diego's wooden face was fresh, his dark pupils turned upward in rapture as he held out his cloth blessed with the image of la Virgen. Carved red roses tumbled to his feet.

I knelt at the pew before it and took the rosary Rodolfo had given me on our wedding day from my bag. I ran my fingers over the crucifix and first five beads, relaxing my shoulders and tilting my chin up to la Virgen as if I were settling in for a full rosary.

Paloma's skirts shifted behind me. She twisted a handkerchief in her hands, her eyes straying to the door, to the white afternoon that spilled into the church. I knew that impatience well. How many times had I worn that same longing expression looking at the open door of a church, watching the silhouettes moving freely beyond it?

"Go ahead, if you wish," I said. "To market or to see friends. I need some time. Today would be my father's birthday," I added.

My father's birthday was in April, but no one knew that. Not even Rodolfo.

Paloma's head snapped toward me, her mouth rounded into a sympathetic O. "My apologies, Doña Beatriz, I did not realize . . ."

The servants knew my sad story, then.

I gave Paloma a wan smile as I waved her away. I began the first of many Hail Marys, brushing my fingers over the wooden beads as the echo of her quick, birdlike steps moved away from me. *Ave Maria, gratia plena, Dominus tecum.* A murmur of voices from the door. *Benedicta tu in mulieribus, et benedictus fructus ventris tui, Iesus.* The murmuring ceased.

A creak of the heavy wooden doors; they closed with a tired, self-satisfied thud.

I lifted my head, blinking to adjust my vision to the dimness.

Padre Andrés's slim form stepped away from the doors. Subtly, barely even a nod, he gestured with his chin across the church, at a wooden confessional opposite la Virgen de Guadalupe's eave.

The sacraments remind us we are not alone.

Of course.

I made the sign of the cross slowly as I rose, the shifting of my skirts and the tap of Padre Andrés's shoes against tile the only sounds filling the quiet cavern of the church. By the time I reached the confessional, Padre Andrés had already disappeared inside.

The wood smelled of recent lacquer; inside the air was close and warm, but not unpleasantly so. It felt like stepping into the solemn quiet of someone else's mind. I sank to my knees, skirts settling around me, my face close to the grate that separated the sides of the confessional.

"Forgive me, Padre, for I have sinned," I murmured, dipping my chin out of habit.

"Something is *wrong* with that house."

My head snapped up. From his visit to my property I had learned that Padre Andrés's voice was low, thickened by a gentle, sleepy rasp. Now, it hummed with urgency.

I tightened my clasped hands as if in a fervent prayer of gratitude. "Thank God," I whispered. The words came out strangled; hot tears had leaped to my eyes and lingered there, stinging. "You *understand.*"

"I felt it the moment I stepped through the gates," Padre Andrés said. "It didn't use to be like that. My aunt is Doña Juana's cook, and I used to—"

A sharp rapping sounded on the confessional door.

I jumped.

"Carajo," Padre Andrés breathed.

My hand rose to my lips in surprise. A priest? Cursing?

"There's a storeroom behind the sacristy," he whispered. "We can talk there. I—"

Light flooded the confessional.

"Padre Andrés!"

His head snapped to the door; a lock of straight black hair fell into his eyes. I had noticed his good looks when I first met him—how could I not have, when sun poured down on him like a saint in a painting?—but now that I was hidden behind the grate of the confessional, I could peer at him unseen. Shadow carved out sharp cheekbones and a severe, aquiline nose; sensitive hazel eyes blinked as they adjusted to the light. He frowned as he looked up at someone out of my line of sight.

"Padre Vicente, a parishioner wishes to have her confession heard," Padre Andrés announced, voice open and innocent.

Padre Vicente. My chest tightened.

"Then why are you in here?" Padre Vicente's voice was aghast. Accusing.

Evidently, confessions were not a responsibility of Padre Andrés's. He was not a full parish priest, then. Perhaps he was too young, or perhaps his mixed heritage prevented him from taking on such responsibilities when criollo priests like Vicente and Guillermo ran the parish.

Padre Andrés blinked. He opened his mouth to speak. A short beat passed.

Then he grasped for something in the confessional and lifted a book in a swift movement. "My book of prayers. Padre Guillermo borrowed it and must have left it here by accident."

Gold lettering winked at me through the confessional grate, peeking cheekily through Padre Andrés's long brown fingers. *The Holy Gospel.*

A giggle rose to my lips. I pressed my hand over my mouth to keep it from escaping.

"Out!" Padre Vicente snapped.

Padre Andrés obeyed. His exit was neither graceful nor immediate; judging from the low thump of a skull against wood, it seemed the confessional was not built for someone of his height.

Padre Vicente settled into the confessional across from me, his pale, thinning hair nearly translucent in the light. He shut the door with a click and settled in with an expectant sigh.

"Buenas tardes, Padre," I said, speaking out of the corner of my mouth to disguise my voice and layering in as much piousness as I could summon. My heart sank. I actually had to confess my sins to Padre Vicente before I followed Padre Andrés, didn't I?

Carajo, indeed.

"Forgive me, Padre, for I have sinned . . ."

TEN EXCRUCIATING MINUTES LATER, I stepped from the confessional and walked quickly to the back of the church. I exited through a smaller side door, deeply grateful that anonymity etiquette dictated Padre Vicente would wait until I was out of sight before stepping from the confessional himself.

Sunlight seared my eyes. I shook my head, blinking to clear my vision, and followed the white stucco wall of the church. What if I walked into another priest somewhere—how would I explain myself? The last thing I needed was to be caught stealing into a sacristy like a common thief, not after running afoul of Padre Vicente mere days ago.

But the alternative was to return to San Isidro without any help. And that was out of the question.

I turned a corner. A worn wooden door, only about as tall as I was, had been left slightly ajar, its angle an invitation. Was that the door to the sacristy storeroom? I slipped through it as quickly as I could and collided very solidly with Padre Andrés.

He leaped back.

"Excuse me!" I gasped at the same time he held a finger to his lips for silence.

I edged away from Padre Andrés as he closed the door, and immediately bumped into an abandoned pew. An old altar, covered in cobwebs and stacked with ceremonial linens, dominated the back of the room; rickety shelves lined the walls, stuffed with bowls and wooden chalices covered in a thin layer of dust.

I slipped back to the altar, sheepishly putting as much space between myself and Padre Andrés as possible. Which wasn't much—even without the clutter, the room was cramped at best. I was surprised Padre Andrés didn't knock his head against the ceiling as he turned to face me.

"My apologies about the confessional, Doña Beatriz," he began. "I think here will be—"

There was a rap at the door.

Padre Andrés froze. Then the gravity of the situation struck me like a blow: what if someone opened the door and found us alone here?

Then—be Andrés a priest or not—I would have something even worse to explain to my husband than asking for an exorcism.

We stared at each other in shocked silence, momentarily paralyzed, realization of our predicament thick as copal on the air between us.

A second rap at the door. "Padre Andrés!"

Padre Guillermo's voice.

I darted around the back of the altar and ducked beneath it, yanking my skirts around my legs and tucking my knees to my chest. Padre Andrés's black trousers and shoes crossed the room in a step and a half; then a box scraped across the stone floor in front of the altar and he pivoted on his heel.

Daylight flooded the storeroom.

"Padre Andrés!" Padre Guillermo huffed. "Padre Vicente told me you were in the confessional with a parishioner."

"I was looking for my prayer book, Padre Guillermo," Padre Andrés said smoothly. "Of course it was an accident."

But this was not. If anything about this conversation went awry, there was no explaining away why I was curled into a ball beneath a dusty altar with Padre Andrés concealing me.

A dusty, faded red cloth covered the middle of the altar, hiding me from sight, but beyond it I could see a dusty statue of la Virgen on a shelf. Her hands were spread wide, her painted face perfectly beatific.

Help, please. The thought flew from my mind before I could summon the shame to stop it. As if that prayer were worth listening to. Who would intercede on my behalf in a situation like this? Our Lady of Dust and Secrecy? Our Lady of Women Disobeying Their Husbands?

Padre Andrés smoothly diverted Padre Guillermo's attention away from the confessional incident and drew him deep into some town affair involving the Sunday bell ringer and his incurable pulque habit. Soon he would usher the priest out and the danger would be gone.

Ducking beneath the altar had disturbed dust; it rose around me in a faint cloud. My nose itched with the beginning of a sneeze. Panic budded in my chest as I fought to suppress it, too afraid to move. If I failed, my hiding place would surely be revealed—

"What are you doing in here?" Padre Guillermo asked at last.

"Oh," Padre Andrés drawled innocently, as if only then remembering his surroundings. "Penance, Padre."

"You're praying in here?"

"Dusting. Organizing. As you instructed me to do two weeks ago, and which I clearly haven't done."

Padre Guillermo's sigh was deep. Long-suffering, but also affectionate. That was a sigh I had often directed at Mamá—the sound of someone who had long put up with the whims of a daydreamer. "Ay, Andrés. What will we ever do with you?"

"The Lord is in all things, Padre," said Padre Andrés. "Buenas tardes."

"Buenas tardes."

A creak; the door shut. Footsteps retreated in the gravel, then faded entirely.

Padre Andrés turned and dropped to a crouch. He shoved the box to the side and lifted the altar covering that concealed me from sight. A thin veil of dust fell between us.

A moment passed. The dust settled. Reality settled: I was sitting on a dusty storeroom floor like a child, my knees pulled to my chest, looking up into the face of an unfairly handsome priest.

I sneezed.

"Salud," Padre Andrés said solemnly.

His seriousness was so incongruous with our position that a sudden peal of laughter escaped my lips.

His finger flew to his lips. "Shh!"

I clapped a hand over my mouth to smother the sound but was unable to stop. I shook with silent laughter, tears leaking from my eyes.

Padre Andrés kept his expression carefully neutral, but I sensed he was mortified as I crawled out from under the altar. He held out a hand to help me to my feet. I accepted it, gasping for breath between stifled peals of laughter.

He released my hand as soon as I was upright, murmuring an apology, his gaze demurely downcast. "I was certain we would be undisturbed here. How Padre Guillermo knew . . ."

I waved a hand, finally catching my breath. "It's all right," I said, wiping tears from my cheeks and brushing dust from my skirts. When was the last time I had laughed like that? Sleeplessness was certainly stretching my sanity thinner than it had ever been. I inhaled deeply to compose myself and looked up at Padre Andrés, at the crease of concern that seemed permanently etched between his brows.

Papá distrusted the Church as a rule. Priests were conservative and corrupt, he said. I had never once told a priest anything aside from what was required from me in bland, unspecific confessions or society small talk. I knew I couldn't trust them, not in my life before Papá's death nor now, when I was alone in my torment in a cold, hostile house. Yet a curl of intuition drew me to Padre Andrés like moth to flame. *You've never met a priest like him before*, it whispered.

"We can speak freely here," he said quietly.

And so I did.

He moved to my side, leaning against the altar as he listened. We had left the confessional behind, but I had never been so honest with a stranger. I laid everything bare, beginning when Rodolfo and I first arrived from the capital, with the red eyes I saw on that first night. I left out no detail. Not even Juana's erratic behavior, believing me one day and dismissing me as mad the next. Nor did I forget Ana Luisa's copal.

Padre Andrés listened, one hand rubbing his jaw thoughtfully, as I described the pounding on the doors and the cold that swept through the house and prevented me from sleeping. As I described the skeleton I had found in the wall that vanished.

When I finished, I glanced up at his face, bracing myself to see a look of horrified disbelief. Instead, Padre Andrés bit his lip, worrying it as he thought. He drummed the fingers of his left hand against the altar. "I think I can help," he said at last.

A swell of relief overtook me. "Please," I began. I tried to force a thank-you to my lips but couldn't—for if I spoke, my voice would break, and take my composure with it. "Please come back to the hacienda."

A long moment passed. I knew it was not an elegant invitation. It was just short of the begging of a madwoman. But I knew with a cold certainty, one that hung around my clavicles with the dread weight of a prophecy, that if I did not get help, I would die.

I had no one else to whom to turn.

Please.

"If anyone asks, say that you want Mass said for your villagers more regularly," he said quietly. "It is common enough that, ah, no one will think more of it."

No one clearly meant *Rodolfo*. So he knew of Padre Vicente's letter and had decided to help me anyway. Another wave of gratitude rose thick in my chest. I wouldn't have to explain that secrecy was required. He knew.

Because he believed me.

I nodded, not trusting myself to speak.

He pushed himself away from the altar. "I think . . . I must ask you a favor, Doña Beatriz. I will need to stay long enough to walk through the house at night."

"Of course. When can you come?" A tremble wound through my voice.

"As soon as possible. Tomorrow." Now his attention was fully on me, he was present, and he was watchful. "Do you feel you will be safe until then?"

No, my heart cried, my chest tightening around it like a vise. *No.*

His gaze fell to my hands. I had been holding them clasped loosely before me, but now they were tight. Too tight.

That was answer enough for him.

"Burn copal," he said firmly. "Fill any room you stay in with smoke."

"What does it do?"

"It purifies your surroundings."

So it *did* work. If I was to defend myself tonight, I needed it. I didn't want protection; I wanted tools with which to protect myself. "I don't have any. Do you—"

He looked over my head, scanning the shelves that lined the back of the room. "We keep some in here, for when we run out of the imported kind Padre Guillermo and Padre Vicente prefer . . . Wait one moment."

The room was so tight, the space between boxes and altar and abandoned pews so narrow. It was impossible not to touch; his hands were ginger, light as the brush of a wing as they guided me by the shoulders to one side so he could step behind me.

From her quiet place on the shelf, Our Lady of Dust and Secrecy met my eyes over the priest's shoulder.

Heat flushed my cheeks. I was certain she saw it.

"Here." Padre Andrés turned and pressed three large pieces of resin into my palm, his fingertips brushing my wrist. He drew his hand back quickly and cleared his throat. "I will pack some things and come to the property tomorrow after Mass," he said, serious once more.

"Thank you so much," I breathed, my fingers curling over the resin. "How could I ever repay you for your help?"

He dropped his gaze, eyelashes brushing his cheeks, suddenly shy once more. "Tending to lost souls is my vocation, Doña Beatriz."

The tenderness in his voice stole something from my chest, leaving me vulnerable and imbalanced.

"Is it not also Padre Vicente's? Yet he had no interest in helping me," I said. My bitterness hung on the air like smoke. That was the tone Mamá scolded me for time and time again, the one that made Tía Fernanda call me ungrateful and sharp.

It didn't faze Padre Andrés in the least. He shrugged, birdlike with those slim shoulders. A slow, knowing smile played at the corner of his mouth. "He lacks expertise with certain things."

"But aren't you less experienced than him?"

Padre Andrés raised his eyes and held my gaze. *Not with this*, my gut said. "Do you trust me, Doña Beatriz?"

I did. I felt it with a certainty as powerful as the sweep of a tide.

I nodded.

"Then I will see you tomorrow. I will arrive at the capilla around noon," he said. "Buenas tardes, Doña Beatriz."

I dipped my chin to him in goodbye, the formality of the gesture so at odds with the intimacy of our conversation, how we stood only a foot apart from each other in a dim room.

I swallowed the thought quickly and raised my head with all the dignity I could muster. "Buenas tardes, Padre."

"Please," he said as I moved to the door. "Andrés. Just Andrés."

11

THE NEXT DAY, I sat on the front steps of the house, waiting for
night to fall. A candle burned on my right, already lit despite the still-
orange skies. At my other side, copal in a censer released a steady, curling
plume of mauve smoke.

A book sat abandoned by my side. Since Papá died, reading had been
my constant companion, my path to escape the confines of my life. Not so
since arriving at San Isidro. Paranoia rendered me incapable of losing myself in words, especially in the hours near sunset. What if I were to become
too caught up in reading and night fell without me noticing? Without being prepared? It was the same fear that woke me with a start from my siesta
that afternoon. With no one to judge me, no one to care, I had taken to
bringing a blanket into the sun-flooded back terrace and drowsing on the
steps that led to the garden, blood warmed by sunshine and lulled by the
presence of lit copal.

Sometimes, I thought longingly of my first nights at San Isidro, curled up next to Rodolfo's heavy warmth. How soundly I slept with the certainty of someone's weight on the other side of the bed, the steady rhythm of breathing.

I would not be alone in the house tonight either, but tonight would be different. Padre Andrés was due to arrive at sunset.

I had met him at the capilla around noon. Ana Luisa cast me a curious look when I asked her to prepare the small rooms that adjoined the chapel for a guest, but she asked no questions. Perhaps she should have. It might have prevented the look of surprise on her face when she saw Padre Andrés walking up the path to the capilla from the main gates of the hacienda, a maguey fiber bag slung over one shoulder, his long legs bringing him into the heart of the estate with an easy grace.

"Buenas tardes, Doña Beatriz. Señora," he greeted Ana Luisa, formal and stiff.

Her eyes narrowed. It did not escape me how hard and cold they remained as I thanked Padre Andrés for agreeing to take up residence in the capilla, to make sure that Mass was celebrated on a more regular basis for the servants of San Isidro.

Though Ana Luisa and I were meant to return to the main house together, she excused herself from my presence as quickly as she could and made for the servants' quarters. To tell Juana, perhaps. But to tell her what? That I, as the mistress of the hacienda, had invited a priest to bring God's word to the men and women who worked for my husband's family? There was no crime in that. Nothing suspicious.

So why did Ana Luisa keep casting stray glances over her shoulder at the capilla as she walked away?

This evening, she came and left after an early dinner as was her custom. Asking myself if she was acting strangely was futile—who didn't, in this house? Even during the day I found myself jumping at the slightest shift of shadow. I began wearing a set of house keys at my waist, not just for the comforting click of iron as I strode through the empty house, but because every time I was certain I had left a door open on purpose, I would retrace my steps and find it locked shut.

The first time this happened, it was when Ana Luisa was still in the house, cooking dinner. I shouted and pounded on the door until she unlocked it with a wry look. I was embarrassed, but it did not escape my attention that if she had not been present, I would have been stuck all night in the windowless storeroom where I was putting away maize.

Without copal. Without candles.

Keys became my constant accessory.

If I were honest, if I were not trying to hold the house at arm's length out of fear it would somehow infect me with madness, I might admit that even in daylight, I could feel the house settling around me. As if I were but a fly on the hide of a giant beast that twitched in sleep.

Now it was waking.

From the moment the sun dipped behind the western mountains on the horizon, it began to shift. Lazy at first, stretching its phantom limbs, then slowly gaining alertness as the dark grew more complete.

Beyond the walls of San Isidro, Apan settled into the cool of its evening. Dogs barked as sheep were herded home; the indistinct voices of tlachiqueros rose as they returned from the maguey fields. The dark form of mountains rose beyond the town, lazily sprawled in a protective circle around the valley.

The slim form of Padre Andrés darkened the arched doorway of the courtyard of the main house. A smaller bag than he was carrying earlier was slung over his shoulder; the sound of gravel beneath his shoes filled the courtyard.

I took the candle and rose to greet him. I was more than a head shorter than him; the result of the candle held before me was that the shadows carved his cheeks hollow like a skull. A chill went down my spine at the thought of the skull in the wall grinning at me.

I barely knew this man. Yet I was placing my reputation, and possibly my life, into his hands.

Why? Was it the black habit and the smudge of white at his collar? What guarantee was that, in times like these, when priests turned over their parishioners, insurgents, to the Spanish armies, when someone as powerful as Rodolfo feared the lingering claws of the Inquisition?

This one was different. I knew it with a certainty that made my bones ache.

"Welcome, Padre," I said.

He thanked me and looked past me into the deepening shadows of the house.

"Ah, San Isidro. You didn't use to be like this," he said. His voice was soft, even soothing, as he addressed the house. As if he were placing a hand on the brow of a feverish patient. "After you, Doña Beatriz."

I crouched to pick up the copal censer, handed it to Padre Andrés, and collected my book from the step.

"What do you mean to do tonight, Padre?" I asked as we entered the dark entryway. I had lit thick tallow candles and left them wherever there was space; they huddled in clusters by doorways, in saints' eaves carved into the walls, lined tidily along the long hall leading to the parlors.

"Andrés," he corrected absentmindedly, his chin tilted up to the ceiling as he scanned the wooden beams. "I'm not sure yet. First, I would like to see the house as you do."

"You would have to be alone for that," I said, leading him up the candle-lined hall. Candelabras were on the long list of things I had sent to Rodolfo, the list that he informed me must have gone missing en route to him, for he never received it. Twice it had gone missing, and I was beginning to lose patience with the men who rode with the mail to the capital.

Padre Andrés nodded. "You may leave me, if you wish. Get some sleep."

Had he noticed the purple shadows beneath my eyes? I laughed, dry and humorless. "I can't sleep in this house, Pa—Andrés," I corrected myself. Addressing a priest by his given name should have struck me as strange, but it rolled naturally off my tongue. Perhaps because he was so young, perhaps because he spoke to me as if I were his peer, not his parishioner.

We reached the green parlor, and I opened the door. Darkness crept from the corners of the room. Cold flushed the stone floors like icy water.

The house was awake.

"This is the green parlor," I said, my voice echoing despite how low I kept it. The room had a single door and the customary high windows; unlike my bedroom, which had the door to the study as well as to a small room with a chamber pot, it was a sturdy, defensible position. One could have one's back to the wall and face the door. It was the kind of room I would have wanted, if I were spending the night on my own for the first time in a house like this. I echoed Ana Luisa's explanation: "It is called the green parlor because—"

"Because it used to be green," he murmured, half to himself, as he stepped into the room. It was still bare of furniture; as Padre Andrés had requested earlier, I brought a few blankets and laid them near the fireplace, near two copal censers and abundant candlesticks. He gestured to the flagstones as he scanned the rafters. "The carpet. It was green."

"Padre Guillermo said you were familiar with San Isidro," I said. "Why?"

He did not immediately reply. He had tilted his head to the side, as if he had caught a strain of distant music. A long moment passed; he was so still, the darkness beyond him so complete, that he almost seemed to bleed into it.

Then he turned; candlelight caught on the sharp panes of his face. "My mother lived her whole life on this land until she married my father. My grandmother lived here as well. I stayed with her often, when I was a boy."

So he had known this house and knew something had changed. That, too, must be the reason why he chose to go against Padre Vicente's orders to help me: attachment to a childhood home. "Where is she now?" I asked. "Your grandmother?"

"Buried beyond the capilla." Padre Andrés set his bag and the lit censer down next to the blankets. "Do things happen every night?" His voice was now crisp and serious as he set to lighting the candles with matches, illuminating the room like a chapel.

I cleared my throat, embarrassed to have pried so much. "The feeling of . . . of being watched never goes away, not even during the day. Some things have happened in broad daylight."

"Your discovery."

The skeleton in the wall.

A clammy veil settled over the small of my back at the thought. "Generally, it is worst between midnight and dawn."

Padre Andrés rose, his height unfolding like a plume of smoke. "With your permission, I will now examine the house without copal."

"You're mad," I said flatly. Or at least he would be by the end of his experience in San Isidro if he insisted on doing that. The red eyes in the dark flashed through my mind. "If something were to happen to you . . ."

What would then happen to *me*? I could protect myself with copal, but it would eventually burn out. I could not be left alone in the dark. Not anymore.

"I will be safe, Doña Beatriz."

But I wouldn't be. If I knew anything about how the house felt—and lately I was beginning to worry I knew altogether too much—I knew that it resented people like him and me. People with plans and ideas. Dread drummed a militant beat in my chest at the thought of going back to my room and sitting in the dark, all the while aware he was poking and prodding around the house's entrails. He didn't understand what this house was. He couldn't.

I did.

"I will accompany you," I said firmly. "This is my house. I am responsible for you."

"Doña Beatriz," he said, taking a candle to match the one I held in one hand. "I know what I am doing."

Then I would be safe at his side. Wouldn't I be? I cast a longing glance past him at the smoke from the censer. No harm could come to me in the presence of a priest.

Or so I told myself.

"We can start with the parlors," I said, forcing more confidence than I felt into my voice. "Make our way to the kitchen, then retrace our steps to the north wing."

He walked at my side as we began, asking to pause in certain rooms. As we approached the kitchen, the house was coy. The tendrils of its feeling kept their distance from Padre Andrés, but I could *feel* it calculating, feel it watching him with care. The sensation writhed under my skin like a centipede.

What if it did nothing to him? What if this were all in my head? If I were imagining the cold, imagining the thundering pounding on the door of my bedroom, imagining—a wash of sweat appeared on my palms—the watching? The cold hands tugging at my hair? The voices? What then? Should I ask him to exorcise *me* instead?

The light from our candles jumped and licked the doorframe of the kitchen. Our shoes met with Ana Luisa's herbs, the ones that grew so abundantly in the garden. Andrés fell into a crouch and brushed his fingertips over them, then lifted his fingers to his nose to smell the sap. He made an indecisive sound, stood, and cast his glance around the room as if looking for something.

His attention fell on Ana Luisa's charcoal markings around the doorframe; his nostrils flared with a quick intake of breath as his eyes skipped over the markings.

"What were you thinking?" he breathed, softly incredulous. It seemed directed more at himself than at me. Something about his voice seemed almost angry.

"Is something wrong?" I asked, voice unsteady. A sudden shift in his energy had accompanied his discovery, and I felt as if I were standing on the deck of a ship that had turned into rough waters.

He did not answer my question. "You mentioned that the north wing was where you found . . ." He paused as if reaching for a word, only to decide the better of it. "Shall we go there next?"

"Very well." I wet my dry lips and turned to the kitchen doorway.

The darkness yawned open, a maw. Nausea swept over me.

It had *heard* us.

Padre Andrés stepped forward, pausing when he noticed I had not joined him. "Doña Beatriz?"

The walls were so close, too close. The darkness too deep. I thought of the flint in Juana's eyes as she pushed me into the dark. How the walls spun around me from mezcal. She knew this house. She *knew* it was like this.

And she sent me into the dark anyway.

"I want the copal." My voice was strained, breathless.

"Would you like to return to the green parlor?" Padre Andrés asked.

Part of me yearned for the sensation of my back safely against a wall. Part of me screamed for light. It begged to light a thousand candles, to throw anything that could be burned into the fireplace and set it aflame.

Part of me wanted to burn the whole house to the ground.

The other part of me could not bear being alone. Padre Andrés was here. He was another creature in the house, one who meant me no harm. Another soul in the dark. Another pair of eyes, to watch my back when I could not. I could not tear myself from that safety, not even to sit in a room of copal and candles, inhaling smoke until I went dizzy.

"My house, my responsibility," I said. "Forward."

I set my jaw and faced the darkness.

The darkness faced me, a tremor of sick joy rippling through it.

We left doors ajar behind us on purpose, to test my perception that something other than Ana Luisa was making them shut behind me. When we reached the staircase, Andrés breathed in sharply.

"The cold," he said hoarsely, barely above a whisper. We could have shouted at the top of our lungs—there was no one to judge us, no one to hear us—but we could not bring ourselves to raise our voices. As if he, too, realized we were being watched, being listened to. I knew the house would hear him anyway.

The cold was like stepping into a current. Three paces back, it didn't exist at all; now it was all-encompassing. It snaked up my spine, wet, slick, heavy as mud, and settled on my chest. My breathing grew shallow and pained; no matter how I tried, I could not breathe deeply enough.

A clacking noise to my right; Padre Andrés's teeth were chattering. "What *is* that?" he forced out.

"A terrible draft," I said, my own jaw stiff from the cold. The house swallowed my joke whole.

"The north wing is where you found . . . ?"

I nodded, too chilled to speak. This was different. Before, when the cold had attacked me, it was a wind, biting and dry, ready to snap me in two. This was like wading through thick water: it tore at my limbs, its heaviness seizing my thighs, grasping at my waist.

We moved into the north wing.

Naturally cold storeroom, I had written. A wild giggle rose in my throat, and I covered my mouth with a hand to silence it.

I let Padre Andrés take the lead in the narrow hall, my heart thundering against the tightness in my chest as we waded slowly through the cold. For a moment, the click of the heels of his shoes on the stone floor was all that broke the silence.

Then he stopped abruptly.

In the flickering light of the candles, I could see that bricks littered the narrow hall before us. The bricks that had collapsed when I—

Red eyes appeared over the bricks, high enough from the ground to belong to a person.

I gasped. Andrés seized my free hand.

The red winked into darkness and vanished.

Candlelight danced on the bricks, on the collapsed wall . . . and glinted off the gold necklace that was still draped around the skeleton's broken neck.

The hair on the back of my neck lifted; a buzzing fear followed, rippling over my flesh. We were exposed. There was nowhere to run, nowhere to create a barrier between us and *that*, nowhere to hide.

Andrés raised his candle, then moved it down and side to side in the sign of the cross. "In nomine Patris, et Filii, et Spiritus—"

I cried out as darkness leaped from the walls, from around the skeleton, from behind us, from before us. The cold sucked shadows toward it with a ferocity that made our candles flicker and jump.

Andrés's candle died.

12

BACK UP." ANDRÉS'S VOICE pitched with fear; his hand tightened on mine as he fell back a step. "Slowly."

A rush of shadows swept from behind us. The keys at my waist rang like wind chimes; the candle's flame bent forward. I wanted him to let go of my hand so I could cup it around my flame. It licked upward, fighting as desperately as if it were being suffocated. As if the air in the hall were too close for it to be able to breathe.

Then it went out.

A low *no* escaped Andrés's mouth as darkness fell over us.

"Back to the parlor," he said. "I face back; you face forward."

We moved as one, our backs against each other, facing the darkness. We had no copal. No weapons to defend ourselves. Nothing to shield us from whatever it was that seethed inside the house, whatever it was that pursued us like the weakened prey we were.

There was no candlelight. Only Andrés's hand crushing mine. It was not enough. Not when the house was all around us. There was no running from it; there was only running deeper into its bowels, and the cold pulling at my legs like mud as we fought toward the parlor where we had left the copal.

I relied on memory to carry me to the fork in the hall, past the staircase, too terrified to reach out to the walls and feel my way forward, for what if they crumbled beneath my touch and revealed new horrors? It was becoming difficult to lift my feet, difficult to breathe, as if something heavy were pushing on my chest. The cold, the dark, was heavy, so heavy . . .

A girlish laugh lilted toward us from the direction of the collapsed wall, faint and wavering, as if carried on a breeze from far away.

Juana, the laughter called, birdlike and thin. *Juana*.

"Go, go." Andrés picked up speed, forcing me forward into the dark. His hold on my hand was so firm I could barely feel my fingers. My feet knew the way, and carried us into the main hall, past the dining room . . .

Juana, Juana . . .

The door of the parlor was shut, though we had left it open. I reached for the handle—it was locked. Of course. God *damn* this house.

Andrés collided with me, pushing me against the door. My teeth jarred against one another and I cried out as my candle fell to the floor. It cracked against the stone floor and rolled away in pieces.

"Carajo," Andrés said. "I'm so sorry, I—"

Juana. Less faint now. It was following us, dropping in pitch, becoming less singsong, less girlish. Its ring was dissonant, setting my teeth on edge. *Juana.*

It drew closer.

"Can you open it?" Andrés's breathing came in rough gasps. My heart throbbed in my throat as I fumbled with the key; finally, we fell forward into the dark room. Andrés slammed the door shut behind us with his shoulder.

The copal sputtered out. All the candles were extinguished. He released my hand. "Lock the door. I'll light candles."

He didn't have to ask me twice. I did so, then followed him as he stumbled forward into the room.

There is nothing more beautiful than the sound of match against paper, the sharp spark of amber and gold, the small crackle of a wick taking flame.

My body shook uncontrollably as I lowered myself to my knees next to the first three candles. He lit ten or eleven in all, his movements sharp with fear as he scattered the thick tallow candles about the room to illuminate every corner. When he was done, he turned his attention to the three copal censers. He placed two on either side of me and the third between us and the door. Then he sat at my right side, breathing heavily, legs pulled to his chest so he could rest his chin on his knees—mirroring how I sat.

His hands trembled.

Slowly, smoke rose from the censers, filling the air with the sharp spice of copal. Andrés sat so close to me our arms brushed.

I was not alone. His presence calmed my racing heart. *I was not alone.*

Andrés drew a long, shaky breath. "I . . . I did not expect that."

His attention was fixed on the door. Beads of sweat were drying on his brow.

"I told you." The words slipped from my mouth before I could stop them.

"And I believed you." His shoulders tensed as a shudder went down his back. "But it is one thing to believe. It is another to see."

We sat in silence, staring at the door. Watching the copal curl toward the ceiling. Slowly, my heartbeat returned to its normal pace.

"I will stay here for the rest of the night," Andrés said softly. "Whenever you are ready, you may leave to sleep. I will be safe."

"You think *I'm* leaving this room?" The indignant pitch of my voice made him jump. "You might be safe, but may I remind you which direction I have to walk to go upstairs? Would *you* want to walk that way alone?"

The shadows made his frown seem deeper than it was. "I could escort you."

"No," I said firmly. *I don't want to be alone.* "I'm staying here."

He shifted, tightening his hold around his knees. He kept his gaze fixed on the door. He was uncomfortable about something; that much was clear.

"If this is about spending the night in a room with a woman," I said, "I might remind you that I am married, and moreover am your host in this horrible place, and therefore I decide what is appropriate or not."

His head snapped to me in surprise. "Cielo santo, *no*, doña," he said, having the infuriating decency to look scandalized. "I beg your pardon. It is only that . . ." He let the thought trail off as he worried his lower lip, as his eyes skipped again to the door. He was weighing something, deciding whether to speak further. Whether or not to allow me to stay.

He *had* to let me stay. Surely he understood what it felt like to be alone in this house. Shadows curled around our small halo of light, reaching for him like tendrils of cloying mist; it was as if they deepened in his presence, grew more alive.

He let out his breath with a hoarse curse, then those long legs stretched out, and he rose to his feet. "If you wish to stay, I must ask that you not tell the other priests . . . anything," he said sharply. "Especially Padre Vicente. Do you understand?"

"Padre Vicente?" I repeated. The demand—for it was clear from his tone it was a demand, albeit couched in polite language—caught me off guard. "I could tell him anything and he wouldn't believe me." I could honestly picture myself declaring the sky is blue to his overfed, red-cheeked face, only to see his eyes widen, his jowls tremble as he reached for a pen to write to my husband to control his hysterical wife.

Andrés looked down at me, somber and unamused. Then his attention flitted to the door. Whatever he had heard, it was enough to tip the scales of his silent debate. He patted his trousers pocket as if searching for something then drew out a piece of charcoal.

Rolling the charcoal between forefinger and thumb, he turned away from me and began to count his paces from the first copal censer to the one before the door. "Siete, ocho, nueve . . ." He crouched, made a mark on the floor, and straightened. He counted again. Crouched, marked, rose. His steps were measured, mathematical, as he sketched a circle of precise markings into the floor around where I sat. Then he picked up a censer and retraced his steps, pacing the circumference of the circle, his stride measured and controlled, murmuring under his breath.

It took me several moments to realize he was not speaking castellano at all. The language was silky, sinuous as the copal that curled around him in thick plumes. I had heard it many times since coming to San Isidro, spoken among the tlachiqueros and their families.

Candlelight danced on the high points of Andrés's face like sunlight on water; incantations wove through the smoke with the lazy grace of a water snake.

He is a witch.

The thought rang in my mind clear as the toll of a church bell.

I shook my head to dismiss it. No. That was impossible. *Padre* Andrés was a priest.

He finished the incantation, crouched on the ground, and began drawing more geometric shapes. Finally, he set the charcoal down and retrieved a small object from somewhere in the black fabric of his habit.

A sharp pocketknife glinted wickedly in the candlelight as he flicked it open and pricked his thumb with its tip.

I gasped.

A large bead of blood bloomed beneath the knife's point. Without missing a beat, Andrés lowered his hand to the floor and smeared the blood through one of the geometric shapes. Then he pocketed the knife and drew out a handkerchief to staunch the blood.

He lifted his eyes to mine, his expression defiant. As if he were daring me to speak the words that he knew were on the tip of my tongue.

"You're a witch," I breathed.

He nodded. Once, solemnly.

"But you're a priest."

"Yes."

He stood, cocking his head to the side as he evaluated the markings he had made on the floor. Then his eyes flicked back to my face. If he had been waiting for an exclamation of fear or any other sort of reaction from me, he received none. I was struck dumb.

You've never met a priest like him before.

"What are you thinking?" he challenged.

"I find it odd that a witch would become a priest," I said flatly.

This answer surprised a bark of laughter from him, its texture low and throaty. "Is there any vocation more natural for a man who hears devils?"

Hairs lifted on the back of my neck. I should be afraid of him. I *should* be. People were meant to be afraid of witches.

But a quiet as soft as dawn fell within the circle. The air felt lighter, calmer. The flames of the candles drank it greedily and danced high, reaching for and illuminating the witch's throat as he turned his head and narrowed his eyes at the door.

"But the Inquisition . . ." I began.

"I feared it, yes. But it has left México." Andrés made a soft, dismissive noise. Though the tension in his shoulders had not relaxed, his movements resumed their natural, languid pace as he adjusted the position of the copal censers. "I don't know if inquisitors even sought people like me," he said thoughtfully. "Their purpose was to destroy political rivals. Control people who stepped out of line, like mystics and heretics. They never found me."

He picked up the charcoal and moved to another part of the circle to resume sketching. His intent, I now saw, was to make a thick band of marks around us.

Like the glyphs on the inside of the kitchen doorway.

"Is Ana Luisa a witch?"

"You're thinking of the kitchen. No." He never looked up from his work. The wax surrounding the wick of the candle nearest to me had lique-fied, and a thick droplet of it rolled lazily down the candle's side. There was a judgmental note on his voice, and a harsh one, as he continued. "She knows these are meant to have power. She also knows that she isn't capable of doing it correctly. It was dangerous. She should have known better."

"Why?" I asked.

The stroke of his charcoal slowed; paused. Perhaps he caught himself speaking too much. Perhaps he realized fear had loosened his tongue and created an intimacy between us that should not be there, that I was not to be trusted with this information, for he raised his head sharply. "You won't tell anyone. You *can't*," he said. "Swear you won't."

"As if Padre Vicente would believe me," I said dryly, but the joke fell flat between us.

"If he were to learn of *this*"—here Andrés made an expansive circular gesture with one long arm—"he would send me away. To Spain, to a prison, I don't know or care. The people here need me. The war left scars. It left demons. It *broke* people." Fervor hardened his voice. "They need to be listened to, they need to be heard, and there are things they can't speak about with the other priests."

"Because they don't speak that language?"

"Mexicano? That matters less," Andrés said. "Neither can I, not any-more. I lost it as a child." To my questioning look, he added: "I memorized what my grandmother taught me. I mean that the other priests . . . they're rich men from the capital and Guadalajara. They cannot speak the lan-guage of the people's troubles. They can't see what I am, and it must stay that way. Apan, San Isidro . . . this is *my* home. I know these people. Their wives are like my mother, their sons my brothers. I *know*. And I listen."

He returned to where he had been sitting next to me, crossing his long legs. Then, there in the center of a witch's circle, he drew a rosary from his pocket. The silver face of la Virgen winked in the candlelight as the center-piece slid past his graceful fingers.

Truly, I had never met a priest like him before.

"I promise," I whispered. "I swear I won't say a word. Thank you. For this. For believing me."

"You didn't even need to speak for me to believe you," he said. His attention on the door was now watchful rather than fearful as his fingers moved from bead to bead with a meditative rhythm. "Your face said it all. And then walking through the door . . . I didn't plan to resort to this"—his slight nod at the circle around us indicated *this* was the dark glyphs—"but in all my years cleansing sickened homes, I have never faced anything like *that*." His voice trailed off for a moment, as if caught and held captive by a memory. "How much have you been able to sleep recently?"

My laughter was dry, its sensation foreign and hoarse in my throat. Perhaps I could count the hours, no more than a handful a night since Rodolfo left . . . nine days ago? Ten? "Does the answer 'I haven't' suffice?"

"Here." He reached for one of the blankets I laid out earlier and passed it to me. "I'll keep watch."

My fingers sank into the thick wool. I could allow myself to fall, to give in to the silence, while someone else stood watch. The peace of being inside the circle enveloped me like mist, cool and soothing. *Sleep.* The idea of it was so intoxicating that I didn't care that it meant sleeping next to a man who was not my husband, whom I had only met a few days ago.

A man who was a witch.

I bunched part of the blanket into a pillow and curled onto it like a cat settling before a warm hearth.

It was so quiet that I could hear the crackle of wicks bearing their flames, the brush of Andrés's calloused fingertips over the beads of his rosary. His voice was a low, steady hum.

I was not alone.

Between one Hail Mary and the next, I slipped over sleep's dark edge and fell, fell, fell . . .

◆ ◆ ◆

IN DREAMS, I FOUND myself on my feet, folding Tía Fernanda's patterned linens in the study of San Isidro, my hands red from harsh laundry soap. Instead of the high small windows that broke up the wall in waking life, tall bright windows were cut into the stucco like the ones that graced my family's home in the capital. One was open, and a breeze billowed through the room, carrying birdsong from a garden. The sheets rippled in the breeze as I folded them. I had a stack of clean sheets and lifted them into my arms as I made my way to the bedchamber. I stepped through the doorway, turned the corner, and stopped dead.

The white sheets and mattress were torn to pieces. Shredded as if by a hundred sharp knives, savagely pierced as if by bayonets. Long marks scarred the wooden headboard; the pillows were carved into chunks, the feathers that had once stuffed them floating serenely on the air, unaware of the carnage they overlooked.

The birdsong had fallen silent.

I stepped forward to touch the bed, to make sure it was true. The sheets I had been holding were gone from my arms in the slippery way of dreaming, and when I put my hand on the bed, it came away red with blood. The sheets were clean. I frowned.

The sound of footsteps on carpet sounded softly from the study.

"Padre Andrés?" I said, because in the dream, it was natural that Andrés should be somewhere in the house. He needed to see this.

I turned to the door. A figure walked into view in the study: a woman with a shock of long hair as pale as corn silk, her dress the fashion of the capital and sewn from gray fabric that shimmered in the light. She faced me, a glint of gold winking from her throat.

Her eyes were pits, pits that burned with the crepuscular glow of embers, of hellfire. Her stance shifted, her shoulders curling like a puma's, and she hissed at me, baring hundreds of long, needlelike teeth that grew longer, longer. She raised her hands, which ended in long, curving flesh-colored claws.

The door of the bedchamber slammed shut.

I woke with a start, my heart in my throat.

Slam.

I shoved myself upright. The candles had burned low—I must have been asleep for hours—but the amount of copal in the room had not less-ened. Andrés was pale; beads of sweat glistened at his hairline. He was still murmuring Hail Marys, his watchful gaze on the door.

Somewhere upstairs, I heard a long creak—a door swinging open. Ex-pecting it to slam shut, I edged closer to Andrés, close enough to be arm to arm, our legs touching, ankles brushing.

Silence lengthened, thick and slow as the creep of a mudslide.

One of the parlor doors down the hall opened with an anguished groan. Then another, closer.

As if someone were going methodically through the house, room by room, looking for something.

I pressed against his shoulder, my heart in my throat.

We waited.

Tense, silent, fixated on the door, we waited. We waited for the door to swing open . . . and for what? For the red eyes to gleam in the dark? To rush toward us, toward the circle?

And then what?

Shredded pieces of dream flashed in my mind's eye: long, deep claw marks in my wooden headboard. Sliced sheets. My hand coming away from the ruined mattress slick with blood. Footsteps behind me . . .

"I have a theory," Andrés breathed, "about houses. I think . . . I believe that they absorb the feelings of the people who live in them. Sometimes those feelings are so strong you can feel them when you walk through the door. And when those feelings are negative . . . evil begets evil, and they grow to fill the house. That is what I usually deal with. But this is different.

This . . ." His pause stretched agonizingly long. "I think whatever you found in that wall—*whoever*—is still here."

"*Here?*" My voice cracked over the word. "In the house? Or *is* it the house?"

"I don't know." He was leaning into me as much as I leaned into him. "It's only a theory."

Somewhere in the north wing, a door slammed shut.

We jumped.

A theory.

Only a theory.

13

I WOKE STIFF-BACKED AND bleary-eyed, a blanket smelling faintly of copal pulled up to my nose. Birdsong and the distant neigh of a horse floated into the room through the windows. With a tumbled rush of images, I remembered where I was.

The green parlor.

The candles were extinguished. A single copal censer remained lit; its smoke toyed with the morning light, drawing my eye to Andrés as he sat back on his heels and brushed charcoal off the palms of his hands. He had been scrubbing the witch's circle from the floor. All that was left was a faint shadow and a smear of blood, oxidized and dark on the gray stone.

"I must go to the capilla," Andrés said. "I said Mass would be at six."

Succumbing to sleep in the faint hours of the morning meant that my head had lolled onto his shoulder. I had a memory, murky enough that I was uncertain if it was a dream or not, of being lowered to the floor, of a blanket being tucked around me. I slept deeper than I had in over a week;

knowing that Andrés had watched over me opened a startling warmth in my chest, something akin to affection.

I shifted and pulled the wool blanket around my shoulders self-consciously. I was a married woman. Feeling a budding tenderness like this for someone who was not my husband—who was a *priest*—could spin perilously close to sin.

"I will spend the morning in the village." The color had sapped away from Andrés's face; his eyes were shaded with the haunted, sleepless wariness I knew well from my own mirror. "After that, I am afraid I must leave."

Leave.

The word struck like a pailful of cold water. My fingers tightened on the blanket. "Why?"

"I have received word that I am needed by the villagers of Hacienda Ometusco," he said. "They're suffering an outbreak of measles."

I frowned. "How do you know that?"

"Prayers travel," he said.

"People *pray* to you?"

"Cielo santo, *no*." He brushed his palms against each other again in a vain attempt to clean them. "I hear . . . I am alerted to people's prayers." A window shutter had cracked open in the night; a breeze slipped through it now, teasing a groan out of its aging hinges. Andrés paused, considering the draft, still as a cat attentive to the far-off call of a bird. *Listening*, perhaps. Then he shifted his weight and, with a long exhale, rose. "I should leave this afternoon, not long past noon. I will return in two days. Three at the most."

He extended a hand to help me to my feet. His palm was broad, calloused. Smudged with charcoal.

"But what if you fall ill?" I had heard many stories from Papá of medics falling ill with the same diseases they tried to cure in his soldiers.

"I never do." He shrugged with the careless certainty of a young man who knew he was invincible. "In my absence, I will protect certain rooms of the house for you. But first we must also discuss . . . possible solutions."

I took his hand. Let him guide me to my feet. Stars sparked my vision from rising so quickly; I tightened my hand on his as I steadied myself.

Then I dropped it. Cleared my throat. "We can eat the midday meal together, if that suits."

He nodded solemnly. "Until then."

A BATH THEN A walk in the sunshine softened the stiffness of my limbs and flushed away any tangled feelings I had about Andrés leaving. I spent the morning dozing on the back terrace of the house, weaving in and out of the misty realm of dreams. Once, a flash of red eyes pierced the gloom, but a low male voice rose and fell, reciting prayers, soothing me into slumber.

When I woke, the house behind me was still. The garden was still. Even the grasses had ceased their whispering.

It was as if the house sensed Andrés's presence. It was weighing it, tasting it. Deciding what to make of the echo of magic that bloomed from the green parlor into its clammy corridors, slipping through the house's many cracks like smoke.

I left the house for the communal kitchen in the village, where I knew Ana Luisa was preparing lunch for the tlachiqueros and other servants.

Voices caught my attention; a group of villagers was gathered near the capilla, dressed in blindingly starched whites and brightly colored skirts. At the group's center was Padre Andrés; at his side, a young woman with festive ribbons in her plaits bounced a small child on her hip. The child looked less than impressed with the spirited atmosphere; her hair was slick with water and shone like a newborn colt in the sunlight as she cast a suspicious look up at Andrés.

A baptism.

Despite the harrowing night, despite how my back still ached from sleeping on flagstones, the young mother's joy was infectious, even from a distance. A smile tugged at my lips as I made my way to the kitchens.

I greeted Ana Luisa brightly, earning myself a suspicious sideways glance. A sudden distrust slicked down the nape of my neck.

"I will be dining outside the capilla," I announced. "With Padre Andrés. If you have something to serve as a tray, I will carry our food there and bring the dishes back so as not to inconvenience you."

I tried to make it sound like I didn't want to disrupt her pattern of work. In truth, I didn't want her near when I was discussing what to do about the house with Andrés.

Ana Luisa said nothing for a long time. I helped her stack a tray with two covered bowls of pozole, spoons, and a cloth laden with warm tortillas. A gentle slick of pork fat rippled across the surface of the rich broth; whole cloves of garlic and thick white pieces of corn spun, following the stirring of Ana Luisa's wooden spoon.

"This will not please Doña Juana."

The sharpness in Ana Luisa's voice took me by surprise.

"What won't please her?" I asked. Surely not the mouthwatering pozole. Starved of rest, my mind was slow to follow what Ana Luisa meant.

She avoided my eyes as she stirred the cauldron of soup before her. Wood from the fire beneath the stove crackled; the silence between us filled with blue smoke. The heat made a bead of sweat drip down her brow.

"That you invited the witch onto her property," she said at last.

Panic threaded through my chest.

The witch, she said.

Laughter drifted over from the direction of the capilla. I looked over my shoulder. The baptism group was filtering away from the doorway; Andrés lingered next to the beaming young mother, head inclined to listen to her. A grin flashed across his face at something she said. When he placed a hand on the toddler's wet hair, the girl peered up at him shyly, eyes wide, then buried her face in her mother's neck.

If Andrés's witchcraft were revealed, if Padre Vicente learned of his true nature, I knew he would suffer a cruel punishment. But moments like this would also be lost. If anything happened to Andrés, it would leave a gaping wound in the lives of people who needed him.

But Ana Luisa *must* know. Her own mother was Andrés's teacher; she herself first demonstrated to me the power of copal. The markings on the inside of the kitchen door were her own work.

But I had promised Andrés I would not tell anyone. Now that oath was seared in my soul by a fierce protective flame. I would keep his secret—and conceal my knowledge of it—even if it meant lying to everyone I knew. Even Rodolfo. Even my mother.

"You cannot possibly mean Padre Andrés," I said, filling my voice with pious offense. I brought my hand to my forehead and made the sign of the cross for good measure. "He is a man of God."

"He is many things," Ana Luisa said flatly. "A friend of Doña Juana is not one of them. I would not have him in the house if I were you."

I set my jaw. This was *my* property, not hers and Juana's. I married the master of the house, and I was the final authority on the matter of guests.

"Thank you for sharing your concerns," I said, keeping my tone crisp and neutral. "But my hospitality will not be compromised by whatever grudges Doña Juana chooses to harbor. No guest is unwelcome in San Isidro, especially not one I invited to bring God's word and the sacraments to a community in need of them." I took the tray primly.

Ana Luisa gave me a sideways look, slicing right through my pretenses. Weighing what I had said, no doubt. Weighing my mettle.

If she knew what Andrés was capable of, *why* wouldn't she want someone who could cure the house within its walls? Why would Juana not?

Ana Luisa reached into a basket of tamales and plucked out four with practiced hands. She set these on the tray, stacked carefully between the two bowls of pozole. Delicate fingers of steam rose from their husks.

"For your guest," she said gruffly. "Never underestimate how much that flaquito can eat."

Andrés and I met at a humble table drenched in sunlight behind the southern wall of the capilla, outside of the tiny rooms that adjoined the chapel for visiting clergy.

Andrés filled the doorway of the rooms when I called his name. His eyes lit with eagerness at the sight of the steaming tray, and he stepped forward—

His head met the top of the doorframe with a solid sound.

"*Carajo.*"

I fought to hide my amusement as he cast a dirty look at the doorway and ducked through it to join me at the table. He thanked me profusely, then fell silent. The pozole and tamales vanished as if swept away by a starving ghost, and color once again bloomed across Andrés's face. While there were not many things I trusted Ana Luisa about, I could trust her assessment of her nephew's appetite.

He sighed and leaned back in his chair, drinking in the sun like a lanky lizard on a warm rock. Purple circles shadowed the skin beneath his closed eyes.

"Did you sleep at all?" I asked.

He made a noncommittal sound.

I ripped a tortilla and used it to fish a piece of pork from my soup. Mamá would cringe at my table manners, but what purpose would putting on airs before Andrés serve? None. There was something about his demeanor that set me at ease. Something in the way he looked at me that made me feel as if he *saw* me, and that there was no point in shoring up the stony walls I had hidden behind for so long.

I chewed the pork and tortilla thoughtfully, feeling life seep back into me with the red broth. "In the capilla . . . is it like the house?" I wondered.

"No. It's quiet," he said softly. "So, so quiet."

Is there any vocation more natural for a man who hears devils? he had said. Perhaps what he meant was that there was no refuge more profound.

"Are all holy places?"

"Some. My mother used to panic because I would vanish in the night as a child. Then she would find me in the church, asleep beneath a pew in the morning . . ."

He opened his eyes, then straightened. Stiffly. The shift of his shoulders hinted that perhaps he thought he had spoken too much.

But something in my heart unfurled thinking about a small black-haired boy curled into a ball beneath a pew, and it wanted to know more. I wanted him to keep speaking.

"Is that why the witch became a priest?" I asked. "Because it was quiet in the church?"

He met my eyes levelly, the curve of his mouth angled slightly downward, as if suspicious I was mocking him. I was not. Was I prying too much? Perhaps. But I still yearned for him to reply.

"That was why my mother wanted me to become a priest." His voice had a distant ring to it, confirming I was indeed prying, and that he was now on guard. "There are few places in the world for people who hear voices. Prisons. Asylums."

"Rome," I pointed out glibly.

His brows lifted to his hairline.

"There are plenty of saints who heard voices. Didn't Santa Rosa de Lima?"

"I am no saint, Doña Beatriz," Andrés said evenly. "And some would think it blasphemous to be so flippant about sainthood."

He tilted his head back and closed his eyes again, effectively shuttering the subject. My eyes followed the raven-black hair falling across his brow, danced down the arch of his throat to his collar, and were caught by the shock of white that gleamed there against the black of his clothing.

Warmth flushed my cheeks. As far as sin was concerned, perhaps blasphemy was the least of my worries.

I dropped my gaze to my soup. "What would you be if not a priest?" Not the most graceful change of subject, but certainly a necessary one.

He did not answer. I was prying again.

"I wanted to be a general." It was I who had asked the question, and in his silence, I who answered it. "My father was a general. He used to show me his battle plans and lecture me on the direction of armies, how to take the high ground and win even when muskets were so scarce soldiers resorted to throwing stones." I remembered Papá's dark hand covering mine and guiding it as we dipped his pen in the pot of red ink. Imagining the scrape of the pen's nib against paper sent a pang of homesickness through my ribs. "I loved his maps best of all. I think that's what I wanted, when I said I wanted to be a general. Maps. I didn't understand leading armies meant leading men to die until I was older."

"So instead you married a pulque lord."

The hint of mockery in his voice *stung*.

"I had no other choice." The words echoed brittle, too familiar to my lips. I had said the same thing to Mamá when she saw Rodolfo's ring on my finger. "Don't mock what you can't understand," I muttered, and thrust my spoon into my soup with more force than was necessary. Droplets of broth sprayed the table. I glared at them, aware that Andrés was watching me carefully now.

"Can't I?" he asked.

It was as if that single soft question broke a dam in me.

He couldn't understand what it was like to be a woman with no means of protecting her mother. He couldn't understand the stakes I faced when Rodolfo proposed.

Or could he?

I lost it as a child, he had said of the language. His skin and eyes were lighter than his cousin's; it was clear he was mestizo, of a lower casta than the other priests. Like me in Tía Fernanda's household. Perhaps he also toed among criollo society on uneasy feet: careful to never misstep, careful to watch his back. Careful to never retaliate when offhand barbs buried themselves in his flesh.

We came from such different worlds, different classes, different experiences: the general's daughter of the capital, the boy of the rural hacienda. At first blush, we had next to no common ground. Perhaps we didn't. But perhaps the lives we had lived were not so different, in this one regard. Perhaps if I let him see that, he might understand.

"My father was intelligent. Kind. He loved my mother so much you couldn't *breathe* being in the same room as them. But Mamá's family cared about limpieza de sangre," I said, letting the spite of a long-nursed wound rake over these final words. *Cleanliness of blood.* The Valenzuelas cherished that poisonous criollo obsession with casta, the belief that any non-peninsular heritage spoiled what was desirable and pure. "They disowned her for marrying a mestizo."

This was the truth I could never articulate to Mamá because—as much as she loved me, perhaps because she loved me—she couldn't see what other criollos saw: *You're nearly as lovely as Doña María Catalina, though quite darker.*

"Look at me. It's obvious that I favor my father," I said. Fears I had never found the words to express rushed out of me, a stream overflowing in the rainy season. Now that I had begun, I did not think I could stop. Andrés did not try. He watched me, thoughtful and silent, as I gestured at my face, my black hair. "Then when he was killed and we lost everything, I knew it would be a miracle if I married at all. What else could I have done when Rodolfo proposed? Turn my nose up at the smell of pulque and let my mother live on scraps from my uncle's table? Let her starve when he lost patience and turned us out?" I gestured in the general direction of the house, fear of what lurked within its walls making the motion hatefully sharp. "*That* was supposed to be a home for her. It was supposed to be proof that I made the right decision. Proof that she was wrong to be angry with me about Rodolfo." My voice trembled—with anger or hurt, I could not tell. Perhaps both. I folded my arms protectively over my chest. "But still she refuses to answer my letters, and I'm stuck with *that.*"

A long silence followed my outburst, punctuated only by distant conversation from the kitchens.

A pair of barn swallows dipped from the sky, looping like butterflies over Andrés's head. He reached for the few remaining tortillas, ripped one into small pieces, and rested his left hand on the table, palm up.

The swallows descended on him. One went straight for the tortilla, perching its small, clawed feet on the base of his thumb as it pecked at the offering in his palm. The other hovered warily on his sleeve. It tilted its head to the side, beady eyes appraising. Then it bounced closer, once, twice, and joined its fellow tearing at tortilla scraps.

"A doctor. For the insurgents. That's what I wanted to be," he said. He kept his eyes downcast, watching the sweetly staccato movements of the swallows, their satisfied preening.

"I saw men who lost limbs to gangrene. Children died of tuberculosis. My older brothers . . . they joined the insurgents and were killed. Two in battle. The third disappeared. I discovered later that he died in prison, just after the war ended. I thought . . ." He trailed off. "I wanted to *fix* things. Fixing people who were wounded—and there were so many—seemed like an obvious choice. I already knew how to heal. But the last thing my mother wanted was to lose another one of us to the war. She wanted me to join the priesthood. My grandmother made sure her wishes were carried out and sent me to Guadalajara."

The swallows chirruped at each other, then lifted from Andrés's arm in unison. I followed their sweeping path up, up, up to the slender bell tower of the capilla.

"They sent you to fight in a different war."

His mouth twisted—sad, sardonic amusement. "Ah yes, the war for souls. The war where we are all soldiers of San Miguel Arcángel, battling the forces of the Devil with flaming swords." He mulled this over for a moment. "I think my mother was more concerned about saving my soul than sending me to save the souls of others."

Because of the voices.

So, so quiet, he had said.

"Do you hear voices in the house?" I asked.

"Yes." A firm answer.

I flinched. I wasn't sure if I had expected him to answer in the affirmative or not, but hearing it aloud still sent a tremor down my spine.

"That alone is not unusual," he continued. "My family has lived in the shadow of that house for seven generations. Any building of that age has memories down to its bones. But its voices are different now. One dominates the rest; its intent is unclear to me. I thought it would be easy to calm, like a spooked horse, but after last night . . ." Apprehension flickered across his face. "I need to think about how I'm going to fix it. Restrategize, if you will." He steepled his long fingers and pressed them to his lips, silently ruminating.

Juana, Juana.

"Do you hear it . . ." I faltered. "Do you hear that voice say any names?"

Andrés lifted his eyes to mine, his brow creasing in concern. A cold, oily fear slipped down my spine.

"No," he said. "No, I do not."

14

ANDRÉS

I LED MY MULE out of San Isidro's stables that afternoon. The sun slipped from its apex toward the western horizon; the chorus of grasshoppers rose with the heat of the siesta hours.

I cast a look over my shoulder at the walls surrounding the house, at its uneven peaks and dips, the spine of an ancient beast.

The house *watched* me leave, its stare baldly appraising.

A tender, bone-deep fear drew its fingertip down the back of my neck.

What had happened to San Isidro in my absence? So often I had sought the company of the house as a boy, ducking past the patrón and his family to find a forgotten storeroom where I could lose myself in its ancient gossip. Back then, the house recognized me as one of the few who could hear it and welcomed me whenever I entered. Centuries of memories lingered in its shadowed hallways, so thick they wove the building's walls a gentle, ageless sentience, one that was distracted and uninterested in the affairs of the living.

But now? This was not the house I had known as a child, its chatter secretive and benign. The earth at the house's foundation was saturated with sickness, a blight, its black veins leading up the hill to the gate and tangling under it like the roots of a cursed tree.

Such a change could not be immediate. It must predate Doña Beatriz's arrival. It must have something to do with the apparition of the body in the wall. There was no doubt that the anger that vibrated deep in the bones of the house had something to do with *that*. It festered like an old, infected wound, open and weeping.

I had to fix it. My loyalty to the house was as complete as that to my family; this hacienda was *home*. I made my decision the moment I stepped across its threshold: I would purge it of its rot.

But how?

My thoughts immediately fell to the locked box in my chest, following the inevitable pull of the current. Every bit of darkness inside it clawed to be let loose.

Last night, cornered in the green parlor by the rage of the house, I acted in self-defense: I unlocked the box. Driven by fear, I reached into myself and released a trickle of the darkness I kept bottled tightly in there.

And now every time I closed my eyes, I saw glyphs carved on the insides of my eyelids. Every time my thoughts wandered, they were drawn with unholy, inescapable attraction to that locked box.

When I was a youth, Titi heard of witches in the north who had been tortured and jailed, accused of an epidemic of demonic possessions. Those who starved in prison or died of torture-inflicted wounds were most often mestizos like me, mestizos or criollos, for Indios did not fall within the jurisdiction of the Inquisition.

"There are some things I cannot protect you from," she told me sadly.

It was true. I was her heir, always had been, but her blood and her gifts were only half of that which flowed in my veins. The rest was a darkness neither she nor I could name.

So Titi sent me to the seminary, where she believed I could hide in plain sight from conscription and inquisitor alike.

Hide I did. And, as much as I initially doubted Titi's conviction that I should join the Church, theological instruction became the structure I hadn't known I craved. It gave me a map with clear markings, explicit indications of correct paths and the wrong, a beginning and an end. Clarity gave me the strength to put my faith in the Christian God—though timidly at first, fearful of being scorned for both my birthright and Titi's teachings. To my eternal surprise, I found myself accepted. Welcomed, even. Trusted.

So long as the sinful parts of my pocked, split soul were crushed into submission, I was given a place to belong. So long as that part of myself was bound with chains, I had His love.

Even since returning to Apan, I had not touched that part of myself. In order to serve as my grandmother's heir, I leaned on what she taught me and that alone. I told myself it was because I did not need that darkness. I had what Titi taught me. I had earned the guidance and trust of the Lord through penance and devotion.

Now I knew it was because I was afraid.

I acted in fear last night. I had earned still more fear for my trouble: would I ever again be at peace, without that heavy, aching awareness of the locked box in my breast? But would I be able to cure San Isidro without it? What if I could not?

Hacienda San Isidro—my *home*—was poisoned. It was hurting. Rot like this would spread beyond the house's walls, leeching life from the earth, blighting the fields, lacing the homes of the village with affliction. It was a sickness. It must be contained, then eradicated.

My thoughts knelt softly before the locked box.

When I opened it last night, when I set a curl of my own darkness free to protect myself and Beatriz from the malice of the house, she did not flinch from me, nor look at me in revulsion. She did not tell me I should burn, as my father had when he learned of the darkness that his bloodline had manifested in me. Even in the candlelight, I could see her eyes filled with trust.

Something in my chest fluttered pleasantly at the memory.

If I were to crack open the box for only a moment, if I were to release only a sliver of what simmered within . . . If I were to control it so completely it had no choice but to return to the locked chamber in which I kept it, then perhaps I could use it to cure the house.

Perhaps it could work.

The mule tossed his head; then, rolling the bit against his teeth in gentle annoyance, he lowered his head and rubbed his forelock against my shoulder. *Walk on*, that said, ornery and impatient—the sooner we began walking again, the sooner he could be rid of bridle and bit and me alike, and rest in the shade.

I obeyed, still lost in thought. My gentle prying with the villagers about the house had mostly been fruitless. They were far more intent on telling me all that had happened to them in my absence, the sicknesses they had suffered. Unfortunately, there was much to discuss. Cholera, from infected drinking water. A rash of measles killing children one spring. Then typhus struck the village. My heart contracted hearing the damage my absence had wrought. Typhus! I shook my head mournfully as the mule and I walked toward the western road. Even at thirteen, I could have rid the village of typhus-spreading parasites with an hour of work.

But I had been banished.

The only mercy was that the plague had taken Doña María Catalina with it.

Paloma had told me how quickly the disease seemed to strike the house. One day, Doña Catalina was her usual barbed self, energetically quarreling about finances with Juana over dinner. The next, the patrón's wife was confined to her room; Ana Luisa said she was too ill to move or be seen. For three weeks she remained in her room in convalescence, only tended by Ana Luisa. Then she abruptly died. Paloma watched her quiet funeral from a distant perch on the graveyard wall: she waited, hands clenched in anticipation, until the casket that held the hateful woman was firmly covered with earth.

And even after Doña Catalina's death, I remained banished from the land my family lived on. For two years, I lived in Apan alone, a stalk hacked away from the heart of the maguey, anger and resentment toward the Solórzanos weeping from my wound. Rumors of Rodolfo's remarriage and return to San Isidro with a new bride had licked through the town weeks before they actually set foot on its dust; when they finally appeared in the church, they were like salt flung on an unhealed wound. I scarcely spared the new wife a glance. Whatever fate she had sealed for herself by marrying that monster was no concern of mine, I told myself.

Until she *made* it my concern.

It was because Paloma was present that I lingered after Mass the day Beatriz sought Padre Guillermo's blessing for the house. Juana and Ana Luisa had forbidden Paloma from coming to town to seek me out; I had not seen her in two years and was desperate to speak with her.

The first words Paloma spoke to me were a desperate hiss. "Doña Juana is hiding something. Mamá too. Something terrible." There was a wildness in her eyes that stopped my heart: that was the feral fear of hunted things. "La señora is going to ask priests to bless the house, but it needs so much more than that. You *must* come help."

She was in danger. I knew then I would fight to return to San Isidro, banishment or no. I had let her be harmed in that house once before. I would not allow it to happen again.

At that moment, I looked up and met the new Doña Solórzano's eyes.

She had dark hair, was small but proud shouldered. Her maguey green eyes were a shock of color against the black lace of her mantilla. These met my gaze and held it fast: she measured me with a frankness that snatched my spirit from my body and set it on the scales of justice.

A thought unspooled in my quiet mind, unbidden, swift and certain as the click of a lock: *this one is different.*

She was. She asked me to come to San Isidro. She opened the gates of the hacienda and ended my banishment.

The sensation of San Isidro's earth beneath my feet after years away was intoxicating . . . until I grew close enough to sense the sickness and rage that putrefied its very air. When Doña Beatriz Solórzano begged me for help, I knew I would not turn her away. Any chance to remain at Hacienda San Isidro and protect Paloma from the poison that seeped through the house was one to be seized. But the desperation in Beatriz's voice unlocked a compassion in me I thought my anger at the Solórzanos had buried for eternity. .

She was alone. No one—not husband, friend, or family—stood by her side as she faced the jaws of that cavernous, sickened house.

Tending to lost souls is our vocation, Titi often said.

That was what I was doing when I covered Beatriz's sleeping body with a blanket in the green parlor last night, my touch featherlight even as it lingered a breath too long. A lost soul sought aid, and I gave it. That was what I was doing. That was who I was, that was the responsibility I inherited from Titi and the Cross I chose to take upon my shoulders.

Then why hadn't I yet sought penance for my moments of failure?

A breeze snaked through the maguey, carrying the voices of the few tlachiqueros who paced the rows of the fields while their fellows took siesta. I worried my lip distractedly as I walked. Last night, I had revealed my true nature to Beatriz. She swore she would tell no one, but the fact remained that outside of Titi's people and the villagers of the haciendas, she was the *only* person with whom I had spoken so frankly. Was it sleeplessness that loosened my tongue? Was it the way Beatriz listened, her head lilting gently to the side?

Or was it a graver failing? A very human failing, one that drew my eye to her more often than not?

A failing that left me following the bend of Beatriz's waist as she set the tray of pozole on the table beside the capilla, tracing the line of her back up to her neck, to the curls that brushed against her skin, to the curve of her throat?

Look at me, she said.

Ah, but I had, and therein lay the sin.

I realized in a sharp flash, the white blow of sun in the desert, that as much as I loathed him, I envied what Rodolfo had.

I should have banished the thought immediately. Sought forgiveness and punishment for it in the same breath. I should have stepped away to collect myself, to regain the cool, controlled detachment I had fought so hard to earn. The hard-won aloofness from worldly desires that I so *liked* about myself.

I coveted the patrón's wife. The map my training gave me was clear on this matter: *repent*.

So why did I continue to turn the sin over in my mind, examining it like an old coin, instead of casting it as far from my heart as I could? Was it because there were graver matters at hand? Or was it because—God forbid—a stubborn part of me did not yet *want* to be forgiven?

A shadow crossed my path. I lifted my chin sharply, tightening my grip on the mule's reins.

Directly before me stood Juana Solórzano. Her feet were planted firmly in the dirt of the road; she looked at me with a bland, almost bored sort of aggression.

"Villalobos." Her voice raked over my skin like a hair shirt. No one addressed me by my surname but her. It was a constant reminder that my father had once served hers, that my family still served her, and that no matter how tall I grew, how far I traveled, how much I studied, how high I rose, she would always look down her nose at me. "You're not supposed to be on my property."

Juana's enforcement of Doña Catalina's banishment even after her death surprised me. Angered me. Perhaps I should have overcome that. Perhaps I should have been able to forgive her with time.

Should is an oddly powerful word. Shame and anger have a way of flying to it like coins to lodestone. I had achieved detachment from so many worldly things, but this clung like burrs. It was a snake that sank its fangs so deep they touched bone, spreading its venom through my marrow.

"Buenas tardes, doña." I reached up with my left hand and tipped my hat to her. Let her read every ounce of quiet insubordination I poured into the movement. Let her know that I could hold grudges just as long as she. "I came at the invitation of Doña Solórzano." *The living one*, I added silently. "And I'll return in a few days at her invitation as well."

I clicked my tongue to the mule and led it forward and off the road slightly, so as to carve a path around where Juana stood.

She told me I was imagining it. Beatriz's voice echoed in my mind as I remembered the hollowed-out, exhausted fear evident in the slump of her posture when we spoke in the sacristy storeroom. *But she* told *me she was afraid of the house. She and Ana Luisa both.*

I believed Beatriz's conclusion was sound. I had known Juana—if from a distance—for most of my life, and I knew her to be sharp-eyed. Attentive. If she avoided the house as much as Beatriz said, then she knew something was wrong with it.

What else did she know?

Juana's face was shaded by a sweat-stained hat, but it was still evident that she narrowed her eyes at me as I passed.

She would not help us.

I mounted the mule and bid Juana farewell without looking back. "Buenas tardes, doña."

I received no reply. When I cast a glance over my shoulder, she was gone, vanished among the rows of maguey, silent as an apparition.

Was there a chance she would go to Padre Vicente about my presence here? Perhaps, but perhaps not—Padre Vicente disapproved of her way of living, how she refused to marry and rarely came to Mass. How her lack of simpering whenever she did cross paths with the priest set the man on edge. In a way, I respected how she grated on Vicente's nerves. She did not give a damn what anyone thought of her, as dangerous as that was for a woman of her station.

But what if she mentioned my presence to Rodolfo? Would he be angry that Beatriz had disobeyed him and sought my help?

This thought sent a bone-deep chill through me.

I knew what that monster was capable of.

But it was still unclear to me what danger Rodolfo posed Beatriz. As cruel as he was to servants, he had not raised a hand against Doña Catalina in life.

From my mind's eye, the skeleton in the wall grinned back at me, naked and mocking in the flickering light of the candle.

Or had he?

15

BEATRIZ

I SLEPT IN FITFUL spurts the nights Andrés spent at Hacienda Ometusco, but enough that I had my wits about me when the first shipment of furniture arrived from the capital courtesy of Rodolfo. With the help of Paloma, the interim foreman José Mendoza, and a handful of young tlachiqueros wrangled away from Juana and the fields for the morning, we outfitted the house. A Nicaraguan cedar table and expensively upholstered chairs in the formal dining room. Rugs in the parlors and bedchambers. Candelabras, love seats, and empty bookcases filled rooms like uncomfortable, stiff company come to dinner.

I left the green parlor empty. The signs of normalcy settling into other parts of the house made its bare walls and long shadows an obvious bruise.

When Paloma, Mendoza, and the last of the tlachiqueros left, the house shuddered, a disgruntled bull shaking flies from its hide. I felt the cold tendrils of its attention on me less often, and with less intent than I had before the priest's arrival: it was as if the house *knew* the protective marks along the threshold of my bedchamber meant Andrés would return, and in his absence, it grew preoccupied with this fact. A sullen energy built beneath its stucco, in the agitated midnight slamming of its doors.

I waited too. With no one to speak freely with about my troubles, my thoughts tangled tight in my mind and chest. Sudden movements caused me to startle; Paloma took to announcing her presence several long footsteps before she appeared in a doorway in a kind attempt to keep me from leaping to my feet, wide-eyed, my breathing shallow and sharp.

If she thought I was mad, she made no mention of it. Perhaps it was misguided hope, or a desperate yearning for company, but I was beginning to think she might believe quite the opposite. Or rather, that she approved of the steps I was taking to combat the house. While helping me gather linens from my bedchamber for laundering on the day Padre Andrés was meant to return, she took one look at the marks on the threshold and made a soft, satisfied sound. Approval, perhaps?

Later, as she was leaving the house for her siesta, she paused before stepping from the kitchen into the vegetable garden.

"I never thanked you, doña," Paloma said softly, speaking through the doorway rather than back to me.

I tilted my head to one side. I had come to understand Paloma's reserve as a matter of fact; her volunteering any emotion—much less gratitude toward me—was enough to give me pause. "What do you mean?" I asked carefully.

"For bringing him back."

And she was gone, sweeping silent through the garden like a raven.

WHEN THE CLOUDS GATHERED over the hills, their rainheavy bellies streaked with dusk, Padre Andrés returned to San Isidro. I waited in the doorway to the courtyard of the main house, twisting my hands over each other. When I caught sight of him walking up the hill to the capilla, the lingering light casting a long, slim shadow through the low chaparral, my hands stilled.

It wasn't that I was no longer alone. It was that *he* was back. A friend. An ally. A shoulder to lean on.

We set up camp in the green parlor an hour past nightfall, two soldiers preparing for a nightlong battle as rain poured outside: blankets and candles, copal and herbs. Charcoal for witch's circles. Holy water. A golden crucifix around Andrés's neck, gleaming in the light of two dozen tallow candles. He stood before me, the witch in priest's clothing, a pocketknife in one hand and a censer in the other. The locked door to his back, the fireplace to mine. A circle of protection surrounding us both.

Andrés set the censer at his feet. Smoke rose like mist at dawn as he then held the knife out to me.

"Ready?" His voice was low as a prayer.

I took the knife.

As mistress of the house, Andrés needed my intent, my will, to help draw whatever *it* was in the walls out. To banish it, and then—if all went according to plan—to purify the rooms.

The sensation of curling my fingers into the worn grooves of the wooden handle was almost like taking Andrés's hand. Candlelight danced off its sharpened tip. I inhaled deeply.

I placed the tip to my thumb, pressing until blood welled ruby bright. Then I followed Andrés's instructions and stepped toward him, heartbeat quickening as he unbuttoned and loosened his collar, exposing the delicate skin of his throat. There, just beneath his Adam's apple, his pulse throbbed, gentle and rhythmic and far steadier than mine.

I placed my thumb on that pulse, smearing blood on skin in a slow, gentle movement.

"I am María Beatriz Hernández Valenzuela, wife of Rodolfo Eligio Solórzano Ibarra and guardian of this house," I recited, my voice coming out hoarse. "And it is as guardian that I grant you authority to speak for me. To call on the powers in this house and beyond and ensure my will be done."

My hand remained on Andrés's throat as his eyes fluttered closed. His voice hummed against my thumb before I heard it speak. He told me in advance what the opening incantation meant, but still the hairs on my arms stood on end to hear a Latin prayer slip into his grandmother's sleek mexicano:

"I call on the Youth, the resurrected lord of smoke and night, guardian of witches and nahuales. Teacher of those who will listen, brother of those reborn on new moons. Guide us through the night. Give us tongue to speak to those whom the lord of the underworld has misplaced, that we may set them on the right path."

The smoke around us began to move.

He had warned me that the copal would dance. I was to stay still, to keep my gaze on Andrés and focus my will on him. To not look at the shapes the smoke might take. In my peripheral vision, I caught the sleek movement of a puma's prowl, the beating wings of a screech owl.

But I kept my focus on Andrés. On the movement of his throat as he spoke, on the gentle beat of his pulse. I focused on breathing in time with him.

This was it. If I followed his instructions perfectly, this would be the end of the sickness of San Isidro. The end of the rot in its walls, the poison in its darkness.

Andrés's prayer finished. The swirling shadows around the periphery of the circle faded; a silence profound as the cool depths of a well settled over the room.

"Very good," Andrés whispered. I raised my eyes and met his. My thumb was still against his pulse. He was calm; I was not, but I was in his hands. He knew what he was doing. He had cured many houses of inhabitants who had overstayed their welcomes, and while this house had taken him off guard the other night, he was now prepared.

"Step back," he said. I lowered my hand from this throat and obeyed. "Whatever happens, do not leave the circle," he added, his voice a low rasp as he spread his arms wide, his palms facing upward.

I nodded. He had explained this as well: the power of the circle drew from our intent and from the circular movement of Andrés's prayers around us, unbroken, constant. This circle itself was a doorway. A path. For whatever plagued San Isidro to be spirited away from here, away from Apan, toward whatever awaited it beyond.

A soft cooing noise lilted down from the ceiling, but it was drowned out by Andrés as he closed his eyes and began a new prayer, one that harnessed the gravelly undertones of his voice and roughened it.

The rich timbre of his voice and of the words he recited slipped into my body, twining around my ribs and spine like vines, like roots, firm and strong and alive. Though I could not understand their meaning, I felt their shift, felt how they grew richer, more seductive, their power curling toward Andrés.

Come, it called, teasing and soft. *Come closer.*

My head spun, giddy with the need to draw near to him, but my feet remained planted on the ground. The call was not meant for me. The blunt force of its power was not focused on me.

It was focused on the house.

For a moment, it listened. Perhaps it, too—perhaps *she*—felt the roots taking hold, felt the heady draw of the call.

Come into the circle.

Then the house rebelled.

A low whine built in the back of my head, thickened to a hum, and grew louder still, until a roar ripped through the circle.

No, my bones screamed. *No. That's not what she wants.*

It was not until my breath began to give out that I realized I was screaming, that my hands were clamped over my ears, that I could barely breathe for the pain of the sound. My skull was about to shatter.

Before me, Andrés stood serene amid the roar. Eyes closed, hands out-stretched, lips moving around the verses of prayer. Copal swirled like hur-ricane clouds, menacing and thick around the circle as Andrés rose.

He rose into the *air*.

It was not a trick of the shadows, a trick of the smoke; his eyes still shut, his arms stretched out like a benevolent saint, crucifix gleaming around his neck, he rose into the air and remained there, his shoes two feet off the ground.

With a violent motion, he snatched his hands into fists.

The roar cut off. As if strangled.

Silence washed over the circle like a flash flood, profound, heavy silence broken only by my whimpering. My hands were still over my ears; a trickle of salty warmth dripped from my nose onto my lips.

My hands trembled as I let them fall away from my ears. Andrés's brow creased with concentration; now, with a sharp jerk, he drew his fists into his chest. As if tugging something. Yanking it toward him.

A furious shriek split the room. I fell to my knees, hands clamped over my ears again.

The air vibrated. It rippled and lashed out, alive with anger.

I tilted my head up to Andrés. *Stop, please*, I begged silently, but the shrieking grew louder, the air shook violently, until—

It stopped.

For a moment, Andrés hung suspended in silence, energy rippling around him like waves.

Then an unseen force snatched him bodily from the air and flung him against the wall of the parlor. He struck the wall with the crack of skull to stone; with a yelp of pain, he fell.

He collapsed on the floor in a heap, boneless as a rag doll.

"Andrés!" I cried, lurching to my feet. He didn't move. Didn't make a sound. "Andrés!"

Do not leave the circle, he said.

I didn't care. The crack of his head striking the wall broke me, shattered whatever sense was left in me.

I raced toward him, throat stinging as I broke through the wall of copal smoke. "Andrés!"

A cold wind swept through the room, buffeting the candles, buffeting the smoke. It seized my chest like a vise, catching my breath, forcing me to my knees. A low wail lifted, then rose to a roar, winding around me, squeezing my chest so hard I thought my ribs were going to snap.

I could not breathe.

Blood dripped from my nose, then my mouth, pouring hot over my chin, choking me; I gasped and sputtered. It dripped onto my skirts, a relentless stream of red; though I coughed and spat it would not stop. I reached a hand to cover my mouth, to staunch the blood; it came away red, with two teeth, pink, fleshy gums still attached to them. The shrieking did not cease. It was a dagger in my skull. I wanted it to stop, I needed it to stop, it had to *stop*, but when I drew breath to cry out, to beg Andrés, I heaved and vomited more blood onto the floor before me.

Andrés. I had to get to Andrés.

I forced myself forward. Crawled to Andrés's side.

I put a hand on his face, over his mouth, feeling for breathing. My blood smeared on his lips. "Andrés. Andrés."

His groan brushed against my fingers.

He was alive.

The shadows carved his face sharp, making it otherworldly, dark and pointed like depictions of the Devil.

A sudden bloom of smoke, smoke that did not smell like copal, caught my attention. I glanced over my shoulder.

A candle had been extinguished. Then a second. A third. Slowly, deliberately. It was as if someone were going and closing a hand over the flames to kill them, one by one.

No one was there.

"Andrés. Andrés, please wake up," I whispered.

The last candle went out.

The house, it, *she*—she was no longer within the walls. Was no longer the cold, the cries of Juana's name, nor even the winking red eyes.

She was the darkness.

Andrés's unfinished ritual had drawn her out and—

I had broken the circle.

Triumph hummed on the air, hard and metallic.

I was flushed with prey instinct, my breathing growing ragged as the two paths that now lay before me came into focus. Either I stayed in this room and was killed, or I fled and survived.

Andrés had not moved. I looked at the heap of his body and saw a little boy, curled under a church pew. I could not leave him behind. Not alone. Not with the dark.

I grabbed his arm and hauled it over my shoulder. I braced one hand against the rough stucco wall as I lifted him; my legs trembled, I wasn't strong enough, I was too small to carry a man of his height out of the room, I—

Darkness coiled around his neck and tugged him down, his weight dragging on my arms.

No. Though clammy sweat slicked my palms, the sides of my throat, the small of my back, I tightened my arms around him.

"Get back! He's mine." My voice came out as a rough snarl; I barely recognized it. I shouted at the dark, a feral, wordless bark. With that, I hauled Andrés up as fast as I could, pushing with all the strength I had in my legs.

His feet caught his weight underneath. He was up. He wasn't perfectly conscious—his head lolled to the side, onto his shoulder—but he could bear weight.

"Run," I whispered to him. His head lifted slightly. "We have to run."

So, so quiet.

We would be safe in the capilla.

Half carrying Andrés, I lurched for the door. The violence of the ritual had blasted it off its hinges; it had struck the far side of the hall and shattered a blown-glass vase. We stumbled over it, shoes crunching broken glass.

To the front door. My legs burned with each step; my damp palms fumbled the handle. We burst through the door.

Rain drenched the courtyard, slicking the path with mud. Rain cooled my scalp, ran down my face, soaked my dress as I staggered into the night.

The farther we drew from the house, the more Andrés seemed able to carry his weight; by the time we slumped against the wooden door of the capilla, he lifted himself back up. I wrenched the door open, and we half fell into the dim chapel.

Someone had lit prayer candles before the humble painted wooden statue of la Virgen de Guadalupe. It was enough light to see by, enough light to make a sob rise to my scream-savaged throat.

The door thundered shut behind us. My legs gave out at last, and we fell forward into the aisle between the pews. My knees struck tile floor; I threw myself out to try and catch Andrés so he would not strike his head a second time, but he had fallen on his shoulder and rolled onto his back, coughing and wheezing in pain.

I was on my hands and knees, like I had been in the parlor, when blood was pouring—

I looked down at my hands.

There was no blood on them. Nor on my skirts.

I jerked myself upward, sat back on my heels, and touched my chin. No blood. Felt my mouth for . . . I shuddered in horror, but my teeth were intact. Firmly attached to my gums and my jaw.

Tears stung my eyes and cheeks as I sucked in greedy lungfuls of air, my breathing and Andrés's the only sound in the empty chapel. That and the thundering of my heart as it slowed, slowed, slowed.

So, so quiet.

Even the darkness here was different. Shadows dyed the corners of the room a soft, deep charcoal gray. The dark of dreamless sleep, the dark of prayers in the night. The dark touched by hopeful fingers of dawn.

Andrés opened his eyes. He frowned at the ceiling. "Where—"

"The capilla." A hoarse croak, barely my voice at all.

His face was gray and gaunt; at my words it went paler still. "No . . . don't leave the circle."

"You were hurt," I said. "It was hurting you more. I couldn't leave you."

"Broke the circle . . ." he murmured at the ceiling.

Had I made a mistake, bringing him here? No, something had gone *wrong*. Something had flung him across the room. It could have killed him. It could have killed both of us. Who cared about breaking the circle when he could have died?

"Damn the circle," I whispered, tears blurring the vision before me: Andrés on his back, blood dripping from his nose, pale and gaunt between the pews. "*You're* broken. That matters more."

"Not broken." A cough wracked his body. He grimaced. "Fine."

"Lying is a sin, Padre Andrés."

A wet laugh. He turned his head to the side, eyes shining up at me, feverish and overbright, as he smiled. Lopsided and without restraint. There was blood on his teeth.

He reached a hand up and gently brushed the back of his knuckles over my cheek. Goose bumps raced over my skin at his touch.

"An angel," he murmured. "Are you an angel?"

His head had hit the wall *hard*. He couldn't be in his right mind.

"Tell me where it hurts," I said, voice cracking.

Awareness flickered behind his eyes; his brow creased with concentration. "I think . . . broken rib." He winced, lowering his hand to his torso. "Or two."

"Shall I get a doctor?"

"No," he grunted.

"But what if you're bleeding on the inside?"

"Doctors aren't witches," he said. "Can't fix broken witches."

We were safe now, safe from whatever mistake we had made, but his behavior sent a wave of panic through me. What sort of damage could a blow to the head like that cause? Would he survive the night?

"Of course a doctor could fix a broken witch," I insisted calmly.

"Pierce with pikes and burn the witch," he murmured, eyes fluttering closed. "Salt the earth and scatter his soot."

The curl of panic beneath my lungs expanded. He wasn't making sense. "No one is going to burn you, Padre Andrés," I said, forcing authority into my voice. "Not on my property. Now look at me."

He opened his eyes, gazing up at me with an open adoration that made something in my chest bend close to snapping.

"You will be more comfortable if you can sleep in your bed."

"Bed," Andrés repeated dreamily.

Yes, bed was the best idea, but there was no way I was going to be able to carry him all the way to his rooms at the back of the capilla. I checked his limbs for any signs of broken bones, but apart from his ribs and his head, Andrés had no other injuries that I could see.

"Can you stand?"

He grunted in the affirmative and began to hoist himself up.

"Wait for me." I scrambled to my feet, head spinning, chest tight. The best way to guide him was to sling one of his arms over my shoulder again. I braced as his warmth pressed against me, with too much weight. "No, you need to stand on your own."

He corrected, and, swaying slightly, we cut a meandering path up the aisle of the chapel. Christ watched us from a wooden crucifix above the altar. The candles on the altar flung shadows across His hollow cheekbones, giving His carved face a condescending air.

"Either help me or stop judging," I muttered under my breath.

"Hmm?" Andrés wondered.

I didn't reply. Thankfully, he began to bear more of his own weight as we neared his rooms in the back of the chapel. I cautioned him to mind his head as we passed through the doorway.

The rooms were dark, but it was a gentle dark. The same safe, soft charcoal dark of the chapel. I followed Andrés's lead to the bed and helped lower him onto it.

I fumbled for candles and matches, finding them near the small round fireplace. I lit more than was necessary—out of habit more than actual fear. Here, we were not watched. Here, it was quiet. Quiet but for rain pattering on the roof and Andrés's sigh as he kicked off his shoes and lay on the thin mattress.

The warm candlelight lit the sparsely decorated room. I cast a look around: a painting of la Virgen hung above the fireplace. Whitewashed walls, a wooden cross opposite la Virgen. A clay bowl and jug on the table. A single chair, a stack of books next to the bed, their spines worn with use.

Andrés curled into a fetal position. Sweat shone on his forehead; sudden distress drew his brows together.

"Are you all right?" I asked.

"I may be—"

I seized the clay bowl and swept across the tiny room to his side just in time. He retched violently. I bit my lip, holding the bowl still until he was done vomiting and set his cheek on the mattress in defeat.

The other afternoon, I had spotted a water pump behind the capilla. I brushed Andrés's hair away from his face. "I'll be right back," I said softly.

I took the jug and the soiled bowl into the rain. It pricked my face and nearly soaked my dress by the time I was through washing the bowl and filling the jug, though it had only been minutes.

I walked back to the door of Andrés's rooms, heavy jug in one hand, bowl in the other, when something caressed the back of my neck, gentle as the curious step of a tarantula.

A feeling of being watched.

I whirled to face it. "Don't you dare," I snarled.

But there was nothing there. Nothing but the thick, impenetrable darkness that cloaked the valley of Apan.

I glowered into the dark. And when I reentered Andrés's little room, I set the jug on the table and fished into the pocket of my dress for the piece of copal resin I had taken to keeping there.

Once there was a curl of smoke at the door, I filled a clay cup of water for Andrés, but he had already drifted into sleep.

I knelt at his bedside and leaned my head against the mattress, careful to make sure it didn't touch his. Panic and fear had drained every drop of energy from me; I was like a wet rag that had been twisted, twisted, twisted, and then hung out to dry.

Andrés's breathing was steady, deep, and mine linked with it, with the rise and fall of his chest.

So, so quiet.

MY EYES FLEW OPEN at a sharp rap at the door.

I didn't remember falling asleep. I hadn't intended to. Bright morning spilled into the room from the high windows, illuminating candles burned low and only the slimmest curl of copal.

The rapping at the door sounded again.

I lifted my head and turned to Andrés.

Carajo, I imagined him hissing.

But he lay still. Said nothing. Blood had dried and cracked at the corner of his mouth, and in the morning light, his face was as pallid as it was last night.

"Andrés!" The rapping gained fervor. The panic in Paloma's voice pitched through the wood of the door. "Andrés, I need you. Wake up!"

It was Paloma. Thank goodness. Then the only excuse I needed for our current state of impropriety was that Andrés was clearly ill, and I had spent the night tending him.

I stumbled up on stiff legs, straightening my skirts as pins and needles ran up and down my calves. Tucked a curl that had torn loose from its knot sometime in the night behind my ear. Cleared my throat. My lips were cracked, parched. I prayed my voice would work.

I opened the door.

Paloma's face was wild, tear streaked. "Andr—"

Her voice cut off and her eyes widened as she took me in, her mouth open in a surprised *oh*.

Then she saw her cousin.

"What *happened* to you?" she shrieked. I jumped back as she shoved into the room and fell to her knees at Andrés's side. "You idiot! What mess did you get into this time?"

"I'm fine," Andrés murmured, patting one of her hands gently. "Don't worry, everything's fine."

Everything was not fine. He could have been killed last night, and my stomach sank when I realized we had not yet assessed the extent of the damage the broken circle had caused. But he lied effortlessly, the rasp in his voice comforting even when he looked like Death hovered near, waiting to snatch him away.

"No, it's not fine," Paloma cried. A sob thickened her voice. "Mamá is dead. She's dead, Andrés!"

16

AFTER ANDRÉS SPLASHED HIS face with water from the pump, the three of us went to the servants' quarters. Andrés walked gingerly, shading his face from the harsh morning sun with a hand. He had not spoken a word since Paloma announced Ana Luisa was dead. If possible, he looked worse than he had when she had woken us.

"What happened?" I asked Paloma as she led us to where Ana Luisa was. Where Ana Luisa's body was.

"I woke up and she was gone," Paloma said curtly. She walked a half step ahead of us, her dark shoes striking the earth with firm purpose, as if their beat were the only thing keeping the tears that hummed beneath the surface of her voice from welling up again. "She wasn't ill, she hadn't mentioned any pain . . . I think it was her heart."

Andrés nodded, then set his mouth in a pained twist. Sympathy tugged at my heart. The blow to his head must have been even worse than I thought.

When we reached Ana Luisa's house, a small crowd of people had gathered outside the door. They parted at the appearance of Paloma, followed by Padre Andrés and myself, whispering to one another as we stepped over the threshold into the darkness of the house.

Paloma took us directly to the sleeping quarters. It was similar to Andrés's room: simply decorated, humbly furnished. But unlike his room, herbs covered the threshold, lined the walls. The air had the inevitable smell of stale copal, mixed with something foul.

Two beds were on either side of the room. One was empty, its sheets in disarray. The other was Ana Luisa's, the floor surrounding it etched with imitation witch's marks.

And there she was.

I stopped, barely a few steps past the doorway. My breath vanished from my throat.

I had not been fond of Ana Luisa, nor she of me. The figure of Juana stood between us, an impenetrable barrier that made us adversaries before we could even learn to know each other. I did not know if we would have ever moved past our differences.

That did not make the sight before me any less shocking.

In death, Ana Luisa's face was fixed in an expression I had never seen her wear in life: her mouth dropped open into a surprised *oh*, her eyelids torn back so far by fear her pupils were naked and round and stark against the whites of her eyes. Her arm was outstretched, stiff.

Ana Luisa pointed to the wall by her daughter's bed.

My stomach dropped.

Though I was beginning to feel my staring was disrespectful, I could not rip my gaze from her stiff, bloodless face.

Fear.

I knew that fear. I had felt it last night. I felt it every night inside the walls of San Isidro.

"I woke up and she was like this." Paloma's voice trembled barely above a whisper. "I can't even close her eyes. I tried—" Her voice broke.

Andrés's posture shifted. He put a hand on Paloma's back; she immediately turned into his embrace and began to sob against his chest. He hushed her gently.

I was suddenly aware that I was intruding on a private family moment. Paloma deserved the same privacy I had needed when Papá was taken away, the privacy I was only able to get at night, sobbing into my sheets with Mamá stroking my back. I took a step away from them and turned to leave.

As I did, I glanced at the wall that Ana Luisa pointed at in her final moments. An unassuming stucco wall, so like the wall Andrés had been thrown against last night. White, rough, plain. My eyes dropped to the floor before it. There was a cross there, a simple wooden cross like the one that hung in Andrés's room.

It was broken.

The center of the cross was cracked, its short arms almost fully detached. It looked as if someone had taken the heel of their shoe and smashed the center of the wood, not once but over and over again, grinding it into the floor.

A chill coated my palms, slick as oil.

Something had been *here* last night.

Something frightened Ana Luisa to death.

I shuddered and left the house, blinking as I adjusted to the painfully bright morning.

Other villagers had stepped away from the door, but still hovered, forming an arc around it. Next to José Mendoza, I recognized the woman from the baptism Andrés had performed a few days ago. She was crying. The child on her hip watched me solemnly.

What was I supposed to say? Ana Luisa had been their friend. Perhaps they had lived alongside one another for years. Perhaps they had known her longer than I had even been alive. Who was I to tell them to go away?

But part of me saw Paloma's back shuddering with sobs and saw myself.

I cleared my throat. "I think Paloma requires privacy," I said. Murmurs quieted as Andrés stepped out of the doorway behind me. He held up a hand to shade his eyes.

"Funeral Mass in an hour," he said. "Burial after. I require volunteer gravediggers. May God bless you."

Despite the grimness of this pronouncement, the tightness in my shoulders eased. I had the sensation that all of us around Ana Luisa's door responded as one to the soft authority in his voice. Something in the air shifted; relaxed. *I am here*, his presence said. *And if I am here, all will be well.*

A few voices repeated the words back to him, and the people dispersed, retreating to their homes or moving to other parts of the hacienda to begin the day's work.

Andrés let loose a long sigh.

"What on earth happened?"

"My aunt had a weak heart," he said, keeping his voice low. Paloma's sobs had waned but were still audible. "A number of people in my family do. It might have been natural, but . . ."

The terror on her face caused both of us to think otherwise.

"Did you see the cross?" I murmured.

Andrés nodded slowly, carefully, as if his head were made of blown glass and shaking it too hard would cause it to shatter. He had not lowered the hand that shaded his face.

"What if when we broke the circle—"

"You broke the circle?" he interrupted.

I stared at him. Was this a joke? "Last night. You broke it first, and then I followed."

The crease between his brows deepened. A shadow of fear passed behind his eyes. "*What?*"

"Do you not remember?"

"I . . ." He chewed his bottom lip. "No." His voice wavered close to cracking over the word. "I know we began the ritual. And then . . . Paloma was pounding on the door."

A long pause stretched between us. How could he not remember? He looked just as panicked by this thought as I felt. "What happened?"

I dropped my voice to a whisper, as dry and raspy as my mouth felt. "The thing—whatever you drew from the house—it hurt you. It threw you against the wall. Your head . . . you were hurt, so I ran after you, and it—"

"It's loose," Andrés finished grimly. What little color remained in his face drained completely. "It must have been here last night."

My gut twisted. I knew he was right. A wild, unfettered darkness was roaming free beyond the walls of the house. I had felt it last night as I drew water from the pump. "Do you think that's why she was pointing at—"

He nodded, the movement slow and ginger. "It *must* have been here."

"Andrés." Paloma's voice snapped through the air with the finality of a book being shut. Andrés jumped; winced at the sudden movement. She was right behind him, her eyes bloodshot, her hands curled into fists. "What are you talking about?" she accused.

"The rain," Andrés said quickly. "It will rain this afternoon. Two hours before sunset." Then he paused, as if weighing whether or not to continue. "I was wondering . . . did you hear anything unusual last night?"

For a moment Paloma stared at him blankly. Understanding, then frustration, blossomed over her features.

"Stop. *Enough.*" Her voice cracked in exasperation over the words. "Why can't you be a normal priest? Sometimes that's what this family needs."

She turned on her heel and disappeared back inside the house.

Andrés watched her go, looking as wounded as a pup that had been kicked. Then his hands rose to his temples and he closed his eyes. He swayed gently where he stood. Was he going to be ill again?

"Are you all right?" I said softly. My hand strayed to his arm; I drew it back quickly.

"I need to go back inside," he murmured. He was ghastly pale.

"I will go clean up the parlor," I said.

"Don't touch the circle." The urgency in his exhausted voice sent a chill down my spine. "Do *not* go inside the marks. I can still feel it. It's . . . active. Please, be careful."

"I will," I promised, and let my hand fall. He ducked his head gingerly beneath the low doorway and melted into the darkness of Ana Luisa's house.

What had we done?

I began the walk up to the house, my feet heavy with dread. What would I find there?

"Beatriz."

I whirled to face the voice. Juana was walking up the path to the villagers' quarters. She held two letters in one hand and waved them at me, gesturing for me to come to her. One was opened, the other not.

My heart lifted with hope. Was one from my mother?

Any other day, I would have stood my ground and insisted she come to me. Dig in my heels for a battle of wills to see which one of us was the true master of San Isidro. But not today. I didn't have the strength to fight her.

There was mud on her skirts. Her hair was mostly undone from its plait and falling around her face; thin blades of hay stuck out from amidst the sandy brown of her hair.

"What happened to you?" I asked.

"I was drunk and fell asleep in the stable," she said bluntly.

I blinked in surprise. What on earth? Before I could ask what she meant by behaving that way, she handed me the unopened letter.

My own name winked up at me in Rodolfo's elegant, sharp-tipped penmanship.

"He's coming back for a short while," Juana said, flat and unamused. "He'll arrive the day after tomorrow."

"What a surprise," I said, for I had nothing else to say. Not to Juana, anyway. My mind was racing past her, up the path and to the house, the house where a witch's circle still hummed with power and the shadows ripped themselves from the walls to prowl the grounds.

"Whatever charlatan's game you have the priest playing up at the house, be done with it," Juana said, her pale eyes fixed on my face with an intensity that made my skin crawl. "He was banished from San Isidro for a reason. Perhaps you're amused by native superstition, but you know how little patience Rodolfo has for it."

I nodded knowingly, though I did not know. Banished? There were many things I had not discussed with Rodolfo; banishment was one of them. Andrés had not mentioned it either. I did not trust myself to speak, not when a hot hum of anger coiled in my throat at Juana's condescending tone.

Charlatan. Native superstition. Who did she think she was, to dismiss Andrés so? Couldn't she see the way the people looked at him, how they needed someone like him? Or did she simply not care? Didn't she know it was his own power that inspired Ana Luisa's protective copal? His work was a gift. It might have the power to save lives in the battle we waged against the house.

A long, thin wail rose from the direction of Ana Luisa's house.

My heart curled in on itself. Poor Paloma.

"What's going on over there?" Juana asked sharply, as if only then noticing the heavy mood that hung over the courtyard.

"Haven't you heard?" I asked. Her expression did not change. She was waiting for me to continue. "The Lord took Ana Luisa in the night."

I wasn't sure what I expected from my sister-in-law. I knew she and Ana Luisa were close—their camaraderie an easy, well-worn thing born from years of being in each other's company. Did I expect her to break into Paloma's sobs? To look as if the wind had been knocked out of her like Andrés?

"Well," she said coldly. "Well."

And that was it.

She turned sharply on her heel and strode to the stables.

THE FRONT DOOR OF the house was ajar, just as I had left it last night when I stumbled into the rain with Andrés. It gaped at me, a dark mouth, toothless and foul breathed. Darkness cloaked the hall beyond it.

It was morning, I told myself. Nothing could happen during the day.

But things *had* happened during the day. Temperatures shifted severely. I found the skeleton in the wall.

But that was in the north wing. I would be in the green parlor.

Sickness lurched in my gut at the memory of falling to my hands and knees, dark blood pouring over my chin onto the floor.

It was an illusion. The darkness could not harm me.

It killed Ana Luisa, a voice wound through the back of my mind. I thought of cold hands shoving me down on the stairs, how frighteningly *corporeal* they had felt. How very real their hatred was. *It nearly killed Andrés.*

Fighting the urge to shudder, I looked up at the red tiles missing from the roof, the brown bougainvillea hanging limp from the stucco walls. San Isidro was supposed to be my victory. My future. My home.

Now all I could do was hope that it wouldn't be my tomb.

I inhaled deeply, curled my hands into fists to steel myself, and stepped inside.

The house sat differently on its foundations. Whereas before it had been slumped and rambling, the limbs of a hibernating beast curled around a central wing, now . . .

Now it was *awake.*

The feeling of being watched no longer brushed gently against me, coy and shy. It was brash, its gaze open and lurid, noting my every move, watching my every step toward the parlor with the naked interest of a dog eyeing a slab of meat.

All I had to do was tidy up the parlor. Andrés would handle the circle. We had to make sure that there was no evidence of what we had attempted—what we had failed at—before Rodolfo arrived.

The door to the green parlor lay in the hall like a corpse, blown off its hinges as if by an explosion. My shoes crunched over shattered glass as I entered the room.

The temperature dipped; I shuddered. It was merely that this room faced west, and the sun's rays had not yet touched it after a long, cold night.

Everything was as we had left it: the candles were in their spots, the blankets piled neatly by the hearth, unused, for Andrés and I had not held vigil as we had initially planned.

My heart skipped against the base of my throat as I thought of Andrés going limp as a rag, flung against the wall. The wall was rough, white, plain. No sign of supernatural events. No blood slicked the floor. No copal filled the air.

I began to clean. I obeyed Andrés's orders to not enter the circle. It was easy to remember the urgency in his voice when I drew near to the charcoal markings to collect the candles. There was a warmth to the ground near them, as if a living body was lying on the stone. As if *life* pulsed through it. It was so at odds with the chill of the rest of the room that when I first brushed against it, I snatched my hand back as if it had been burned.

It's active, Andrés had said.

I had no intention of discovering what that meant.

As I tidied, I preoccupied myself with an equally pressing concern: how on earth I was going to welcome Rodolfo back into this home. The very taste of the air inside these walls had changed since he was last here. I could not be inside the house at night without the comforting shroud of clouds of copal smoke. I could not sleep in the dark, as Rodolfo would wish.

Maybe I could take the blankets I had just stowed away and run to the capilla. Perhaps I could sleep beneath the pews as Andrés had as a child.

Perhaps I could tell Rodolfo . . .

You know how little patience Rodolfo has for it, Juana said.

Whether that was true or not, Rodolfo had admonished me in his letter and told me not to seek help from the Church again. When he looked at Andrés, he would see a priest. He would see the Church. He would see someone who had been *banished* from San Isidro, though I did not yet know why.

He would see that I had disobeyed him.

I had never upset Rodolfo in our short marriage. Fear skipped down my spine, its steps uneven and discordant, at the thought of how he had snapped at Juana at dinner. How quickly could that same anger turn on me? What would it look like?

"Beatriz."

Andrés filled the high doorway, a basket of something that smelled of warm masa in one hand.

I frowned. That was the first time he had said my name without *Doña*, and it felt naked, almost profane.

He pointed at the wall, eyes wide in his gray face. The wall he had struck last night.

I turned my head.

Thick strokes of blood splayed across the white stucco, forming a single word, repeated over and over:

RODOLFO RODOLFO RODOLFO RODOLFO RODOLFO

It had been blank. Mere minutes ago it had been white and plain. And now—

A single droplet of blood rolled from the last O. It was fresh blood, as wet as new paint and dripping.

RODOLFO RODOLFO RODOLFO

I couldn't look away. I couldn't breathe.

RODOLFO RODOLFO

"Did she . . ." Andrés trailed off.

She. *She.*

I heard she died of typhus. I heard she was kidnapped by insurgents.

"Did you know Rodolfo's first wife?" I demanded.

"I . . ." Andrés paused. "I met her. Yes."

"What did she look like?"

"Like she came from a peninsular family," he said softly. "Tall, white. She had the palest hair I have ever seen. It looked like corn silk."

I tore myself away from the wall to look at Andrés. If he had eaten or rested, it hadn't improved his appearance—his face was sickly, his expression queasy.

"Andrés. I had a dream when you were last here."

I told him what I had dreamed: the woman in gray, her hair like corn silk, and her eyes like embers. Her flesh-colored claws. The shredded sheets, the marks carved deep in the wooden headboard of the bed.

He listened silently, still hovering in the doorway, either too ill or too stunned to move until I delivered the final piece of what I had to say.

"Juana told me Rodolfo is coming back in two days."

Andrés looked back at the wall. His eyes followed a thick bead of blood as it carved a fresh path down the stucco. The scrawl was rough, frantic. Could it have been written in fear?

Was it a warning?

"I think you are in danger, Beatriz," he breathed.

That I knew was true.

But from whom?

17

ANDRÉS

COLD RAIN SLICKED THE road from Apan to Hacienda San Isidro, leaving my clothes splattered with mud. The walk took the better part of the day; I arrived as evening darkened in the west.

I had returned to Apan nearly six weeks ago, but finally I was home.

Passing through the gates of the property was like passing into a memory that no longer fit. I was a foot too big for a shoe, deformed by the world beyond as I returned to the landscape of my boyhood. The road to San Isidro felt like a path into a dream. I had left the quotidian world of the Church and townspeople and passed into a beyond where the bellies of the clouds hung low and listening, where the coyotes were afraid to draw near Titi's house. Where all the pieces of me had once made sense. Where I hoped they would again.

It was a false hope, of course. The muddy earth of the hacienda grounds was no different from town. My troubles were not immediately lifted from my shoulders the moment I arrived.

Tía Ana Luisa greeted me with her usual stiffness. Never a warm woman, I doubted she would ever forgive me for the crime of being born with the innate potential she lacked, for becoming my grandmother's pupil when Titi refused to teach her.

"Paloma is up at the house with the others," she said, taking my water-logged bag of few belongings. "I imagine you'll be staying at the capilla, now that you're . . ." Here she gestured vaguely at the collar at my neck. "This."

I let Ana Luisa take my bag to the capilla and followed her instructions to go to the kitchen of the main house. There, Paloma would warm dinner for me, and I could sit by a lit fire and read the Bible to the women of the house as they mended or did embroidery.

Night deepened as I approached the house.

Hello, old friend, I thought as I strode through the softening rain.

It grumbled in reply, shifting cantankerously on its foundations.

I couldn't help but smile. The house had more moods than a swallow had feathers. I was fond of its peevish spells; its impatient creaks and groaning inspired an urge in me to pat its side affectionately as I would a stubborn but lovable mule. As a child I knew this ancient house of spirits was unlike anything else I had ever seen. Now, after having stepped through the doorways of countless old houses, I knew it was unique.

"Cuervito!" A woman hovered impatiently at the glowing doorway of the kitchen, calling my childhood nickname: *little raven*. It was Paloma. Aside from the procession, I had not seen her since she was twelve or thirteen, and to see her so grown still caught me by surprise. "Hurry up!"

She ushered me into the warmth of the kitchen, taking my soaked wool sarape and hanging it by the fire. Then she turned, hands on her hips in an uncanny imitation of Titi. "Will you ever stop growing?"

I shrugged, sat where she ordered, and waited patiently while she prepared a plate for me. Years apart had not changed my role in the family: the sole surviving boy among a loud, bossy host of women, my job was to sit and listen, eat the food placed before me, and reach things stored in high places.

Warmth seeped into my waterlogged clothes and windswept bones.

This was home.

When I was dry and fed, Paloma brought me to the green parlor to meet the wife of the patrón.

A fire roared in the hearth. The silhouette of Doña María Catalina Solórzano, the spun-sugar mistress of Hacienda San Isidro, rose to greet me. I knew from Paloma's chatter in the kitchen that the staff referred to her as Doña Catalina. A handful of household staff rose as she did—I recognized one as Paloma's friend Mariana, transformed by adolescence like Paloma.

"Padre Andrés." Doña Catalina's voice was crisp as a new sheet of paper. Firelight took to her pale hair like dye; it was as if a halo of red gold framed her small, pointed face. "How good of you to join us. Ana Luisa says you have a wonderful voice for reading, among your other fine qualities."

Desagradecido, sin vergüenza . . . Throughout my childhood, Ana Luisa had many things to say about me, but never that. I donned the pious, bashful smile I had learned to wear in Guadalajara, the one that concealed any apprehension or distrust I felt while speaking with parishioners, and took the Bible from her with a respectful bob of my head.

I sat opposite her and opened the Bible to the letters of St. Paul to the Ephesians.

The room was silent but for the crackle of the fire.

I paused, letting my fingertip skip down the page of the Bible without seeing the lines it crossed. How odd that the house should choose to be so quiet in this room. I could always hear its complaining, its sly gossiping, its murmuring commentary in the background of every conversation.

It was *quiet*.

This was not the pious silence of holy places, nor the respectful hush of graveyards. This was . . . odd.

I cleared my throat, aware that Doña Catalina still watched me, and began to read.

Paloma took her place next to Mariana and picked up her needlework. Dark, wispy hairs flew free of her plait; she worried her bottom lip as she stitched, like Titi did when she had something on her mind. There was a heaviness in the room that wasn't from the warmth of the fire; a tenseness that I could not place. And when Paloma insisted on walking with me to the small rooms that adjoined the capilla, a pile of blankets in her arms, I did not protest.

The room was humble: a fireplace, a table, a bed. Packed-dirt-and-gravel floor, polished smooth with varnish and generations of footsteps. One shelf for books and an austere wooden cross on the wall. Paloma shut the door and put the blankets on the table. She lit a few candles, then hovered as I crouched before the hearth and began a fire. Once or twice I glanced at her out of the corner of my eye. She was worrying her bottom lip again; now that her hands were not occupied with needlework, they toyed with the tassels at the end of her shawl.

I knew the look of someone who had much to say but was afraid to speak. I lowered my voice to make sure it was soft, and would not frighten her away, the way I spoke to birds.

"Something is worrying you," I said. "Maybe I can help."

"Help is exactly what I want," she blurted out, lifting her head. She pulled a chair out from the table and sat on it, then drew her knees to her chest protectively. "Your help, specifically. You see . . ." She trailed off, her gaze on the fire. "My friend is too afraid to ask you directly, even though I told her you were harmless. She . . . Mariana, the one sitting with us tonight. She's shy." I nodded. *Shy* was not the word I would have chosen. Mariana had flinched whenever I shifted my weight, her shoulders coiled tight. She pricked herself while sewing at least twice from the sudden movement.

That was the way my mother had moved, when she was still alive.

"Titi must have taught you," Paloma said. "She must have. You have to help her."

Our grandmother taught me many things. I didn't immediately follow her meaning. "I don't understand."

Paloma searched for words, clearly flustered. Her eyes shone with tears of frustration, and when she spoke, her voice trembled: "When he was here, the patrón forced himself on Mariana."

I stared at her, grasping for words, shock stinging like a slap to the face. I found none. My God, why do You forsake Your people? Why do You not protect them from the gilded monsters that prowl the earth?

I thought of bright-haired Solórzano smiling at Padre Guillermo, his lissome wife at his side; my stomach turned to stone, and sank deep, deep underwater. I was wrong to think old Solórzano's son was any better than his father. The pulque dons were poisoned men.

"Don't look so stupid. You know exactly what I mean." The women of my family sheathed their fears and sorrows in knives and claws; the sharpness of her voice did not offend me, but drove home how distressed she was. "She's with child now. She's meant to marry Tomás Revilla from Hacienda Ometusco, but if he finds out, if anyone finds out . . ." Her wavering voice broke off, as if she were simply unable to continue.

My heart turned over in my chest. I rocked back on my heels.

"When is the wedding?" I asked softly. "Perhaps there is a way for Mariana to hide the pregnancy, until . . ."

"You're not listening," Paloma snapped. "*She doesn't want it.* Isn't that reason enough?"

Her words fell like an enormous pine in the forest, leaving a long silence in their wake. The fire smoked; a soft crackle indicated the kindling was taking the flame. I did not turn away from Paloma.

"You need to help her. You know what I mean." Paloma's voice was still frail but grew steadier as she struck her final blow: "Titi would."

Titi was not a priest, I wanted to cry, but bit my tongue. Could Paloma understand how fear had been my only bedfellow since leaving for Guadalajara? She did not live cheek to jowl with Padre Vicente; though the Inquisition had left for Spain amid the upheaval of the insurgency, it still beat in the veins of many clergy, flooding them with the vigor of the righteous.

I had to continue to hide myself. That was how I had survived, and how I would continue to survive. There was no question about that.

I dropped her gaze and turned to the smoking kindling.

"I need to pray about this," I said to the fire.

"Prayers are empty talk." I flinched at the acidity in Paloma's voice. She stood sharply, her jaw set fiercely as she tightened her shawl around her shoulders. "She needs help."

She left and let the door slam behind her.

AFTER CELEBRATING MASS IN the capilla the next morning, I left the chapel, taking a shortcut through the graveyard of generations of dead Solórzanos. My feet followed the path with the habit of many years; hopping over the low wall, I was a boy of eight again, or twelve, or fifteen, visiting my grandmother on an escape from town with its endless days of school and chores and endless nights of dodging my drunken father's outbursts.

The house watched me out of the corner of its eye. Rather than toying with me, plying me with centuries-old gossip and whispers in singsong voices as it had when I was a child, it kept a cautious distance. Perhaps it could smell the change in me. Perhaps it knew how deeply I had buried the parts of me it found the most interesting.

A hush fell around me as I wove between the graves and the aged, humble headstones. Paloma was the seventh generation of our family to live on this land; one day, she, too, would be buried here, and her children would continue living beside the house, her daughters working under its roof, her sons taking up the machetes of tlachiqueros or herding sheep. Another generation would make its living in the shadow of the golden Solórzano family and their maguey.

I walked down the hill to where the villagers buried their dead. I had spent the better part of the night staring at the ceiling in the dark, wondering what I should do. It was time to stop wondering and ask Titi directly.

I followed Ana Luisa's direction to where my grandmother was buried, my shoes leaving deep impressions in rain-saturated earth. I felt it before I read her name on the grave: *Alejandra Flores Pérez, d. Julio 1820.*

July. I was ordained that month. I left Guadalajara in the fall; I was slow on the road, deterred by moving armies and the threat of bandits, but I had returned as soon as I could.

Yet it was not soon enough.

Why couldn't you have waited for me? I sank to my knees at her side, not caring if the earth dirtied my trousers, not caring for anything at all but my own sorrow, my own self-pity. Tears welled thick in my throat; I shut my eyes and tilted my head back, to the sky and its pale winter sun. *Why couldn't you stay with me?*

The wind lifted, shifting my hair, then fell again. Clouds slowed over the hills that ringed the valley. Far past the walls of San Isidro, a shepherd whistled to his dog, his note riding thin and high through the clear air.

The graves were quiet.

I received no reply.

All I wanted was her voice telling me what to do, correcting me, instructing me as she had since before I could even read.

Another lift of the wind. It swept tender over my face, and a memory bloomed behind my closed eyelids. I was a boy, watching my grandmother tuck wool blankets tight around a child with a fever, murmuring prayers I could not understand. We were in the village of an hacienda to the northeast of Tulancingo. Often, I accompanied Titi as she visited villagers on other estates surrounding Apan on an ornery gray donkey one of my cousins had named el Cuervito in jest.

That year, a fever had swept through many of the haciendas, seizing children in swift waves. I watched my grandmother tend to the child before her, a censer on the floor beside the cot and an egg in her right hand. The copal twined like a lazy snake toward the low ceiling of the room. A shadow hung over the child, as if someone had draped a smoky veil over the scene before me, and only my grandmother could pass through it unharmed.

Titi stood. Her back was already hunched, even then, her long braids white as milk, but an undeniable strength settled in her posture as she took the child's mother in her arms and embraced her. Let the woman cry and comforted her softly—in castellano, I remembered, for the pueblo of that hacienda spoke otomí rather than our dialect of mexicano.

As we left, Titi took the censer from me. We walked a short distance from the house.

"What did you see when you looked at the child?" she asked.

The vision of the veil clung to me like the smell of smoke. Something was watching the boy, waiting. "He's going to die, isn't he?" I whispered.

Back then, she looked down at me and not the other way around. She nodded solemnly. "Yes."

"What good did we do, then?" I asked, my voice cracking over the words. "If we can't stop it?"

Titi stopped and took me by the elbow. I glared at her worn sandals. "Look at me, Andrés." I obeyed. "What else did you see?"

I thought back to the dark room, the closeness of the air inside, how the only light came from the door and the fire lit to help sweat out the child's fever. "His mother?"

"Some illnesses we cannot cure," my grandmother said. "Others we can soothe. Sorrow is one of these. Loneliness is another." She searched my face. "Do you understand? Tending to lost souls is our vocation."

Our vocation. It was meant to be *ours*, shared, the burden slowly distributed from her shoulders onto mine with time. With years of working together. For it was Titi who taught me to listen to mortal and spirit alike, who taught me her own grandmother's herbal cures and how to banish mal de ojo by passing a chicken's egg over a child's feverish body. She taught me all she could, all she knew.

"I fear it is not enough, not for you," she once said. "One day, you will walk paths I do not understand. You must find your own way forward."

My heart ached every time I recalled this, for I both loathed and feared the fact it was true. All I wanted was to walk the path Titi had. Even before I became a priest, it was clear I couldn't.

I was the son of Esteban Villalobos, a Sevillan who came to Nueva España seeking his fortune and found work on Hacienda San Isidro.

And when he crossed the sea from the peninsula, he had brought his only sister.

I only saw her once. Not long after my mother died, when I was twelve years old, I returned to my father's house in Apan after a few days spent with Titi and Paloma to find a tall woman in the kitchen. She had the presence of a bull, with broad, calloused hands, coppery brown hair, and dark eyes that sparked like gunpowder. My father called her Inés and introduced her to me as his sister; despite this, they were stiff and formal with each other. She said she had come to see him to bid farewell before returning to Spain and meant to leave for Veracruz the following day.

The next morning, after my father had left to attend the prison—part of his duties as the caudillo's assistant—I woke to find that Inés had pulled up the edge of one of the floorboards in the kitchen and was in the midst of wedging a sheaf of papers beneath it.

I thought I had not made a sound, but she lifted her head. She went very still, locked her gunpowder eyes on me, and squinted, the corners of her eyes forming crow's-feet.

"You," she said. Her voice was archly matter-of-fact, as unfriendly as it was flat. "You've got the Devil's darkness, don't you?"

"I—I don't know what you mean," I stammered, shocked. I crossed myself for good measure. "God forbid."

Her fair eyebrows bobbed once toward her hairline, sardonic. "Don't lie. I knew it the moment I saw you."

A sour feeling of shame mixed with fear washed over me. I had vexed her, though I did not know my sin nor how to fix it, and that frightened me. I watched in silence as she finished hiding the papers and thumped the wood back into place.

"Consider this your inheritance." She patted the floorboards once; palm struck wood with a hollow, strange note. "Keep it hidden, if you know what's good for you."

Without another word, she gathered her belongings and left.

This. But what was it? It was barely a week after Inés left that I succumbed to curiosity and pried up the floorboard. The papers she had hidden were bound into a pamphlet, stained with age, their edges heavily thumbed with use. I had learned to read in school, and though I had little talent for it at that age, I recognized that though the glyphs on the page had the measured choreography of language, they were neither castellano nor Latin.

Behind me, the voices in the walls of my father's house cooed. The hair on the back of my neck stood on end as I felt them peer over my shoulder at the glyphs, the darkness of their interest like wet mud slipping down my spine.

I took the papers to Titi that same day. Though she had never learned to read, we discovered interpreting the pamphlet Inés left did not require that skill: guided by the intuition of her own gifts, Titi was able to deduce the purpose of the glyphs. They were spells of protection and healing, exorcism and curses; Titi paired these with her own incantations and taught me how to harness the darkness she sensed in me. If Inés had owned this pamphlet of glyphs and had spoken of the Devil, then Inés herself must have also been a witch, albeit a very different sort than Titi. And whatever gave Inés her powers had been passed—either through blood, the gift of the pamphlet, or both—to me.

I had invented a way of transcribing Titi's teachings in mexicano for myself, but when I was sixteen, my father discovered notes I had stuffed haphazardly beneath my cot in his house.

I thought I knew his temper like I knew the weather. With a flood of pulque would come predictable storms, slamming doors, raised voices. With enough patience, I could skirt the worst of it; I learned to melt into the walls as if I were one of the voices myself. But if my own temper thinned, or if I snapped back at him, I courted danger. When I tried to snatch the papers back from him, I expected to be shouted at, shoved, or struck for my trouble.

Instead, my father shrank away from me.

"They burn people like you, you know. You, Inés . . . they should *burn* you." His eyes popped from his skull with fear, bloodshot but for the bright white above and below his irises. "Send you to Hell where you belong." Sharp as a darting animal, he reached for a wooden cross on the wall, yanked it off, and flung it at me. I ducked. It struck the wall behind me with a dull thud and fell to the floor, cloven in two. "*Go to Hell.*"

I left for San Isidro that night. I never saw him again.

Word came from town that he packed his belongings and left Apan. Some said he meant to go north, to Sonora or Alta California. Others said he spat on the earth and swore he would return to Spain.

It was not long after that Titi insisted I go to Guadalajara. That I fulfill my mother's dying wish by becoming a priest.

"You must," she said as she bid me goodbye. "This is what is right."

I was far less firm in my conviction. I was afraid of insurgents and Spaniards on the road, of bandits, of the Inquisition circling me like Daniel in the den of lions. What wisdom was there sending a damned soul straight into the Church's jaws, when I ought to be hiding from them?

The fear in my father's eyes as he shrank away from me had seared me like a brand. Its mark would never heal over, never scar.

They should burn you.

"How can you know this is right?" I said, fear cracking my voice. *"How?"*

"Ay, Cuervito." She patted my hands. The touch of her gnarled hands was soft, but her dark eyes were steely in their confidence. "You will learn to feel it. When the time comes, you will know what is right."

Years had passed, and that time had not come.

I balled my hands into fists, the winter wind cold on my face, my knees pressing into the damp dirt of her graveside.

How could one simply *know?*

In Guadalajara, I endured homily after homily on faith and belief. On placing my fate in the hands of the unknown. In my splintered self, God was one thing. God was invisible and unknowable, but I learned to have faith that He was there, even if I doubted He paid as much attention to the smudge of earth that was Apan as He did other places.

But in Titi's teachings, I learned that some things *could* be known. I always heard the voices, no matter where I was. Now that I had returned to Apan, I felt the movement of weather; I knew when thunder would open the heavens over the valley. I knew when the riverbeds would flood with the spectral presence of the Weeper and how to placate her. I knew when the wildflowers would blossom, when horses would foal. I felt the presence of spirits in the mountains, how they shifted even in their deep slumber.

So why didn't I *know* whether or not I should help Paloma and Mariana?

I thought of Mariana in the firelight, flinching away from my every movement like a wounded dove, a frail shadow. I knew she hurt. It was written across her spirit clear as ink. I knew Paloma's fierceness. Her conviction.

I knew when I looked at the small congregation that morning at Mass

that my grandmother's absence was a wound. The people of San Isidro—
the people who were my home—were in pain without her.

Priest or not, I *knew* I was meant to fill that absence.

But no one would instruct me how. No one could.

It was up to me to find my way alone.

18

BEATRIZ

PRESENT DAY

AFTER ANA LUISA'S FUNERAL, Andrés followed me gingerly into the parlor. He stared at the blood dripping from the wall for a long time.

At last his chapped lips parted. "I have to close the circle." His voice was barely above a whisper.

"Is it possible?" I asked.

"I hope so." He inhaled through his nose and exhaled long and slow. "Cielo santo. I hope so."

He faced the circle, his eyes fluttering shut, and began to chant softly. His hands extended out in front of him, palms facing upward like a supplicant's. I fell back a step.

The humming I had noticed earlier increased. It rose in volume and pitch, a swarm of bees filling the room; pulses of it rolled over my skin in waves, raising gooseflesh. Quickening my heartbeat.

Soon, I became aware that Andrés's voice faltered. Though I could not understand him, I thought he was pausing, and starting again. The humming hovered at one pitch and then dropped, and began its slow rise anew.

Finally, Andrés stopped chanting altogether. I waited for him to turn to me, I waited for solace to flood over us like dawn after a long night . . . but the determined line of his shoulders collapsed. He lowered his head, held it in his hands.

The hum of the circle continued. If I closed my eyes, I could still see the circle as if it were etched in red marks on the inside of my eyelids. My intuition told me he was not finished yet. "Did you close it?"

"No."

A long moment of silence passed.

Distantly, a trill of mocking laughter. Cold shot down my spine.

"Are you going to try again?" I asked.

He inhaled deeply. "I can't."

He couldn't? What did that mean? I drew forward a step, the click of my shoes on flagstone echoing through the room. He had steepled his hands before his face, pressing them to the hard line of his mouth. His face was gray, his gaze fixed on the circle, unmoving, not even as I drew close.

I thought of him on his back on the floor of the capilla, gray faced and coughing, his teeth stained with blood. *Can't fix broken witches.*

Last night and the shock of this morning were trying for me, but even more so for him.

"You need to rest," I said. If I were honest with myself, I would admit that I wanted to say *let me care for you.* If he was my protector through the night, I would be his in the day. *Share this burden,* I meant to say. *You're not alone.* Instead, I bit my tongue. Resisted the desire to take him by the arm. The situation we found ourselves in was dangerous enough. Becoming too familiar with him could lead nowhere but more trouble. "Come, let's go to the kitchen."

"I can't remember." The tremble in his voice struck a hollow note. His expression as he stared at the circle—was that fear behind his eyes? "The right prayer. I can't remember it. I can't close it. I *can't.*"

His voice cracked over the last word. Sympathy yawned in my chest; now I did let myself put a light hand on his forearm. But deep in my bones, I did not believe him. How could I? Andrés cured the sick. Andrés rose into the air like a saint. Andrés was capable of anything. "Do you have it written down somewhere? Among your things in town?"

"No."

The defeat in his voice chilled me. Was it that that drew gooseflesh over my arms, or was the temperature of the room dropping? Were the shadows thickening, growing stronger as they fed on the taste of our fear, or was it my mind playing tricks on me?

"Then how—"

"I memorized everything," he said sharply. "It is too dangerous to write. And I—" His voice caught. His eyes had taken on a glassy cast. He was on the verge of tears. "*I can't remember the words.*"

I saw him being flung against the wall as if he were no more than a rag. The darkness had not killed him. But by smashing his head against the wall, by injuring him so, it had taken something almost as precious as his life: his ability to protect us all.

A sharp spike of fear dug into the back of my skull.

"Is there anything that doesn't require words?" I asked, fighting to keep rising panic out of my voice. "Something where you act on instinct, or you could improvise, or use castellano . . ."

"Absolutely not," he snapped. Anger crackled like lightning over his words, drawing his shoulders back sharply as he turned to me. He said, "This—what I did in this room last night—it must be *controlled.* It's dangerous. You don't understand what you're talking about."

A flush rose to my cheeks and smarted there. No, I did not understand his witchcraft. But I understood that it was dangerous to be without protection in this house. Without his power, we were bare and defenseless against the darkness. Yet here we still stood, unshielded and unarmed, surrounded by the house, by the malice that festered and spread in its walls like an infection.

We were its prey.

Beatriz. I stiffened. A voice called my name, rising in my mind though I heard nothing. The hairs on my arms stood on end. *When is nightfall, Beatriz? When is day?*

My fingers curled tight around Andrés's arm; I cast a wild look around the room.

No one was there.

"Andrés," I hissed. "I hear a voice. Do you hear it?"

In a fluid movement, he seized me tightly by the shoulders. My breath caught, startled by the harshness of his touch.

Aren't you frightened?

"Andrés—" I cast my eyes around the room again.

Don't you know what he is capable of?

"It's here," I breathed. "*She's* here."

That which we had set loose last night. Whoever had frightened Ana Luisa to death and smashed the crucifix. She was in the walls, in the rafters, around us—

"Look me in the eye," Andrés said forcefully, shaking my shoulders when I did not immediately obey. His grip was so tight it would leave bruises. "Look at me." His tears had evaporated; his eyes burned feral, and ... yes, it frightened me. This passion made him a stranger, commanding, *dangerous.* "Do not listen to her. Cast her from your mind this instant."

He has secrets, Beatriz ...

"Do you hear it?" I asked, raspy and uneven. "Tell me. Please."

"Cast it out." His command had the brassy ring of the priest he was, one who cries for his congregation to repent of their sins, whose condemnation of the Devil fills cathedrals. "*Cast it out.*"

I shut my eyes.

Beatriz, Beatriz, Beatriz . . .

I curled my hands into fists and thrust it away with all my might. *No*, I told it. *No. Out.*

The voice stopped.

Footsteps rang in the corridor, announcing someone's approach to the parlor.

My eyes flew open.

Andrés dropped my shoulders and turned to face the door.

Paloma stepped into view. "Ay, Cuervito," she said, drawing the syllables out as she took in the half-tidied mess of the room, the melted-down candles, the censers, the broken glass. She made the sign of the cross. "You've outdone yourself this time," she added dryly.

"Palomita, you should be resting," Andrés said. In the blink of an eye, he had transformed. His face and voice were soft with concern, his posture once again full of gentle authority. Everything about his presence exuded calm.

But I was rattled to my core.

"I can't sit still," Paloma said. "Give me something to do."

Andrés walked toward her and put a gentle hand on her shoulder. "You could rest in my rooms, if you'd prefer. I understand—"

She shoved him away, clearly frustrated. "You're not listening. Give me something to *do*," she said. "I can't sit alone doing nothing."

I was desperate to be out of this room. I needed to be away from Andrés. I wanted the safety of being outside, where there were no voices, or at least—

"Will you help me cook?" I said abruptly.

They looked at me in one motion, surprised—as I had been—at the strange pitch of my voice. I cleared my throat. "I . . . I need to make something." *As we no longer have a cook*, I added silently. "I would appreciate some help."

Paloma raised a brow. "You cook?" she asked dryly.

"I do," I said. "And I will need to ensure that I have a plan for when my husband returns day after tomorrow."

Paloma stiffened. "The patrón will be back? Santo cielo, Andrés. You need to clean up."

My whole body trembled as I crossed the room to Paloma. As I stepped through the doorway, I cast a look at Andrés over my shoulder.

The wall behind him was perfectly blank.

No blood. No name.

It was gone.

THE COLD IN MY bones did not lift as Paloma and I entered the kitchen. While she lit the oven, I knelt in the doorway to light the censers that stood guard there. It took me longer than usual to get the resin to light; my hand shook violently. Finally, smoke twined upward like columns, filling the kitchen with the distinctive aroma of copal. I inhaled of its comfort. My heart slowed. This was safe. This I could rely on. This would not falter.

Andrés, on the other hand . . .

I bit my lip as I glanced down the hall. Before me, it was a cool dark, a neutral dark that did not watch me. Perhaps the house's attention was on Andrés. *He has secrets, Beatriz . . .*

A shudder tripped over my shoulders.

How was I going to survive the night? How was I going to survive at all? How on earth was I to receive Rodolfo? Would he humor my many censers ringing our bed? Would he think me superstitious, or worse, mad?

Was I going mad?

The darkness smirked at me.

I jerked back from the doorway and turned to Paloma. The kitchen faced south, and she had thrown its wide door open to the garden. Sunlight streamed rich and warm into the room as she stoked the fire.

"What are we making?"

Her voice was taut. I knew that feeling. She itched to work with her hands, to forget.

"Something simple and filling," I said. "Arroz con pollo," I decided. "It will be easy to make a lot. Padre Andrés is exhausted, and I worry . . . I think he might be ill."

"What happened?"

I did not know how to reply.

"You won't shock me. He and I have few secrets between us," Paloma said flatly, leaning against the side of the kitchen doorway. She scanned the garden beyond: a few chickens wandered in a wide pen abutting the kitchen wall. "I'm not like him, but I was our grandmother's shadow, just as he was."

She stepped into the garden and approached the chicken coop. I turned away. Yes, I cooked. But though Tía Fernanda's cooks tried to teach me, I could not stomach the killing of fowl. Later, when she had plucked and gutted the chicken and I was washing my hands after helping dispose of the unneeded parts, Paloma said: "So how did Andrés hurt himself this time?"

I cleared my throat. Wiped my hands on the rough apron I had thrown on over yesterday's dress.

"To be frank," I began in a low voice, low enough that I hoped the house could not hear, "Padre Andrés tried to exorcise whatever it is that makes this house . . . what it is."

Paloma made a soft noise of understanding. Evidently, talk of exorcisms in the same breath as her cousin did not surprise her in the least. She jerked her chin to the shelves. "Pots for rice are there."

I stepped around her as she reached for a meat cleaver, found the pot, and placed it on the enormous stove. I wiped sweat from my brow. The warmth of the kitchen felt clean and whole after the bone-deep chill of the rest of the house.

"He hit his head," I said. "So hard that he vomited and cannot remember half of what happened in the night. And now he cannot recall prayers your grandmother taught him."

Paloma looked up at this, cleaver held aloft over the chicken carcass. "That's not good."

"I'm afraid," I said, averting my eyes to the pot. My hands moved without my thinking, and soon, the smell of browning rice enveloped us like a rich blanket. "How long has the house been this way?"

A long moment passed. Paloma continued cutting up the chicken into the appropriate-sized pieces. Instead of answering, she asked another question: "How is it that a woman of your class is like this?"

"What?" I said. *Mad?* I wondered.

"Useful."

I stared at the rice, moving it around the bottom of the pot with a large wooden spoon. I added more ingredients; cumin bit the air, mixing with the sizzle of broth hitting hot oil.

Useful. From Paloma's tone, I knew it was meant to be taken as a compliment. But how I had loathed being called *useful* by Tía Fernanda. As if being of *use* to her was the only way I could earn any worth.

In faltering sentences, I explained my family's past: my mother being turned out by her family for marrying my father, how we relied on Papá's extended family in Cuernavaca, living with them in an ancient stone house on an hacienda that produced sugar. Papá inherited a little from those relatives, and his rise through the army and position in the emperor's cabinet meant we catapulted to as high a class standing as Mamá had started. I explained how we fell just as quickly: when Papá was murdered, refuge with Mamá's cousins was our only choice. How Tía Fernanda treated me. How when an offer of marriage was extended to me, I seized it like a drowning man clings to driftwood. For what other choice was there?

Paloma sighed softly when I came to the end of my tale. She was chopping tomatoes for the sauce.

Her face had an odd look on it.

Pity, I realized with a start. Paloma pitied me for my story. Pride flung up hard walls around me.

"So that is why I am *useful*," I said. "Because my family will have nothing to do with me."

"I thought you would be like the other one, when you arrived," Paloma ventured in a small voice.

The other one. *María Catalina.*

I waited for her to elaborate, but she did not. One by one she put the tomatoes in the pot, salted them generously, and remained silent as she stirred.

"What was she like?" I prompted.

Her face changed again at this question. It lost its open look and shuttered. She stirred a few moments longer. "Like the patrón," she said at last.

"How so?"

She worried her bottom lip as she withdrew the spoon from the pot. "I wouldn't say this to most people, but you seem to have a level head about the world." I glanced at the censers in the doorway. *Levelheaded* was not how I would describe myself after living inside these walls. "I think you see the world more clearly than the hacendados," she continued. "We don't have a choice when it comes to our patróns. We tolerate them. We survive them. Some have a harder time of it than others. Our patrón makes life difficult for young women who work in the house. Do you understand?"

My face must have betrayed my confusion, for with a small, frustrated noise, Paloma pivoted to blunter language. "Girls feared working in the house, near the patrón, because some of those who did became pregnant. Against their will. When the señora found out, she was furious. She said that she didn't want him leaving a trail of bastards across the countryside." Paloma set the heavy lid on the pot with a resounding clang. "She got her wish. She made sure of it."

My heartbeat echoed in my ears. I was swept back to my first day at San Isidro, when Rodolfo led me on a tour through the cold, dark house. In the dining room, he forbade me from going up to the ledge that ringed the room.

A maid fell from there once, he said.

I could not speak for shock. Not only had Paloma accused my husband of raping servants, but he and his first wife of *murdering* them.

She folded her arms across her chest, her flint-hard eyes challenging me to defy her. To lose my temper, to tell her to stop lying.

I couldn't.

For I believed her.

I sank into one of the small chairs by the kitchen table and put my head in my hands.

Mamá hated Rodolfo because of his politics. But perhaps that had cloaked something else, an instinct, an intuition. Rodolfo was not who I thought he was.

And his first wife?

Red eyes, flesh-colored claws . . .

"I've overheard the patrón talk about the Republic," Paloma said. "About abolishing the casta system. About *equality*." She snorted. "I don't think he knows what that word means. Not when he and his treat their dogs better than us."

From the moment I had woken to Paloma pounding on Andrés's door, the morning had dealt me blow after blow. Ana Luisa dead. Rodolfo returning. The voice. Andrés's loss of memory.

Now *this*.

"Why are you telling me this?" I asked weakly.

Paloma did not look up when she answered. "You said your family doesn't want you. That means you're one of us, now." Her voice grew distant, cold, as if it were coming from the mouth of a much older woman. "That means you're trapped in San Isidro, just like the rest of us. And you'll die here like the rest of us."

19

THE SHADOWS AROUND THE house grew long. The afternoon rain Andrés predicted came and filled the small central plaza of the hacienda village with mud.

I adjusted my wool shawl around my shoulders, making sure its longer end covered the basket I carried. It was still heavy with copal, though Andrés and I were now halfway through our task.

He walked a step ahead of me to the next small house and rapped on the door. It opened; warm light from inside slicked his rain-soaked shoulders, caught on the drops that fell from the rim of his hat as he dipped his chin.

He greeted the young woman at the door cordially, smiling at the baby on her hip as he introduced her to me as Belén Rodríguez. Briefly, he explained that he thought it best that all the villagers stay inside once the sun set. Belén followed Andrés's movements as he turned to me and took copal from the basket. Assessment flickered behind her eyes when they lingered on me, even as she accepted the incense Andrés offered.

I thought you would be like the other one, Paloma said. Was this woman also wondering why the wife of the patrón stood next to the witch priest in the mud and the pouring rain?

The answer to that was simple: Andrés was still injured, and I had not let him out of my sight since finally bringing him out of the green parlor at midday. There were moments he swayed on his feet; memory recall seemed to cause him intense physical pain. His frustration with himself was palpable. It simmered beneath his calm exterior, turning ever inward. I had watched over him as he napped on the terrace, and now we were preparing for nightfall.

There was something about battle that changed the way a man felt about his comrades, Papá said. Andrés and I had seen a fierce battle together and barely made it out alive. I had known him for such a short time, yet I felt bound to him. I called it loyalty. Perhaps it was something deeper.

But the villagers did not know that. As far as they knew, he was still their invincible son; the blow to his head had not touched Andrés's air of quiet authority.

Our work done, Andrés and I walked side-by-side in silence toward the capilla. He had agreed with me that spending the night alone in the house was dangerous, and that I should not endure it. With little fanfare, he decided that I would spend the night in his rooms.

This was what I had wanted, too, without knowing how to broach it. Still, I couldn't help but feel a touch scandalized by how quickly he had come to such a conclusion.

Andrés opened the door, and I immediately understood his reasoning.

There was a fire lit in the hearth and leftovers from the afternoon's meal on the small table. Paloma knelt in the corner, unfolding blankets and spreading them on the ground opposite Andrés's cot.

She looked up in surprise when I stepped over the threshold.

"What is she doing here?" she cried as Andrés entered and shut the door.

Ah. Rather than brave the small house where her mother had died, Paloma was going to spend the night under the same roof as her cousin. And Paloma's presence made mine permissible.

"I think it is clear that the situation requires unusual measures in order to ensure everyone's safety," Andrés said softly.

"But—"

"Would you want to spend the night alone in the house?" I added. It was without question that the house was unsafe. To be alone anywhere on the hacienda grounds was unsafe. I was sure that was why she was here— so that Andrés could keep her safe from whatever prowled in the darkness outside.

Paloma stared at me, somewhat aghast. She opened her mouth to speak, then met her cousin's gaze over my shoulder. Whatever look he gave her was enough to settle the matter.

We ate in relative silence. After Andrés said the blessing, Paloma asked him the occasional question about villagers and their reactions to our crepuscular visits bearing copal. She did not invite my input, so I kept to myself until it was time to prepare for sleep.

Then Andrés pointed to the cot. "Doña Beatriz, you can—"

"Absolutely not," I said.

"Don't be an idiot, Andrés."

Paloma and I met eyes. We had spoken in the same breath, our voices ringing with twin chastisement. Neither of us would let Andrés sacrifice a good night's sleep in this state, my status as the lady of the property be damned. He was outmatched two to one for stubbornness. And he knew it.

"Ya, basta," he sighed in defeat.

I moved my makeshift sleeping pallet—a bundle of blankets on a thick patterned rebozo—to a space near the door and sat, relieved that Paloma seemed to have forgiven my presence. I busied myself with taking my hair down as Andrés sat obediently on the bed at Paloma's instruction.

"Can't you do anything to heal yourself?" she asked softly. "Remember what Titi said about severe headaches, that—" Then, mid-sentence, her voice spilled into their grandmother's language.

My fingers slowed as I braided my hair. Had she been speaking castellano all this time for my sake?

Andrés made a soft noise of understanding, then touched fingertips to his temples gingerly. "If I could remember how, I would," he replied in castellano. *I lost it as a child.* Not fully, it seemed. He seemed to understand Paloma perfectly as she carried on speaking in a low voice, switching from one language to the other until she abruptly burst into tears.

Poor Paloma. I turned my body away from her and Andrés as I nestled beneath my blankets, hoping to give her some semblance of privacy. I curled into a fetal position, thinking of the nights Mamá and I spent in the narrow bed at Tía Fernanda's. How hard I sobbed—for Papá, for the loss of our life, for the loss of my future. Paloma was proud and would likely not accept spontaneous sympathy from me. But if she ever asked, I knew then it would come pouring out of me like a flood.

Presently, their conversation calmed, and slowed; I heard Paloma settle into her bundle of blankets and, after a few minutes of silence, start to snore lightly. I shifted to put my back to the wall. Though by then I had closed my eyes, sleep did not come so easily. I listened to Andrés rise and rake the embers in the fire, the brush of bare feet on the ground, the shift of fabric being folded, the strike of flint and the blooming aroma of copal. A soft shuffle back to the bed.

I slitted my eyes, peering out through a veil of lashes. Andrés lay on his bed with one hand under his cheek. The crease of pain that he had carried all day between his brows had softened at last; his chest rose and fell slowly. If he was not asleep, he soon would be.

The fire lowered to embers. Its cast dyed his face the deep orange of twilight after a storm. Shadows hollowed his cheeks and the circles beneath his eyes.

Aren't you frightened? Do you know what he is capable of?

I should be afraid of everything he did last night: calling on spirits, rising into the air. Everything I had ever heard from a pulpit or a whispered ghost story told me that witches were dangerous. They were cronies of the Devil.

Perhaps I was frightened of him. But one could fear and trust at the same time: whether because of that curl of intuition that drew me to him when he first came to San Isidro or because of the way he looked at me as if I were the sunrise at the end of a long, harrowing night, I believed he would not harm me.

These thoughts swirled through my mind as the embers died, their weight drawing me down into sleep at last.

I woke with a start. The room was silent, its dark the soft charcoal of safe places, but—

Behind me, the lock rattled. I pushed myself sharply up on my elbows, lurching away from the door. Andrés and Paloma were asleep, unaware.

Something was behind it. Something that caused a buzzing to build in the ground beneath my blankets, a persistent hum, like a far-off swarm of wasps drawing inevitably closer, closer . . .

I seized the copal censer, holding it in both hands between me and the door like a weapon.

Still the door groaned against its hinges, the whine of aging wood against a powerful winter storm. Cold seeped through cracks, reaching toward my blanket, shifting over my feet and legs like a physical weight.

"Don't you dare come in here," I hissed through gritted teeth. "Get *out*."

For the length of several heartbeats, nothing happened. I could not breathe.

Then the door settled in its frame. The cold drew back. The humming slowed. Then it, too, faded, until I could hear nothing but Andrés's and Paloma's steady breathing behind me.

I don't know how long I sat at attention, the censer in my hands, my focus honed on the door. My heart beating thickly in my throat.

Peace filled the room, settled, complete, disturbed only by the frantic pounding of my heart. It was so quiet.

Had I imagined it all?

IT WAS STILL GRAY the next morning when Paloma insisted that she fetch José Mendoza to come to the house and fix the door of the green parlor.

"The patrón is on his way, and we've wasted enough time already," she said, her tone of voice brushing Andrés's concern away as sharply as a gesture. "The house is a disaster. We have no menu. How long is he staying? Only God seems to know, and now I have to plan for everything."

She stepped outside, tying her apron strings with staccato gestures. Fingers of pale mist shrank away from her as she turned toward the village.

Andrés crossed the room in two steps and called after her from the doorway. "Do *not* go inside until I get there, do you understand?"

Paloma waved a hand dismissively. "You don't have to tell me twice," she said dryly over one shoulder. "But hurry up. I'm hungry and I won't wait forever to get into the kitchen."

Andrés sighed deeply as he watched his cousin's retreating back. A full night of sleep brought life back to his face; the look of constant pain that creased it yesterday had softened. A new look of concern settled in the line of his mouth as he looked at me pulling my shawl over my shoulders.

That concern was echoed in my own posture.

The patrón was returning tomorrow.

RODOLFO RODOLFO RODOLFO

"I've been thinking about that dream," Andrés said softly. "The one you told me about yesterday."

Flesh-colored claws, eyes burning, burning, burning . . .

"And?"

He clicked his tongue. "I should have thought of it yesterday. I need to see something before we return to the house. You don't have to accompany me, if you don't wish . . ."

"Tell me."

"The grave of Doña María Catalina."

I inhaled sharply. I had never liked graveyards. Even before I knew what it felt like to be watched by something beyond the veil of earthly creation, my skin crawled among the headstones. Long before I ever set foot on Hacienda San Isidro, I had hated the trailing sensation of being watched. I was always worried that something might follow me, tangled in my hair like smoke or stray leaves, as I walked home.

But this time, I straightened. Curled my fingers tightly around my shawl. I was battered, exhausted, and frightened, but I was the daughter of a general, and I would not back down. I would not sit in the priest's rooms alone, waiting for my fate to come to me. If Andrés thought visiting a grave could give us answers, I was ready to accompany him. "Let's be quick about it, then."

A thick carpet of dead leaves blanketed the graveyard behind the capilla. Though the mist had lifted, and the promise of sun teased warm over my face, the walk through the headstones left a cold feeling of rot in my bones.

Marble angels reached for the dying mist, their faces chipped or yellowed with age; thick lines of dust settled into the halo of statues and engravings of la Virgen. I followed a few paces behind Andrés as we wove through the statues; our shoes sank into earth still soft from the night's rain when we paused to check names, searching for the correct grave.

Seven generations of Solórzanos were interred in the shadow of the slim bell tower of the chapel. *You'll die here like the rest of us.* Would I, too, become another layer in this cemetery, rotting forever under the weight of the name Solórzano?

For every name on every stone was that of a don or doña Solórzano. Each date on the headstone a solemn reminder of how long the walls of Hacienda San Isidro had stood. *1785. 1703. 1690. 1643* . . .

"Where are your people?" I asked Andrés.

He rose from where he crouched by one of the markers, brushing away leaves to check the name. He shielded his eyes, then pointed at the low stone wall that marked the northern edge of the cemetery.

"Over there."

And he returned to his task.

Beyond the wall were more graves. No marble angels marked the earth, no grand statues of la Virgen. The divide between hacendados and the villagers extended beyond life.

"Beatriz."

I turned.

Andrés stood before a tasteful white headstone. I stopped next to him, averting my gaze from the stone until my arm brushed his, as if merely looking at the name I knew was carved there could harm me.

Doña María Catalina Solórzano de Iturrigaray y Velazco, d. 1821.

My fingers trembled as I made the sign of the cross and pressed my thumb to my lips.

Andrés cursed under his breath.

I looked up at him in surprise, hand dropping from my mouth. "What?"

He lifted a foot as if to stamp it on the grave.

"Andrés!" I gasped, seizing his arm to stop him. "Are you crazy?"

"*She* did this to my home. She did this to my family," he spat. But he set his foot down beside the grave. "Besides, it's empty earth. I can sense it," he added. A dark tremor of feeling underscored the words. "She's not here."

Her body.

It wasn't here.

The plaster crumbling and slipping beneath my fingernails. The skull grinning at me from the wall. A glint of gold in the darkness. My heartbeat throbbed in my ears. "Does that mean . . ."

"Yes."

María Catalina's body was interred in the walls of San Isidro. But—

"Who put her there?" I cried, voice pitching high. "*Why?*"

"I don't know," Andrés said quietly. "But now that I know for certain *she's* behind everything, I think I know what to do to close the circle."

IN OUR ABSENCE, MENDOZA had joined Paloma waiting for us in the courtyard, and together, all four of us stepped inside the quiet, watchful house with the caution of lost travelers seeking shelter in a cave. Would its predatory occupant return? When?

I cast a glance at the north wing, and a chill snaked down my spine. María Catalina was *there*. Someone had bricked her body into the wall and hidden the evidence.

An earthquake, or water, I can't remember which, Rodolfo had said. *I will have Mendoza look into repairs.*

"Señor Mendoza," I said, fighting to keep my voice casual as our group continued to the green parlor. "Did my husband ask you to do any repairs on the house before he left? Mend any . . . water damage?"

Mendoza cleared his throat. "No, doña. He didn't."

His voice trailed off when he saw the door to the green parlor on the floor, and the circle on the floor of the empty room beyond. He let out a low whistle. "Do I want to know, Padre?"

"Probably not," Paloma piped up from Mendoza's side. "I certainly didn't ask."

Andrés swept into the room, each of his movements sharp with anxiety. He paced around the circle twice as I picked up a broom and began sweeping the final remnants of shattered glass and broken candles out of his way; Mendoza shook his head, then he and Paloma began work on the door.

"Palomita," Andrés said. I looked up, surprised by the tenseness of his voice. "Could you please stop speaking castellano? It would help my memory if . . ." He left the sentence unfinished.

Mendoza shot Paloma a questioning look. Paloma answered with an obliging shrug, and seamlessly slipped into their grandmother's tongue as she and Mendoza positioned the door on its hinges.

I flitted in and out of the room, slowly moving pieces of furniture, forbidding Andrés from helping me as I dragged in a heavy rolled rug. By then, Paloma and Mendoza had left. Andrés stood at the edge of the circle, fingertips at his temples, eyes closed. Shoulders tight.

He began to pray. First in Latin, then not. When the words *María Catalina* slipped between one portion of Andrés's prayer, an unpleasant hum built in the back of my skull and spiked into pain. I winced, closed my eyes, and placed my hands over my ears as he continued.

I was glad I did.

A shriek split the room, white and bleeding with fury, stretching breathlessly, impossibly long, raking over me like talons. I cried out. My eyes snapped open; I half expected to see the window shutters splintering and shattering from the sheer rage that was flooding the room.

Andrés had not moved. Fingertips pressed to temples. Shoulders wound with tension. I could see his lips move through continued prayer, though I could not hear him over the noise.

The shriek cut off.

The room was still. It was the emptiness of a tomb, airless, its belly filled with the absence of life rather than the presence of silence.

Andrés released a long breath and rolled his shoulders back. No power hummed from the circle at his feet. No buzzing filled the back of my skull.

He looked over his shoulder at me. Despite the exhaustion in his posture, the stubble on his jaw, a fey sort of victory burned in his shadowed face. "I did it." He took a deep, shaky breath. "She's confined to the house again."

Behind him, a pair of red lights winked from the corner of the room, then vanished.

Terror shot through me, lodging itself in my throat.

Yes, Andrés had succeeded. He had muscled the darkness back into the house and closed the circle.

I did not feel the same victory. The danger was contained, yes, but the fact remained that Ana Luisa was dead. We knew that the body of María Catalina was in the wall and that her spectral rage fed the activity of the darkness. But we did not know who put her body there.

Nor why.

Rodolfo returned in the morning.

The closing of the circle was but a slap of plaster on a crack in a swollen dam. Water surged behind it, ready to burst forth; the crack grew wider and wider with each passing hour.

And we still stood directly in the path it would flood.

20

ANDRÉS TOLD ME THAT while Paloma and Mendoza were fixing the door in the green parlor, Mendoza had invited her to stay with him and his daughter. His eldest daughter had married away to Hacienda Alcantarilla in the spring, and there was ample room in their home for Paloma to stay as long as she needed. When they left, it was to move her belongings across the village to Mendoza's house.

Which meant that without Paloma present, spending another night in the safety of the capilla's rooms was no longer appropriate.

I would have to sleep alone.

Heavy rain opened over the valley midafternoon and continued with silent flashes of lightning. As the gloomy skies darkened further still at twilight, Andrés arranged censers in a particular pattern around my bedchamber, especially near the door and window, and lit them. The darkness followed his movements closely, drawing back with a soft hiss when he

began to murmur a prayer. He lifted his chin, squared off with the darkness, and closed the prayer with a territorial stamp of the heel.

The darkness shrank away.

He turned back to me, victory glinting in his face as it had earlier. He
was recovering from his injury. Perhaps I would be safe tonight after all.

"Have you heard any voices since this morning?" he asked.

Tightness gathered in my throat, thinking of the red eyes appearing
behind him in the green parlor, of Andrés's intensity when he told me to
cast out the voice.

I shook my head.

He must have watched all of this cross my face, for he said, "I fear for
you. Your dream . . . it is evidence that your guard was down, left open to
that. It is dangerous."

I did not have to ask why. "How dangerous?" I breathed instead. If I
were in danger of losing my mind, what could I do?

You'll die here like the rest of us.

Andrés worried his bottom lip, an echo of Paloma's expression when
she weighed how much to tell me. How much of the truth I could stomach
as I faced the inevitability of night. And with that inevitability, the threat
of fear so profound it could drive me to madness.

"My grandmother once brought me to a house that she determined was
making its inhabitants irritable. It brought the marriage of the couple who
lived there to the edge of ruin. They loathed each other by the time she
arrived. These forces have the power to pry your mind open and enter it.
Shift what you see, how you feel. Shift your reality. I am afraid . . . I am
afraid to leave you alone." He rubbed a hand over his face, his palm scraping over the shadow of stubble. "Do you want me to stay?"

The meaning underscoring his tone was clear: he asked because he
wanted to stay. Something in the determined placement of his feet, or the
way his attention curled around me, calm, sentry-like, and watchful, made
it clear that he had no intention of leaving me alone.

My God, there was nothing more I wanted. "Yes," I breathed. But . . .

The room around me was bathed in flickering candlelight. The boudoir, my vanity, the plush bed that was so absurdly different from Andrés's hard cot. The very air was imbued with an intimacy that spending the night next to each other in the green parlor did not have. Nor even Andrés's austere rooms after the disastrous exorcism. We had fled there in desperation and collapsed defeated.

This felt intentional.

He met my eyes. Though his face was carefully impassive, there was something there that told me he saw what I saw. He, too, felt how close to a cliff's edge our sudden, desperate friendship danced.

He still chose to stay.

I took some linens out of the dresser and placed them in his arms, then changed out of sight on the far side of the dresser. When I finished, I found him sitting on my vanity's stool, which he had taken and positioned next to the door. The blankets and pillow I had supplied lay in a neat pile, ig-nored. Didn't he intend to use them?

I glanced up at him: a rosary in hand, his attention fixed straight ahead, deliberately diverted away from me.

Perhaps not yet.

I sat on the edge of my bed, then loosened my hair from its knot and braided it. I, too, kept my attention shyly averted from the other person in the room. If I thought I felt his gaze dance over to me, linger, then dart away, I ignored it out of propriety.

Instead, I let the quiet of the room sink into my tired, aching bones. I imagined myself plaiting copal smoke into my hair, weaving in Andrés's protective powers, the sound of his low voice beginning the rosary. When I curled beneath the blankets, I was asleep within minutes.

For a time, I slept dreamless and deep. Then, red eyes appeared in the dark; I dreamed of being pushed from a high place, and falling, falling, falling . . .

I woke with a start, heart pounding. Sunlight poured over the bed from the window. A chorus of birds sang outside, lilting up from somewhere in the garden. Everything had a crystal, clean sheen, as if I had blinked water from my eyes and were seeing clearly for the first time.

"Buenos días," a low, musical voice said.

I looked to the doorway.

Andrés was gone.

The woman with the corn silk hair sat where he had been, her chin resting in her palm as she watched me. A golden necklace glinted coyly beneath her lace collar.

María Catalina.

Dread washed over me. Had she been sitting there, watching me sleep, the whole night? Her skin gleamed like candle wax in the light; then she grinned, and whatever color her eyes had been before, now they turned red. In an instant, her skin transformed, dried and desiccated into leather, and her teeth grew long and needle sharp.

She sprang toward me, arms outstretched—

I woke with a strangled cry. *Truly* woke this time. My heart hammered as I sucked breath in, in, in, my ribs straining from the effort.

Dawn paled the sky outside the windows. It was morning. Andrés was still at his post, his long legs stretched before him, his head leaning against the door. His chest rose and fell rhythmically.

The rosary had slipped from his fingers to the floor, the crucifix face-down on the floorboards.

The candles had burned down. The copal was not thick enough.

I rose with trembling hands and lit the censers and the candles. Yes, it was nearly dawn, another night was nearly over. But that did not mean I was safe.

When is nightfall? When is day?

I shook my head to clear it, and quietly scooped up Andrés's rosary. I kissed the crucifix, a reflexive apology for letting it touch the floor. I kept it curled in my palm as I put my back to the wall opposite Andrés.

He woke as I slid to the floor, drawing my knees to my chest.

"You all right?" Though his voice was rough with sleep, he was instantly alert, scanning the room for danger.

Did you not sleep well last night? Perhaps you dreamed it. I used to have terrible nightmares as a child. Juana's voice twined through my head. Juana, who refused to believe me when I said someone was buried in the wall. Did she not know the grave in the capilla was empty?

All I could see was a golden necklace around a skeleton's broken neck, glinting through clouds of dust and crumbling bricks.

I shook my head, pressing my back firmly against the wall as he approached and sat next to me.

I offered him the rosary. His knees were also drawn up to his chest, his shoulder so close to mine they touched when he took the beads.

The touch of hands can be an innocent thing. Andrés seizing my hand in the dark: that was the touch of human connection burned pure, a bastion against fear.

Then there was *this*.

The brush of Andrés's fingertips against my palm sparked a flush of intimacy, a rush of heat deep in my chest.

It was a sin, and I knew it, and suddenly I realized that I didn't care.

For if sin was all I had standing between myself and the darkness, I would take it.

THE SERVANTS LINED UP to greet Rodolfo, just as they had when I first arrived. I lingered in the doorway of the house's courtyard, feeling oddly detached as I watched. The sky was cloudless, blazing lapis, the air crisp and fresh after the night's hard rain. It was a perfect imitation

of the first day I had set foot on San Isidro's soil, the day I had unknow-
ingly handed my soul over to the house and its demons. I half expected to
see myself step from the carriage, a cloud of silks shadowed by a wide-
brimmed hat, placing my delicate city shoes on the cursed earth.

You don't belong here.

I leaped away from the doorframe.

No one was in the courtyard. I did not have to turn to know that.
Paloma was with the others in a row next to José Mendoza; Andrés was in
the capilla, avoiding sunlight while his head healed.

Cast it out, Andrés said.

But because I did, because I left my mind open for spirits to pry open,
I knew who that voice belonged to.

I heard his wife died of typhus. I heard she was kidnapped by insurgents.

What had truly happened to her? I fought the urge to turn around and
stare at the house, fought to keep away the image of Rodolfo's name in
blood dripping from the stucco. Who would bury a body that way?

The hairs on the back of my neck lifted as a cool breeze brushed over
my shoulders, coming from the direction of the house.

If I died in this house, would I, too, be bricked into a wall?

If I were killed in this house, would I, too, linger in an unholy way, and
watch the perverted fairy tale repeat itself as the gleaming prince brought
a new wife home? Watch her emerge from the carriage, all shining silks
and a face open with trust, only to be brought to my waiting jaws like a
sacrifice?

A girlish giggle lilted behind me, toward me, carried by the breeze over
my shoulder and into the courtyard before me.

You'll die here.

Curling my hands into fists, I banished the voice from my thoughts as
forcefully as if I were slamming a door shut: with both arms, all my heart,
and all my anger.

I whirled on the house and met its gaze head-on.

If I died in San Isidro, so be it. Perhaps Paloma's bleak, oracular words had a power that bound me to this land. To this house. Perhaps one day I would stop fighting the voices and give myself over to madness at last.

But it would not be today.

I was the daughter of a general, and I was not done fighting yet.

"Behave yourself," I snapped, the words loaded with a threat.

The house did not reply.

I turned my back on it and walked down the easy slope of the path. Rodolfo stepped from the carriage and began to greet the villagers.

His hair was bright bronze in the sunlight, gleaming like a cathedral retablo. He was perfect. Of course he was. He was Rodolfo, and he was full of promise and light.

RODOLFO RODOLFO RODOLFO RODOL—

Or was he?

His face was smooth and calm; if he noticed Ana Luisa's absence, he gave no sign of it. But how could he not, when she had lived and worked on this hacienda all of her life? All of *his* life?

He and his treat their dogs better than us.

Did they mean so little to him?

"Querida!" he cried, and strode toward me, arms outstretched. I took his hands and offered my cheek to kiss, keeping my face still and angelic to hide the revulsion that bubbled beneath my skin at the brush of his beard, at his dry lips.

"Welcome home." I smiled my brightest as I looked up at him, blinking and shielding my eyes from the midmorning sun. "How was the road?"

"It felt longer than ever," he said, taking me by the shoulders.

"As was the wait for you," I said. "Were you able to deliver my letters to my mother?"

His smile faded.

"I'm sorry," he said, putting a hand on my cheek. My spine stiffened, but I focused on the disappointment I felt to keep myself from flinching away from his touch. It was not hard. It pulled me down, its weight like wet wool. "She would not see me," Rodolfo added. "I sent the letters through a messenger instead, and though I sent him back daily for a reply, none came."

Mamá would not listen to my pleas to come to San Isidro. And what if she had? San Isidro was in no state for her to arrive.

Not yet.

"Don't worry," Rodolfo said softly. His voice crawled under my skin. "She will come around. Perhaps all she needs is time."

I nodded, then lifted my eyes to meet his. He was searching my face, looking for something; a slight crease formed between his brows.

"You're not wearing your hat," he said, his voice pitched strangely.

I wasn't. Nor had I been for days at a time, not in the garden, not as I slept on the terrace in full sunlight in the afternoons, desperate for rest and respite. I had barely spent any time in my bedchamber out of fear, and that was the only place where I had a mirror in the house. Without Rodolfo around to remind me, I had completely neglected my complexion.

And I knew what happened when I did. When I was careless. I fought to keep my face still, though panic rose like acid in my throat.

You're one of us, now, Paloma said.

Rodolfo had not even noticed Ana Luisa's death.

If he had it in him to kill his first wife, who was criollo pale, waxy as a doll, then what of me? What if he saw me as just as expendable as the villagers? As the maids?

I could not believe I had let myself slip. What would Mamá say?

I waved one hand, a delicate dismissal of his concern. "Oh, how my mother would harangue me for how careless I have been while preparing the gardens." If my mother had any idea what was truly going on at Hacienda San Isidro, she might say many things. If she began with *I told you I was right, you married a monster,* I would not blame her in the least. "Come inside. I'll get it and show you where I put the furniture."

The house hummed at Rodolfo's return. It shifted around me like a colt ready to bolt; if Rodolfo felt it at all, his face remained infuriatingly impassive.

After my brief tour of all the things I had accomplished in his absence—an underwhelming litany, if I were to be frank, since my primary concern had been staying alive—Rodolfo met with José Mendoza. To my relief, he spent most of the day with the foreman, breaking only to have lunch with me on the terrace. I made sure to wear my thickest hat, as if that could change anything now, and listened as he glowed about how well the pulque was selling. How the economy was beginning to settle at last. I weighed this, thinking of how my father said that at the end of the war, the insurgents didn't even have guns and fought with stones. No one had money coming out of the war, yet somehow, my husband did.

I started when Rodolfo mentioned something about the hacendados of Haciendas Ocotepec and Ometusco coming for dinner. "What did you say, querido?"

"Didn't you see my last letter?"

I pasted a smile on my face. I had not read it. The news that he was returning was enough to occupy my mind in the wake of the failed exorcism and Ana Luisa's death.

"Ah yes," I said. "It had slipped my mind in the excitement of your return. I look forward to welcoming them into our home."

I did not, not in the least. After lunch, Rodolfo rejoined José Mendoza; the minute he was out of sight of the house, I ripped off my hat and rolled my dress's sleeves up to my elbows. "Paloma!"

PALOMA AND I WORKED in hurried silence, each of us doing the jobs of two people as we prepared an elaborate meal for eight. Rodolfo insisted that if a priest was on the property, it was appropriate that he join us for dinner as well as Juana, the two hacendados, and their wives. My mouth soured at the idea of Doña María José seeing me *quite darker* than I had been when she first met me, but I shoved this to the back of my mind.

"How is Padre Andrés?" I asked Paloma in a spare moment where I stoked the fire, relishing its warmth on my face. The winds had risen, and though the afternoon was as bright as the morning, the air had a bite of chill of the oncoming winter.

She made a noncommittal noise as she chopped onions. "His head still aches."

"Did you say to him—"

"Yes, I told him you said he shouldn't feel he has to come." Paloma shrugged. My skin felt like it was too tight at the thought of him and Rodolfo facing each other across the dinner table. Would Rodolfo realize what I was trying to do with the house? Would he peel away my thinly affected adoration of him and see how the priest had as powerful a hold over me as he did the villagers?

For it was true: somewhere between sleeping and waking, suspended in pale, quiet dawns, Andrés had slipped into my heart.

Perhaps it was that the thick walls my mother claimed I had built around myself in the wake of Papá's death were nothing to a witch. Perhaps it was how he was strength to lean on, safety in a storm. Perhaps it was that, despite all he was capable of—rising into the air like an angel riding a cloud of darkness, bringing peace to a room with a prayer and his raspy voice—he, too, admitted he was afraid. He, too, seized my hand in the dark. Needed my shoulder against his until dawn.

"He refused to listen. I was able to make him sleep more, though. That's victory enough for one day."

She returned to chopping. I sighed, staring at the fire.

"Has he always been like this?" I asked.

"Hmm?"

"Stubborn as a donkey."

This startled a bright peal of laughter from Paloma. It took me by surprise. In my mind she was a serious woman, burdened with too many sorrows from a young age. Perhaps she was. But that did not mean she was without humor, nor without a laugh that rang like church bells on a feast day.

"Doña, you don't know the half of it," she said, her own smile a sharp echo of Andrés's. "Titi used to smack him upside the head for trying to play the hero when simply doing what was expected of him was enough. He wanted to be an insurgent, but she would have none of it." She wiped a trickle of sweat from her brow with the back of one hand. "She knew he was a boy made of gunpowder. That letting him play with fire would be his end."

"He said it was his mother's wish for him to become a priest," I said, brushing soot from my skirts as I rose.

"It was Titi's too. She knew it was best," Paloma said with a nod. "I thought she was crazy, sending someone like him into a horde of priests. But she was right. It straightened him out. It gave him peace. And it gives him the perfect role to play while serving the pueblo like Titi did. He purifies houses our way after giving final rites to the dying. He deals with troubles the other priests can't see, or won't." She grew quiet. A long moment passed as she stared at the chopped onions. She sniffed; hastily brushed at her tearing eyes with her forearm. "But he doesn't go looking for trouble, not anymore. Not unless people bring trouble to him."

Though it was clear her cousin was several years older than her, I suddenly understood that Andrés was a younger brother to Paloma in all but name. And that if he were hurt any more on San Isidro's property, more than he already had been, Paloma would never forgive me.

"I'm sorry," I said. "I was afraid."

Paloma shrugged. Apology accepted, in her own brusque way. "He would have come poking around here anyway, banishment or no. It was only a matter of time. It's our pueblo who suffer most because of it, after all."

She was right. Her mother had died because of the darkness. She and the other villagers lived in fear because of it. But why had Andrés been banished?

I opened my mouth to ask, but Paloma interrupted me. "Now get out of here," she said crisply. "I'll do the rest. The patrón won't want his wife smelling like onion and smoke when the other hacendados arrive."

I obeyed and went straight to my bedchamber. There were more people in the house than there had been in all my weeks here; people Paloma had summoned from the village dusted and arranged furniture. They steered clear of the green parlor—whether by instinct or instruction, I did not know.

My bedchamber was still in shambles from the night before: a sea of candles and censers greeted me. The last thing I wanted to do was clear them away, but I inhaled deeply and set to work.

I washed in cold water, letting it shock me into wakefulness. I didn't want to wash my hair—there was not enough time for it to properly dry— but Paloma was right about the smell of smoke. I dried it as best I could, and let it hang down my back as I dressed in silk and pearl earrings for the first time since Rodolfo left.

Afternoon sun streamed in through the window, reflecting off the mirror and filling the room with light. I sat before my vanity and studied my reflection for the first time in days. It was as I feared: the sun had deepened my face. In the capital, I had kept my complexion as fair as I could through hats and avoiding sunlight. I was never as pale as Tía Fernanda's daughters, nor as Mamá, for even the palest parts of me had a sallow cast. Now, the high points of my face had deepened to light brown, bronzed by sunlight in a way that made my hair look even blacker.

You're nearly as lovely as Doña María Catalina, though quite darker.

My mouth twisted. So I was.

I reached for my powder.

21

WHEN I FLOATED DOWN the stairwell of the house, perfumed and powdered pale as an apparition, Rodolfo met me at the foot of the stairs with a beautiful smile.

He was standing with his back to the door of the north wing. Could he not feel the cold? It seeped into my bones with each step I took closer to him, closer to the north wing.

I let him kiss my cheek. His lips were warm.

Did the callousness of guilt inure him to the cold? To the madness that sank its claws into me as deeply as the chill?

I met his smile with my own, pasting it firmly across my cheeks as we went to the green parlor to welcome our guests.

Mamá said Papá was so charismatic he could charm guns out of the hands of his enemies. I believed it until I saw him led away from our house at bayonet point. Perhaps he was not quite that charismatic. But he had a way of talking through a room that somehow drew even the most reserved members of a party out of themselves. A seed of that still lived in me; though it was barricaded behind thick walls of pride, I drew on it now as I entertained Doña María José Moreno and Doña Encarnación de Piña y Cuevas. We sat on one side of the room, bathed in delicate candlelight, our skirts spread around us like the petals of exotic flowers. Their husbands and mine drank on the other side of the room, discussing crops and sheep. The fine European glassware in their hands and the silver candelabras from the capital gleamed in the glow of the fire. From the look of the room, one could almost believe we were in the capital.

Almost.

The presence of Andrés and Juana was blatant evidence of just how far from civilization this parlor was. They were stiff islands of silence each apart from the groups. As hostess, I had ensured that Andrés would be seated strategically on the rug that covered the faint witch's glyphs whose shadow still remained ghostlike on the flagstones, in case it flared from the energy of too many people. He sat with a Bible on his knee, his face drawn and shadowed, pretending to listen to the men's talk of pulque. Opposite him was Juana, his reflection in discomfort as Doña María José talked of further furnishing the house.

"Oh, I completely understand," she cooed when I apologized for the sparse decorations. "It was empty for years. I remember when Atenógenes and I took the house from his brother, oh, it must be forty years ago now. It was in such a state of neglect. The work it took to bring it back to life!"

Over her shoulder, I caught sight of Juana scowling. She made no effort to disguise it.

"At least now, with the war over, it is easier to get things from the capital," Doña Encarnación added, nodding sagely before launching into a discussion of the benefits of lining the courtyards with Puebla talavera.

My eyes flicked to Andrés. His face was a perfect mask of interest as the men discussed rumors of Church reform and lightly mocked him for knowing as little about it as they did.

I wished I could whisk him away from all these people. For a hot, swift moment, I hated this room and everyone in it but him. I wanted to burn San Isidro to the ground and build it up from the foundation, a sanctuary for the two of us.

Mercifully, we moved to the dining room not long after. I was terrified that I had ruined dinner, that the hacendados and their wives would turn their noses up at what I had spent hours preparing with Paloma. That terror—unlike so many others in the house—turned out to be unfounded.

"You must give our compliments to Ana Luisa," Doña María José said, sipping her wine with a flourish.

"She's dead."

Heads turned to Juana, for it was she who had spoken. Her posture was relaxed, too relaxed, and her words slurred ever so slightly.

She was drunk.

I shot a swift look at Rodolfo. His jaw was tight as he stared at his sister. I had to intervene before she caused any damage—to her reputation or ours alike.

"Doña María José, I'm so sorry to bear this news," I said softly. "Ana Luisa passed away recently. It was sudden, and quite a shock to lose someone so beloved to our family."

The hacendados' wives made sympathetic sounds; their men nodded solemnly, following Andrés's example in crossing themselves and sending words to heaven for Ana Luisa.

"Her daughter, Paloma, is taking her place as head of the household," I said. "Despite the tragedy, I think we can all agree she rose to the occasion marvelously."

More sounds of agreement, and the energy in the room relaxed. I made to catch Rodolfo's eye and failed. He dabbed his mouth with his napkin, but he fixed a cold look on Juana, who swayed slightly as she worked through her dinner.

Crisis averted. Dinner was nearly through. Rodolfo had always said country socializing never went into the small hours of the morning like in the capital. Depending on how much the men drank and talked, the whole evening could be over in an hour or two. The hacendados would leave, Andrés and Juana would leave, and then . . . it would be Rodolfo and me in the house. Alone.

I swallowed, laughing airily at some joke Don Atenógenes made. I turned to Andrés as if to ask him a question. He looked a touch nauseous; he had barely touched his food. I pursed my lips, then froze—

The chair next to him was meant to be empty.

It wasn't.

The woman from my dream sat there. Gray silks and a golden necklace gleamed in the candlelight as she perched her sharp chin in her hands and gazed down the table at Rodolfo, thoroughly engrossed with each of his gestures.

María Catalina, the first Doña Solórzano, looked so painfully real, so flesh and blood, it sent a dagger of terror through my heart.

As if she heard my heart slam against my rib cage, her head snapped to me, avian sharp, and she caught my eye with her own glowing red ones. My chest contracted, so tight it was akin to a spasm, as she grinned savagely at me. It was too wide, with too many teeth, too long teeth, and—

She vanished.

Gooseflesh rolled up my arms; an iciness poured into the room, one so profound it was all I could do to keep my teeth from chattering.

Yet the conversation carried on. Doña María José laughed along with Rodolfo, opening her mouth and revealing half-chewed rice and pork; Juana shot her a murderous look and slumped glumly in her chair.

Did none of them see? Could none of them feel it? I set my fork down. It clattered onto my plate; I quickly put my hands in my lap to conceal their trembling.

When Doña María José expressed her concern at my shaking, I forced a broad smile.

"Only a chill," I said. "The house can be terribly drafty at times."

Andrés shot me a concerned look; I refused to acknowledge it. I kept my peace for the remainder of the meal, answering questions only when they were directed at me, watching as Juana sabotaged every attempt to draw her into the conversation with brusque replies.

I should have found her retorts excruciating. Rodolfo certainly did: the more strained the expressions of our guests became, the more his jaw tightened. The colder his eyes grew.

It washed over me in dull waves of noise. My attention was consumed by how the house shifted around us, waking and stretching as the night deepened. By my own heartbeat, its staccato and persistent drum just below my ear.

The house hated this charade of normalcy. Its loathing seeped through the walls, tangible and thick as mud. I waded through it as I followed the guests from dining room to parlor for nightcaps in a haze; everything moved too slowly, dragged by the thickness of the cold, the weight of the house's watching.

It was all I could do to make myself obey as Rodolfo waved me over to join him in bidding good night to the guests. I kissed their rouged cheeks dutifully, echoing their empty compliments with my own empty gratitude, echoing Rodolfo's promise that we would join them at their haciendas. I let Rodolfo lead me back to the parlor on his arm.

Andrés sat with the Bible closed on his knee. Juana was opposite him as she had been before, glowering at the fireplace.

Rodolfo released me suddenly. He crossed the room in three strides and seized his sister by the arm, yanking her to her feet.

Andrés rose to his feet in surprise. "Don Rodol—"

"You beast," Juana spat, cutting him off. "Let me go." Rodolfo ignored them both and dragged Juana out of the parlor, kicking the door shut behind him.

It bounced off the doorway, swinging open an inch or two into the hall.

"I am at the end of my rope." Rodolfo's voice carried easily into the parlor.

"So hang yourself with it," Juana spat.

"It will be a miracle if they do not immediately tell the whole district Juana Solórzano is a drunk and a whore." Rodolfo raised his voice to speak over her. "A miracle if I marry you off and get you the hell out of my house."

"Father said the house was—"

The smack of palm on cheek. I jumped; Andrés and I locked gazes, eyes wide in horror.

"Do not ever dare to call him that in my presence again," Rodolfo roared. "You and I both know he is no father of yours, and I will no longer tolerate your lying bastard tongue. You will change your behavior and act as befits the station we pretend you deserve, or so help me God, I will throw you out and make sure you inherit nothing of his honest work. *Get out of my sight.*"

Juana's boots struck the flagstones, sharp, determined, leading to the front door. She slammed it shut behind her.

Surprise brought a tinge of color to Andrés's wan face. If what Rodolfo said was true—that Juana was a bastard, that she and Rodolfo did not share the same father—it was as much a surprise to him as it was to me.

The sound of Rodolfo's shoes striking the flagstones drew near; hastily, Andrés and I both sat in the chairs closest to us. I seized some needlework. Andrés opened the Bible and began reading in the middle of a sentence. I focused on rethreading the needle as Rodolfo entered.

I lifted my head, keeping an innocent look pasted on my face. Rodolfo seemed as calm as if he had been strolling through the garden with his sister, not shouting obscenities at her and threatening to throw her out of the house. The dying fire cast him in a soft, reddish glow; the only signs he had been angry were the twitch of a muscle in his jaw and a single lock of hair falling into his face. This he brushed aside in a smooth, controlled movement.

He was Janus-faced, my husband. A creature of rage and violence on one side, a serene, gilded prince on the other. He was a staunch defender of the Republic and casta abolitionist who raped women who worked on his property.

I could not trust him. Either side of him.

I could not anger him either. Too many women had died in this house for me to test his patience.

There was nothing I could do as Andrés, my only protection, stood and bid good night to Rodolfo.

"Yes, I think it best we retire," Rodolfo agreed, turning to him. "I have had a long day of travel."

I rose, shooting Andrés a look from behind my husband's back.

Don't leave, I longed to cry out. I was sure he could read it on my face, in the desperate glint of my eyes in the firelight, as he nodded farewell to me.

No. But there was no reason for him to stay.

"Buenas noches, doña." A turn of the shoulder, and he departed.

My last defense gone.

From somewhere in the hall, a trill of dissonant laughter echoed. How long the night before me stretched, a black maw without beginning or end. I now stood alone in the parlor with Rodolfo, surrounded by walls that had once borne his name in fresh blood. Walls that still hummed with thick hatred for my presence, that watched my every move.

Over the course of my time at San Isidro, I had learned the different tastes of my fear: the sickening awareness that I was being watched. The dread of the sentient cold sweeping through the house, the spears of terror at a flash of red eyes in the dark.

The fear that rooted my feet to the floor as I stared at Rodolfo's back was different. It was new.

I now knew what it tasted like to be truly trapped.

22

Rodolfo stared into the fire. His hands were clasped behind his back, and he worked a golden signet ring on his left hand with the right, lost in thought.

I sat, my needlework limp in my hands. There was no more use in pretending I had been counting stitches, that my attention was occupied by anything but awareness of Andrés's presence passing through the gates of the courtyard. The moment he did, the weight of the darkness shifted. It twitched, first here, then there, as if shaking off an irritating fly, and refocused on the only two people left in the house.

It coiled around us, darkness thickening with each passing moment. A chill crept under the closed door and drew near, slinking across the floor with the sinuous determination of a centipede. Closer, closer, snaking around my ankles.

Beatriz, Beatriz . . .

My heart stopped.

"Come, querida," Rodolfo said sharply. "I'm tired."

I stowed my needlework with trembling hands. "Yes, you must be exhausted."

He grunted in agreement and held out his arm to me. I rose and took it, biting the inside of my cheek as he set a firm kiss on my hairline.

I wanted to throw him off. To run—but where? I had nowhere to go.

I followed him out of the parlor and into the dark hall.

Paloma had left it illuminated by candelabras. I told her she must do so, but also to depart the house as soon as she could and leave the washing up in the kitchen for the morning. I was glad she had, though the opening and closing of the front door had extinguished a few of the candles.

Or had it?

The light from the candles barely penetrated the black stretching before us. At the end of it was the staircase to our bedchamber, but also the doorway to the north wing.

Rodolfo walked confidently down the hall, taking me with him. The cold parted around him like water, catching me in its wake. It watched me gasping for breath from every corner, from the rafters, from within the walls.

The hairs on the back of my neck stood on end.

She was here.

Beatriz . . .

"I think you did very well tonight," Rodolfo said.

Beatriz, Beatriz . . .

The closer we grew to the north wing, the more the barriers I put up against it threatened to split like the skin of overripe fruit. I could not keep that voice from slipping under my skin like a knife.

"Oh?" I said, hoping my voice sounded light rather than strained. I should have kept my eyes straight ahead, or better yet, fixed them on my feet, but I swept the darkness before me. As if seeing could help me defend myself. I was raw and vulnerable, a lamb before slaughter.

And the house knew it.

"Yes. I think Doña Encarnación and Doña María José were rightly impressed with your hosting," he continued. "I do think, however, that . . . some things need to change around here."

Beatriz, Beatriz . . .

We drew near to the staircase. As we took the first step, my eyes drifted to the doorway leading to the north wing.

There, in the hall, a body lay facedown on the floor, clothed in ripped, moth-eaten rags. It was pale, streaked with blackened blood from a wound in its back. I shouldn't have been able to see it in the darkness of the hall, but there it was, clear as day.

Someone had been killed.

I jumped, colliding with Rodolfo, who reached out for the banister to balance himself.

"What?"

"Do you see that?"

"See what?"

I looked to his face—the creases of concern deepened with shadow—and back to the hall.

The hall was empty.

"Oh, a mouse." My voice came out so high it nearly cracked. Rodolfo's expression deepened to a frown. "I'm jumpy because it's so cold in here, querido," I babbled as he led me up the stairs. "It's quite drafty, isn't it?"

"I don't think so." He reached to his collar to loosen it. "If anything, it's too warm. Keeping a fire like that in that small parlor on a night as mild as this was too much. You must speak to Ana Luisa about that."

I nearly tripped over the next stair, stunned. *Ana Luisa is dead*, I wanted to shout. *I told you.* I wanted to seize him by the arm. I wanted to scream at him, to shame him. How could he not remember? How could he not care?

But the cold paralyzed me. It clawed at me as Rodolfo and I ascended, as if it wanted to draw me down, down, down . . .

As we reached the top of the stairs, I glanced over my shoulder.

The body lay at the foot of the stairs. It had moved. It *was* moving. It lifted one arm—half bone, half rotting flesh—and seized the first pillar of the banister. It hauled itself up a step and raised its head to grin at me.

It was a skull; like its arm, shreds of flesh clung to it, and matted hair stuck to its crown with blackened blood. Lidless, empty eye sockets locked on me.

Then I blinked, and it vanished.

Cold sweat slicked the small of my back. Rodolfo was saying something about the decoration of the upstairs as he led me into the room that I had made a study, and then into the bedroom. I wasn't listening. I was stunned, my heart hammering violently against my ribs, my eyes peeled wide.

I was going to die in this house.

I was going to shatter into a thousand pieces in the dark, crushed by the cold, by the agonizing malice of the watching, the knowing. I would die.

"Don't you think?" Rodolfo was saying as he closed the door to the bedchamber behind us.

None of the candles were lit. I ignored him and seized the first box of matches I could find. I was aware of him watching me as I lit them on the table of my vanity; slowly, that awareness drew me back into myself. I could see the tremble in my hand, the frightened hunch of my shoulders. I could feel the concern in his posture.

Concern was dangerous. He was dangerous.

"So many candles, right before bed." There was a light laugh in his voice.

"I . . . I was so lonely without you, you see," I sputtered. I did not turn to face him but straightened. In the mirror, the light of the candles was reflected and expanded; beyond the line of my shoulder, Rodolfo was a dark silhouette, moving closer, closer, closer—

He took my arm.

I whirled to face him. He lifted my hand to his face and kissed the soft skin on the inside of my wrist.

An ancient instinct lifted in the back of my skull and sent a ripple of panic through my body.

I was prey. I was trapped.

"I was lonely too." His voice was low, a rumble in his chest as he took me by the waist and pressed me to his body.

I needed to run.

I pushed against his chest. He did not release me but instead buried his face in my hair, kissing it, and moving to my neck.

I needed to throw him off, to wrench away. But I was nowhere near as strong as him—his hold on my body was like iron, and his shoulders curled around me in easy dominance.

"Querido, not tonight," I breathed. My voice was strangled. He kept kissing my neck anyway. I imagined him growing fangs, long needlelike fangs, too many for his mouth, and flesh-colored claws, and—"Rodolfo. No."

He loosened slightly, gazing down at me. If the intent of him was to look amorously at me, the candlelight shattered the effect: shadows emphasized the depth of his eye sockets, making them seem too deep, almost hollow—

I pushed him away.

He frowned, tightening his hold on my wrist. No. He could not become angry. He could turn on me in moments, he could—

"It is my time of the month," I sputtered, forcing a smile to stretch my lips wide over the lie. My blood had come two weeks ago. Early, to my displeasure. Mamá once said the same used to happen to her in times of distress; if my experiences of the last weeks did not amount to *distress*, then I didn't know what to call them. "It is quite uncomfortable, you know."

Please. Please. I don't know where I sent the prayer, but it was received.

Rodolfo's face realigned in a swift fall; he placed a soft kiss on my forehead and released me. "Of course."

Of course he did not question. Men do not trouble themselves with women's bodies, save when they can be of use to serve or to sate them.

I did not relax.

Not as I prepared my toilet and loosened my still-damp hair from its knot, not as I fussed over my undergarments in the small chamber adjoining our room in a half-hearted attempt to maintain my lie. Not as I returned to the room and saw he had extinguished all the candles and already lay down in bed.

It was too dark. This was not a natural dark. It was too thick. It curled too intimately over the bed. I needed copal. I stepped toward my vanity; the floorboards creaked under my bare feet. I could not—

"Leave it," Rodolfo murmured, half asleep. "I can't sleep with light."

I froze. Should I try to light the copal, or would that irritate him? It was the only thing I had, the one piece of safety.

"Come to bed," he said.

My feet were like lead as I trod across the floorboards and slipped into bed. I lay stiffly on my back, neither moving toward him nor away.

He drifted off immediately. The rise and fall of his chest was rhythmic, slow. So incongruous with the drumming of my pulse in my ears as I stared up at the wooden rafters.

Somewhere between one blink and the next, I tripped into uneasy dreaming.

The air thickened with smoke. I was in my house in the capital, my father's house. Red light leaped and danced around me, wild as a tempest, tearing at the dark plumes. The house was on fire; I knew with the perfect, terrible certainty of dreaming that Papá and Mamá were deep in the house. They were in danger.

I called for them, but smoke choked me, swallowing my screams, slinking tight around my throat like a clawed hand. I stumbled forward, but my legs were too heavy. My head was too heavy. The floor came up to meet me and I was pinned to the floorboards, flames licking through their cracks from beneath, smoke clouding my vision. I had to get to my parents. I had to. But I could not move.

Somewhere in the house, a door slammed.

I wrenched myself awake. In this house, in San Isidro, I sucked in lung-fuls of air crisp and free of smoke. But that air *crackled*. It was alive, alive with the fey energy of kindling about to catch.

Another door slammed. Closer, this time.

My heart echoed the act against my ribs.

There was no one in the house. No one but myself and Rodolfo, who turned in his sleep, murmuring something unintelligible.

Slam.

I was going to die in this house. The knowing swept through me, heavy with grief, cold and oracular as the whispered words of a saint.

San Isidro was my tomb.

But not tonight.

I threw the blankets off my legs. The room was black as the Devil's shadow. I could not see my hands before me as I pawed desperately for matches. Two strikes; light spat into being. My reflection peered back at me as I held flame to wick.

Yellow flesh peeled away from my face, dry as parchment. Like the corpse at the foot of the stairs, it stretched too thin, revealing the hollows of my eyes and a line of too many teeth stretching back to my ear.

I shut my eyes. It was a vision, like the night of the failed exorcism; it could not hurt me.

Or could it?

Ana Luisa was dead, her heart stopped by fright. Andrés was snatched from the air and flung against the wall of the green parlor. In the capilla, the blood on his face did not vanish. Injury inflicted by the house did not vanish like the visions as dawn streaked the skies above San Isidro's roof. Death would not dissipate like a nightmare.

I stood and stepped toward the doorway. Reached for the handle, hands shaking. I did not care if Rodolfo woke.

If I stayed, this house would kill me.

I opened the door and fled.

Darkness clawed at me; cold hands yanked my hair, pawed my nightdress. Drumming erupted beneath my bare feet, thundering through the floor and following me to the head of the stairs. Unseen hands planted on my shoulders. Cold as ice. Hard as death.

With a powerful shove, they pushed me down the stairs.

The world spun; the candle went flying. Was this how I died? I flung out my arms to slow myself, but cold hands forced me down, down toward the flagstones with steely determination. Poor Doña Beatriz, fell down the stairs. Shattered her skull. Spilled her brains everywhere. Poor Doña Beatriz, such a tragic accident . . .

Not tonight.

Anger caught light in my ribs. I curled myself into a ball as if I had been thrown by a horse: knees to chest, elbows tucked in, hands curled over my ears.

I caught the flagstones forearms first, then rolled. Cold air stung my grazed elbows as I sprang to my feet and stumbled to the door.

Beatriz, Beatriz . . .

I wrenched the door, almost pulling my arm out of its socket. It did not move. Yet it was not locked. I could *see* it was not locked, but it would not open.

Cold enveloped me like a wet cloak, covering my nose, my mouth, smothering me. I clung to the door handle. I could not breathe. I gasped and felt nothing; my lungs burned, my eyes strained against the dark. The darkness would strangle me. Unless I fought, I would drown.

Not like this, I thought.

I gathered all the strength I had and slammed a balled fist against the wood of the door in frustration. Soft, pale sparks haloed my darkening vision. I needed *air*. My chest was caving in, collapsing from the weight of the darkness. I struck the door again. Harder. Anger sparked in me like kindling, catching and blazing with a hunger that lit me anew. *She* was holding me here. She was trying to kill me.

I would not let her.

"Not tonight, you bitch," I forced out.

I reached for the handle and yanked.

The door opened. I stumbled backward with its weight, catching myself as air rushed into my lungs. A shock of cold, wet wind struck my face. Sheets of rain slaked the courtyard, the sound of it striking the earth like shattering glass.

A gust of wind tolled the bell of the capilla once. It echoed through the courtyard, a hollow, lonesome knell.

I sprinted toward it.

23

ANDRÉS

When I woke, the fire was embers; my room was silent. The slam of a door echoed through my mind. Had I dreamed it? Did the house plague my nightmares?

No. Something tugged at me. I touched bare feet to floor; from beneath it, the earth reached up into me, stirring my clouded mind into sharp wakefulness.

Someone was in the capilla.

I felt the hum of distress like someone grasping my wrist, and I followed it.

I kept thick candles lit in the capilla all night long, to let the villagers know they had a refuge at any hour.

I froze when I saw who the light fell on.

At first glance, I thought it was the apparition we called the Weeper. A woman in white with black hair falling into her face. She stumbled up the aisle, sobbing uncontrollably. Water trailed behind her, leading from the door.

But I knew the Weeper well. It was not her season, not her time. Nor her place to appear.

This was not a spirit.

Beatriz.

She reached out and clung to the side of a pew, half collapsing into it. Her knuckles were white where she clutched the pew; her whole body heaved with sharp, gasping breaths. They came too quickly, too suddenly.

I should not have left the house. It was an irrational flash of feeling—of course I could not have stayed. Rodolfo's presence prevented it. But it was a mistake.

She looked up at the sound of my approach, her green eyes so wide I could see the whites around her irises. Ana Luisa's face flashed in my mind. Her heart had stopped from terror, her eyelids peeled back, leaving her gazing into the void in horror for eternity.

"Beatriz. Shh," I said, my voice low. I crossed the last few steps to her, my hands held out as if I were calming a spooked horse. "Shh."

Her arms gave out. I sprang forward to catch her before she fell against the pew. She was soaked to the bone and shook forcefully. Her face was pale with fear. I tightened my grip on her upper arms to steady her. "Shh."

She lifted her chin. A red graze cut across one cheekbone; her eyes were glassy with unshed tears as they tracked over me, searching me hungrily, perhaps trying to see if I were real or phantom. Then she looked around me, her chest rising and falling staccato. "It's so quiet." Her breath hitched. "So quiet."

My heart tightened. How many times had I fled from the roar of the darkness as a child? How often had I been tormented by voices after sunset, and sought solace in the peace of the church?

"You're safe here," I said.

Her face crumpled.

The world slowed: a yearning like a tide swept through me, an unbear-able need to protect the woman before me. At the same moment I drew Beatriz to me, she threw her arms around my body. One movement, per-fect as dancers. One tight embrace. Her arms wound around my rib cage; her fingers dug into my back. Damp seeped from her dress onto my shirt, warmed by the heat of our bodies. I pulled her head into my chest, resting my cheek against her wet hair. She smelled of rain. She smelled of fear.

"You're safe," I murmured. She shook against me as she sobbed. "Shh. Breathe. You're safe."

I stroked her hair, my other hand pressed against her lower back. Slowly, her hitching breaths calmed; her hands relaxed. Her weeping soft-ened and stopped altogether.

Neither of us loosened our arms. I do not know how long we stood there, twined tightly as lovers in the soft glow of the candles on the altar. Rain beat the roof of the capilla; deep in the night, an owl's soft call echoed across the valley. She was safe. *She was safe.* I did not know why she had fled, but I knew this: as long as my feet felt the earth beneath me and my heart the heavens above, I would not let any harm come to her.

I felt the muscles of her back stiffen, ever so slightly, beneath my palm.

Reality fell into place around me. I should not hold her so tightly, no— I should not be holding her at all.

She loosened her arms, and I took a quick step back. Something akin to grief tightened in my throat.

Holding her felt *right.* The feeling swelled in me with the inevitability of rain, my certainty an ache that cut to marrow. An ache that knew no language. It was *right.*

"I know what you're thinking," she said, a flat determination in her voice.

My heart stopped.

"I am *not* going back. I can't." Her voice cracked.

I cleared my throat. I had not been thinking that at all. Was that what she thought of me? That I was foolish enough to send her back to the husband from whom she had fled in the middle of the night? To that house?

No. I wanted to beg her to stay here, to slip into my arms, to dig her fingers into my back—

"I'm going to sleep on a pew," she said. She inhaled deeply. "And you can't stop me."

Different thoughts tumbled through me, tangled, half articulated: her husband would wonder where she had gone. No, her husband would be angry if he woke and found her with me. The house was awake, alive, and she could not go back alone. Not until dawn broke. But she could not spend the night here.

Could she?

Hadn't I sought refuge by doing the same, so many times in my life? Titi knew I fled my father's house in the night because of the voices. When I grew old enough to begin learning from her, she lectured me about the powers that sought to slip under one's skin, to seize their hosts like bats gorging themselves on a weakened bull.

You must cast them out, she would say. *You are your mind's sole master. Banish them. Tell them to mind their own business and leave you be.*

Even when she walked into the most sickened of houses to purify their energy with copal and smudging of burnt herbs on the walls and hearths, houses so diseased she ordered me to stand outside with the inhabitants, the voices rippled off her like water off silver, her aura as impenetrable as a warrior's gleaming shield. She was a prophet in a land that had been stripped of its gods: a healer of the sick, a beacon in the night. She reached into steel-dark clouds to control the storms of the rainy season, seizing lightning as her reins and bending them to her will to turn harvests into gold. She called the voices to heel and banished them.

I was not her.

I had failed, and Beatriz suffered because of it.

Perhaps I was weaker than Titi. No matter how hard I tried to walk her path, how hard I fought to be good, to do good, I failed. No matter how hard I thrust the darkest parts of myself into their box and worked only with Titi's gifts, they endured. Worse, they had tasted freedom and hummed with life. They mocked my failure. They strained at their chains, demanded my attention. Reminded me that I was damned.

Damnation was not something Titi concerned herself with. She believed in an underworld for all, a smoky, dark peace into which all souls folded. But she had not spent years studying scripture as I had, nor praying for her sins in dark seminary cells, convinced the very soul she was born into marked her for burning. Because of what I was, I feared Judgment Day. Aside from Titi, anyone who knew what I truly was—not just her heir, as the pueblo did, but something darker—feared me. This was a pillar of my life, as fixed as the pattern of seasons.

Yet in her flight, in her own fear, Beatriz had sought the capilla. Beatriz sought *me*. After all she had endured in my company, all she had seen, any practical mind would associate my presence with danger, and therefore cast me out of their life as fast as they could.

But she didn't.

Even as she folded her arms across her chest in preemptive defiance of words I could not bear to speak, she stood here, barefoot and drenched in the capilla, because she trusted me. Her nightdress was so soaked that it clung to her arms, stomach, and thighs. Against my better judgment, I let myself notice this for a moment longer than I should have.

Heat climbed up my throat.

I did not deserve the trust she placed in me.

"You'll catch your death of a cold." Was that my own voice? It echoed far and foreign. It *was* mine, though the words it spoke were those of an imbecile.

"I don't care." She stepped into the pew and sat on the bench, dropping her weight with the heavy determination of a child. "I'm not going back."

I could not argue with that.

I turned to walk back to my rooms.

"Where are you going?" I caught how her voice pitched toward fear and cast a glance over my shoulder. Though her hands rested on the back of the pew in front of her, her body was tensed, as if she were ready to rise and follow. This sent an arrow of compassion through my heart, further bruising what was already too tender for her.

I could rationalize this decision away. It was easy, too easy. She was a lost soul who sought help and I gave it; thus was my vocation. I could repeat that sentence like a litany, like a prayer, a meditation of pious deceit, but it still would not change the truth. I was giving in to temptation. Every decision I made that kept me close to her, that offered the opportunity to be close enough to touch her hand or smell her hair, was a sin.

I wanted it all the same.

"You'll need blankets," I said. "I'll be right back."

I returned with an armful, some still warm from my sleep. Beatriz was shivering when I reached her; I stepped into the pew to set most down next to her, then chose the softest and draped it over her shoulders.

"Thank you," Beatriz murmured. Her fingertips brushed mine as she tightened it around herself.

Her eyes fell from my eyes to my mouth.

A soft dizziness settled in my chest, curling around my lungs and robbing them of air. I had to get ahold of myself. I sat on the other side of the blankets, clasping my hands before me.

"What happened?" I asked, willing my voice to be steady.

"I saw things." Her voice was hollow; a shadow of distress flickered across her bloodless face. "I tried to do as you say and cast out the voices. I tried not to listen. But I have begun to see things. I *feel* things, as I never have before."

Her hands trembled, even as they clutched the blanket around her.

I knew precisely what Titi would say. *Get the family out of the house. Quickly.* She would wag one gnarled finger at me. *Then purge it of its rot.*

I had tried. I had opened that dread prison within me and released a limb of the darkness within. I held it with a pale-knuckled grip, tightened the reins of incantations around it though it yanked and champed at its bit. I was in control. I used every prayer precisely as it was meant to be used. There was not a breath that was unplanned, not a step that was not precisely timed.

And yet I had failed so profoundly that I could have been killed.

My aunt was killed.

The rot in the house was a plague. Who would it fell next? Paloma? Beatriz?

I could risk neither. I could not fail either of them again.

But how could I proceed with Rodolfo back from the capital? If he was any bit as suspicious or intolerant as Doña Catalina, I would have no luck convincing him that allowing me to draw his wife's blood in the middle of the green parlor and speak to unseen spirits was for the good of his household.

Unless he, too, was as tormented by the house as Beatriz was.

"Does . . . does he feel it?" I asked softly.

"Rodolfo?" She made a disgusted face. Even that moment of animation was enough to make her seem alive again, and I was grateful for it. And for other reasons, too, reasons that I then suppressed with the force of slamming a chest shut. "No, he doesn't. I don't think he can feel anything at all." She shifted uncomfortably, then took another blanket into her lap. A long moment passed before she spoke again. "Paloma told me he has done horrible things."

I lowered my gaze to her hands, watching them methodically shred the end of a tassel. Paloma must have told her about Mariana. I closed my eyes and made the sign of the cross for her. I had failed her too.

"I know," I murmured.

"Then you know he is too evil to feel it," Beatriz said.

"I don't believe it works that way." Even my father had felt what dripped from his walls. Perhaps it was one of the many reasons he turned to pulque: to dull his senses, to blind himself to the shadows that slithered from the corners of his house. "A house like that . . . he *should* feel it."

"Do you know what he said?" She turned to me, tightening the blanket around her shoulders. Most of her hair was still in a long plait that fell down her back, but much had worked its way loose and fell around her face. "He complained that the house was too warm. Can you imagine?"

I could not. "Perhaps he is mad."

"Perhaps I am," Beatriz muttered, the animation in her face dulling. Her shoulders slumped as she leaned against the back of the pew. "I have nightmares. I see things no one else can. I hear things no one else can."

"Perhaps you are a witch, Doña Beatriz."

Her laughter was the bright, sudden snap of castanets, its surprise echoing in the dome of the chapel. She cast a coy look at the crucifix and crossed herself. "God forbid, Padre," she said, a little breathless as she touched her thumb to her lips.

Despite myself, a smile tugged at the corner of my mouth. God forgive us, blasphemers both.

I moved to the side, slightly away from her down the pew, and patted the pile of blankets that remained. "Rest," I said. "I will wake you before dawn and escort you back to the house when it is tolerable." I almost said *safe*, but I wondered if it ever would be.

It was as if she heard this, or saw the thoughts written across my face. "You should rest too," she said. "Your head . . ."

"It will heal, God willing," I said. Then, soft and determined: "I will not leave you."

She considered this, her expression grave. This was the fifth night we had spent in each other's company, each more unpredictable and dangerous than the last.

"Do you promise?" she asked.

When a man makes a promise, he makes it on his honor. When a witch makes a promise, they feel it in their bones. Titi believed words are power:

they may lay your destiny in stone or shatter a legacy altogether. Words can damn or bless in equal measure, and are never to be used lightly.

"I promise," I breathed.

Then I knelt on the knee rest before us, reaching out of habit to my pocket for my rosary. I met the soft cloth of my sleeping clothes. My rosary was in my room, resting on the stack of books next to my bed. No matter. I made the sign of the cross and began to pray in a low voice. I had learned visiting orphanages in Guadalajara that there was no easier lullaby than someone else's meditative prayer. Behind me, I heard Beatriz lay herself down on the blankets, shift, and settle. Her breathing softened, then deepened.

When I was certain she was asleep, I let my voice drop to a murmur, then fell silent.

She was curled in a fetal position on the pew, one arm tucked under the blankets she used as a pillow. Dark hair tumbled over her cheek and her mouth, rising and falling with her breathing.

I brushed curls away from her face, mimicking her own gesture by tucking one gently behind her ear. I ached to leave my hand on her hair, to stroke it gently, but I drew it back. She shifted; her eyes fluttered open.

"Sleep," I murmured. "You're safe."

Her eyes drifted shut. She believed me. She had seen all I was—darkness, damnation, and doubt, my failings, my fear—and still trusted me enough to fall asleep by my side.

I listened as her breathing resumed its deep, steady pattern.

"I promise," I whispered.

24

BEATRIZ

Beatriz."

Sleep was deep and soft and dreamless, and I was reluctant to be drawn out of it. Let me be, let me sink deeper into silence. It was only when there was a hand on my shoulder that I floated to the surface of awareness.

I was curled on my side on a bench. Candlelight draped over me like a blanket. I blinked. There were pews before me. An altar. Where was I?

"Beatriz." That was Andrés, his warm hand on my shoulder.

The night before flooded me: fleeing the house, racing through the rain to the capilla. How Andrés found me here and stayed with me through the night.

The Andrés who stood over me now was not the one I had embraced last night, whose black hair was messy from sleep, whose ragged nightshirt I had soaked with my tears. He was dressed in his austere black habit, and was freshly shaven, his hair slicked away from his face. He smelled of a piney local soap and, faintly, of copal.

I tightened the blanket around me. I was now—in a way I hadn't been last night—acutely aware of how little I wore. I hadn't cared in the middle of the night. Safety was what mattered then. Nothing else had crossed my mind.

Almost nothing else. Looking up at Andrés now—*Padre* Andrés, I emphasized to myself—should fill me with a sense of shame. I should not admire the dark line of his lashes or the placement of the small mole on his cheek. I should remember last night more innocently, not lingering on the warmth of his body, nor the weight of his hands on me. I hadn't cared then. But as the daylight strengthened, so would my shame.

I didn't want it to.

I wanted to stay in the capilla forever, abandoned in sleep, not a shred of guilt to be found within me.

I did *not* want to go back to the house. Which was precisely what Andrés had woken me to do.

Seeing I was awake, he sat next to me on the pew and offered me a cup of water. I snuck a glance at his face over the rim as I drank deeply.

He was staring into space, or perhaps up at the crucifix. His mouth was firm, and the lines forming around it seemed deeper than ever. There was no peace to be found there.

I lowered the cup and followed the line of his eye up to the crucifix. The carver and painter had fixed Jesus Christ's gaze upward in agonized rapture, but a small, curling feeling of shame told me His attention was focused on the more earthly affairs before Him. I set the cup down and tightened the blanket around my shoulders.

Maybe He could turn that attention on the house and lend a hand, for once. That I would not mind.

"You said you saw things," Andrés began, his voice rougher than usual—by a night of praying, by sleeplessness, or both?

I nodded.

"How distinct?"

"Like she was there." My voice came out hoarse, cracking over the words. I cleared my throat. "She sat next to you at dinner."

He shuddered. The grimness in his face deepened. "Not good."

"Do you think Rodolfo killed her?"

"Beatriz." There was a measure of surprise in his voice, of chastisement.

"Things changed, when he returned. Couldn't you feel it?" The line of his mouth told me he did. "And the writing on the wall . . . Andrés, when did she die? Was he here?"

He searched my face. Looking for madness, no doubt. I did not blame him. Something in the house had slipped under my skin before I could stop it, and it had been growing, spreading, festering ever since. I could not know if I would ever be rid of it.

You'll die here, like the rest of us.

"I couldn't say," Andrés said at last. "You would have to ask Paloma. There was a period . . . when I was not welcome here."

His banishment. Part of me had assumed it was Rodolfo's doing, but Rodolfo had no problem with inviting the priest to dinner, nor having him on the property. They were not warm with each other, certainly, but there was no open enmity between them either.

Something in Andrés's face warned me from pressing that point further. I would have to ask Paloma about that.

"Maybe we could learn from him whether he did it or not," I said. "You could sneak into the confessional in town as you did with me, but actually hear his confession, and—"

"*Doña Beatriz.*"

His scandalized tone made heat rush to my cheeks. "It's a good idea," I challenged.

"It is flawed for a number of reasons, the least of which being I will not break the vow of the confessional."

The quiet fervor with which he spoke stung me. "But you would only tell me. To warn me. To protect me."

"No." He shook his head.

"Even if he told you he murdered his wife?"

He raised clasped hands and, pressing his fingers to his lips, gave me a measured look. "That is a complicated ethical question."

"But what if he means to hurt me?"

"That is what I am afraid of."

The dark sobriety of his words sent a chill through me, into my gut. "How then would speaking to protect me pose a *complicated ethical question*? Do you want me to end up a skeleton in a wall?"

He closed his eyes. I could almost hear him saying *cielo santo* in his mind. "That is *not* fair. We do not know what happened to Doña Catalina."

And yet he did not revise what he had said.

I scowled, tossing one of my hands up in frustration. "I prayed for help, and what good did it do me? God has sent me the only incorruptible priest in México."

He opened his eyes. This time, when they met mine, there was a shade of intensity in them that caught my breath and held it fast. "I would not go so far as to say that."

A ribbon of warmth unspooled in my belly, its curiosity piqued by his words. I could not ignore it, not when heat bloomed in my cheeks, not when he sat barely a foot from me. Perhaps the yearning was forged from loneliness, from a lack of touch, but it was real all the same. It was a rope drawn taut, firmly anchored in me, and reaching to . . .

"Whatever happened to her, the fact of the matter is that she cannot move on," Andrés said. There was a sobriety in his voice that brought reality over my shoulders, heavy as a leaden cloak.

"Do people often struggle to . . . move on?" I asked.

"No." He lowered his hands, folding them in his lap. His eyes grew distant, lost in thought. "My grandmother had her theories about people who left behind unfinished business, who could not, for whatever reason, let go of their mortal lives. But there are also souls who are confused. Lost.

Who need some guidance to find their way. Then there are the spirits who remain tied to this world by their anger."

"Anger?" I repeated.

Andrés nodded. "It holds a great deal of energy."

"Why is she so angry?" I wondered aloud.

Andrés's brows rose to his hairline. "Doña Beatriz, we know someone killed her."

"But *I* didn't do it," I cried, gesturing at myself emphatically. "So why torment me?"

A vision from the night before flashed before my eyes: the apparition of María Catalina in my dining room, her hellfire eyes fixed on the other end of the table, staring with naked adoration at my husband.

Her husband.

If I were her, if my husband had remarried and my home been invaded by his new wife . . . wouldn't I, too, be angry?

My thoughts were interrupted by Andrés. "Because she was like that in life," he spat. "She struck Paloma. Ana Luisa hated her. They all did, because she was cruel and liked seeing people suffer. She—"

"Paloma thinks she killed Mariana," I said softly. "Is that true?"

Andrés froze mid-gesture. His hand hung in the air for a long moment. He did not breathe, as if time itself had stilled around him and stolen the breath from his lips. Then he swore, twice, blunt and wretched, as he covered his face with his hands. "This is my fault. It is all my fault. I made her angry. I should never have . . ." He swore a third time.

I stared at him, mouth falling open in silent surprise as the pieces fell together in my mind. "*She* banished you," I breathed.

Banishing Andrés from the land where his family had lived for generations meant separating him from the people he loved and served. I thought of Paloma shyly thanking me for bringing him back—María Catalina had separated him from his family. That was the one thing that could truly spark an anger so powerful it overcame his steadiness.

He lifted his head. Nodded curtly. "I *hate* her for it. For everything she did." His voice trembled with it. "It is a sin, but no matter how much I repent, I cannot shake it."

My heart shifted in my chest, disquieted, off-balance. I trusted him so earnestly, but how well did I know him, truly, if it took me aback to hear that heat in his voice? Since I met him, I had placed him on a pedestal as my savior, my protector against the darkness, my own private saint who kept the nightmares of San Isidro at bay. His injury rattled my faith in his omnipotence, but not my trust in his perfection.

Now, taking in the way he worried his hands in his lap, the shame that curled at the corners of his hard mouth as he looked away for me, I felt as if I were seeing him for the first time: yes, he was the priest who baptized children, who sat next to me in the chapel praying novenas until his voice went hoarse. Formal, sober, measured. He was the witch who drew my blood to exorcise a house at midnight, around whom copal and darkness and chaos bloomed, who heard voices and held a quiet power over the living. Over me.

But he was not perfect.

He doubted himself. He failed to forgive. He lost his temper. His was a bruised soul like my own, pitted with wounds and unhealed grudges.

A sudden wave of fondness for him flushed my chest, its sweet ache catching me off guard. Before I could stop myself, I reached out and put my hand over his fidgeting ones.

He stilled. His eyes dropped to our hands, but otherwise he did not move. For a moment, the capilla was so quiet it was as if both our hearts had stopped beating.

"What happened?" I asked.

For a long moment he did not reply. Perhaps he was weighing whether or not to tell me. Perhaps he did not want to shatter the silence of the chapel, the delicate, pale stillness that hung between us.

At last, he released a slow exhale. "It is a long story. And the sun is rising."

I took my hand back, my throat tightening with dread. No. I wanted to stay here forever. Couldn't he speak to still the sun and preserve this peace, this silence? Keep the softness of the gray light from melting away?

But instead I nodded. My thoughts strayed to Rodolfo, asleep in bed, as I rose. Pinpricks stabbed my lower legs; my shoulder was stiff from being pressed against wood for hours. I shook myself out. I had to return before he woke. For if I returned, looking like this, I would have to explain myself.

And that was the last thing I wanted to do. To anyone. Much less my husband.

I stepped out of the pew, the tiles of the chapel aisle cold against my bare soles. Andrés stood and followed, genuflecting and making the sign of the cross as he did so.

Then he turned to me. "I'll walk with you," he said, voice even. "I don't trust her." *The house.* "You must tell me when your husband plans to be away in the fields, or with José Mendoza. I will try again to cleanse the house."

"He's meant to see Don Teodosio Cervantes of San Cristóbal. He wants to buy land from us." But that was in three days, maybe more—I could not remember. The conversation of the night before blurred in my mind, punctuated only by the appearance of the woman in gray. Of María Catalina. I shuddered as we stepped through the door of the chapel.

A low mist hung over the courtyard, veiling the house in silken gray. No birds sang; far away, the baying of dogs echoed from elsewhere on the property.

"How will I survive until then?" My words died on the cold cloud of my breath. I still clutched the blanket around me like a shawl, but it was not enough to keep the morning from seeping into my bones.

A warm hand against my upper back. A voice, its rasp soft now, and tender: "I am here."

I knew he was worried. I knew he was frightened—but if he felt these emotions as powerfully as I did, he did not allow them to show. An aura of calm radiated from him; I basked in it as I would before a roaring fire on a damp night.

Priest and witch, a source of curses and comfort.

Truly, I could not understand him. Truly, I was more grateful for him than I had ever been for a man in my life.

His hand stayed on my back as we retraced my flight from the night before. The walls of San Isidro emerged through the mist, white and impenetrable. He stayed with me as we passed through the arch and crossed the courtyard. We did not speak. A reverent sort of silence hung around the house like shadows. Its attention was elsewhere, and—or so I thought—did not note our arrival. The front door was open. Tendrils of mist curled away from the sound of Andrés's shoes as he and I walked up the low stone steps.

The darkness inside was gray and quiet. More still than I had ever seen it. But I had long ago learned not to trust appearances as far as Hacienda San Isidro was concerned. I inhaled deeply and squared my shoulders. Andrés's hand dropped away.

Our eyes met. Wordlessly, I knew this was where he left me. That he could not pass farther, however much I wished him by my side.

I stepped into the house. He did not close the door behind me, but lingered, watching me cross the flagstones solemnly to the stairs. I did not look back. I did not know how long he waited there, nor when he closed the door. He must have stood there for a long moment, listening to the strange, gaping silence of the house. Wondering at it. He must have lingered far longer than anyone else would have, only stepping away from the threshold after heavy minutes. He must have walked slowly through the mist, lost in thought, wondering at the path we had set ourselves on.

For he was still close enough to the house to hear me scream.

25

ANDRÉS

FEBRERO 1821
TWO YEARS EARLIER

WHEN I RETURNED TO Apan from San Isidro, I stole hours away from my duties in the church to walk far from the town, beyond the fields where townspeople grazed their goats and few sheep, into lands that belonged to no hacendado. Far enough that the earth became rockier and the ayacahuite pines grew thick.

I combed the forest floor for herbs Titi used to collect, following a path she and I had trod many times to a stream that flowed down the craggy faces of the hills. Shadows had grown long by the time I found my quarry; complete night draped over the church when at last I returned to the rectory. I mumbled my apologies to Padre Vicente, as I knew there was no need to apologize to Padre Guillermo. The latter shook his head when he saw how soaked I was from the rain, how I smelled of the pines far from town.

"I'm surprised you even made it back," he said, casting me a knowing look over his crooked reading spectacles. While the leaping firelight made Padre Vicente look like a vision from Judgment Day, it softened the lines of Guillermo's aging face. We had both grown and changed since the days he would find me asleep beneath the pews of the church, but much had remained the same. He often joked that I was like a green horse, one that couldn't stop moving and paced deep grooves into its paddock.

"Let him stretch his legs," he told Vicente. "He was born in the country. He needs the air or he'll go mad."

Unlike Padre Vicente, Guillermo saw no problem in turning me loose to celebrate Mass or perform baptisms and other sacraments in the various capillas of the haciendas. Nor did he care about stamping out what he euphemistically called the *traditions* of the villages, so long as these did not interfere with the people paying the correct levy to be baptized and married as the Church required.

Vicente was different.

I had overheard him confiding in Guillermo that he doubted that a priest with mixed heritage could serve as a civilizing influence on the villagers.

"He is too naive. He simply isn't capable of being as rational as he needs to be," he argued. "It's in his blood."

Bitterly though I admitted it, in one respect, Vicente was perfectly right about me: I had no gift for *civilizing*, not as criollos like him defined it. Nor had I ever wished for it.

I slipped away from the other priests; once in the safety of my room, I lit a candle and emptied my small cloth bag of treasures. If brewed correctly, this was the medicine Paloma requested.

Titi taught me everything she knew rote. She never learned to read or write; I was able to keep in contact with her during my years away because she insisted that I teach Paloma her letters before I left for Guadalajara. This foresight benefited Paloma as well: as the war drew on, fewer and fewer educated young men lived on the hacienda, and in the absence of an official foreman, José Mendoza began to rely on Paloma to help him transcribe records and calculate earnings, though he never told the patrón. He claimed it was because his eyesight was growing too weak to work into the night. I knew it was because of Paloma's fierce alacrity with numbers. Her penmanship was blocky but clear; a steady, determined hand wrote the letters I received from her and my grandmother while at the seminary.

Titi says it will be cold near the feast day of San Cristóbal, and you should dress warmly, Paloma's letters would read. *She says you must go for long walks, as this will cure your sleeplessness. There was a rainbow yesterday as the rain began, and even though there were fresh puma tracks near the house of Soledad Rodríguez and her daughters, all of the lambs were accounted for this morning. She says it is a good omen. She says the pueblo is praying for you. She says I pray for you. The birds pray for your return to San Isidro.*

I memorized each letter with the same fervor as I had memorized every prayer my grandmother taught me, every recipe, every ritual, every symbol. I carved them into my heart, into the muscles of my arms, into my palms and the soles of my feet.

My mind wandered as my hands parted the herbs into groups, then divided them into the correct proportions. Raíz de valeriana. Milenrama. My grandmother quizzed me often, pride settling in the corners of her wide, kind mouth each time I answered or repeated back the recipes for drafts that soothed coughs and fevers and colicky infants.

My hands stilled in their work. I stared at the herbs.

I thought of the faces of villagers when they watched me during the procession on the feast day of la Virgen de Guadalupe. The strained face of Mariana in the firelight, the suddenness of her flinches.

She needed my grandmother. They all did.

You must find your own way, Titi told me.

But I couldn't. Not now. Not when what they needed was someone like her.

I WAS NOT AFRAID of crossing the empty countryside in the dark. Once past the last stables and chicken coops of Apan, I gave a soft call into the night, barely a breath. The night replied: it settled over my shoulders like a cloak, gifting me a measure of itself. Invisible to man and beast alike, I walked on. Even the most curious of the nocturnal creatures smelled the presence of night on my back, recognized the watchful eye of the skies, and cut me a wide berth.

This time, my arrival went unannounced. I slipped into the kitchen where Paloma and I had agreed to meet. When she bade me sit, I hesitated. I should give her the herbs and instructions and leave as soon as I could. But the warmth of the kitchen coiled around me. Paloma's promise of a mug of warm atole would make the long, cold walk back to town more tolerable . . . I gave in. She put a pot on the embers of the kitchen fire, stoking it enough to warm the liquid contained within.

When Paloma turned her attention back to me, I placed the small pouch of carefully selected herbs on the table. I had prayed over them as they dried, imbuing them with the correct intent. Ideally, I would have brewed them immediately. Titi had the luxury of being able to brew cures in her own home; as a priest, I had neither the privacy nor the impenetrable disguise of a woman hiding in plain sight in her kitchen.

Fortunately, Titi had predicted this might be a problem I would face, and gave me alternative instructions. These I began to recite to Paloma, beginning by stressing how important it was to brew the herbs in the correct order.

"Stop," she interrupted. "I can't remember all that. Write it down."

"No." Written instructions, if found, could implicate Paloma and Mariana, even though Mariana could not read. The girls could be punished. "It's too dangerous."

"What if I confuse the instructions?" Paloma said when I voiced my concerns. "That's also dangerous."

"Titi would not want us to get caught," I said.

"Titi would not want Mariana to die on our watch," she hissed.

I had no reply to that. Titi made that explicit when she first taught me the recipe—error could harm the recipient, perhaps irreparably.

Sensing my weakening resolve, Paloma rose. "There's paper in the drawing room," she whispered.

"Paloma, wait," I said, but she was already gone. She slipped into the hall, her bare feet whispering along the flagstones. I was achingly aware of how hard my frightened heart beat as I waited for her return; it was so loud it nearly drowned out the sound of a door opening and softly clicking shut. *Let this not be a mistake*, I prayed silently. I sent the prayer up to the heavens; it caught in the rafters of the house like a cobweb. Voices of the house approached it, cooing with curiosity, passing it from presence to presence like children with a new toy. Before I could scold them, ask them to release my prayer to the heavens where it belonged, Paloma returned.

She set charcoal and paper on the table crisply.

"Be quick about it," she said.

I kept my instructions shorthand and as spare as possible. Paloma knew the names of the herbs; it was a matter of which ones to crush in a molcajete and how much broth to boil. What symptoms Mariana should expect after drinking the mixture. That the cramping would pass within a week, but if the bleeding continued for longer, to send for me.

No sound but the scratching of the charcoal on paper disturbed us. I did not notice how silent the voices in the rafters had fallen until a new voice—a real, mortal voice—shattered the peace of the kitchen.

"What is this?"

Paloma and I jumped, our faces whipping to the door.

Doña Catalina, the patrón's wife, stood in the doorway of the kitchen, the lit candle in her hand illuminating her frighteningly pale face.

"Padre Andrés came to discuss my mother's illness," Paloma blurted out. "She has a weak heart but is quite proud and often refuses help, doña. He is our kin, so—"

Doña Catalina swept into the room like a cloud of white smoke, a dressing gown swathing her like a saint's robe. She narrowed her eyes at me; seeing I was in the middle of writing, she drew close enough to read.

When I moved my hand and forearm in a vain attempt to conceal the writing, she snatched the paper away.

Even in the light of her candle, it was clear how color rose to the high points of her pale cheeks as she read.

She put the paper down, then seized Paloma by the forearm with a sudden violence that brought me to my feet. *"Is this for you?"*

"No!" Paloma and I cried in unison.

"Silence," Doña Catalina spat at me. "Get out of my house."

I stepped forward instinctively, meaning to put myself between my cousin and the snake that bared its fangs at us, ready to strike.

"Release her," I said. "This has nothing to do with her."

Doña Catalina took a step back, yanking Paloma to her feet with her. She was tall and had no trouble looking me dead in the eye.

"That is enough." Her voice was deathly soft. Paloma yelped; Doña Catalina's long fingernails dug into my cousin's skin. "You have no business contradicting me before my servants, nor encouraging them to sin. I knew when I first came to this godforsaken place that a mestizo priest meant corruption among the villagers, but I expected drinking and licentiousness. I did not expect *this*."

"I protect their health and their souls, doña," I said archly. Stung pride goaded me, loosened my tongue. "It is not easy, when they suffer so at the hands of their patrón."

"You *dare* speak of my husband that way?" she said.

"Let her go," I snapped.

"I think not, Padre Andrés." Then her face shifted, mercurial as smoke. Anger carved the delicate lines of her face deep, transforming her beauty into something brutal as a coy, sharp smile played across her lips. "*Leave.* Or I shall tell Padre Vicente you not only trespassed on my property, you spread satanic beliefs among the villagers."

This robbed my reply from my lips. Padre Vicente was just waiting for an excuse to condemn me, and I had just put all the proof he needed in writing. All my years fighting to remain hidden would be for naught; already robbed of my grandmother, the villagers would be robbed of me too. If the Inquisition was merciful, I would be removed from Apan and appointed elsewhere after a thorough reeducation. If not . . . I could be imprisoned. Tortured.

Fast as a snake's strike, Paloma twisted out of Doña Catalina's grasp. She snatched the paper and the cloth bag of herbs and flung herself across the kitchen.

"Don't!" I cried.

Paloma threw the dried herbs and paper into the fire. The embers flared, leaping and devouring evidence of my work like kindling. Even if Doña Catalina held true to her word and told Padre Vicente I had been on the property and what I had intended to do, neither he nor inquisitors would have any evidence with which to condemn me. In moments, only the acrid smell of burning herbs clinging to the air and soot would remain.

Doña Catalina crossed the room and slapped Paloma across the face.

The breath left my lungs. Paloma had hinted that the patrón's wife was cold and unpopular among the villagers. She had said outright that Ana Luisa loathed her and would do anything to be rid of her white-knuckled control of the house. Now I understood why. I understood why Paloma rarely spoke of her, why Mariana flinched at sudden movement.

I sprang between them, fury leaping bright and hungry as the kitchen fire in my chest. That box I kept locked in my breast strained until its bindings loosened; tendrils of what lay within seethed out and rippled off my skin like heat.

"Don't touch her," I shouted.

The fire matched me, licking high as it devoured the darkness that began to roll off me. It reflected in Doña Catalina's light irises, opening a window into Perdition. I loathed her then. I hated her with more wicked, burning power than I had ever felt toward any living being.

"You should leave," Paloma murmured behind me. I glanced at her. She held a hand to her face, a weary resignation heavy in her posture. "Go."

But I couldn't leave her in the hands of a woman like this. There were tlachiqueros who whipped their donkeys with more shame than Doña Catalina possessed. Paloma was in danger in this house.

"I'm taking you to your mother," I told her. "Come with me."

"Stay," Doña Catalina commanded.

I moved toward the door, but Paloma did not follow.

She hung her head, her hands loose at her sides as Doña Catalina took her by the shoulder and yanked her away from me. Paloma did not protest, though her plaits swung from the force of the movement.

My anger died in an instant, as if drenched by a bucket of cold water.

I gave in to my temper and my hatred of Doña Catalina. But it was Paloma who would now suffer because of it.

"Get out of my house," Doña Catalina said. "And pray that I don't tell Padre Vicente of your visit." At the look on my face, she added: "My word against yours, Padre—to whom do you think he will listen?"

There is no draft more bitter than that of helplessness. It bruised my throat as I looked at my cousin held fast, her proud head hung.

Doña Catalina marked my pause. She smelled my fear, my hesitation, my grief at knowing Paloma's pain was my fault. She found the most tender part of my body and struck her final blow:

"I banish you from San Isidro," she said coldly. "If I ever find you have been here against my wishes or hear that you have sent messages or otherwise brought Indian superstition to this place, I will give Paloma to the Inquisition."

The smugness in her voice struck me like a physical blow.

"Go, Andrés," Paloma begged. "Just go."

I retreated into the dark of the kitchen garden, stunned, then turned on my heel and strode away. I had caused Paloma pain, and now there was no way for me to protect her. No way for me to fix the damage I had wrought.

I had tried to do precisely what Titi would, but I failed. I had put Paloma in harm's way. I had not helped Mariana. I had failed them all.

A light rain began to fall. It struck my burning cheeks like ice, mixing with the tears of rage it found there. A hooded figure passed into the kitchen courtyard just as I left it; Doña Juana, the daughter of old Solórzano, pulled back her cloak's hood to frown at me through the rain.

"Villalobos?" she said, genuine surprise coloring her voice. My surname smarted; it was what old Solórzano had called my father, when he was San Isidro's foreman. What old Solórzano called me or any of my brothers. *The Villalobos boy.* As if we had no other identity but the legacy of the Spanish foreman forcing himself on an hacienda maid and being ordered to marry her. That name was a living, breathing scar of the criollo stranglehold on this land. At times like these, I wanted to strip it from my body like so much flesh and burn it. "What are you doing here at this hour?"

I could feel more than see how Juana's look swept me appraisingly, from the thunderclouds on my brow to my balled fists.

My family had lived on this land longer than the Solórzanos had even *been* in Nueva España. To be banished from my home, forbidden from contacting my family . . .

I shouldered past Juana, leaving her unanswered in my wake. I had no patience for any Solórzano. Not tonight, not when loathing raked the inside of my ribs as I strode through the night. Loathing of the Solórzanos, of Doña Catalina. Of myself, for putting Paloma in danger.

Paloma was not safe here. Not with these monsters.

I would find my way back to her, to this place, if it was the last thing I did. No Solórzano could keep me from my home. My grief crystallized the thought into a white-hot prayer, branding it on my bones like a promise.

God help me, I will be back.

26

BEATRIZ

I WAITED WITH PALOMA in the study outside my bedchamber. The latter was filled with more people than I thought it had ever seen: Padre Andrés, José Mendoza, and the caudillo Victoriano Román, who was the local military officer charged with maintaining order in the district of Tulancingo. He and his men had arrived with surprising alacrity, given the hour at which we sent for them. Román's men now walked the property, looking for evidence of bandits.

We had asked for the doctor as well, but he was not in town. His wife told our messenger that he was nearly a day's ride away at Hacienda Alcantarilla, tending to the feverish pregnant daughter of the hacendado. He would come to us as soon as he could.

Paloma stood at the doorway. At her insistence, I had changed into actual clothing, but I had not touched my hair, nor put on stockings or shoes: my feet pacing the rug were still dirtied with cracked mud from the courtyard.

"Doña Solórzano." Román called for me from the bedchamber.

I looked up, startled. Paloma's brow furrowed with concern. "They need you," she whispered.

I knew that. Still, I hesitated. I didn't want to pass through the door to my bedchamber, but I had to.

I swallowed the dread in my throat and stepped into the room.

Andrés and José Mendoza stood closest to the door, near my vanity. Román was on the far side of the room, opposite them. He gestured up at the wall, brusque and authoritative. "Is this window normally left open at night, doña?"

I meant to keep my eyes on him. I tried as hard as I could. But against my will, as if drawn by gravity, or the weight of horror, they fell to the bed.

Rodolfo lay on his back, tangled in sheets. His face was pale, his eyes open, glassy and frozen wide with horror, just as Ana Luisa's had been.

Like Ana Luisa, he was dead.

That was where the similarities ended.

Blood soaked his shirt and the sheets, blackened and gruesome in the light of morning. It reached the foot of the bed; it spilled on the floor. It had even fanned out to the stucco wall beneath the window where Román stood, waiting for my reply.

His throat was slit from ear to ear like a butchered sheep. The red edges of the cut were profane in the light, but I could not look away.

I could not.

Not even as Rodolfo's head turned to the side in an avian-sharp movement, his eyes jerking side to side, scanning, then falling on me. His beautiful bronze hair fell back against the pillow as his back arched, as if he were lifted by a thread tied to his rib cage.

His eyes were fixed on me, but they were unseeing. Glassy and vacant.

Then he spoke.

Or rather, something animated his lips, moving them in stiff, wrenching movements. The voice that emerged was not his, nor even a man's. It was a girl's voice, a young woman's voice, shrill with anger.

"Answer him, bitch."

Silence rang in my ears. I tore my eyes from Rodolfo, looking wildly to Andrés. José Mendoza. Román. They all looked at me expectantly.

They had not heard the voice that came from Rodolfo. They had not seen him move his head so sharply it made the loose ends of the cut in his neck slide against each other like the lips of a monstrous mouth.

"Answer him!"

My gaze shot back to Rodolfo. That *voice*. Those movements distorting what should be a dead, stiff face, moving my husband's features in uneven, spasm-like jerks.

"Tell him the truth!"

Darkness crept along the edges of my vision.

Distantly, I heard the words *she may faint*; Andrés was at my side, taking my arm and backing me out of the room.

"*Tell him the truth!*"

No one else could hear that voice. Nor see that movement, though it happened right before their eyes, in the cold light of morning.

It was Paloma who took me down the stairs and out the front door as quickly as she could, who knelt by my side as I fell to my knees and vomited into the dead flower bed next to the entry stairs.

I heaved violently, until acid stung my nose and my eyes burned. Paloma took a kerchief from a hidden pocket and wiped my face, her own still and solemn. She guided me back to the steps and sat me down at her side, holding me upright with a firm, steadying grip on my upper arm.

"I'm sorry," I said, crumbling the kerchief up in a tight fist.

Paloma released her hold on my arm and rubbed my upper back with an equally firm hand.

You're one of us, now, she had said. *You're trapped in San Isidro, just like the rest of us.*

And there was nothing I wanted more than to be anywhere but San Isidro. I wanted to be back in the capital, scalding my hands and my pride with hot laundry water as I washed Tía Fernanda's dirty underclothes. At least Mamá was by my side. At least I slept soundly. At least when the dead passed, they stayed dead.

My eyes filled with tears. How scornful I had been of Mamá insisting I should marry for love. How convinced I was that I was right to be practical, to sacrifice a loving partnership like she and Papá had for an estate in the country and financial security.

But what had my sacrifice won me?

Hacienda San Isidro. Madness and torment. This could never be a home for my mother, no matter how hard I worked to fix it, no matter how much porcelain and glass arrived from the capital. No matter how many exorcisms tried to drive the evil from its bones. Mamá would never plant flowers in this garden, nor orange trees nor birds of paradise nor the olives that the hacendados had discussed introducing to their own properties at dinner.

It was a cursed place.

It could never be home.

Not for her. Not for me.

"I want to leave," I whispered, head in my hands. "I want to leave and never come back."

Paloma resumed rubbing my back. "Where would you go?"

"I have nowhere." The realization cracked my chest open like a tlachiquero's machete opening the heart of maguey. A single, true strike, severing off a part of me that I hadn't known was there. A hope that somehow, I could convince Mamá that all would be well in the end.

"Are you sure your family won't have you?" Paloma asked softly.

I shook my head. Mamá wouldn't even receive my letters, much less me.

Perhaps she interpreted it as no, I wasn't sure, for she kept speaking. Her words held a comforting weight. Perhaps the soothing, magnetic quality of

Andrés's voice was not the trace of a witch's power, but rather a mark of their family.

"Family is all we have when things fall apart," she said. "I am glad Andrés is here. You know . . . he was gone for so long." A moment passed, heavy with words unspoken. I sniffed pitifully and wiped my nose with her kerchief. "It was a good thing that you brought him back to us. We need him."

"I know," I said. The words came out nasal from the tears.

"His return earned you much respect among the pueblo," Paloma added. "That is not something easily won. We have had little love for the Solórzanos, least of all the wives they bring from the capital. Especially not when the last one banished Andrés."

"What happened, that he was banished?" I asked, grateful for something to focus on. Anything but the idea of Mamá turning away letter after letter from me.

Paloma looked out at the garden. The mist had lifted, but the day was gray, and in its light the flower beds looked especially lifeless and forsaken.

Though she was a servant and I the patrón's wife, that did not mean I was any more entitled to what she knew than she was to my own troubles. Any other time, I would have backed away. Respected the sorrow that so clearly hung around her like a shroud.

But a deep intuition, or perhaps dread, or perhaps even fear told me I *had* to know.

"What happened?"

She inhaled deeply through her nose, and her dam burst:

"I told you I heard rumors that the patrón raped someone who worked in the house. That was a lie. Mariana *told* me it happened, then later, she told me she was with child. She was frightened. I asked Andrés for help. Titi . . . I mean, our grandmother, had many cures, and I knew she had taught him the one to end pregnancies. He had just returned from Guadalajara. I think he brushed up against the Inquisition there—he was afraid. But I pushed him to do it. Doña Catalina saw him bring me the cure. She threatened him. Cast him out. And then she turned on me." She barely drew breath, she was speaking so quickly. "We watch each other's backs. That's how we survive. But I—" Her breathing hitched; tears made her eyes glassy, reflecting the gray light of the morning. "She was cruel. She told me she would not tolerate bastards and kept beating me until I told her who the cure was for. Mariana wouldn't have. Mariana was stronger than me. But I gave in, and a week later, Mariana was *dead.* Doña Catalina ordered her to take candelabras up to that ledge in the formal dining room, even though we never had guests and no one used that room. Only Doña Catalina was there when Mariana fell . . ." Her voice cracked. "Doña Catalina killed her, I'm sure of it, and *it's all my fault.*"

Sobs seized her. She leaned into me; I slid an arm over her shoulders and held her tight. The clouds did not part, but the sky was lightening. I tilted my face up to it. I wanted to spirit us away, lift her and take her with me somewhere, anywhere but here.

But there was nowhere to go. Nowhere to seek refuge. Nowhere to find peace.

Slowly, Paloma caught her breath. She sniffed. "That bitch got what she deserved," she whispered.

I stiffened. "I thought she died of typhus," I said slowly, my voice sounding distant as it echoed the words that Tía Fernanda had once stage-whispered maliciously behind my back.

Paloma lifted her head. "Who buries someone who died of typhus in a *wall?*" she cried.

Juana, Juana . . .

From the crumbling wall in the north wing, the skull grinned out at me, mocking me with its too-wide smile and crooked, broken neck. I thought of Juana mocking me for thinking someone was buried in the wall, releasing me so I fell back into the cold dark of the north wing.

As you wish, Doña Beatriz. Your word is the patrón's.

Juana hated me because I threatened her authority. I was her brother's wife, a check on her power in the kingdom of San Isidro. She must have hated María Catalina because she, too, was a symbol of Rodolfo, how Juana's life of privilege and freedom was nothing but a lie. That it could all be taken away in a moment.

For Juana was a bastard.

Rodolfo kept this secret. Out of misplaced loyalty to her or his own pride, he had never told a soul. Not even me. And when he threatened to treat her as he believed she deserved, when he threatened to disown her . . .

It wasn't the house that killed Rodolfo. Not like Ana Luisa, no. He never felt the cold, he saw no apparitions nor heard dissonant laughter, because the house—María Catalina—*liked* Rodolfo.

But Juana?

Juana killed him.

She must have killed María Catalina too, for the same reasons. She was the one who buried her *in the wall*, covering up evidence of her crime and showing her brother the grave behind the capilla.

Shouts and swift footsteps sounded from beyond the courtyard gates. Paloma and I looked up as Juana appeared in the open doorway, flanked by two of Román's troops.

"There she is!" she cried, voice wretched from weeping. She was a portrait of perfect anguish, her hair dirty and wild around her tear-streaked face. The men broke into a run, charging me and Paloma.

It was as if the world slowed and went silent as realization dawned on me. That was why the caudillo and his men had arrived so quickly: they had already been on their way. For Juana had summoned them.

Paloma yelped and leaped to her feet. But where was there to run?

The clean skirts of Juana's work dress swirled around her legs as she stopped walking. She lifted a finger and pointed at me.

I was frozen to the spot, even when Paloma grabbed my arm and tried to wrench me to my feet. For when Juana met my eyes, my blood ran cold: there was a hardness in her gaze that pierced me like a bayonet.

She had planned this.

"That's the bitch who killed my brother," she said.

27

ANDRÉS

I PACED THE COMMON room of José Mendoza's house. Though the area before the hearth was no broader than four strides, I walked those four strides back and forth, back and forth, as desperately as if the act alone could solve our troubles.

Mendoza and Paloma sat at the table on wooden chairs, watching as I wore the flagstones down. Then they exchanged a look I could not parse. They knew each other well, Paloma and Mendoza. Not only was Paloma friends with the foreman's daughters, she had become his protégé in all but name when the patrón was in the capital. I was glad he had offered her a place to stay—she was still too shaken by the suddenness of Tía Ana Luisa's death to stay in her own home alone. I turned to him for his steadiness and his wisdom, now that the tide had changed and the world had been turned on its head.

Doña Juana accused Beatriz of murdering Rodolfo. She was placed under house arrest. The caudillo Victoriano Román left the keys of the house with Juana, and two of his men standing guard as he returned to Apan. He needed to check the state of the prison, he said. During the war, the small jail on the outskirts of Apan was barely more than a way station for captured insurgents, men who spent mere hours under its roof before being dragged from their cells and shot against the stucco walls at dawn. Now it was populated by town drunks and the occasional bandit; apparently, it would be inappropriate to place a member of the landed class among their ilk, even if that person was accused of murder.

Fury filled me when I heard this. What was *inappropriate* were these monstrous accusations against an innocent woman.

"She didn't do it," I said for the fifth time. "She was in the chapel all night. I know. I was with her." At this, Mendoza and Paloma exchanged a second pointed look. I stopped in my tracks and whirled to glower at them with all the righteousness I could summon—a skill much practiced and perfected by men of the cloth. I had learned from the best. "*We prayed.* She fled the house weeping, so we prayed. All night. And then, as Paloma said, she saw us return to the house at dawn."

Mendoza set his hat on the table between him and my cousin and ran a hand over his weathered face. "I believe you, Padre," he said. It was so strange to hear him call me that. Mendoza was gruff, but not unkind—his primary way of expressing affection for the children of the village was calling them malcriados. All my life before I left for the seminary, I was simply *chamaco* to him. Part of me still expected him to address me so. "But couldn't she have killed him before she went to the capilla?"

I fought the urge to shudder remembering the scene in the bedchamber. "You saw the amount of blood," I said. "She would have been drenched. And she was wearing white!" I exclaimed. "A white nightdress. It had mud on it from the courtyard, but no blood. Paloma saw it. Didn't you help her change out of it, when Mendoza went to town?" I barreled on, too impassioned to wait for a reply. "If one of us could sneak past the guards and get the dress, it would be proof of her innocence."

"Padre." Mendoza rubbed his temples. "It won't change what has already been done."

"How can you say that?" I had promised to keep Beatriz safe, and I would not stop until I had succeeded. The darkness bound deep in my chest hummed in accord, straining at its chains. "You said you saw someone run away from the house in the night. I saw no blood on her, was at her side all night, and returned her to the house in the morning. We have witnesses! We have proof!"

Mendoza lifted his head. "But it is our word against Doña Juana's," he said. "And forgive me for saying so, Padre, but in their eyes . . . your word is only as good as ours."

In their eyes. The eyes of the caudillo, the eyes of a judge, the eyes of the hacendados . . . they bore down on me, scrutinizing me, my cousin, my friend. Scrutinizing who we were. What we were. The casta system was abolished, of course, but the courts outside the capital carried on with business as usual: legally, the word of a criolla like Juana was still worth that of two Indios in court. The word of hacienda workers against their hacendado? Worthless. The word of a low-ranking mestizo cura like me?

Not enough.

"I will come forward anyway," I said.

But as I spoke, my mind lingered on Juana. She had not waited for any other evidence. Clearly, she had decided to take advantage of the tragedy and rid herself of Beatriz.

Or had she designed it?

Bastard, Rodolfo said last night. He threatened to disown Juana. Now he was dead. The woman who would inherit all his property accused of his murder. Who, then, stood to profit from the blood spilled in San Isidro?

"Did you know that Doña Juana is a bastard?" I asked Mendoza suddenly.

Paloma gasped. Mendoza looked up, wide-eyed. "Your pardon, Padre. What the *hell?*"

"I heard Rodolfo discussing it with her last night," I said.

"When?" Paloma said. "I didn't hear anything."

"Outside the green parlor, after dinner," I said. "You must have left already. He called her a bastard, shouted at her for calling their father hers. Then he said that if she did not behave, she would inherit nothing of old Solórzano's property. And now . . ." I let the words trail off suggestively.

Silence hung over the room like a shroud.

Mendoza swore softly.

"Blackmail," Paloma said, firm with conviction. "We blackmail her. Make her withdraw her accusation, or you'll tell all the hacendados she's a bastard. She must have cousins somewhere who'll gladly descend and take the land from her."

"Not a bad idea, Palomita," Mendoza said. "But you need proof, and the man who knew the truth is dead. If I were to go through old Solórzano's documents . . ."

God forgive us, I thought, running a hand over my jaw. Talking of blackmail and bastards and stealing papers from the dead.

"Those would all be in the house," I said.

"Carajo," Paloma said, and thoroughly ignored my chastising look.

"I will go into the house tonight," I said. "I will find the papers, and I will stay until dawn."

"Are you crazy, chamaco?" Mendoza cried. "That house!" He crossed himself.

"I won't leave Doña Beatriz alone in there after nightfall," I said.

There was no need to explain why. I had seen the villagers cut the house a wide berth. They could feel it. They *knew*. They crossed themselves at the mention of it, and there were rumors that the reason Juana had abandoned the house was not simply because of money, because of the war, because of the lack of guests and family on the property. They knew it had done something to her: Juana had always been headstrong, almost churlish, but there was a wildness to her now, one that spoke of something shattered within her.

She heard things, perhaps even saw things. I saw it in the way she took her drink last night. That was how my father drank when he heard voices.

Doña Catalina's cruelty was trapped in the rafters of the house, bound by her hatred into its very walls. Her essence was the sickness, and the house was festering, rotting with her from the inside out. Poisoning the foundation and spreading like disease. What emanated from its walls was a storm brewing, building in strength and venom. When it was unleashed . . . anyone within its walls could be harmed.

"I'm afraid . . ." I inhaled and let the breath out sharply. "I'm afraid the house may try to kill Doña Beatriz."

"You're right to be afraid," Paloma said. "But you're forgetting something."

"What is that?"

She met my eyes levelly, her mouth set in a grim line. "Juana might kill her first."

28

BEATRIZ

THEY LOCKED ME IN a storeroom while Rodolfo's body was removed from my bedchamber. My wrists were bound with rope. I lowered myself to the floor, curled my knees to my chest, and rocked back and forth in the dark. Hunger gnawed at my belly; I had not eaten all day, nor had water since the cup Andrés offered me in the capilla. The lack of food was making me dizzy and caused my hands to tremble.

The house curled around me with all the tenderness of a rattlesnake. Its rank breath trailed over my arms, curled around my neck. Too close. Too airless.

Visions intruded in my mind. At first they pushed like hands through curtains: prying and grasping, a dozen of them or more, their rhythm unpredictable as the thunder of fists on my bedroom door. But their ability to seize me was ultimately blunted by thick fabric.

The hands grew claws. Long, flesh-colored claws. They sliced through the curtains, through the barrier between me and *it*, carving my defenses to ribbons. They sank into my flesh, forcing visions that were not my own into my mind:

> *Juana's face loomed over me: calavera-white, her footstep soft as a puma's, appearing out of the gloom. The burning of alcohol in my nostrils. The steady beat of rain on the roof. Blooms of smoke; the fading of Juana's face. I felt circled by her, trapped. I knew she disliked me, even resented me, that our argument that night was heated, but this—*
>
> *The glint of steel in the darkness. Once, twice. Again. Pain blooming in my throat, my breast. A sour swoop of vertigo. The sensation of falling; a sickening crack. Darkness broken only by the thunderous drumming, of rain.*

I tried to push them away. These were not *my* memories. Their metallic tang was someone else's fear. *Cast it out,* Andrés said. But the claws of the house held me too tightly, their needle tips sinking fang-like into the flesh of my throat. Cracking the fragile casing of my mind and sinking deeper, deeper, deeper . . .

> *Ana Luisa's voice snapped through the gloom.*
>
> *You acted too soon, Juana, she said. This wasn't the plan.*
>
> *Distantly, she came into focus over me, disgust carved into her face's every line. She loathed me, I knew.*
>
> *We cannot dig with the flooding, she said. It is impossible. Where will we hide her?*
>
> *Juana materialized in the darkness. Her bronze halo of hair; a splatter of red bright on one cheek.*
>
> *The north wing's collapsed wall, she said, her tone flat and determined. I was fixing it today, she added. The mortar is still wet.*

Distantly, I saw Ana Luisa nod curtly, and heard her voice; I could not make out words. I was falling, falling . . .

I struck stone. I was being dragged by two people, one hauling each of my arms, flagstones peeling away the skin of my cheek. Heavy panting; the scrape of brick on brick. Brick on brick on brick . . .

Juana, Juana. I know what you are, Juana. I know you slaughtered Rodolfo, Juana. I will rip your throat out with my teeth. Crack you like eggs. Grind your wretched bones in my jaws. Tear your flesh to shreds. Juana, Juana . . .

I rocked back and forth, sobbing silently. I was hallucinating. In the broad light of day, I was losing my mind. When the shadows grew long, when the sun set . . . I did not know if I had the strength to survive another night of the house.

Voices echoed through the gloom. Men's voices. Real, mortal voices, with cadences that rose and fell with breathing, with echoes that began and stopped.

And Juana's voice.

A sudden flood of light blinded me; I jerked away from it, startled. Unable to catch myself with my hands bound, I nearly lost my balance. The caudillo's men had wrenched open the door. One seized me by my bound wrists and hauled me to my feet. If they saw my face streaked with tears, if they saw how I shook with the terror of the mad, they gave no indication that they cared. They led me down the hall, closer and closer to the chill of the north wing. My heart hammered against my ribs. My God, if they were taking me there, I should beg them to shoot me now. I could not face that cold, the glint of red in the dark . . .

They turned to the stairs.

I dug in my heels; they yanked me forward. Pain burned dully in my arms and shoulders.

"Where are you taking me?" I asked.

They did not reply. I discovered soon enough: Juana waited by the door of the study, my ring of keys in her hand. She tapped her foot impatiently.

"You know I didn't do it."

"That's quite enough from you," she said. "I will not tolerate further insult to my brother's memory."

She made a motion as if to wipe a tear from her eye and turned to the caudillo's men. "She's mad, you know," she said in a voice so sweet I wouldn't have recognized it as hers if I hadn't been watching her move her lips. "Ask Padre Vicente, he knows the truth. She thinks this house is possessed."

They couldn't believe this act. Did they not know Juana Solórzano? She was no victim. She was rotten, as rotten as the evil that blackened this house.

"Best step away, Doña Juana," one of the men said, a tone of concern in his voice.

Juana obliged, tucking a lock of her hair behind her ear. Her hair was dirty, yes, but her clothing so clean.

Though the door to the bedchamber was closed, I could still smell butchery. In my mind's eye, all I could see was blood. Staining the floorboards, the walls. The sheets. My copal censer was in there, and candles—things I would need for the night ahead, but I could not brave it. I turned my face away for fear I would vomit again.

Juana was a monster. A gilded monster with my keys on her hip, looking beatifically at me as the caudillo's men turned to leave the room.

I held her gaze until the door shut, picturing her covered in red, Rodolfo's blood dripping down her face, splattering her clothes. I wanted to scream.

Slam.

I flinched. The tongue of the lock slid shut. A jangle of keys; the sound of footsteps descending the staircase.

I was alone.

A plate of cold tortillas was left on a table. My stomach growled. What if they were poisoned? I wouldn't put it beyond Juana to do so. I glared at the food. Even if it weren't, I couldn't stomach the thought of food so near to where Rodolfo had died. Not when the smell of blood still hung in the air, drifting in from the next room.

I crossed to the far side of the study, away from the door to the bedchamber. The rug was damp beneath my bare feet. It hadn't been earlier this morning. I was barefoot then too—I would have noticed.

I squinted up to the ceiling. Was there a leak? If there was, it was significant: the rug was soaked, the floor on this side of the room was dark and slick with . . .

I inhaled, and my nose crinkled at the strength of the smell. *Alcohol.* It reminded me of the night Juana and I drank mezcal, when I woke with a sour headache and knowledge that something was wrong in the house.

How long ago that seemed.

I frowned. Rodolfo had not drunk mezcal, as far as I knew—though, then again, I did not know.

And I never would.

He was gone.

It was a strange realization. It had not struck me that morning, when I found him, nor at any point during the day thus far. Judging from the color of the light coming in from the western-facing windows, it was late afternoon. Hours had passed. And still—

Rodolfo was dead.

I had cared for him, when we met. I was hungry for him and all he stood for. That hunger soured to fear and disgust in the last weeks, as I learned of his cruelty and his hypocrisy. But he was dead. As dead as my dream for a home.

Now what awaited me? Prison? An asylum? Execution, for my supposed crime? My heartbeat quickened at the thought. The vapor of the spilled alcohol was making me dizzy, but at least it masked the smell of Rodolfo's death.

His chest lifting; his head turning. The jerk of his lips and the sharp movements of his glassy eyes . . . these were imprinted in my mind, burned there in a way more powerful than any nightmare. Andrés and the caudillo and José Mendoza staring at me, completely unable to see or hear.

Tell him the truth, that strangled voice said.

The truth was Juana killed him. Juana killed anyone who stood in her path. And she had won. With her crocodile tears and authority as an hacendado's daughter, she had won. She told the men I was mad.

The truth was I *was* mad.

Andrés had come too late. The house cracked my mind open and shattered it like china before I even knew of his existence, before I knew a witch could purge the house of evil intent.

Cast it out.

I could not, not now. Perhaps I never could have. I was vulnerable and ripe, and doomed from the first night I saw red in the dark. The house knew me as prey the moment I crossed its threshold, and now, it would devour me.

Lifting my eyes, I saw my father's map on the wall. I had pinned it above my desk weeks ago, the day Rodolfo left for the capital. I was so occupied with the north wing and the green parlor that I had not thought about this room much at all, not since the day I discovered my silks covered with blood. That was the only point at which Juana and I had spent any time together.

Apparently, it was enough to convince her I was to be gotten rid of.

My eyes stung with tears. What had I done wrong? Nothing. What could I have done right? Nothing. I married Rodolfo and presumably would bear heirs to inherit this property away from Juana. Perhaps I was not even a flesh-and-blood person to her: I was but a symbol of her brother taking away what she wanted, what she believed to be hers.

Hadn't I longed for the same? Wasn't that what an hacienda represented? Rodolfo's money was liberation from Tía Fernanda's reign of humiliation. Deliverance from desperate reliance on the fickle kindness of relatives I barely knew. I had sacrificed any hope of love in my marriage to secure my autonomy.

Juana sacrificed María Catalina. She sacrificed her brother. I had no doubt she would spill my blood, too, if she saw it beneficial to her.

I had to fight back.

I was not my mother, ready to give up when the blood was spilled and the muskets leveled. No. I was a general's daughter.

But I was so, so tired.

My feet squished across the wet carpet as I went to the desk and kicked the chair back. I sat beneath my father's map and rested my elbows on the desk. My arms ached, my wrists ached. My throat stung from bile, and my mouth tasted sour. I wanted to lay my head down on the desk. But even that I could not do. My hands were bound and going numb from it.

The shadows in the room were lengthening. Tears filled my eyes.

I rested my forehead on my hands, my position so similar to praying it brought the image of Andrés in the chapel last night to my mind.

How many times had I heard priests lecture about prayer from their pulpits and let the words wash over me, unbelieving? I had never trusted them. Never truly trusted the existence of God. Yet a few weeks ago, I would have said I never believed in the existence of spirits.

Or witches.

Help me, I prayed. *Give me the strength to fight.*

I began a rosary. I built a barrier to protect myself with words, layering them around me like an impenetrable skirt, like stones, anything to keep the house at bay. Whenever I lost track of where I was, I thought of Andrés's voice beginning the words of the next Hail Mary. It was a trick of my mind, I knew it was, but I followed, whispering when my voice grew hoarse and cracked. When I reached the end, I began again.

For the length of another rosary, the house was silent.

The sun set, its dying light bleeding across dark storm clouds. The dark deepened, from blue to gray and finally black. A distant roll of thunder.

I heard the cold before I felt it. It scraped along the floorboards like claws, the sound vibrating in my teeth more than my ears: like metal on metal, glass on glass.

I lifted my head.

Blood rushed from it. My hands were numb and bloodless. Hunger dizzied me, sucked the strength from my legs and left them trembling.

The cold slinked around my ankles, curling up my calves.

I jumped up. The rug was clammy, squelching beneath my feet. Unbidden, I envisioned it drenched in blood, like the sheets in my bedchamber that morning.

Beatriz. A whisper, girlish and light.

Cast it out.

Darkness filled the room, crackling and snapping with potential. It was kindling ready to light.

Light. Candles were in my bedchamber, I knew that. And copal.

But I would have to enter the bedchamber.

My heart curled in on itself at the thought. I couldn't.

Deep in the house, a door slammed.

"No," I whispered. "No, I'm so tired."

My voice cracked. A long moment passed. My shoulders were wound tight, taut as rope. I braced, ready for the next slamming door.

It never came.

Instead, a drumming began. First it was faint, distant, from the far side of the house. Distant enough that I thought it was another roll of thunder. But it never ended. It was a drumming on the wooden floorboards, as if a thousand heavy fingers struck in quick, violent succession. The sound marched toward the north side of the house, growing, becoming louder, so loud my bones rang with it. I could not cover my ears, could not hold out my arms to protect myself.

It drew closer, closer, then it stopped at the door of the study. There it drummed an irregular beat, growing louder, frantic, so powerful the door shuddered on its hinges.

The drumming stopped.

Sweat poured down my temples and slicked my palms.

It was there. It was there outside the door, and there was no copal to stop it. No candlelight. No Andrés.

A wink of red appeared in the dark, then vanished.

No.

It was here.

The red eyes appeared by the dark doorway to the bedchamber, then vanished.

It was coming closer. My heart beat so hard against my chest, so desperate and irregular it ached. Would it give out and leave me stiff and wide-eyed as Ana Luisa? Was this where it ended?

Hands grasped at my skirts, near the floorboards. Three or four hands, long fingered and icy; I could see nothing in the dark, but their too-soft flesh seized my ankles and yanked at me.

I shrieked and sprang away.

"Don't touch me!" I cried.

A girlish, lilting laugh from somewhere in the rafters. *She* was mocking me. She was enjoying this. Anger swelled in my chest. I jerked my head up, scanning the dark desperately for something, anything to direct my furor at. The laughter now sounded from my bedchamber; I whirled to face it.

Enough.

"What do you want?" I cried.

A pair of freezing hands struck my shoulders forcefully, knocking me off my feet. Unable to throw out my arms to stop myself, my skull struck the rug with a dull thud.

Nausea heaved through me, from chest to rattled skull. I rolled over onto my side. The rug dampened my cheek; the smell of distilled alcohol overpowered me.

I coughed and, fighting the urge to retch, forced myself to my knees. I staggered upright, head spinning, breath coming in ragged gasps. Lightning illuminated the room for a moment; then darkness fell again.

"I didn't hurt you," I spat. "I didn't even *know* you. Leave me alone."

Something hurtled toward me through the dark. Instinct seized my chest; I ducked.

Glass shattered on the wall directly behind me, and pieces went flying. A few struck my back; they rolled across the floor. A vase? It didn't matter what—I was barefoot and blind. Moving would rip my feet to shreds.

"So you're angry," I said to the dark. I picked my way carefully over to the desk, where there was a glass vase. I picked it up in both hands and faced where I had last heard that infuriating giggle.

"I am too!" I shouted, my throat ripping from the strain of my fury. I threw the vase as best I could while bound at the wrist. It shattered against the opposite wall. "I wanted things too! I wanted to be safe. I wanted a home. And I got stuck with you."

The darkness hissed—like a cat, but with a depth to it that assured me that no mortal beast could make a noise like that. Then a growl rose: an inhuman growl that set the hair on my arms standing on end.

Red eyes appeared in the dark, blazing more brightly than I had ever seen them.

I had nowhere to run. I was backed into a corner, barefoot in a sea of shattered glass. I wondered if I could even open the door with my hands bound.

"I bet you want to avenge yourself," I said, forcing the words to be steady, past the tremble in my voice.

The eyes drew closer; the darkness closed in on me, pressing down on my chest with a weight I only knew in nightmares. Breathing became difficult. But I did not retreat. Though my heart screamed against my rib cage, my head and shoulder throbbed, and my legs shook, I dug my heels into the damp carpet and looked the Devil in the eye.

I was not done fighting.

"Is that it? You want vengeance? Then go find it," I spat at it. "Killing me won't sate you."

Another growl. A cold flush of fear swept over my skin. That was a challenge. A dare.

The darkness pressed on my chest, on my throat. I gasped for air like a fish on land.

"If you kill me," I forced out. My voice was strangled, a snarl robbed of breath but full of venom. "I'll be stuck here, same as you." Air, I needed *air*. "And I swear on my father's grave *I will make you miserable*."

The darkness released. I gasped, lungs aching as they expanded; I fell forward onto my knees. Glass dug into my kneecaps through my skirt, but I didn't care. I breathed, I breathed.

The darkness's attention had lifted to the rafters. I frowned. Footsteps tracked across the roof. Mortal footsteps. Familiar footsteps. They settled overhead; clay struck clay as terra-cotta tiles were ripped from the roof and stacked on top of one another. Metal struck wood. Once, twice; the ceiling began to splinter.

Someone was breaking through the roof with a machete.

"Andrés?" I tried to call the name, but it came out a whisper. Had he come to rescue me? Was my torment at its end?

A boot kicked in through the ceiling, widening the hole cut by the machete.

Liquid poured into the room through the roof in a swift, short torrent, as if from a well bucket. Droplets splashed my dress and my face, and where they touched my lips and eyes, it burned.

That smell. It was alcohol. Pure, distilled alcohol. Like the rug. Like mezcal, but even stronger.

From overhead, the sound of a match being struck; a torch blazed to life.

Its light illuminated a woman's face. Bronze hair, a thin-lipped visage, the shadows carving distinctive cheekbones, skull-like in their sharpness.

Juana's mouth was set in a grim line, her gaze dispassionate as she took in my desperate appearance.

In an instant, I was back in the capital, watching Papá led away at bayonet point. Watching the remaining soldiers throw oil on the house and set it alight with torches. Smashing windows; waves of rippling heat. The acrid taste of smoke, my weeping, stinging eyes.

Fear enveloped me. I forgot all my pain. Every sinew of me was focused on that torch, on how it leaped and danced and cast wicked shadows across Juana's face.

Oh, no. *Not like this.*

"No. Get me out of here," I begged Juana. My throat was shredded; the words came out half a sob. "I'll lie. I'll cover for you. I'll leave and never come back. I swear I'll never come back."

Something flickered in her face. Perhaps it was a trick of the light. Perhaps it was my own desperation, tricking me into thinking she would actually consider my plea.

She did not.

Without a word, Juana dropped the torch into the center of the room.

29

ANDRÉS

THAT AFTERNOON, RODOLFO SOLÓRZANO was buried, hastily and with little fanfare, in the plot behind the chapel next to the empty grave of Doña María Catalina. After conducting the brief ceremony, attended by no one but myself, José Mendoza, and a smattering of other villagers—Juana had vanished without a trace—I retreated to the capilla.

I dipped inside and knelt in the pew closest to the door. I clasped my hands and thought of Mariana, the victim of my and Paloma's attempts to help her. I prayed for her forgiveness. I prayed she found peace in the embrace of our Creator. I forced myself to search deep in my heart and find what little mercy I could summon for the man I had buried today, a man I had never loved, who represented everything I loathed.

And I prayed for his wife.

I reached for the house as I prayed, sending Beatriz comfort, sending her strength. I promised she would be safe. I had promised myself I would heal the house and free my home from its blight. These aims were now one and the same, and there was only one way to achieve them.

I prayed to the Lord for forgiveness for what I was about to do.

A roll of thunder drew me from deep in my mind. I stepped from the pew, genuflected before the altar, and let my eyes rest on the crucifix.

Deliver us from evil, the Lord's Prayer pleaded. At the end of days, Jesus Christ would indeed deliver us from evil. In that I had faith and fear. Whatever end descended on Creation in the apocalypse was God's to command, and it was His hand that would divide the faithful from the sinners for eternity.

But mankind had already seen much evil and not been delivered. It would continue to see so much pain between now and the end.

I made the sign of the cross. Yes, the Lord was my Savior. But I had spent years in the silence of unanswered prayer, years that taught me that I must also learn to save. The question that plagued me was *how*.

Prayers are empty talk. She needs help.

It was not enough to be a priest. But my hubristic insistence on trying to replicate Titi's path had only harmed Mariana and Paloma.

You must find your own way.

My home and Beatriz were in danger. How could I do anything but take up the tools I had to deliver her from evil?

Deep in my chest, that locked box of darkness hummed, trembling with expectation.

Forgive me, I begged.

Then I rose, turned, and walked briskly to the door of the capilla. For better or for worse, I had chosen my path. I could not think of what I was sacrificing to do so, nor what punishment might await me at the end of my days.

There was no time to waste.

I STRODE DIRECTLY TO Ana Luisa and Paloma's house in the fading light. Its windows gaped dark in the twilight, hungry and empty.

The door swung open before me; as I crossed the threshold, I sensed something in the house invited me in, drawing me toward it like a moth to flame.

It was here, as I suspected. My inheritance. My birthright.

I fumbled in the dark for flint and a candle. When the flame's pale light illuminated the room, I turned to the beds against the wall.

Ana Luisa must have gone through Titi's belongings after her death and found it. How else could I explain the bastardized markings in charcoal that lined the doorway of the main house's kitchen? How else could I explain the instinct that drew me to my knees beside Ana Luisa's cold bed, to a small wooden box beneath its head? When I was last here, the morning Paloma found my poor aunt dead from terror, I was too ill from the blow to my head to think clearly; nausea deadened my senses to the dizzying pull that now drew my hands to the box. I set it on my knees and lifted its lid.

There it was. The pamphlet my father's sister had left me.

Smudges I did not recognize darkened some of its pages. A thrum of grief beat through my heart. When the house went rotten, when the poison of Doña María Catalina's anger began to spread, Ana Luisa had been afraid. She sought help from this. She should have come to me. Why didn't she?

Pride, perhaps.

I thought of the day Paloma first told me of the problems with the house, the day she spoke to me outside of the church in Apan.

Doña Juana is hiding something. Mamá too. Something terrible.

How many times had Paloma told me Ana Luisa loathed the patrón's first wife? If Juana had meant to rid the hacienda of Doña Catalina, would she have sought Ana Luisa's help as an accomplice?

Would my aunt have given it?

Then perhaps . . . perhaps it was guilt that prevented her from seeking my help when the house turned on her with its cold, strangling fingers. Perhaps she knew that if I returned to San Isidro, Titi's gifts or my own darker ones would reveal the truth eventually.

"May God forgive you, Tía," I murmured.

Then I set to work.

I flipped through the pamphlet. Though I had not laid hands on it in nearly a decade, my fingertips traveled well-worn roads through its pages, guided by memory as I searched for the most powerful exorcism contained within. The one Titi tapped with her index finger and of which she said, *Not yet, you are not strong enough for this one.*

As I searched, I saw the gunpowder eyes of my father's sister peering up at me through the glyphs. The terror I felt when I first beheld their dark spark. I saw disgust carving my father's face, heard his voice echo behind me as if he stood just feet from me in the dark of Ana Luisa's house. *They burn people like you.*

Burn, burn, burn. Perhaps that was what awaited me in death.

But in life, I would fight. I would fight to save the soul of San Isidro and the woman trapped inside its malicious walls because that was what was *right.* I knew it like a brand on my flesh as my fingertip found the glyphs I sought. It felt so right it had to be sinful.

The dark box in my chest trembled as I scanned the page. I felt its anticipation like the taste of pure cane sugar on my tongue.

Stand down, I told it. I had chosen to turn to this part of myself, but I would still keep my hands tight on the reins. I knew precisely the rituals and incantations to combine with these glyphs, and I would adhere to them with the utmost care. There was no room for error. No time to second-guess myself.

I looked up to the window over Ana Luisa's bed. Full darkness had fallen.

It was time.

The air hissed with anticipation as I shut the door to Ana Luisa's house behind me, pamphlet tucked under my arm. A storm hung over the mountains, teasing the tension in the valley with the crack of boulder on boulder. I could taste in the air that the valley would have no respite tonight; the wind had other designs, and carried the clouds away from us, sloping southeast toward the distant sea.

I gave a soft call into the dark; the night settled over my shoulders like a cloak. Invisible to the eyes of men, I slipped soundlessly through the gates of the courtyard.

My heart thrummed against my ribs; the darkness within me strained to leap forth, now that it knew I would call on it. I had to keep it in control. Beatriz's safety depended on my success. I would enter, find where she was. Exorcise the house and stay with her until dawn broke and we proved her innocence. It was simple. All I had to do was act according to my plan.

The caudillo's two men were stationed at the front door of the house, the closest to the capilla. One slept, the other stood watch. Though they had not lit their post with torches, the wakeful guard looked out into the night, alert to my silent approach, perhaps aware, as beasts were, of the presence of a predator.

Yes, I was here.

I slipped up the steps, around the man, behind him. A moment was all I needed to recite in his ear the prayer my grandmother used to sedate patients. He slumped against me. As he fell to the ground to the right of the door, I seized his gun, catching it so it would not clatter to the flagstones. I set it down at his side, then repeated the act on his sleeping compatriot just to be safe. I did not envy the throbbing in their heads that would plague them when they woke with the sun high in the sky.

It was time to enter the house.

I tried the handle of the door. It was locked, of course, but I had learned to bend locks to my will before I lost my first tooth.

Open, I bid it.

The house bucked; it threw me back a few steps, but I caught myself. I came back to the door. I touched the handle again, then snatched my hand back with a strangled cry—it was like ice, so cold it burned my palm.

I placed my stinging palm against the door and leaned into the cedar.

"Yes, it's me," I hissed through gritted teeth. "Yes, you hate me. I don't care. *Obey.*" This time, I lifted the lid of the box inside me a crack, just wide enough for a sliver of darkness to accompany my whispered incantation.

Then I seized the handle, ignoring the cold that jammed my joints stiff. I braced, preparing to force the door open.

Somewhere from the copse of trees beyond the village, the hooting of an owl caught my ear.

I paused. Tilted my head to the side, listening. It was calling to *me.* Once, twice, pause—a third call. That was a warning.

I released the door handle and took the steps in a single bound. Once my feet were on earth, I centered myself and swept my awareness around the perimeter of the house. All my senses were alight, sharpened by the darkness awakening within me, by the taste of fear on the night.

Something was deeply wrong. My skin crawled with it.

Acting on instinct, I left the front entrance of the house, crossing the garden to its southern wing. First striding quickly, then running, I beat through the weeds and emerged near the chicken coops at the back of the kitchen. My heart pounded in my throat as I pulled around the corner and skid to a stop, and the long terrace that lined the back side of the house came into view.

A ladder was set against the side of the house, but that was not what stopped me dead in my tracks.

It was another taste, heavy as metal on my tongue. *Smoke.*

A dark figure perched on the roof. A plume of black smoke billowed near it, barely visible against the dark sky. My eye fell to the window of the study above the drawing room: it was illuminated from within by flickering hellfire, its lurid glow an affront to the night.

Juana may kill her first.

I fell back a step, my mind utterly blank, my limbs turned to lead by shock.

Juana had set the house aflame. Within minutes, Beatriz could be dead, either by smoke or flame or any other violent means Juana had.

My heartbeat hammered in my ears. My hand trembled as it reached for the pamphlet, then froze. I did not have time to search for the right glyphs, to plan and draw and chant. Unless I acted, and acted now . . .

I had to get to Beatriz. Through the kitchen, up the stairs . . . and if the room were already alight, what then? Titi could pass through flame if she willed it; once she had taken a child from a burning house and emerged unscathed, though she was barefoot and bareheaded. I had no idea if I was capable of the same. Beatriz certainly was not. I had to fight on two fronts, strike two foes at once: extinguish the fire and get her out.

I had to be *fast*.

I dropped the pamphlet and backed up several steps, lifting my face and arms to the heavens, seeking, seeking, seeking as Titi did when the valley was parched.

The black clouds were slung low on the far side of the mountains, their bellies heavy with rain.

You, I called. *Heed me.*

The clouds did not turn their steely heads. The wind that ushered them, steady as a shepherd, swept me away like a fly from its hide.

I was not strong enough. I was a man divided, weak, uncertain. Not as strong as Titi. I did not have her conviction, nor her command over the skies. The wind had no master; it bore allegiance to no power. Any other night, I would have accepted this. I would have recognized how I was not strong enough. Any other night, I would have retreated. Sought other solutions. Taken the path that was safer.

But Beatriz was in that house.

Her words rang in my head. *Is there anything that doesn't require words? Something where you act on instinct, or you could improvise . . .*

Even though she saw the darkest parts of me, she looked at me with kindness. I had failed, I was damned, and still she looked at me as if I were someone worth having *faith* in.

I could not let her die. I would not let a Solórzano harm another person I loved.

I reached inside myself to the box. Darkness seeped from its lid like smoke; it was already straining at its lock. Without bracing myself, without questioning, without another thought, I did what I swore I would never do.

I flung it open.

Darkness surged through me like a flash flood. It swept through me and over me, deafening power coalescing into a dark storm in my chest, one that crackled, one that was *alive*. It quaked with the rumble of a thousand galloping hooves, with the strength of a long-sleeping volcano brought to the brink with fire and thunder and the Devil's brimstone.

I released it on the clouds.

"I am the witch of this valley!" I roared. "Heed me!"

Thunder rumbled. I *was* my fury, my anger, soaring through my chest and the crown of my head dizzyingly high, cracking as lightning across the low, leaden bellies of the clouds. Lightning struck once, twice, brilliant green.

I bound the clouds with all my strength and yanked them toward San Isidro. They resisted, but I dug in my heels and pulled harder.

Come, I commanded. *Come.*

The clouds released rumbles of thunder, but I kept pulling until, groaning, they shifted course. They breached the mountains, then spilled down into the valley toward San Isidro.

I sucked in a breath. Suddenly, I was no longer in the vast black of the skies, but in myself. My feet on the ground, outside the back of the kitchen. Sweat cut tracks down my hairline, down my spine. My very skin vibrated with dark power; I was stuck with a thousand needles over every inch of me, I was outside of my body and within it in the same breath. I was *alive*.

The clouds opened; sheets of steely rain struck San Isidro. Rain poured over my hair and face. My bones ached with it. My ally was here to fight the fire.

Now it was time to get Beatriz.

I seized the pamphlet from where I had dropped it on the earth and crossed the garden in three steps. I threw myself into the kitchen and flung the wet pamphlet on the table. I had no censer, no copal. No plan as I strode to the door, shaking and savage with power.

I was the storm. Witch's lightning crackled over my knuckles; though it scorched my skin, I felt no pain as I placed my hand on the locked door.

Open.

It flew off its hinges, landing with a sharp crack on the flagstones.

The darkness beyond turned to me. It seethed with anger; its hackles raised when it realized who—or rather, *what*—stood in its belly.

"Yes, it's me," I said, a feral grin pulling my lips taut. I shifted my weight, and with a flush of will, seized the darkness itself and held it in a stranglehold. "Now stay out of my way."

30

BEATRIZ

THE TORCH FELL. THE rug was soaked. The floors were slick. The door to the hall was on the far side of the room, and it was locked.

The bedchamber.

I didn't care about Rodolfo's blood anymore. I had to get away from the torch.

I bolted.

With each of my steps the torch grew closer to the ground; I was on the other side of the carpet, on floorboards that were dry, stumbling into the stench of—

The torch struck the carpet.

Flame exploded: blue and white, like lightning. It devoured the rug and shot to the sides of the room, engulfing it in seconds. When it reached the chests of my silks, those, too, exploded into flame: one, then the next. Any remaining glass vases shattered from the force of it.

I dropped into a crouch, shielding myself as best I could with my bound forearms.

From above, another bucket of alcohol poured into the room. Juana angled it so it splashed toward the locked door to the hall and the staircase, my only escape. I cried out as some splashed on my hair.

The flames consuming the carpet had caused the floorboards to catch flame; they licked toward the door. On the opposite end of the room, the desk began to crackle with heat. Through the rippling air, I watched as the edges of my father's map curled, blackened, and burst into flame.

This time, there was no Mamá calling my name. There was nowhere to run.

No way to escape.

I was going to die in this house.

Foul black smoke billowed through the room, stinging my eyes and blinding me. I coughed, but each breath I sucked in was hotter than the one before. I hacked, gasping for breath, and forced myself to my feet. The air rippled; the floorboards scorched my soles as I inched closer to the bed-chamber door.

I put my hand on the handle. I hissed as it scalded my palm but forced myself to try to open it.

It was locked.

I slammed a balled fist on the door in frustration, in panic. A door slammed elsewhere in the house as if in response. The darkness around me bucked and howled; wind fanned the flames higher, higher. The heat seared my cheeks; I shut my eyes against its onslaught.

Damn the house. It would whip the flames into an inferno and we would both be eaten alive. I would go first, and far more painfully—the floor would give out, and I would fall, and be buried beneath piles of flaming debris if I did not first break my neck.

"You want vengeance?" I cried out to the house. "Then take it. She's the one who killed you, isn't she?"

"Shut up," Juana shouted. Creaking overhead told me she was shifting away from the hole in the ceiling. She was retreating—fire or no, she was still wary of the house's unholy power.

Because she knew what she had done. Why the house was filled with rage. Why it called, *Juana, Juana, Juana,* into the darkness. Why the darkness of the house had sought Ana Luisa, her accomplice, in the night and given her a fright so powerful her heart stopped from terror.

I struck the door again. "She's right there. Take your revenge."

A groan shuddered through the house. Was it thunder? Was it madness and heat and smoke distorting my senses?

With a fearsome crack, the roof gave way.

Juana screamed.

She fell into the center of the flames. There was a wet *snap* that flipped my gut, for the instant I heard it, I knew it was not tiles or broken beams, but bone shattering.

She shifted, rose; shuddered and fell down again. A jingle of metal rang from her waist.

The keys. She had the keys.

"Juana!" I cried, then coughing seized my chest. We would both die without the keys.

The flames had seared away all the material to be burned on the rug; there was a path, of sorts, to where Juana lay crumpled amid broken wood and shattered tile.

My eyes teared with smoke as I reached to the floor and picked up a piece of broken glass. I tore at the hem of my dress with it; then, with shaking, bound hands, ripped strips of fabric away to wrap my feet. I worked clumsily, slowly, coughing all the while as black smoke filled the room. It would kill me before the flames did, I was sure of it.

You'll die here like the rest of us.

No. *Not tonight.*

I walked toward her, using my bound hands to cover my mouth with the last piece of cut cloth, praying my skirts were now too short to brush the embers scattering the floor. Oh, please, dear God, don't let the floor give way.

She looked like a broken doll, even as she forced herself up to her knees, coughing. Soot smeared her face. Her ankle was bent at a strange angle—it was broken.

My heart pounded as I looked down on her. I had called on the house to help defeat her but couldn't let her die in here. I could not bear to leave another human being to burn alive. I couldn't.

"Get up," I said, hoarse from coughing. "Keys. Let's go."

I held out my hands to her.

She looked up at me, panting, transformed by wild fury. A flash; the movement was so quick I didn't know what happened, not until white pain tore across my ribs.

The machete she had opened the roof with had fallen near her; she had snatched it and struck. Now it dripped with blood glinting orange in the firelight.

My blood.

Another flash; this time I dodged it. I stumbled backward, tripping on the rags that I had bound around my feet. I caught myself just before falling into a burning chest of silks.

She lurched to her feet, swaying, the machete in hand.

"This is my house. It's your fault"—she was cut off by a fit of coughing—"for trying to take it from me. You and Catalina." The heat rippled between us as she took a staggering lurch toward me. "You think you can come here and take what is mine? Go to *hell*."

The house shuddered around us. Unable to throw my arms out for balance, I fell. My shoulder ground into shattered glass; my head swam with smoke. I squinted up at the ceiling; it was alive with embers.

It was going to collapse on us.

This was the end. I had fought and I had failed. Would Papá be waiting for me, on the other side of agony?

Slam.

Damn those doors, I thought, coughing. My vision darkened. The shadows were moving. The shadows looked like someone's legs cutting through the flames . . .

"Beatriz!"

Andrés. He was here. Hands—*his* hands—hauled me to my aching feet. My awareness spun with smoke and heat as he lifted me into his arms.

A sickening crunch carved through the heat overhead. Tiles cracked as they struck one another. Beams groaned and snapped.

The roof fell.

"*Carajo.*"

Andrés ducked his head and bolted forward. Rather than trying to stop us or smother us, the attention of the house—of María Catalina—pulled away from us. It blazed down on Juana, on the inferno, and let us pass unassailed.

An explosion of sparks and heat; but it was behind me, it was behind us now. Cold air washed over my face. Andrés was taking the stairs two at a time, leaning against the banister for balance as he used our weight to sprint for the door.

Whispers I had never heard before swept around us from the walls of the house. Cobweb soft, they drew us forward, supporting us down the stairs, across the flagstones. To the front door.

It flew open of its own accord.

Andrés stumbled down the steps into the courtyard. Curtains of dark rain poured over us as he fell to his knees, his arms tight around me, holding me to his chest like a child. I realized, distantly, that he was speaking to me, that his breath hitched as if he were weeping, but everything around me faded to darkness.

To silence.

31

DARKNESS GRAYED; THERE WERE voices over me, light
and deep. Andrés's voice was among them, its soft rasp cutting through the
thick haze hanging over my mind. "Paloma, will you write down what he
said?"

"Shh, she's waking," Paloma's voice said.

I opened my eyes.

Wooden beams hung low overhead. A wool blanket rested over my
lower body and legs; cool air brushed over my stomach. A man with white
whiskers who looked vaguely like Padre Guillermo examined my side. A
touch of something warm that stung; I gasped, from surprise more than
pain.

"Gentle, doctor." Andrés's voice carried a dark warning.

"Padre, for the last time. Keep your peace or leave." The old man hovering over me harrumphed, but not unkindly. "Meddling know-it-all," he

added under his breath as he dabbed more poultice on the wound across my ribs.

I turned my head to the side. Paloma sat next to me, biting her lip as she scribbled furiously on a piece of paper—instructions from the doctor.

Andrés stood before the hearth, staring into the fire. His hands were bandaged in thick white strips, clasped as if in prayer with his fingertips pressed to his lips. Was he all right? What had happened?

Did Juana survive?

Andrés glanced over his shoulder, as if he heard my building distress, and met my gaze.

Rest. He did not speak, but I heard him as clearly as if he had. Whatever had happened, it was over. I could sleep.

I let myself melt away into soft, gray unconsciousness.

WHEN I WOKE SOMETIME later, it was to the sound of someone chopping vegetables.

Sunlight streamed over the blankets covering me. I turned my head to the side. There was a chair next to the cot I lay on. It was empty but for a stack of letters. Beyond was an open door; Paloma was outside, working in what looked like an open-air kitchen. The smell of frying onions brought me fully awake. I was famished.

I tossed off the blankets, wincing as I sat upright and brought my feet to the floor. The bandages around my torso were white and fresh, and the pain along my ribs had lessened to a dull throb.

I glanced at the chair. A single letter lay open atop a handful of envelopes; it was signed by the hand of Victoriano Román and absolved me of Rodolfo's murder. I lifted it; my breath caught.

The envelopes. They were addressed to Doña Beatriz Solórzano, of course, but in Mamá's handwriting.

I didn't notice the pain in my side as I reached for them. There were six, perhaps eight. My vision blurred as I tore the first open.

Mamá was back in Cuernavaca. The matriarch of Papá's extended family had died and left Mamá the little stone house in the garden where I had grown up. I saw her clearly as I read, as if I were in the room myself: Mamá sitting in its small kitchen, writing to me, surrounded by vases of flowers, the smell of her perfume mixing with chocolate warming on the stove. Her soil-stained gardening apron hanging on its hook on the door. Morning light curling into the room through the thick vines that hung rebelliously over the window.

Mamá invited me to visit. Mamá wanted to make amends, Mamá wanted . . . she wanted *me*. It was evident from Mamá's letters that she was concerned by the lack of reply, but that she understood my stubbornness, and prayed I would forgive her.

Later, after I had read them all and forced myself to stop sobbing for the pain it caused in my side, I limped to the doorway.

The wind shifted; smoke from the cooking fire carried over to me, and I shuddered. Paloma looked up from stirring a vat of pozole over the fire.

I lifted the letter I held in my hand, too shaken to speak.

Paloma's face transformed with pity. She set her ladle aside and wiped her hands on her apron. "I found them among the patrón's belongings," she said softly.

I shook the letter once, still speechless. *He lied.*

"My mother . . ." I fumbled for words. "She wants me to come to her."

"Will you go?"

I nodded. My voice was hoarse from disuse; could I trust it to carry me through a sentence? "I have to," I said. "I can't stay."

Paloma held out her arms to me. I cried in her embrace like a child.

"Now that's enough," she said after a minute or two, pulling me away by the shoulders. "If you cry any more you'll reopen your side, and it's me Andrés will be angry with."

I sniffed and looked around us. We were somewhere in the village. Small houses nestled up against one another like sparrows against a winter wind; a few curious onlookers peered at us but quickly turned away or vanished into their houses when they saw me looking.

"Where is he?"

Paloma shrugged, turning back to the pozole. "Back at the house, trying to get it to listen to him," she said. "He'll wear himself out eventually. And when he does, he knows where to find us."

32

ANDRÉS

AFTER A DAY AND night of hovering at Beatriz's bedside, using my grandmother's gifts to ensure that her recovery was seamless and quick, Paloma unceremoniously ushered me out of her house.

"She can't rest properly if you keep meddling. Go be useful elsewhere," she said. With a meaningful tilt of her head, she gestured out the doorway at the main house of the hacienda. "You know what I mean."

I did.

The morning was gray and misty as I walked across the courtyard to the house, my aunt Inés's pamphlet in hand. Its pages had been damaged by rain, but its glyphs survived without a smudge. I suspected something a bit stronger than ink bound them to the page.

The house watched my approach, silent and apprehensive. Its stucco was stained with soot from the smoke, but the fire had primarily damaged the far side of the house. From the front, it was the same it had always been: a few tiles missing from the roof, wilting bougainvillea. Flower beds weeded, then abandoned.

I could almost feel it narrowing its invisible eyes as it sized me up: like it, I looked the same as I had before the night of the fire. But a different man opened the front door and stepped into its cavernous quiet. It smelled of rain, wet wood. The aftertaste of smoke lingered heavy on the mist that seeped into the ruins of the dining room and, above it, Beatriz's study and bedchamber.

The night of the fire, the roof had collapsed on Juana. Mendoza and I searched for her body there the next day and found it in the formal dining room, shattered and scorched. The floor of the burning room had collapsed into the room below before rain could extinguish the flames.

We buried Juana in the Solórzano plot with even less fanfare than her brother . . . and as far from her brother as we could manage. The caudillo Victoriano Román abandoned his investigation against Beatriz when Paloma brought forth a blood-blackened knife and dress from Juana's rooms; her evidence was compounded by Juana's arson and the blatantly clear attempt she had made to kill Beatriz.

I shook away the memory of finding Beatriz ringed by flames. It haunted me like my own shadow. In my brief, stolen hours of sleep since that night, I saw nothing but her silhouette against Perdition's rage. In dreams, I could not move. I cried out to her but was voiceless. My feet were too heavy, my arms feeble and unable to move as fire devoured her, as her screams for help whipped the flames higher, still higher.

I woke drenched in cold sweat, her name knotted in my throat.

Never again would I allow her to be so threatened. I swore no more harm would come to anyone under this roof. I was there that morning to ensure that.

But would it be enough?

Paloma told me that she and Mendoza had found a stack of letters addressed to Beatriz among Rodolfo's papers, that she suspected they came from Beatriz's mother.

She wants to leave, Cuervito, she said. We must let her.

I wanted to flinch away from the softness of her voice. I found my beloved cousin's brusqueness fortifying. I longed for her sharp edges, a blunt retort. To receive her sympathy made me fear she saw too much. It made me fear she saw even more clearly than I how powerfully I wanted Beatriz to stay.

But would I want to stay, if I were Beatriz? So many Solórzanos had died in this house over the years. Some violently, some not. Their voices would always live in its walls, as would the memories of the hundreds of people of my family who had served them. Such houses were what they were. I could not remove those voices any more than I could remove the foundation of the house. Some people could live in such houses utterly unaware of the company they held. For others, the walls were halfway to sentience, as difficult to live with as an overly intrusive relative.

But there was one force I needed to release. One body left to bring to the graveyard once its spirit had passed.

I could only hope it would be enough to convince Beatriz to stay.

Evil twitched in the shadows of the house, unnaturally inky black. It slipped through the halls, following me as I stepped into the green parlor. I left the door open, inviting it to follow, as I walked toward the center of the room. I began to move furniture and rolled the green rug away, my movements even and deliberate as I took a piece of charcoal from my pocket and set it to stone. I drew the first line of an exorcism glyph.

The door slammed behind me.

My heart skipped a step, then steadied as I flexed my hands. Scars were forming beneath the bandages wound around my knuckles, sustained from the burns of lightning.

I was not the same man who had faced the darkness before.

I continued sketching the correct glyphs under the watchful gaze of the darkness, my hand steady even as the hair rose on the back of my neck. Newfound power did not mean I was not still prey. I could smell my own natural fear rising, its tang metallic and sweet.

She was here.

Of course she was here. I would not grant her the satisfaction of seeing me afraid of her. I inhaled deeply, turned the page of the pamphlet, and continued working for long, silent minutes until the circle was closed.

Then I rose, stepped into the center of the circle, and faced the shadows.

"Buenos días, doña," I said.

A soft hiss. A rattlesnake's hiss, but deeper in timbre. A predator's hiss.

"Enough," I said, voice ringing with chastisement. "It is time."

My arms loose at my sides, I turned my palms out to the shadows.

That simple act was all it took. Like an arroyo glutted by a flash flood, I was flush with dark power. The darkest parts of myself were no longer bound, no longer confined to the box. It no longer weighed heavy in my chest, chained with shame and self-loathing and fear of what awaited me after death. It spread over my limbs with the weightlessness of dew, a steady comfort. I wore it with the ease of my own shadow, even when I turned to my grandmother's gifts. Even when I celebrated Mass and led the people of San Isidro in prayer.

The darkness howled, building around me with the electricity of a storm.

You must find your own way, Titi always said.

If I continued walking the path I knew was right, one day, I would find my own balance. My way. My calling.

I reached into the darkness and took the spirit of Doña María Catalina in my fist. It flung its weight away from me, battling for release with sheer force of will as Titi's incantations unspooled from my lips.

"Enough," I repeated in castellano.

I yanked down with all my strength.

A sound like a cord snapping split the darkness. The house's stormy rebellion died.

The spirit of Doña María Catalina stepped into the parlor, as real as she had been when I saw her in this room years ago. She shimmered like a mirage as I drew her into the circle. She was as delicate and sugar-spun as when I first saw her in the plaza de armas of Apan years ago, dressed in gray, her corn silk hair haughtily upswept. The enmity she felt for me in life, that she directed at me through the house, was perfectly etched on her features as she crossed her arms over her chest.

Hate like hers was a cancer. It was time to excise it from my home, once and for all.

"I think you know what I'm here to do," I said.

Her mouth twisted into an elegant scowl.

I hope you burn, she spat. *Burn, burn, burn.*

The thrum of her voice struck my ears like drumming. Like the pulse of unholy fire that lit my dreams.

They burn people like you.

How long those words had wounded me.

I gave Doña Catalina my most beatific smile. Yes, I still feared discovery, by Padre Vicente or someone worse. Yes, I feared the hereafter. I was a sinner. I was a witch. I had sinned and would sin again, like all men. But whatever my decisions meant for life after death was between me and the Lord. All I could do was serve the home and people I loved using every gift I was born with.

I squared off with the apparition of Doña Catalina.

It was long past time for her to face the Lord herself. She and I both knew it; an expression of resignation shadowed her features as I lifted my voice with incantations, as my power wound itself thickly around her. In a moment, I would sever her from the house for eternity. If she feared what waited for her on the other side, she gave no indication of it.

"There is only One who decides who burns and who does not," I said.

With a sound like the ripping of paper, the apparition of Doña Catalina turned to ash. It hovered on the air, then drifted slowly down through the silence to the charcoal glyphs on the floor. There, they curled in on themselves like burning paper, shrinking and melting away.

I made the sign of the cross.

"Let His will be done," I said.

33

BEATRIZ

THOUGH THE SUN SHONE bright in an azure sky, I wore a thick wool shawl over my shoulders as Andrés escorted me to the house. He had succeeded in healing it several days ago; it was safe enough that Paloma had salvaged some of my clothing from the wreckage of the fire. The dining room was damaged, for it was beneath my study, she said, but otherwise the majority of the house remained unscathed. My belongings were not so lucky. Smoke had damaged much of what had not burned, but I didn't care.

The next morning, I was leaving. I was taking Mamá up on her invitation and going to Cuernavaca for a long, long time. Perhaps forever.

Part of me was wary—was Cuernavaca truly the solution to my longing for a home? I had thought as much of San Isidro.

Perhaps it wouldn't be.

But I knew that returning to Mamá was.

Birdsong lilted overhead as we entered the courtyard and walked toward the house. Swallows swooped toward the pockmarked tiles of the roof; nests had emerged in the hollows beneath tiles.

I stopped before the door, my heart hammering.

Andrés took the steps leading up to the door two at a time and reached for the handle before he noticed my reticence or the color draining from my face. I would not be surprised if he could hear the panicked thundering of my heart against my rib cage.

"It's all right," he said softly. "She's gone. The house is back to its old self."

The house looked the same, but I could sense—somehow I could, somehow I could *feel* it, through my feet on the ground, through the taste of the air—that he spoke the truth. The energy of the house had softened. Whatever attention it had turned inward, on itself. I was not its focus. I was no longer a mouse walking into the jaws of a cat.

Andrés backtracked down the steps. He held out a hand. "It's completely inhabitable now. It's safe."

For a moment, I wavered, considering his upturned palm. Perhaps I could step inside, if only to see for myself that he was right. That he had healed it.

Alcohol catching flame blazed through my mind. The flash of the machete. The certainty of heat, the inevitability of catching flame . . .

"No." My throat tightened. I could still taste acrid smoke, hear Juana's cry as she fell, hear the wet snap of bone. No, I could not go in. Not now. "It's too much."

"Beatriz." His hand was still outstretched, his voice soft. "I spent the night here, without copal, to make sure of it. It's very peaceful."

I considered him warily. Why was he so eager to show me? Why did he feel the need to prove he was right? Didn't he understand?

When I met his eyes, the answer opened before me, bright as the toll of the capilla bell.

Because he wants you to stay.

But I couldn't.

I had once called the house before us *mine*. I came to its threshold with the confidence of a conqueror, of a general, ready to put down its rebellions and bend it to my will. I was wrong to. San Isidro could never have been mine. Never would be. It had never been Juana's. Nor Rodolfo's, nor any other Solórzano's.

If it belonged to anyone, it was to the people who lived here, like Paloma and Ana Luisa and Mendoza. To Andrés. Or perhaps it belonged to no one, and would forever remain a willful, ancient domain unto itself. A pale stucco giant slumbering in this valley, its high walls looming, forever watchful, over the fields of maguey.

For me, it would remain a place of painful memories, lingering fear woven thick over the place like a shroud. I knew that if I stayed, I would suffocate beneath its weight.

"I can't stay," I breathed. "I'm leaving."

Andrés lowered his hand. "Cuernavaca."

"You must understand," I said. "This house, the money. None of it matters unless I have Mamá. She apologized, in her letters, and I . . ." I trailed off, my voice wavering precipitously close to breaking. "I have to go to her."

The lines of his face settled; his breathing shifted. "I know."

We went for a long walk, my last survey of the property before leaving the next day. We crested the hill overlooking the neat rows of maguey and stopped to catch our breath. Or for me to catch my breath, rather—like the first time I had seen him walk up the hill to San Isidro, Andrés was infuriatingly at ease, as if he had expended no more energy than crossing a parlor on his long legs.

The wind had changed, and clouds thickened the blue sky. I pulled my shawl tighter around my shoulders. I traced the sweep of the valley before us, into the dark rolling hills of the mountains far away. A breeze swept through high golden grasses, a bite of winter on its breath. Far away, a boy whistled to his dog as they followed a herd of cloud-white sheep trotting across the valley floor.

"Will you ever come back?"

I turned to Andrés. His hands hung loose at his sides. I had noticed the backs of his hands were roped with strange new scars. I had not yet asked him about them, and I would not now.

He looked down at me with an expression I knew immediately was a mask, for it showed a calm too carefully composed to be natural.

"Don't look at me like that," I said. "Say what you mean to say."

A long moment passed where only the wind spoke. It lifted and whispered through the grasses, passing the quiet gossip of the valley to the hilltop.

I turned my face away from him, toward the shepherd and his flock far away. I had misspoken. I should have never agreed to be alone with him, not like this, not when I was raw. Not when my ribs ached with a sweetness that was not from mortal wounds.

The soft touch of fingertips at my wrist.

I looked up as he took my hand loosely in his. My breath caught as he lifted it to his mouth and pressed my knuckles to his lips.

Now his face laid his emotions bare: brows drawn together, a mournful earnestness in his hazel eyes that made my heart trip over itself.

Don't go, that look said.

My pulse pounded in my ears. The breeze that rose stung my cheeks; they burned with a flush as we stood, locked in each other's gaze for many heartbeats, still as figures in a painting.

He did not speak.

How could he? There was too much to say. The road we stood on led to nowhere but parting.

Somewhere over the mountains, a soft roll of thunder sounded.

Andrés cast a look up at the sky, soft annoyance crossing his features. As if he were displeased with the heavens for interrupting.

"Is it going to rain?" I whispered.

He still held my hand to his lips. I could almost feel his indecision against my skin. Of course it was going to rain. It always did, this time of year. But rain meant turning back, and turning back meant . . .

"I don't think so." His breath brushed against my knuckles, sending a shiver over my skin.

The wind tugged at my skirts. One cold drop, then another, struck my cheeks.

"Liar," I said, and pulled my hand toward me. He released it, though his expression remained unchanged.

I turned away. I couldn't bear to see it. Better to bid goodbye and get it over with than linger with him here. Better not to think about how perhaps, he was as lonely as I was. How perhaps he felt the tautness between us as I did, as a living, breathing thing. A creature of featherlight longing that bound us, though it rippled fragile as mist at sunrise. Perhaps he was afraid that my leaving meant losing it forever.

It would.

And that was the way it *should* be.

I repeated this over and over to myself, setting one foot in front of the other. I walked ahead of Andrés so I would not have to look at him and filled myself with stern determination. This was the way it must be. Loneliness had been a part of my life before, and perhaps it would be again—it was not something that would kill us.

But oh, the weight that had lifted from my shoulders when I slept next to him in the capilla. When we sat shoulder to shoulder, facing the darkness together. The rush of knowing one was not alone was a heady thing, thicker than mezcal in the way it made my head spin.

We were still a half kilometer from the village when the clouds broke open. The rains in the valley never began shyly: it was as if the skies had made a trip to the well and dumped bucket after bucket into the valley with cackling abandon.

At first I made to outrun it, pulling my shawl over my head in a vain attempt to keep dry, then I pulled up short. I was breathing too hard; my wound hurt faintly. Andrés was at my side then, and I laughed up at him as I opened my arms to the skies.

"I surrender," I called to the clouds. "You win."

We reached the capilla before the village. By then, the rain was coming down in sheets so thick the ground was slick with mud and the stucco walls of the chapel gray in my vision.

"Come inside," Andrés said, raising his voice to be heard over the tumult. I followed him to his rooms off the chapel. He struck his head in the low doorway for the umpteenth time; he cursed colorfully. I broke into breathless laughter as I followed, shaking from the cold and from running through the rain.

He shut the door behind me. His hair was slicked dark across his forehead, his outer coat completely soaked. I lifted my shawl and held it out before me. It poured water onto the floor.

"I'm so sorry," I gasped between peals of laughter. "I didn't mean to—"

I broke off, laughter dying on my lips. He had taken a step closer to me. My pulse pounded in my throat as he tucked a curl behind my ear and, ever so delicately, took my face in his hands. My cheeks burned; the brush of his thumbs was cool relief.

He met my eyes and saw all the answer he needed there.

He kissed me.

There was no hesitation. No shyness. Only *need*.

I dropped the shawl. I leaned into him and kissed him back, winding my arms around him. Holding his warmth close. Fleetingly, I thought of how Rodolfo was the only person I had ever kissed, and how this was *nothing* like that. Time was lost to me—here, there was no calculating, no wandering thoughts. I was *here*, breathlessly *here*, and seized with a dizziness that left me clinging to Andrés as if he alone could keep me on my feet. As if there were nothing in the world but Andrés, the smell of rain on his skin,

◆ ◆ ◆ THE HACIENDA

his lips on the sensitive skin of my throat, his hands traveling down my back and pressing me to him with a strength I did not know he had.

I dug my fingers into his back. Hard.

A small gasp against my neck. "*Beatriz.*" Then his mouth was on mine again, hard, with a deep and searing need.

I knew then I would not look back. I would not look forward.

There was only now, there was only stripping soaked clothes from burning skin and the labored creak of his cot as he sat on it and drew me roughly into his lap. There was only *now*, the skin of his chest against mine, running my fingers through his damp hair as he kissed my neck and breasts, holding me so tightly to him I could barely breathe.

He loosed a small groan as I rocked against him. "Don't leave." There was a note of helplessness in it, a plea, a prayer.

"Come with me," I said into his hair. "To Cuernavaca. Leave all this behind."

He lifted his head and looked up at me.

All this.

For the briefest second, his eyes skipped past me, to where I knew a cross hung on the wall. A flicker of apprehension across his face; a soft lilt of panic in his voice as he forced his attention back to me. "I can't think about that now. I can't."

"Shh." I cupped his face in my hands, running my thumbs over his cheeks. I wanted to memorize the feeling of his stubble against my palms, the shape of his lips as they parted. His dark eyelashes, framing eyes that looked up at me with utter trust. With a longing so open and deep it sent an ache through my chest.

No looking back. No looking forward.

"Then don't." I lowered my face to his. "Just be with me now," I breathed against his lips. "*Be.*"

◆ ◆ ◆ 327

34

THE NEXT MORNING, PALOMA and José Mendoza helped me put my trunks in the carriage. Mendoza held his hat in his hands awkwardly as Paloma and I embraced and both burst into tears, promising to write.

I watched them walk back through the gates of San Isidro.

Using José Mendoza as an intermediary, I had sold the land that our neighbor Hacienda San Cristóbal so greatly coveted. I had made Mendoza and Paloma keepers of the property in my absence and drafted a plan with them for how the new income would be used and invested. Reopening the hacienda's general store for the first time since the death of old Solórzano, with all the villagers' generations-old debts wiped away. Building a school for the children. It was the talk of the village, passed from hand to hand with loaves of pan de muerto as families prepared for the first of November, as they gathered in the graveyard behind the capilla and exchanged news over the crackling of small bonfires.

I had spent the holiday evening indoors with Paloma. We scattered bright cempasúchil petals around a small ofrenda for her mother, but she did not want to go to the graveyard. And I had no desire to go into the graveyard bearing offerings for the Solórzanos. Some wounds were too fresh. Perhaps they would heal, when we were ready for them to. Instead, we sat by the fire and talked long into the night, our conversation marked by the rising and falling of laughter, by the blue of a single plume of copal at the door.

I would miss her. Her bluntness. How her sense of humor bent wicked more often than not. But I knew she and I would correspond regularly. I had officially made her Mendoza's heir as foreman. She would see the house repaired and cleaned; cover its furniture with dust cloths and keep the gardens alive. If I or my descendants ever found ourselves in need of its use, Paloma would see to it that the house would be ready and waiting. If I ever healed enough to return.

If.

"Are you ready, Doña Beatriz?" the driver asked.

"A few more minutes," I said. There was one person I still had not yet said farewell to.

Andrés stood off to the side of the carriage, his shoulders stiff. He, too, watched the gates where Paloma and Mendoza had melted away, and did not look down at me until I walked the few steps between us and stood before him.

Finally, he met my eyes.

Neither of us said anything for a long moment.

"You could come with me," I blurted out at last.

There was still time. The carriage could wait as we gathered his few belongings from the rooms adjoining the capilla. We could leave together, start a new life. Something unmarred and perfect and—

He dropped my gaze and turned his face to the side, looking away from me.

My heart sank.

"I can't." His voice cracked. "This is who I am. This is my home."

Andrés the priest. Andrés the witch. He was a fractured creature, stretched between darkness and light. He belonged to this place in ways I could never comprehend, and he chose to keep belonging: the village. His family. The Church. His land.

"I know," I breathed.

But I offered no apology for what I had said. It was what a deep, selfish part of me wanted: I wanted to steal him away and make him mine. I wanted to keep him always by my side; I wanted his hand clasped, warm and strong, over mine. I wanted him *near* with an ache that carved bone deep.

And I understood it was not possible.

As I took a step backward, he lifted his head. For a moment, I thought of his face last night, how its lines were softened by the dark. How his eyes had fluttered closed as our linked breathing drew us slowly toward sleep. How young he had looked. How at peace.

Now his eyes were bloodshot, his mouth set in a hard twist that betrayed how he fought to keep his composure.

If only I could speak. If only I could say something to alleviate his pain and mine, but I couldn't. There was a tempest inside me, thoughts jostling one another back and forth, struggling to be set free: I could say how I would carry him with me always. How he had saved my life and I would be forever in his debt.

How I longed for him to choose *me*. How I was angry he would not leave everything behind for me.

How ardently I wished for him to never, ever change.

But for all that, I had no words.

In that moment, we were two people standing opposite each other on the road. We had walked it together, holding each other close in the dark, but now our paths forked. His led one way, back to the village, back to his family, back to San Isidro.

Mine led another way: to Cuernavaca. To Mamá. To a wealthy widow's freedom, a freedom that was so frighteningly my own I barely knew how to hold its reins.

But I would learn how. I would learn to carve my future into whatever I wished it to be.

I had Andrés to thank for that. For believing me when I could not believe myself, for reaching into a nightmare and drawing me to a dawn.

But now the gray mists of dawn had burned away, and day was garish bright around us. He had given me a new chance at life. The only way to repay such an act was to *live*. I knew the only way for me to heal, to fully live again, was to leave San Isidro behind.

"I will always trust you," I breathed. "Adios."

Then I turned my back on Andrés, on Hacienda San Isidro, and stepped into the carriage.

35

ANDRÉS

THE CARRIAGE WAS GONE. I knelt in the dust, staring at an empty horizon.

You will learn to feel it. Those were some of the last words Titi said before I left for the seminary in Guadalajara. *When the time comes, you will know what is right.*

Holding Beatriz in my arms felt right. Giving in, losing myself in her dark hair, in the warmth of her body, the brush of her lips over my skin— that, too, had felt *right*.

And yet . . . so did this.

All this time, I thought knowing what was right would bring me peace or contentment. Instead, sorrow draped leaden across my shoulders as I watched the empty horizon, every fiber of my being willing the carriage to turn back.

But it was *right* for Beatriz to leave.

Her need to heal was profound, and I knew it simply could not be accomplished beneath San Isidro's roof. Yes, I had purged the house of its malice, cleansed its energy. But when I saw the fear that bloomed in her eyes when she looked up at the house, I knew there was nothing more I could do. She deserved a life free of such fear.

I had to let her go.

Beatriz leaving San Isidro would give the hacienda the space *it* needed to heal. I had sensed when I met her that she was not like the other Solórzanos, and I had been right—but not everyone who lived on this land knew and trusted her as I did. So long as she remained, she would be the symbol of the family that had carved so much damage into the land and its people. For too many generations, there had been a Solórzano to fear in the great house of this hacienda. Too many generations of pain. If the people who owned this land in deed never again lived on its soil, I could only envision peace coming of it for my family and the others who lived here.

But thickness welled in my throat at the thought of Beatriz never returning. Selfishly, I could not bear the idea. Her presence in my life the last few weeks turned my world on its head, pulled me out of my festering resentment for the Solórzanos and into action. It was her intercession that had ended my banishment and brought me back home. Without her, who knew how long San Isidro and my family would have suffered from haunting and hacendado alike.

Slowly, I rose. My limbs were stiff; my head ached from a night of little sleep. My eyes burned from tears shed and unshed, from the dust the carriage left in its wake.

It was *right* for Beatriz to leave. Just as it was right for me to stay here, on this land, with the people who needed me most.

That did not mean saying goodbye would be easy.

IN THE WEEKS THAT followed Beatriz's departure, I often sought solace in the house. During the siesta hours, when I knew Paloma and

Mendoza would not be frequenting their realm—a small drawing room off the kitchen in the main house repurposed for their bookkeeping and general use—I would walk the path through the front garden, up the low steps, and into the shadow of the threshold.

One day, six weeks after Beatriz's farewell, I entered the house and felt a tug of awareness from the rafters. I closed the front door behind me, surveying the dim foyer with narrowed eyes.

The door of the green parlor swung open with a low creak. An invitation. A quiet beckoning.

The house wanted me to go into the room. With Doña Catalina gone, it went through phases of deep sleep and sentience, the latter frank and guileless, if occasionally prone to mischief. I was not afraid as I walked straight to the green parlor and stepped through the open door.

A white envelope lay on the carpet in the center of the room, its intentional placement and the contrast of paper against dark green rug capturing my attention.

How odd. Paloma and Mendoza were not fond of this room, and therefore it was unlikely they had forgotten any of their bookkeeping notes here. Though weeks had passed since the night of my failed exorcism, the night the darkness unleashed its full fury on me, the walls of the room still hummed with my touch. Memories swirled through my mind as I drew near: Juana slouched in this chair ignoring the hacendados, Doña Catalina resplendent as a demon in the firelight. Mariana flinching away from me. Beatriz sitting on the flagstones when the parlor was bare; her face, framed by dark wispy curls and illuminated by candlelight, open and unafraid.

You're a witch.

I savored the memory of her voice. The way her whisper held a profane, exquisite power over me, how its brush could send an aching trill down my spine.

When I was near enough to make out the name written in a looping, thin hand, I froze mid-step.

It was addressed to *me*.

Distantly, I was aware of my heart losing its rhythm, caught off-balance by a swift updraft of hope. I did not recognize the handwriting when I picked it up, but when I turned it over, the unmistakable Solórzano seal was embedded in dark green wax.

Beatriz.

I knew Paloma had her address, for she had mentioned their correspondence over dinner one night. When at last I could not resist any longer, I went looking for it. Without asking her permission—out of fear that doing so would raise her suspicion—I snuck into her and Mendoza's realm.

How I would confess this sin to Padre Guillermo was a thorny question. And what of confessing the reason *why* I wanted to write to Beatriz? I thrust the thought away whenever it crossed my mind. I guarded the memories of her last night in San Isidro fiercely, protecting them from the harsh light of reality. I was not ready to repent. I was not ready to let go.

Perhaps I should have respected the finality of her farewell, let my path and hers continue to diverge. But I was weak. I wrote her a letter and sent it. Hastily followed by a second, dashed off when anxiety spun me awake in the black of the night; this was briefer, formal, apologizing for assuming she wanted to hear from me, apologizing for the contents of the first, which were decidedly . . . raw. Perhaps inappropriate. Certainly stupid.

I had not let myself hope for a reply. How could I? What if I had, and a reply never came? Or what if she did reply . . . ? I did not know what I would do then.

Now that it had happened, I discovered that my hands had begun to shake.

The house shifted around me. Could I interpret its creaking as self-satisfied? As pleased with itself? Perhaps it had filched this from Paloma and Mendoza's bookkeeping room. Perhaps, over the course of my quiet visits, it had sensed that a hole was gouged open in me as well, that I was healing from wounds just as it was.

Perhaps it also sensed the reason why. A curious presence tugged at my attention from above. I heard no words—houses, healed as I had healed this one, were not capable of speech—but I understood its question.

Where? it wondered. *Where is she?*

I knew which *she* it referred to. Not María Catalina, no—it was relieved to be rid of her. The *she* it had helped save, by whisking us down the stairs and out the door the night of the fire. She who had left with the intention of never returning. She whose letter I slipped into my pocket.

"Gone," I whispered. "It's just you and me, now."

I walked to the doorway and patted it as I passed through, as one would pat the flank of a horse at the end of a long, exhausting journey.

Somewhere upstairs, a door slammed.

I jumped, snatching my hand back with a curse.

Soft laughter spilled overhead. I looked up at the rafters, heart thumping against the inside of my chest. That was not the shrill, girlish giggle that plagued Beatriz and me over the last few weeks—no, this was a harmony of different voices, some smokier and older than I had ever heard before.

I willed my heart to slow and scowled at the rafters.

The house was *teasing* me.

"Cielo *santo*," I snapped. But an affectionate smile toyed at the corner of my mouth as I turned to the front door.

Hacienda San Isidro was healing from its wounds.

I stepped into the sunlight and took Beatriz's letter from my pocket. I brushed my fingertips over my name written by her hand, over the green wax with which she had sealed the letter, a reverent thief with his stolen treasure.

With time, God willing, so, too, would I heal. But I was not ready to. Not yet.

I opened it.

AUTHOR'S NOTE

It BEGAN BECAUSE I am afraid of the dark.

Over the course of the first eighteen years of my life, my family lived in nine houses. I learned by the fourth of these that not all houses are the same. Some are still. Empty and quiet. Others have long, long memories, hung thick like curtains and so dense you can taste their bitterness the moment you cross the threshold.

I have a theory about houses, says Andrés.

From the age of thirteen, as my family settled into its eighth house, I found the sensation of being watched unbearable. I began to sleep with the lights on. For years, I have endured teasing from my sisters. I still fear the intimate horrors houses see and keep, what grudges build over decades and stain their walls like so much water damage.

But it's only a theory, after all.

A theory that planted the seed of an idea.

◆ ◆ ◆

AS A YOUNG MEXICAN-AMERICAN reader, I struggled to find representation in genre fiction. It simply didn't exist. I clung to any brunette on the page, desperate for mirrors that reflected my experience of feeling out of place in spaces that *should* feel like home.

I knew from the opening sketches of this idea that this book—a sacrifice at the altar of my childhood fears, an homage to Shirley Jackson and Daphne du Maurier—would feature characters who looked like me and my family, who acted and sounded like us. I also knew I wanted it to take place during or after Mexico's War of Independence, a period that has fascinated me for years.

As I am a historian by training, I flung myself into researching the crucial, complicated period directly following the end of Mexico's War of Independence. A historical period is more than the dates of its battles and politicians jockeying for power in affluent capitals. It is the sum of a thousand strokes of a mad artist's brush: it is droughts and floods, new inheritance laws, fabrics and building materials becoming cheap or too expensive, taxes imposed to be paid or ignored, the privileging of one language over another. It is the rhythms of daily life in towns that are silenced, the spirits that move in the shadows cast by the conquerors' history books.

I knew that in the year 1823, two years after the end of the draining eleven-year War of Independence, money was scarce. I also knew I wanted my novel to be shaped by the classic Gothic trappings of a grand old house and a mysterious new husband. As I sifted through the ashes of the War of Independence, searching for the right setting, I followed the money.

It led to pulque.

It led to an hacienda.

And as I wrote, *The Hacienda* began to engage with the ugly themes of the period: the racist *casta* system, the racial and socioeconomic dynamics of the hacienda and land ownership, colonialism, and oppressive religion.

The novel evolved. It became more than the story of a house, for in this period, a house like Hacienda San Isidro was more than four walls, more than a home.

It was power.

The Hacienda is a story about the terrible things people will do to cling to power. A story about resilience and resistance in the face of a world that would strip you of power. A story about a young mestiza woman's battle of wills with a house and all it represents, a house haunted by both the supernatural and its colonial history.

THE HACIENDA IS NOT intended to be a source for the study of this period of Mexican history. At its heart, it is a horror novel, a suspenseful yarn about witchcraft, forbidden romance, and things that go bump in the night. I am leaving the academy to devote myself to the life of a novelist, a métier that demands that I close the history books and lie colorfully in the name of plot and character.

For example, Padre Andrés's belief system is fictional. I wanted to build a worldview for this character that was respectful of and informed by folk beliefs I learned from my mother and other family members, but also influenced by the specific colonial context of nineteenth-century Mexico and its religious syncretism. I am deeply indebted to the primary texts and secondary analysis included in *Local Religion in Colonial Mexico* by Martin Austin Nesvig, *Nahua and Maya Catholicisms: Texts and Religion in Colonial Central Mexico and Yucatan* by Mark Christensen, and *The Witches of Abiquiu: The Governor, the Priest, the Genízaro Indians, and the Devil* by Malcolm Ebright and Rick Hendricks.

I encourage readers who are interested in the facts of this period to look up overview texts like *Everyday Life and Politics in Nineteenth Century Mexico: Men, Women, and War* by Mark Wasserman and *The Women of Mexico City, 1790-1857* by Silvia Marina Arrom.

If reading *The Hacienda* encourages you to pick up these books and others, I hope you will discover what I did: that homes like Hacienda San Isidro were haunted by more than the supernatural.

Colonialism has carved the landscapes of our homes with ghosts. It left gaping wounds that still weep.

Reading historical fiction can teach us about worlds long gone, but in doing so, it must also inspire reflections on the present. As a historian, a Mexican-American woman, and a fellow reader, I hope this novel inspires the courage, anger, and compassion we all need to face the ghosts of colonialism that linger today.

ACKNOWLEDGMENTS

I must first thank my agent, the indomitable Kari Sutherland, the most passionate advocate of my writing and career. Words cannot describe how grateful I am to have signed with someone who fights so hard for my work, whose business acumen and editorial eye I trust, and who so kindly humors my need for utterly arbitrary deadlines to chase. I raise my glass to you and to many books to come.

To my fierce champion Jen Monroe, whose sharp editorial insight helped me push myself to the best of my current capabilities and shape this novel into something I am truly proud of: thank you. I have grown so much working with you. I can't wait to see how high we soar with the next one!

To the incredible team at Berkley, whose hard work I deeply admire and appreciate: Lauren Burnstein, Jennifer Myers, Christine Legon, Marianne Aguiar, Jessica Mangicaro, and Daniela Riedlová, and the publishing team: Claire Zion, Craig Burke, and Jeanne-Marie Hudson. I especially thank Vi-An Nguyen and Kristin del Rosario for bringing my first novel to life—it is a long-held dream to hold this book in my hands, and I am so grateful for your part in making that a reality.

I am endlessly grateful to the Clarion West class of 2018, but especially to B. Pladek and N. Theodoridou's insightful critiques, daily encouragement, accountability, and love in our beloved Slack channel. I thank the '21–'22 Berkley debut group (a.k.a. the Berkletes), CPs I have had the brilliant luck of meeting over the internet (Tanvi Berwah, Rae Loverde), and my brilliant agent sisters (especially Kelly Coon) for laughter, levity, wisdom, and commiseration. Thank you to my PitchWars mentors, Monica Bustamente Wagner and Kerbie Addis, and to writers I met through that cohort, especially Hannah Whitten and Marilyn Chin: your advice and critiques made this book real. Thank you.

Teşekkür ederim, Hakan Karateke, for your early and continued support as I juggle fiction with finishing my dissertation (inşallah by the time you read this we'll be at the finish line). To all my friends from the University of Chicago—Sam, Annie, Kyle, Mohsin, Betül, and Sarah L.—I appreciate you so much. To Mireille, who cheered me through my first NaNoWriMo and many manuscripts besides. To Christine and Liam, whose reading enthusiasm renews me every time.

Some friends require special thanks for being pillars of strength through tumultuous years. To Debbie, for laughter and companionship during seasons of rejection and success alike, but especially for championing the bad boys in every book. To Erin, a dear friend, artistic inspiration, and confidante without peer for the last thirteen years and counting. To Kara, my rock in this publishing adventure, for your boundless loyalty, sharp eye for story, character troubleshooting, career scheming, and salt on the toughest days.

I thank my beloved in-laws, Mary, Michael, and Alison, for love, food, and cheerleading through many discouraging rounds of submissions and for celebrating every hard-earned accomplishment. (Alison—I promise I will rewrite *Fang*, I swear.) I adore you all.

I am endlessly grateful for my crazy family: for inspiration, encouragement, loving teasing, and for reading my writing (even when it spooked you!). You are my home. To Elvira Cañas and Arnulfo Flores: every book I write is because of you and for you. Te amo mucho.

I owe my littermates the world for literal decades of untangling outlines, filling in plot holes, shaping character backstories, and pointing out underlying themes that I would not have realized otherwise. Thank you, Aurora, for being my first ever first reader, but especially for suffering my cringe-worthy juvenilia. Special thanks to Honore, valued violence adviser, for helping me kill characters with (enough) medical accuracy and bloody aplomb. To Pollisimo, for safeguarding my beloved baby brother and teaching us the meaning of super spook. And dear J: pew pew pew u r my sister too.

I thank my mother for raising me hard-working and definitely too daydreamy, but especially for listening when I begged to be taken out of public school. For cultivating a freewheeling homeschool education where we ran barefoot through books, where I had the space to read, dream, and most importantly, to write. I love you.

Last but certainly not least, I thank the man who holds my hand through every meltdown and every victory, who has taught me the compassion and patience that makes me the writer I am and the writer I will become: Robert, I could not have done this without you.